DEATH'S ANGEL

SECOND BOOK OF

THE GODDESS'S SCYTHE

COLIN LINDSAY

This book is a work of fiction. Names, characters, places and incidents are products of the author's imagination or are used fictitiously. Any resemblance to actual persons, living or dead, events or locales is entirely coincidental.

No part of this publication may be reproduced, stored in a retrieval system, or transmitted in any form or by any means, electronic, mechanical, photoccpying, recording or otherwise, without written permission of the author.

Text and cover art copyright © 2020 by Colin Lindsay

All rights reserved

for Katherine

Artic Sea
Trax
Skye
Edith
Kala
Petra
Refuge
Western
Sea
Dhara

Brinn
Eastern
Sea
Amber
Addis
Dayl
Eryl
Priestess
Bayre
N
W
E
S
Southern
Sea

Preface

Soren leaned forward in the saddle, examining Kala and the sorry state of her companions, his army surrounding him impatiently. "I won't insult you by offering you a chance to switch sides," he told her, "but I do have a proposition for you. I'll negotiate the terms of your survival…" He paused to let the hope he'd just dangled in front of her sink in. "…if, you can best my champion."

Kala didn't need to consult with her loved ones to decide that any chance of their survival was worth more than hers. "I accept," she replied without reservation.

"Excellent," Soren responded with a smile and turned to his hulking general. "Trax, do you think you can handle this little girl?" he asked.

The man barely restrained his fury at the insult but was forced to accept the challenge, framed as it was. He swallowed his curses and turned to face Kala. "Let's get this over with," he spat, drawing an enormous broadsword and swinging it around him to loosen his muscles. Kala, beyond exhaustion, simply watched him. He circled her slowly like a predator playing with its prey, then, without warning, swung at her blindingly fast for a man his size. Kala barely dove aside in time to avoid being cleft in two. She looked up, uncertain of whether she had the strength to rise.

"Get up and die with some dignity," Trax sneered.

PART I
BAYRE

1
Kala

"Kala?" Skye asked hesitantly, assuming he was dreaming, were it not so vivid. The girl that had haunted him every night for the past two years stepped out of the airship. In his dreams, she'd always been frozen in time as she'd been when he'd left her, but now, she was older, more beautiful, and radiating a steely self-assurance that bordered on threatening. She still wore leathers, but these were jet black and hugged her figure in a way that he found newly suggestive. Her hair had grown too, but she let it hang loose, flipping it back to glint darkly in the sunlight. Her eyes bored into his, and he found himself speechless.

"You called. I came," she replied.

"But how?" he asked, still unwilling to believe that this could be real.

Kala placed a hand on her hip, the corners of her lips twitching upward. "I've learned a thing or two about the airships," she explained. "Now, are you going to crouch there all day or come give me a proper greeting?"

Skye rose hesitantly, scanning the airfield for guards as he did. There were none in sight at the moment, but it didn't tend to stay that way for long, especially if the ship that Kala had arrived in had just landed. He advanced toward her slowly, careful not to dispel the illusion if that's all it was.

Kala remarked that their time apart hadn't changed Skye much. He wasn't his usual cocky self, but he'd grown more handsome and muscled. She'd imagined their reunion a thousand times, and it always involved either their embracing passionately or her slugging him for leaving her. Now that it was actually happening, she desperately wanted to do both.

Skye closed the distance until he was close enough to feel her breath on his neck. He reached out tentatively to touch her, feeling her solidity. She looked up at him as though he'd lost his mind, exactly the way Kala would have. "You're real," he concluded, the shock of his prayers being answered finally registering.

"Last time I checked, yes," she replied with an eye roll, then grabbed him firmly by the shoulders. "We have unfinished business," she declared.

He was about to ask what that business was when she shut him up with a deep kiss. His initial shock gave way to an all-consuming passion until his worry about the guards finally intruded, and he pulled away.

Kala was more than a little nonplussed that the kiss she'd waited two years for was being interrupted and showed no concern whatsoever about the precariousness of their situation.

"We've got to get out of here," Skye urged her, feeling exposed and vulnerable.

Kala grimaced but relented at seeing him so nervous. "Fine," she agreed reluctantly. "Where to?"

"Anywhere but here," he replied, then took her hand and led her briskly toward the fence that enclosed the airfield. Kala was maddeningly unhurried as they wove between the crates that littered their path. Skye almost had to drag her with him.

Just as he'd feared, a patrol emerged from a building, spotted them, and raised the alarm. Skye prepared to bolt, but Kala wheeled around and started back toward the guards.

"What are you doing?!" Skye asked, spinning her back around. "Do we really need to pick a fight?"

"I guess we don't *need* to, but does *want* count for anything?" After having been cooped up in the cramped airship for days, Kala was spoiling for a fight. Skye looked at her as if to say that it wasn't the time for sarcasm, so she sighed, nodded, and followed him as he sprinted for the fence.

When they arrived at it, Skye clambered up it while Kala simply flipped over with effortless grace. She was waiting for him on the other side when he reached the ground, rooted and reluctant to leave without a fight. Skye retook her hand and pulled her toward a nearby alley. The guards made it to the fence, yelling, but didn't pursue them beyond it. As Skye and Kala got further and further away, his holding her hand to ensure that she stayed with him gradually morphed into their simply walking hand in hand.

"You left without saying goodbye," she accused him.

"Technically, I did say goodbye," Skye countered.

Kala stopped and turned to face him. "You know what I mean."

"I know," he conceded, "but what could I have said that wouldn't have made things harder?"

"Anything. You could have said anything."

"I never got the chance. The ship came while you were away."

"I wasn't 'away,'" she corrected him. "I was banished."

"Either way, I had no way of reaching you." He tightened his hold on her hand. "I wanted to; I swear."

"You could have waited. You didn't have to take the first ride out of town."

"That's not fair. I wasn't itching to leave."

"So why didn't you wait?"

"The Council would have sent someone else, and it could easily have been one of your friends, Lily or Cera. I didn't want that on my conscience. We could just as easily be having this conversation with you asking why I did nothing to stop *their* being sent away, especially when I'd sworn to leave anyway. I'd have had no answer, and you'd never forgive me."

Kala had no reply – the thought of Lily or Cera experiencing what she'd been through was almost too much to bear. Skye was right, but his leaving still hurt.

He softened. "Leaving you was the hardest thing I ever did. It turned me inside out."

"And still, you left," she concluded bitterly.

"I had to. I promised my mother that I'd find a way back to her. She's all alone at the mercy of people that it would be an understatement to call uncharitable."

Kala understood what it was like to be at the mercy of unkind people, so she didn't begrudge Skye his vow, just that it didn't have to be a choice – his mother *or* her. "What about me? Didn't *I* count for something? What was I to you? What am I now?"

"I've been trying to figure that out since I first met you," he replied.

Kala stared at him, clearly unhappy with his response.

"All I can say is that you're all I see when I close my eyes, and it breaks my heart to open them."

"That… is an acceptable answer," she said and relaxed the stare that held him impaled. "You could have waited," she repeated, more to herself than him. "We could have figured it out together."

"I was afraid I'd lose myself in you and with it my resolve."

"Would that have been so bad?"

"If I'd abandoned my vow, what kind of person would I have become?"

"*My* person," Kala protested.

"You are," he promised, squeezing her hand.

She dropped his hand and looked away. "I'm not the girl you remember. I've done things… terrible things. Darkness dwells in me," she admitted, shuddering.

Skye could not believe it and pulled her back to him. She refused to meet his gaze, so he gently lifted her chin until she was looking him in the eyes. "No amount of darkness could ever put out your light."

She pulled away testily. "You have no idea how deep it runs in me."

"That may be, but if you have demons, we'll face them together," he promised.

She wished it was that easy. "That's sweet of you, but those guards scare you…"

"With good reason," he interrupted, defending himself.

"What *I* am is far scarier," she finished gently.

"You've always been scary," he assured her. "I'll just have to get used to a new level of scary." He held out his hand. "I'm willing if you are."

She stared at his hand for a long while, really wanting to try but not believing she could. She finally took it. "Okay, I'm willing, but I can't make any promises."

He pulled her into a tight embrace. "I'll be at your side every step of the way. I won't ever leave you again," he promised.

She nestled in slowly, a glimmer of hope kindling in her heart. After a time, they separated, and Kala looked around. "Shall we go to wherever you're staying?" she suggested.

"We could, but your old treehouse was more luxurious," he admitted discouragedly.

"Right now, I'd be happy with anything."

"Okay, follow me," he replied, guiding her down a quiet side street. "Best to keep a low profile," he explained.

"Why's that?" she asked.

"Well, for starters, it seems I'm not that popular with the local clergy, but more importantly, you look like you're ready to wage a one-person war."

Kala's hand strayed to the dagger at her thigh.

"It's more the swords strapped to your back," Skye informed her. "Well, maybe it's also the collection of daggers you're sporting. How many do you have?"

"Eight," she replied.

"Eight! Where?"

"Want to search me?" she teased.

"Forget I asked," he muttered. *A new level of scary*, he reminded himself as he crossed to the shadowed side of the street.

Kala shrugged and followed. "Low profile it is, then."

They still encountered town guards on the way, but Kala had a knack for timing that allowed them to slip by without being noticed.

"How do you do that?" Skye asked.

"Do what?" she replied.

"That thing you do where you know which way the guards are going to look or turn before they do? And not just the guards – everyone."

"It's a dance," she replied cryptically.

He gave up trying to understand and carried on under Kala's bizarre form of invisibility until they arrived at his building.

"You'll like this," he promised her. "I sleep on the roof. The sunsets are wonderful. I'll show you," he told her as he led her up the long staircase. He was winded by the time they reached the top, although Kala didn't seem the least bit bothered by the climb. He shook his head and turned the knob. "Welcome to my home," he announced and pushed open the door.

Monks lying in wait drew their weapons and grabbed Skye before he could react.

"Run, Kala!" he yelled as he struggled to free himself from their iron grip.

Kala did no such thing – she simply stepped through the door, not even bothering to draw a weapon.

Great, thought Skye. *She's insane.*

Kala stared patiently at the monks, who took a moment, then released Skye.

"Sorry, milady," they said in unison.

Skye took a step back, looking from Kala to the monks, who sheathed their weapons and filed out, nodding respectfully to Kala as they did.

"Do you mind telling me what just happened?" Skye asked once they'd left.

"I'm kind of a big deal in certain circles," Kala replied innocently.

"In death cult circles?!" he asked incredulously.

Kala just shrugged.

"No, seriously. Please explain."

Kala sighed. "I can't, really. Let's just say, 'they think I'm someone I'm not.'"

"Well, that clears things up," he concluded. "But I guess I should thank you for getting me out of whatever was going to happen to me."

"You're welcome," Kala replied and watched him apologetically as he sorted through his belongings, which were strewn across the roof. His journal was missing, to his dismay, and he debated asking Kala if she could get it back but decided to broach the subject later.

"If I'd known I was bringing a girl home, I'd have cleaned up," he joked instead.

"Do you bring a lot of girls home?" Kala asked.

"I wouldn't say that," he replied, but something told him he was walking into a trap.

"Eden might say otherwise."

Skye froze, then turned slowly and asked, "She's all right, then?"

"Your concern is touching, lover-boy," Kala replied. "When I left her, she was nursing a broken heart."

Skye deflated. "I think I can conclude that I acted badly."

"You think?"

"I was desperate for a way home," he justified. "When I stumbled across Eden, she presented a way."

"That's no excuse. There's always a way to do right by someone, especially an innocent like her."

"I tried to make things right, but I was run out of town by your friends," he explained, gesturing at the door the monks had just exited.

"How about not having things to set right in the first place?"

"I'm not good at these things," he admitted. "I'm just doing the best I can. I didn't exactly set about to worm myself into the hearts of young ladies across the continent."

"And yet you have," Kala concluded, then exhaled resignedly. "Can you see how this makes it hard to trust you? Was *I* just a way home? Am I just that still?"

"You know you're not. You're special."

"How can I believe you?"

"Because it's not me, it's you – you draw me like a moth to a flame."

"You know what happens to the moth, right?" she asked. "That appears to be my specialty."

"I'll take my chances," he declared.

Kala still felt unsettled but accepted his offer. "Promise me... no more girls."

"How can I refuse someone carrying six daggers?"

"Eight," she corrected.

"Just checking."

"You haven't promised," she reminded him.

"I promise that from now on, my sun rises and sets on you alone."

"That's a good start," she accepted.

Skye had no bedroll, but they lay down side by side to refamiliarize themselves with each other. To his credit, Kala thought, Skye wasn't tentative about it – he stared into her eyes and unabashedly ran his fingers through her hair. He basked in her closeness while Kala relished the feeling of being wanted, of belonging. She might have stumbled across Skye, but she'd found herself in the process.

The setting sun lit the sky in a riot of orange and red. It was as beautiful as Skye had promised, but the monks' appearance reminded Kala that she'd been prophesied to plunge the world into fire. She tensed.

Skye misread her apprehension and stilled his hand. "How is everyone?" he asked, hoping to cheer her thoughts. "Your grandfather, Lily, Cera, Meadow…?"

"Meadow is Forest now," Kala informed him, then, sensing his confusion, added, "It's a long story." She missed her young protégé. It was painful to think of everyone she'd lost, but she knew that Skye had come to care about them, too, and he shared in her loss. She steeled herself and opened her mind to the past.

"I don't have much to tell," she had to admit. "I left pretty soon after you did. Forest took your room, by the way. Lily and Cera were as adorable a couple as ever."

"Speaking of which, how's Calix? I'll bet he was happy to see me leave," Skye guessed, remembering that Kala's friend harbored feelings for her.

"He probably was," she laughed.

"Did you two ever…?" Skye asked.

"Hell, no," Kala replied firmly, making Skye feel even worse about his dalliance with Eden.

"I miss your granddad," he deflected. "He was so kind to me."

Kala's grandfather's absence remained a gaping hole in her heart. Tears welled up in her eyes. "I miss him too."

Skye kissed her forehead and stroked her cheek. "You'll see him again," he promised.

Kala wanted to believe she would, but she didn't share his unflagging optimism. *Never promise something you can't deliver,* she thought. Still, her village was undoubtedly exactly as she'd left it, like a scene captured in a snow globe. It would never change, only her; she'd changed so much already. Even if she found her way back, would she be welcome? She'd killed Lily's abusive father, which she'd do again a hundred times over, but it branded her a murderer. *Is that how my friends and family think of me?* she worried.

It registered with Skye that if Kala had left her village soon after him, that she'd been out in the world for two years. "What did you do after leaving?"

"A lot, most of which I don't want to talk about," she deflected.

"I'm sorry," he told her earnestly, intertwining their fingers.

"It's not your fault," she assured him. Thinking about the past fatigued her, so she rolled into him to signal an end to their conversation.

Skye stroked her hair, wondering what she'd been through. She'd always been fearless. Hell, she'd faced down dire wolves, a jaguar, and the gods-know what else prowled the woods. And now, she was even more capable. The guards and monks hadn't fazed her because she knew she could handle them. Despite that, something still terrified her, and he felt woefully inadequate to protect her from whatever it was. He vowed to do what he could and pulled her close, soothing her to sleep in his embrace.

Kala woke stiff but content in a way that she hadn't felt in ages. Happiness, in her experience, tended to be fleeting, so she resolved to enjoy it while it lasted.

She watched Skye sleep, his chest rising and falling in a steady rhythm. She worried that he wouldn't accept her once he grasped what she'd become. The girl he'd fallen in love with was a distant memory. She was no longer a doe-eyed village girl, naïve to the evil of the world. She'd become that evil, she'd hurt people, killed them, and she hated herself for it.

Kala wondered if Skye might also not be the person she fell in love with. Maybe it wasn't him that she'd fallen in love with at all, but rather what he'd represented – a world beyond the confines of her village? Now that she was out in that world, would she still feel the same about him?

Her worries made her restless, and she shifted to extricate herself from his embrace without waking him, rolling quietly away. She rose and walked to the roof's edge to distract herself. The sunrise illumined the city's various quarters, bathing them in warm tones and revealing just how sprawling the city actually was. The sounds of its inhabitants stirring rose by degrees. *Far more people live here than all that I've ever encountered combined*, she thought, amazed.

She watched people move about despite the early hour. Markets opened, and tents flaps were drawn back to reveal all manner of goods. Shop owners circulated, acquiring supplies before the populous called on them. The heartbeat of the city quickened.

Kala guessed from her map that she was in Bayre, on the east coast. She and Skye needed to find a way back to the distant west. While she'd discovered how to stow aboard an airship, she still needed to figure out how to make it go where she wanted.

A groan alerted her to Skye waking, then his stretching like a cat.

"You're still a treat in the morning," she observed, thankful for any sign that nothing meaningful had changed between them.

"I try," he replied, yawning. "I need some kai," he decided. "Do you think you could leave your arsenal behind while we hunt some down?"

"Way ahead of you," she replied, gesturing at her lack of visible weaponry.

"Great. You've put away your daggers."

"Four of them anyway," she replied.

Skye rolled his eyes and freshened up at a rain barrel while Kala hid the weapons she was leaving behind.

"You clean up well," Kala remarked.

Skye beamed. "That's why you love me."

She shoved him playfully, and they made their way down to the street, then off toward the nearest market. Kala wrinkled her nose at the assault of smells. She was used to fewer of them, ones that were more subtle, and definitely ones that were more pleasant.

Skye noted her discomfort. "It takes some getting used to," he encouraged.

"I'm not sure I want to," she grimaced.

Skye put an arm around her and guided her onward.

"I'm sorry I wasn't very chatty last night," Kala apologized. "The journey here was exhausting, and running into you sort of threw me for a loop."

"No apologies necessary," he assured her. "We have all the time in the world to catch up now that we're together, and I know just the place to do it – it serves the best kai in the city. I found it during my explorations," he informed her. "This place is huge," he added unnecessarily.

"I got that impression from the view," she confirmed.

They strolled through the city just like any other couple, and Kala reveled in the normalcy of it. The market they entered was filled with brightly colored awnings and vendors competing for their attention. People milled about browsing and haggling.

Skye guided her to the vendor he'd mentioned, and she waited at a quiet table while he bought two cups of kai with the meager supply of coins he had left. They found themselves surrounded by an odd assortment of people indulging in their morning rituals. A boorish merchant hunched over a steaming cup, not yet fully awake, a couple of schoolgirls chatting about boys they fancied, and a sullen waif of a girl sitting alone, nursing a tiny cup of twice-boiled kai. Everyone was consumed by their own thoughts, but Kala and Skye kept their voices low regardless.

Skye had a million questions. "How did you find me?" he began.

"I wasn't really looking for you so much as following the same path you took. It was just luck that I met you at the landing port."

"Lucky me," Skye chuckled and took a tentative sip. The drink burned his mouth, so he put it down. "So, the Council picked you to send away after all?"

"No, they picked Lily. I took her place."

"Great minds think alike," Skye beamed.

"I didn't really plan it," she explained truthfully. "It just felt like the right thing to do."

"Lily…," Skye mused. "She's an angel. I can't believe they chose her."

"Well, her father is a devil, or was anyway."

"I'm sure he still is."

"Only if there's a hell," Kala replied cryptically, leaning back. She was reminded of the hell she'd lived through under Baron's control and decided she wouldn't let it define her. "You asked me what happened after I left the village," she reminded him.

"Yes?" Skye confirmed, not wanting to pressure Kala into talking about anything she wasn't comfortable with.

She could read it in his eyes. "It's okay," she assured him. "Let's just say that I found myself employed, forcibly, by a petty crime lord." She left out the part about the job involving extortion and murder.

"Sounds terrible," Skye commiserated, recalling all the tyrants he'd run across in his travels.

"Believe it or not, it wasn't all bad. I met some good people," Kala responded, thinking of Amber and Hawke. Hawke had told her that her lost soul would eventually return to her, and she clung to that hope.

"How'd you get away?" Skye asked.

"The fellow's business empire sort of collapsed," Kala replied obtusely. "So, I moved on to the city where I met Eden."

It was Skye's turn to be uncomfortable at the memory of his mistreatment of the poor girl. "She's sweet," he admitted.

"She really is," Kala agreed. "She reminded me of a lot of Lily in that way." *Maybe that's why we bonded*, she thought. "Eden helped me remember that there's still good in the world, and corny as that sounds, I think my spirit healed during my time with her."

What happened to you? Skye thought but kept it to himself. "How did you meet her?" he asked instead.

"The Head Librarian introduced us."

"The older, stern-looking woman."

"Tallie? I guess that's an apt description."

"She didn't like me much."

"What's not to like?" Kala laughed.

"Apparently, I make a bit too much noise."

"That would bother Tallie, but really, she's quite nice. She gave me books about airships and introduced me to Eden when I asked about maps."

"Speaking about maps," Skye added, thinking of his stolen journal, "do you have any idea how we get home from here?"

"I made a copy of one of Eden's maps that showed the directions the winds typically blow. It seems like we have two options – we can either take an airship east over the ocean or south until the winds turn westward. East is a straight shot, but it's a long way across the ocean. Going south, then west, would involve multiple shorter hops, but through places we know nothing about." She traced her finger around her cup's rim while she thought. "I don't like either option, but we have to choose one."

"Our decision may be made for us," Skye replied. "I've watched ships land and take off for days. None of the ones heading east take passengers, ever... only the ones going south. There has to be a reason for that, so we might just have to go south, whether we like it or not."

Kala furrowed her brow and took another sip. "Before we rule out going east, I want to know why the airships going that way are all unoccupied. Any idea of where to start with that?"

"We could ask your religious friends," Skye joked and braced himself for Kala to smack him.

"Very funny," she responded. "I've read everything the Church had about the airships in its main library, which was gigantic. And I had a very helpful librarian assisting me. So I doubt we'll find anything useful here just poking around."

"There's always the airfield, but I didn't see any clues there when I was staking it out. Plus, the guards there might be keeping an eye out for us now that we eluded them."

"We have no leads," Kala concluded. "We're going to have to create some if we're going to find a way back home." She hunched forward in thought. "I think I'll scout the temple," she decided. "The city must have one if there are monks here."

"Oh, they're as thick as flies," Skye confirmed. "So, it must be a super-sized temple." He didn't relish having anything to do with the monks. "I'm going to either stick really close to you or stay way the hell away. I haven't figured out which is smarter yet."

It occurred to Kala that while they both spoke of returning home, they hadn't talked about which of their homes they were trying to get back to. She feared that their choices would eventually split them apart again. She suppressed the thought with an effort. *One problem at a time*, she told herself.

The waifish girl got up to go, leaving her unfinished kai on the table, which felt like a fitting conclusion to Skye and Kala's conversation, so they downed the remains of theirs and rose as well.

They walked toward the city's center, and as they did, Skye studied Kala to see if he could figure out how she performed the trick of staying invisible to the guards they passed but failed utterly. *Where did she learn that?* he wondered, *and why?*

Kala interrupted his thoughts. "We're being followed," she informed him.

Skye looked behind them but saw no one.

"Subtle," Kala scolded him.

He felt chided but accepted that she was the expert in this area while he was woefully out of his element. *Not that I have an element*, he thought. *I have no element*, he realized and found himself bothered by the realization.

"Will you pay attention?" Kala asked, annoyed.

"Right. Don't pay attention, but pay attention – check!" Skye concluded exasperatedly.

"You're learning," she replied sarcastically and steered them toward a nearby alleyway.

"Are you sure a dark alley is the best place to lead whoever's following us?" he asked.

"No better place to dispatch them," Kala replied coldly.

Skye cringed. *This version of Kala is not my favorite*, he thought.

Kala whirled and threw a dagger that Skye hadn't even seen her take out. He turned to see it vibrating in the wood of a door frame, a hair's breadth from the head of the waifish girl from the market.

The girl didn't seem overly fazed by her brush with death, however, and her eyes sparkled as she reached up to grab the dagger's hilt. She pulled on it, but it didn't budge, so she had to brace her foot against the door to yank it out. Freeing it at last, she brushed the blond hair out of her eyes and walked casually over to Kala, handing the weapon back.

Kala took it impassively and returned it to its sheath inside her tunic.

"I sort of lost all of my cool struggling to free that, didn't I?" the girl asked.

"You're still breathing," Kala replied, "so I'd count it as a win."

The girl smiled. "Don't think I don't appreciate that."

"Why were you following us?" Kala asked.

"You piqued my curiosity."

"You're going to have to do better than that," Kala replied with a hint of menace.

"Okay. I've met a lot of people your age, and without fail, they're trying their hardest to stay *out* of the airships, and here you two are discussing how to get into one. Forgive me, but that's curious."

"Who do you work for?" Kala pressed, communicating a thinly veiled threat of violence if the answer didn't please her.

Skye looked at Kala with shock. The girl couldn't be more than fourteen years old.

"I'm with the Resistance," the girl replied, straight-faced.

"Now you've piqued *my* curiosity," Kala replied.

"Thought so," the girl replied confidently. "If you want to know more, follow me," she said and turned to go.

Kala stopped her with a hand on her shoulder. "And if you're leading us into a trap?"

"Do I look like an assassin?" she asked, rolling her eyes.

"Do I?" Kala asked sternly.

"Well, are you?"

"Yes."

The girl whistled, impressed. "My first assassin." She gestured at Skye, who'd been silent so far, and asked, "Is he one too?"

Kala laughed. "Only of rocks and trees," she replied, recounting his failed attempts at archery.

"Gods-damn skittish deer," Skye grumbled.

"He talks," the girl observed.

"Of course, I talk," Skye replied, mildly annoyed before relaxing. "Allow me to introduce myself properly. I'm Skye," he said and offered his hand awkwardly.

The girl just stared at it until he withdrew it. He motioned toward Kala. "She's..." he began.

"Raven," Kala finished for him.

"Skye and Raven," the girl mused. "That's rich. Are we using code names?"

"That's my actual name," Skye replied, now decidedly annoyed but raising an eyebrow at Kala's choice of Raven as a name."

The girl sighed. "I'm Celeste, and that is my real name, for the record. I'm also definitely not an assassin. Satisfied?"

Nothing about the girl raised any warning signs with Kala, so she replied, "Satisfied. Lead on."

Celeste led them through the city, oblivious to who saw her, much like an anti-Kala. Because she was so confident in her surrounding, no one paid them any attention, just like Kala's mysterious talent, but in reverse. Skye was wondering if everyone had superpowers except him when Celeste guided them into a dead-end alley. Kala tensed as they stopped in front of a dilapidated building without doors or windows, just water-stained plaster peeling off the brick walls. "We're here," Celeste announced cheerfully.

Kala looked closer at a rough sheet of wood leaning against the discolored wall.

"Good eye," Celeste noted and pulled it aside to reveal a person-sized hole. "Welcome to the Resistance," she said and stepped through.

2
Dhara

Dhara paddled down the muddy river that cut across the southlands in the direction that the airship had taken her sister, Caia. Her shoulders ached from the strain, which was made harder by propelling a two-person canoe on her own, but she needed it to bring back her sister, assuming she was still alive. The blood moon was mere days away, and if Caia wound up somewhere that shared the customs of their tribe, she'd be sacrificed that night. Their mother hadn't just sent her away, she'd sought to end her.

Dhara's back still stung from the caning she received from her mother's guards for interfering in Caia's send-off. If her older sister, Zara, hadn't pulled her away, it would've been far worse. Zara had restrained her, telling her, "The will of the tribe is final."

"You mean mother's will," Dhara had spat.

"Mother's will *is* the tribe's," Zara reminded her, then pleaded, "Please, Dhara, stand down. I can't lose you too." She held Dhara firmly as she struggled helplessly.

Dhara hated Zara for taking their mother's side. She'd come to terms with their mother's callousness long ago, but sisters were supposed to look out for each other, especially in a world in which no one else did. She spat in the water, but it didn't rid her of the sour taste in her mouth.

She hated feeling exposed on the open river but, judging from the sun's position, it wouldn't be for much longer – the river's path would soon diverge from the direction the airship went. She looked for a place to beach the canoe and continue on foot, scanning the river's edge for any distinctive tree, beside which she could hide the canoe and find it again later. She paddled toward such a tree and pulled the canoe onto the shore.

The soaring canopy shaded the jungle floor, and the sparseness of the undergrowth allowed her to make swift progress inland. She disliked being on the ground when her tribe dwelt high above it in the trees. The ground was reserved for hunters and the hunted.

As the vegetation became denser, Dhara had to hack through it. It was stiflingly hot in the southlands, and rivulets of sweat stung the cuts on her back. The slow going only fed her anger as the image of Caia being forced into the ship replayed over and over in her mind. Her sister's eyes had pleaded, "Don't let this happen!" and the disappointed look that followed shamed Dhara deeply. She'd failed her sister then, but nothing would make her fail her now, least of all some damned plants!

She'd disobeyed her mother by leaving the village in search of her sister. As the tribe's matriarch, her mother would probably have her gutted for it when she returned, if she returned, but at the moment, Caia's survival was all that mattered. She had to rescue her before the blood moon. If she was still alive, she wouldn't be for much longer if Dhara didn't make faster progress.

Dhara's muscles glistened as she raised her machete again and again. She hacked and cursed, cursed and hacked. No sane person would attempt to pass this way, but she had no choice if she was to follow the airship's path. Her machete struck something so hard that it jarred her up to her shoulder. She sheathed it, grimacing, and brushed the vines out of the way to reveal a jet-black pillar. She mouthed a prayer to the Goddess to protect her from ancient evils. She'd heard of such places from the tribe's elders, dark places hidden in the jungle where evil dwelled.

To stay true to her path, she had no choice but to pass the pillar. The vegetation thinned slightly beyond it, and she spotted several more of the black columns. She felt like she was walking through the skeletal ribcage of a massive beast. The hairs on her arms rose, she felt pressure in her temples, and her stomach revolted. The feeling of wrongness was overwhelming.

The jungle had gone utterly silent. Even the hum of insects had disappeared. It was as though Death had covered the jungle under Her cloak. Dhara shuddered and hurried to get out of this place before it consumed her. She couldn't bear the assault of silence any longer and covered her ears to block it, which eased the pressure in her head and the upset in her stomach slightly. She uncovered her ears and immediately felt worse. She pulled some leaves off a vine, rolled them in her palm, and stuffed them into her ears, making her feel marginally better. She cupped her hands over her ears, and the feeling of being assaulted subsided a little more.

It was awkward to run with her hands over her ears, but the alternative was much worse. She found herself moving parallel to an obsidian wall and spied an opening that was distinguishable only because it yawned blacker than the darkest night. Her skin prickled. She felt watched by an entity so ambivalent about her existence as to be malevolent. Her head swam. She tore her gaze from the opening and ran faster, crashing through brush that clawed at her face but caring only about getting away.

She burst between two more of the pillars, and the feeling of unease abruptly ceased. She tentatively lowered her hands from her ears, and the sounds of the jungle returned faintly. She pulled the leaves out of her ears. Her hand shot for her machete, only to find it safely sheathed. *Thank the Goddess!* She was sure that if she'd had it in her hands during her flight, she'd have dropped it, and it would have been lost forever.

She turned to look at the way she'd come, and it seemed no different than the rest of the jungle. She shuddered, said another prayer, and continued on her way. The jungle was less dense on this side of the evil place, and she advanced by squeezing between the plants rather than hacking through them, allowing her to make faster progress.

She came across a snare set for small game and immediately grew cautious – she couldn't stumble across a hunting party. She trusted her skill with a blade, but she was only one, and they could be many. She crept onward, keeping an eye out for more signs that people inhabited this corner of the jungle.

Tribes rarely interacted, but every few generations, one would wage war on another. The result was typically wholesale slaughter, which was why Dhara's tribe trained since youth to be warriors, not just hunters. Her mother would never let her tribe come out on the losing end of a conflict. Dhara was raised to be ruthless but not foolhardy, so she moved warily through enemy territory, hopeful that if the airship had carried her sister this way, perhaps she'd be found nearby.

Dhara came across more signs that people had passed this way, then heard distant sounds of labor. She advanced cautiously, and peering through the brush, saw a crew of men ferrying stone blocks from a sled to the foundation of a building. A handful of female guards oversaw them and kept the men's pace with the crack of a whip. One of the guards was leaning against a tree with her back to Dhara.

Dhara compared the woman's clothing to her own, which clearly marked her as an outsider, then withdrew a short distance and stripped naked. She looked at her dagger and sighed. *Can't get blood on my new outfit*, she thought and put her knife down. She crept forward without a stitch of clothing or even a weapon. The guard, to her credit, heard the faint rustling and turned to see Dhara standing before her nude. She paused in confusion, then lifted her whip and brought down a lash that bit into Dhara's shoulder.

Dhara winced. *You're going to regret not going for your knife*, she thought and closed the distance between them before the woman could raise her whip again. Dhara punched her hard in the stomach, and as she collapsed forward, reached around and snapped her neck. She lowered her body to the ground and looked to see if she'd been seen, confirming that fortunately, she hadn't.

She dragged the woman's body into the trees, then stripped her of her clothes and dressed herself in them. The guard had at least been lean and well-muscled, so her clothes fit Dhara's lithe form reasonably well. Dhara also took the time to arrange her hair in the same style as the guard. Once she'd done her best to resemble her, she buried the woman's body beneath a pile of leaves and hid her own pack in a nearby tree. She traded her machete for the woman's whip, despite thinking it pointlessly less deadly.

She emerged from the bush but skirted the work party. Her intention wasn't to take the woman's place, only to pass as a local. She avoided people but tried not to draw attention to herself by skulking. She passed small plots of vegetables, then found herself at a village comprised of squat buildings. *Uncivilized*, she thought with disdain for the ground-dwellers. The nearer buildings were made of mud bricks, but the ones closer to the village's center were constructed from quarried stone and surrounded an enormous pyramid that towered over the community.

Dhara scouted for places where the villagers might keep captives, likely somewhere central. Slaves were abundant, but they seemed sufficiently cowed by the ruling class that they weren't locked up the way her people did theirs. She moved closer to the village center, where she spotted a bamboo cage containing a small figure. Even at that distance, she recognized Caia. Dhara seethed and rejoiced. The cage was well guarded, but Dhara needed to see her sister up close to confirm that she was okay. She took a meandering path past the cage, strolling purposefully and fingering her whip.

Caia looked up at her sister's approach. *Good girl*, Dhara thought. Caia's eyes widened when she recognized her sister, but Dhara shook her head slightly to warn against drawing attention. Caia nodded and glanced to the enormous pyramid facing the square. Dhara understood her meaning and proceeded past her to cross the courtyard.

Peering back from the jungle's edge, Dhara examined the pyramid, conceding that it was a remarkable structure, one that would have taken generations of slaves to build. Stone steps ascended the side that faced the square, but the other sides presented no easy way up. Atop it was an altar surrounded by an irregular circle of columns. This would be where Caia would be sacrificed at the height of the blood moon, which, by her reckoning, was only one night away.

Dhara bided her time until dark, then ascended the pyramid from its back side. It was an effort, but it could be done. She carried a rope that she'd stolen from a storehouse earlier in the day. That prize had necessitated another kill, and she worried that if people kept going missing, it would alert the village to her presence, but for now, its pulse seemed the same, as though death was as common here as it was in her home.

A single guard was standing atop the pyramid as Dhara peered over its lip. It wasn't a large space, with room for only a few people. That would make her task somewhat easier, she concluded and climbed down, leaving one end of the rope wedged into a crevice out of view and uncoiling the rest as she descended. She only had to wait for the next night.

The village was abuzz with energy when the time came. Dhara watched from her hiding spot as guards dragged Caia from the cage. Even though she didn't resist, one of them punched her in the stomach, and the other slapped her face. Dhara bit down hard. *They'll pay for that with their lives,* she vowed. The guards flanked Caia and dragged her up the pyramid's wide steps. Dhara judged it time to move into position before the village priestess arrived to plunge a dagger into Caia's heart when the moon reached its zenith.

She climbed the back of the pyramid and arrived at its lip, panting from the exertion. She willed herself to control her breathing so it wouldn't give her away, and gradually her racing heart slowed. She glanced over the edge to take in the scene, which was well-lit by torches secured to the columns. Caia had been tied to the altar and lay calmly with unshakable faith in her sister. The guards stood on either side but as far back as the limited space would allow.

The crowd quieted, and Dhara sensed that the ceremony had begun – the priestess was making her way up the pyramid's steps. The old woman reached the top and stood before the altar, raising her hands to quiet the crowd, taking her time before she spoke, savoring the attention and the rising tension. She sermonized to the assembly about their need to appease the gods so that they might be blessed with rain. When the moon was finally at its apex, she retreated behind the altar and mounted a wooden step that allowed her to be better seen by the masses.

She pulled a curved dagger from her belt and held it up to the sky. The crowd hushed as the crone entreated the gods in a voice loud enough to carry to those below. When she'd finished her prayer, she gripped the dagger and raised it high over Caia to bring down through her heart. She hesitated, and the crowd held their breath in anticipation. She slumped over instead, however, revealing Dhara behind her with her own knife in the woman's back.

The crowd erupted in fury, and the guards atop the pyramid pulled out wicked-looking blades and closed on Dhara, who just yanked her knife out of the crone's back and hurled it into one of their chests. She ducked under the swing of the other and used the woman's momentum to send her sailing off the pyramid. Her impact made a sickening sound as she struck the stone midway down. The crowd surged up the steps, murder in their eyes.

Dhara raced to the first guard's body, pulled her knife from her chest, then spun and hurriedly sawed at Caia's restraints. The crowd was halfway up the steps and roaring for blood by the time she'd cut Caia's hands free. She handed her the knife to cut the ropes that still bound her legs and turned to secure the rope she'd hidden the day before as high as she could around a sturdy-looking column. Caia, now freed, joined her just as the crowd crested the top of the steps. Dhara handed her sister a length of leather she'd cut from the whip she'd taken from the first guard she'd slain, then flipped her own piece over the rope and used it to slide down to the jungle below. She looked over her shoulder to see Caia do the same just as the villagers reached for her, several of them tumbling off the pyramid in the process.

Dhara flew toward the trees, and it occurred to her that she hadn't thought about how to arrest her speed. She twisted the leather tightly around the rope, and it slowed her enough that she wasn't torn apart by the branches she crashed through before hitting the ground and rolling. She looked back to see that Caia had figured out how to slow herself earlier than she had and was coming to a more controlled stop. Her sister's mind had always worked quicker than hers.

With Caia safely on the ground, Dhara jumped up to saw at the rope. Cutting it free, she heard the thump of several bodies falling to the jungle floor.

Caia hugged Dhara tightly, and she hugged her back before pulling away and grabbing her by the arm. "Stay close," she told her and tore off at a run. The glow of torches and sounds of pursuit were not far behind.

Caia was weak from hunger and mistreatment but didn't let it stop her from keeping up with her sister. "We can't outrun them," she pointed out.

"We don't have to," Dhara reassured her. "Just stay close."

Dhara swore she could feel the breath of their pursuers on her neck as she led her sister between two black pillars. The sound of pursuit ceased abruptly, but Dhara did not assume it meant they were no longer followed. The villagers were so incensed that Dhara doubted that even this evil place would dissuade them from pursuing them here.

Dhara grabbed a fistful of leaves and handed them to her sister. "Stuff these in your ears, then cover them with your hands." Dhara did the same and resumed moving forward, looking back to ensure that Caia stayed with her. She ran until she came to the obsidian wall, then followed along it, despite feeling increasingly like throwing up. Flickers of torchlight reflecting in front of them confirmed that the villagers had indeed followed them.

Dhara shouted to her sister, "Close your eyes and stay right behind me." Caia's head pounded, and she was equally sick to her stomach, but she did as she was told. Dhara guided her forward until she found the opening in the wall. Her mind revolted, and terror overwhelmed her, but she threw her sister into the yawning darkness and dove in after her.

3
Kala

Celeste led Kala and Skye through the opening in the wall to a large, dimly lit room containing a few beds and several wide-eyed children. "This is home," Celeste announced.

"This is the Resistance?" Skye asked. "It looks more like an orphanage."

"Close enough," Celeste replied. "We are these kids' only hope."

"Hope of what?"

"Of not being sent away in an airship to an unknown and altogether unpleasant fate. We provide refuge to the street kids that the guards like to round up to fill the ships. People think these children are expendable because they have no home, so we provide them with one."

"You've said 'we' a few times. Who is 'we'?" Kala asked.

"My friends Petr and Twill, and myself. They're out making coin so we can feed all these mouths." Celeste looked around lovingly at her charges and sat down on a bed beside a young boy. She pulled a bread roll from her bag, handed it to him, and rubbed his head. "This little guy here is Frey. His parents had him as insurance against their older son's getting sent away in an airship. When his brother aged out, his parents stopped paying attention to Frey, and it wasn't long before he was on the street, and we found him."

"Should you be saying these things in front of him?" Skye asked.

"Shielding them from the truth of the world is no kindness," Celeste replied, placing a hand on Frey's shoulder.

A little girl strolled by. "I'm a bastard," she announced.

"Own it," Frey encouraged.

"Go to hell," she replied.

Celeste gestured to the girl, "Her parents couldn't bring themselves to love her for fear that she'd be taken from them, so she grew up not knowing love. Can you imagine?"

Kala couldn't, and a vision of her grandfather swam into her memory. She sat down beside Celeste and placed a hand on her leg. "It is a good thing you do here."

Celeste smiled wistfully. "We do what we can, but it never seems to be enough – we still lose kids." She clenched the blanket in her fist but otherwise looked unruffled. "You're welcome to stay here," she said, brightening.

Kala and Skye looked at each other.

"Come on. I can tell by the look of you that you don't have a roof over your heads. I have an eye for these things," Celeste accused them bluntly.

"Guilty as charged," Kala admitted. "It's kind of you to offer."

"Are you kidding? We'd have our very own assassin. How cool is that?"

"Pretty cool, I'd say," Skye replied, smiling. Celeste's enthusiasm was infectious.

The children stared at Skye in wide-eyed wonder.

"Not me," he set them straight. "Her," he added, gesturing to Kala.

The children turned to Kala and looked her over appreciatively.

"You two can have the bed in the back," Celeste continued. "It's not too big, but it'll give you a measure of privacy."

Kala blushed at the implication, and Skye looked at his feet.

"Thank you," he finally replied, then looked about the run-down room and asked, "How can we help?"

"The protection of your assassin girlfriend is golden all on its own, but if you're up for it, you could help me put dinner together."

"I'd be happy to," he replied. "Do you like spicy food?" he asked, growing excited at the prospect of making a real dinner.

"I'll go fetch our belongings," Kala declared and headed back toward the hidden door.

"Can you find your way there and back?" Skye asked uncertainly.

"More easily than in the forest where every tree looks like every other tree," Kala assured him.

"I guess," he replied. "Be safe."

"Always."

Kala returned with her weapons and Skye's things. The children at Celeste's sanctuary mobbed her, fawning over her weapons – only guards and monks walked around armed in Bayre. Kala sighed and demonstrated precision knife throwing to a chorus of *oohs* and *aws*. The children regarded her as a shiny new toy, and she had to pry herself away to join Celeste and Skye in the kitchen.

Skye was stirring a pot and waved with his free hand. Celeste smiled at Kala but kept chopping carrots. Across the room, two eighteen-year-old boys were sitting at the kitchen table. Kala surmised that they were Celeste's friends. "Petr and Twill, I presume," she greeted them.

The taller, wistful-looking boy got up and offered his hand. "Petr, at your service, miss," he said.

The second boy had loosely bound, long hair and deep blue eyes and stayed seated. "Twill," was all he said, nodding to Kala. "I'd get up, but…" he added, rolling his wheelchair back from the table.

"Pleased to meet you both," Kala said. "As Skye probably told you, I'm Raven."

"I heard you're an assassin," Petr asked skeptically, seeking her confirmation.

"It's not who I am, but it's what I've done," she replied flatly.

"So, you've killed people," Petr stated.

Kala tensed.

"Petr, you're insufferable," Twill rescued her. "I apologize for him. He's a musician and completely unfiltered."

"Well, you're a tortured artist and a bit of a prig," Petr countered and sat back down in a huff.

"See what I mean?" Twill asked, and from his expression concluding that he was winning some ongoing contest between him and Petr.

Kala relaxed and sat down with them. "How did you two come to meet Celeste?" she asked amiably.

Twill laughed. "It was the other way around. We're two of her first rescues when we were still of age."

"Not that the bastards care that we've aged out," Petr grumbled. "Especially Twill – he could pass for fifteen, and the guards love nothing more than ridding the city of a cripple."

"Thanks, Petr," Twill bristled.

"I've got your back, buddy," Petr replied.

"With friends like these?" Twill said conspiratorially to Kala.

"In all seriousness," Celeste jumped in, "if you look anywhere remotely close to fifteen or sixteen, you're at risk."

"That's why Petr sports that pathetic attempt at a beard," Twill explained.

To curb Petr's offense, Kala assured him that his beard did indeed make him look older. Celeste didn't even look fifteen and yet had somehow created a clandestine orphanage, so Kala asked, "How old were you when you started all this?"

"Old enough," she replied. "I grew up in a family with ample coin, which probably buys me some measure of protection from the guards, but street kids near my school would disappear. It wasn't right, so an idea was born."

Petr piped in, "Celeste didn't just find me; she really did rescue me. A few years back, I was busking and didn't see the guards approaching."

"Someone gets a little too into his music," Twill added.

Petr whacked him. "They were hustling me off when Celeste marched out the gates of her school. I'd seen her a few times, but I'd never met her. Well, this girl of eleven years…"

Celeste coughed.

"Sorry, Celeste. I know you're sensitive about your age. So, this girl, old beyond her years…"

Celeste nodded that that was an acceptable alternative.

"She marches right up to the lead guard and demands that he unhand me at once. He stared at her as though considering adding her to his collection, but she gave him a tongue-lashing about my playing in the school band and being needed for their upcoming play. If I were carted off, there'd be hell to pay. She basically bullied the man into letting me go."

"Hence this place," Celeste interjected. "I needed somewhere large enough to house Petr's enormous ego," she joked.

Petr smiled broadly. Celeste could do or say no wrong in his eyes. Twill looked at Kala as if to say, *She gets a pass, but I get nothing.*

Celeste changed topics. "Skye's a great cook, by the way. You're lucky to have him."

"I only recently reacquired him," Kala said.

"Events conspired against our being together for a while," Skye said in his defense.

"*Skye* conspired against our being together," Kala said, half-joking and half-accusing.

Ever the peacemaker, Twill interjected, "So you're only recently back together?"

"Yes," Kala confirmed.

"Fabulous. Then you should go on a date," he declared.

"They don't need you as a matchmaker, dummy," Petr said, dismissing Twill's suggestion. "They're already together."

"You have no sense of romance," Twill replied to Petr. "Celeste's performing tonight. You *have* to go hear her. She has the voice of an angel."

"I do not," Celeste blushed.

Clearly, everyone in this place is a big Celeste fan, Skye thought but found that he was being similarly won over by her.

"We've got enough coin between us to get you in the door and a drink in front of you. It'll be our re-engagement present, or whatever," Twill proposed and wouldn't take no for an answer.

"Sounds like fun," Skye concluded and looked so eager that Kala had to agree to it too. "No sharp pointy objects, though," Skye requested of Kala.

"For *one* night," she acquiesced.

"You don't have much time," Twill pointed out, shooing them out of the kitchen. "You'd better get changed."

On a whim, Kala had brought the grey dress that the Priestess had given her. She found one of the few rooms with a door and changed into the dress. Peeking out the door, Twill was the first to see her.

"Perfect," he declared. "Now you look more like a girl on a date than an assassin. Can I help you with your makeup?" Kala nodded emphatically, and Twill dug about for his art supplies. "I have to be careful to only use stuff that'll wash off, or you'll be pretty permanently," he joked.

"Good idea," Kala replied, then added light-heartedly, "Remember that I can kill you."

"It's never far from my mind, I assure you," he chuckled and set about dabbing her face with various powders and oils. He rolled back and moved a few candles closer, muttering, "Better," before resuming accenting some of Kala's features and smoothing out others. After a while, he leaned back to take in his masterpiece. "You'll turn heads for sure," he concluded.

She got up to look herself over in the mirror and was impressed with what she saw. "You're a magician!" she declared. "You're even more skilled than my old house-madam, and she had a lifetime of prettying up her girls."

Twill looked at her to elaborate on how she had come to be made up by a brothel's madam.

"A tale for another day," Kala dodged with a wink.

"I just highlighted your natural beauty," Twill deflected, putting away his supplies.

"I think you might have invented some too," Kala replied, turning her face side to side to examine it in the mirror.

Skye walked in, and his jaw dropped. "The gods have blessed me with an angel," he declared when he'd composed himself.

Kala bristled. "Please don't say that," she asked, to Skye's confusion. *How can I tell him that I'm widely believed to be an angel of death?* She sighed and took his arm to reassure him.

Celeste emerged in a diaphanous dress that was scandalous as hell on a girl of fourteen years. Kala's eyes went wide. "This old thing is great for tips," Celeste said, smoothing it over her body. Skye had to look away.

"Good for you, girl," Twill declared as Celeste's personal cheerleader.

Celeste led them out, and the three of them were careful not to dirty themselves when they stepped through the hole in the wall. They all helped move the sheet of wood back into place. Celeste guided them to a tavern that was a bit more upscale than Kala was used to. It was lit by an array of twinkling lanterns suspended from the ceiling, and true to Twill's description, it was very romantic.

Celeste guided them to a tiny table near the stage and bade them sit down before heading to the performers' room. Skye ordered them drinks, and they sat across from each other, bathed in the soft light of the lanterns, wondering what to say to each other.

"I still can't quite believe we're here together," Kala began and reached across the table to put her hand on Skye's. She looked about the room at tables of couples and close friends. "This is the life I've always dreamed of," she said wistfully. "A life in which a girl and a boy can just be a girl and a boy. No predators, no airships, no tyrants…" She looked at Skye and blushed. "It's silly, I know."

"Not at all," he replied, squeezing her hand. "Your life is anything but ordinary. Ordinary is good, although tonight, you're making it extraordinary." He held her hand, and they gazed into each other's eyes, drinking in every moment, acutely aware of how easy it was to be torn from each other.

The band stopped playing, signaling a change in performers. Celeste walked onto the stage, candlelight glinting off silvery powder that she'd applied to her skin. She looked ephemeral, and the room hushed. She sat on a stool and motioned for the band to start playing her music. It was lilting and haunting. She closed her eyes and began to sing. Twill hadn't been wrong to say she had the voice of an angel. Her song started low and built with passion, her voice winding around the listeners, coaxing every emotion from them. Kala was enthralled. Celeste's song flowed through her, and in it, Kala heard the story of her life. Tears coursed down her cheeks.

When the last echoes of her song faded, the room fell silent, then erupted in applause. Skye and Kala found themselves on their feet, not remembering having risen. Celeste nodded to the crowd modestly and retired from the stage.

Kala wiped the tears from her wet cheeks. "She's amazing," she exclaimed. Skye was speechless and merely nodded.

"I want this life," Kala declared, looking around the room as hot tears flowed anew. *I don't want to be a murderer, banished, a weapon, a savior... I just want to be a girl, a friend, a granddaughter*, she thought.

Skye shifted around to her side of the table and put an arm around her. He knew he couldn't promise they could have this life – the lie died on his tongue. He could hold her though, and that's what he did.

"I'm sorry," she sniffled as she regained her composure.

Skye cradled her head in his hands, wiping away her tears and telling her, "Never be sorry for feeling what you feel. That's your strength leaking through, not weakness."

Kala smiled hesitantly, then kissed him chastely. "Thank you."

Skye squeezed her hand and retook his seat. They enjoyed the rest of their evening, pushing aside the fact that they were a couple of lost souls, and contenting themselves that they'd at least found each other. They made their way back to Celeste's sanctuary later that night, finding her waiting for them.

"You were incredible!" Kala exclaimed, hugging her and meaning it with every fiber of her being.

"Thank you for saying so. It's my passion. Well, other than this lot," she said, looking at the children lying on beds about the room.

"Why didn't you join us after your set?" Skye asked.

"You two looked to be having a moment," she replied.

"I guess we were," Kala admitted bashfully. "Thank you for that too. I'll never forget tonight."

Celeste squeezed her hand and retired to sleep wherever it was she slept. Kala left Skye talking with Frey and went to bed herself. Sleep didn't come easily though, as she lay awake waiting for her perfect world to combust. The longer she spent with Skye, the more her anesthetized heart thawed, and unpleasant memories surfaced along with the pleasant.

Her dreams that night were filled with images of the drug addict, Chantal, who she'd been forced to fight, her fists bloodied from pummeling Beryl, Tito stiffening as she drove her daggers into his neck, and the gambler's daughter shouting, "No, daddy!" as she was dragged away. Kala thrashed and sobbed in her sleep, and Skye pulled her to him, whispering soothing words as he held her tight.

Kala woke in the morning to an empty bed. She bolted up and rushed out of the room in a panic, only to hear Skye's melodic voice as she burst into the kitchen.

He looked up, concerned. "Are you okay, beautiful?" he asked.

"Of course, of course – just desperate for some kai," she lied and set about looking for a cup.

Skye strode over, handed her one, kissed her on the cheek, then returned to regaling the gathered children about Kala's exploits, waving a spoon for emphasis. The children stared at her reverently.

She waved lazily at them. "What are you telling these kids?" she asked Skye.

"Your story."

"How does it end?"

"That remains to be seen, but I'm told it's a happy ending," he smiled.

She smiled back, but inside, she felt nagging apprehension. "I'd better get started on the next chapter," she declared, putting down her kai. "I'm going to scout the city's temple. Are Celeste, Petr, or Twill around?"

"Celeste is out, Petr never gets up before noon, I'm told, and Twill is at his studio painting," Skye replied.

"Darn."

"I know where it is," little Frey piped up. "I can show you."

"Celeste wouldn't mind?" Kala asked.

"As long as I'm with an unkillable killing machine, I don't think she'll mind."

"What did you tell these kids?" Kala asked Skye in exasperation.

"Only the truth, darling," he replied mischievously.

She turned to Frey. "Okay. You're my guide today."

"If it's okay with you," Skye asked her, "I'm going to stay here and do some repairs. Apparently, not a single person here knows how to use a hammer."

Kala nodded her consent. "We all have our strengths, carpenter-boy. You get this place squared away, and I'll see you back in time for dinner."

"Sounds good, and oh, if you run into any mushrooms in your travels, dinner would be grateful."

"Noted."

Kala didn't have any outfits beyond the dress she'd worn the night before and her skin-tight leathers, neither of which were particularly subtle, so she took the liberty of borrowing some of Celeste's clothes that were loose on her and so fit Kala passably well.

"Celest won't mind," Frey assured her as she returned to her room to get changed. Moments later, he was guiding her toward the temple at the center of the city. It was an imposing structure with its own high walls. Black standards emblazoned with skulls flapped in the wind high on the parapets. It had all the charm of a crypt. Kala wanted to scale a nearby building and spy into the temple grounds, but no adjacent building was higher than the temple walls. *More fortress than temple*, Kala mused. Their best alternative was to position themselves across from the temple gates, which were open to allow people with business at the temple to come and go.

"We need a reason to loiter outside the gates," Kala told Frey. "Any ideas?"

"I could busk, and you could be my 'handler.' I never go out without juggling balls."

"Well, aren't you resourceful?" Kala smiled, and they set themselves up on the corner across from the gates. She looked for all the world like Frey's guardian but kept a surreptitious eye on the goings-on in the temple.

Near noon, Frey was tiring, and nothing exciting had been visible through the gates when Kala spotted a woman in flowing black robes approaching down the street. *It can't be*, she thought. *How can she be here?* The High Priestess from the town that Kala had just left strode through the temple gates. It was unmistakably her with her long black hair, high cheekbones, and darkly shadowed eyes. *I have to find a way inside and find out what she's doing here*, Kala concluded.

Kala grabbed a bewildered Frey and raced back to Celeste's place with him in tow. She burst in and announced to Skye, "She's here! I don't know how she's here, but she's here!"

"Who's here?"

"It doesn't matter, but it means there must be a way to direct the airships, not just stow aboard them. The Priestess proves it," Kala exclaimed, her mind racing. "I need Twill's help."

"I'll go get him," Frey offered.

"Thank you. Please make haste, my little man."

Frey rushed out and returned with Twill.

"I need your help making me look not like me," Kala told him.

"I guess that can be done," he replied, thinking it over.

"Oh, and I need to look like a priestess."

"That'll be tougher, but let's see what we can scrounge up." He got the kids running around looking for a list of items which they treated as a hugely entertaining scavenger hunt. "Our assassin needs a disguise!" they crowed. By the time Twill was done with her, Kala judged that she was unrecognizable enough and might just pass for a young priestess on pilgrimage. She hugged him, being careful not to smudge his carefully applied concealer, and hurried back to the temple as quickly as she judged she could without drawing attention to herself.

Arriving, she focused on the dance of infiltrating the most challenging building she'd yet encountered. She became invisible in her mundane manners and movements and slipped through the gates with a party of vintners, looking equally purposeful and scattered. Once inside, she used her knowledge of the layout of the temple where she'd recently stayed to navigate this one, or at least recognize their common elements. *Where would you be?* she asked herself. *Here to reveal prophecy, I bet*, she concluded. *I need to find the auditorium.* She scanned the grounds for a structure that looked the most like a classroom building. She picked one based on the spacing of its windows, and as she entered it, found that she'd judged correctly.

She hurried down the empty corridors toward a room whose door was guarded by two muscular monks. She approached them, looking rattled. "I'm here for the Priestess's address. Is it here? Did I miss it?" she asked, flustered.

"Through here, yes, but go around to the back door, so you don't interrupt her talk."

She looked about for the most likely placement of a back door, but nothing was apparent.

"You're not from here, are you?" the monk asked suspiciously, and his hand drifted to the hilt of his sword.

"No. I just flew in from another temple. The winds were terribly slow. I'm *so* late," she said despairingly.

The guards didn't bat an eye about her "flying in," confirming her suspicions about travel by airship.

"This way, priestess," one of the guards sighed and guided her down the hallway.

She thanked him profusely, and he left her at a nondescript door, which she entered as unobtrusively as she could. The High Priestess was in the middle of her talk, so no one noticed Kala slip to the back of the audience.

"Soren's forces advance from the northlands," the Priestess was saying, "laying waste to everything in their path. He's playing his role perfectly, although maybe a little too perfectly. It won't be many more years before his armies set every corner of the continent aflame."

"Should we begin evacuating to the Wastes, Priestess," a matronly-looking woman sitting at the head table asked her.

"Not yet, but soon, yes. I think it'll be two years before Soren is at the gates of Bayre and two moons more for him to sack it. He's already disrupting trade by air. Communities will collapse for that reason alone, if he doesn't put them to the sword first."

Kala was reminded of her village's dependence for its survival on the contents of the airships. Worse, Skye's village was entirely dependent on supplies from outside. *If the ships stopped coming, how quickly would they starve?*

"And where is our champion?" the elderly woman asked impatiently.

"She's currently unaccounted for – although I've heard reports that she's here in Bayre."

Murmuring filled the room.

"The Ancients have faith in her," the Priestess reassured them. "She will rally forces and push back. The world will be decimated, and balance will be restored for another millennium."

"With all due respect to you and your sister oracles, the Ancients' thinking can be difficult to infer, and the three of you do not always agree with each other's interpretation."

"In this, I can assure you that we are in agreement," the Priestess defended, hiding the annoyance she felt at being doubted.

"So, we do not need to take matters into our own hands?" the old woman pressed.

"Not at this time, no, but we must remain ready in case the girl fails."

It struck Kala like a blow that the "girl" they were speaking about was her. She reeled, and the priestess beside her looked at her worriedly. "Breakfast isn't agreeing with me," Kala told her, and she did genuinely look green. Priestesses moved out of her way as she made for the exit. The room had become a sea of raised hands and urgent questions, and Kala was able to slip out unnoticed, despite the tightening in her chest.

She stood in the hall, trying desperately to catch her breath. *The world was going to burn. It was burning already. People she cared about were going to die. What could she do to stop it? She was one girl — she had no allies, no army.* She couldn't breathe. She swooned as a guard approached. "Help," was all she could manage to say before passing out.

She woke sometime later to find a kindly woman peering down at her. It took her a moment to deduce that she was lying in bed in the temple infirmary.

"Feeling better, dear?" she asked Kala.

The juxtaposition of her concern and the Priestess's cold recounting of the end of the world nauseated Kala again. The woman handed her a bucket and patted her on the shoulder. "I'll be outside if you need me," she said and stepped out. Kala threw up before the door had even closed.

She slowly regained control over herself. She had to make it back home to her grandfather, Lily… everyone. The world was going to hell, and despite the Ancients' misplaced faith in her, there wasn't a gods-damn thing she could do about it. If she could at least save the ones she loved, then maybe her small life wouldn't be in vain. She spat out the bitter taste, got out of bed, and rushed out. The kindly nurse tried to stop her, but Kala pushed past her with a string of apologies and thanks.

She made her way out the temple gates without recalling how she'd accomplished it and stumbled back to Celeste's sanctuary. She burst in, looking like death. Skye raced to her side.

She raised a hand to forestall his questions. "We need to get home now," she said breathlessly.

"Yes, of course," he soothed her.

It had the opposite effect. "We need to leave. NOW!" Kala shouted. "The Church has airships – I'm sure of it, and we're going to steal one."

4
Dhara

Dhara sat up in the dark confines of the tunnel she'd dived into with her sister. She tentatively removed her hands from her ears and found that the panic that had assailed her earlier had vanished. Staying silent, she gently pulled Caia's hands away from her ears and helped her up as they both pulled the bits of leaves out of them. Torchlight flashed outside the tunnel, but it was dulled, as though viewed from deep underwater.

They didn't want to be discovered near the entrance and couldn't leave the tunnel, so their only option was to move deeper into it. It quickly became so dark, however, that they were entirely robbed of their senses. Without a hand anchored to the wall, they felt like they were floating.

They advanced side by side, holding hands and tracing the tunnel wall with the other. The tunnel descended slightly, and they thought they heard skittering ahead. They felt watched, too, but neither sensation felt entirely substantial. Caia squeezed Dhara's hand tighter, and she squeezed back.

The air was as still as in a tomb but without the stale smell of death. The walls, curiously, weren't covered with dust. Caia removed her hand from the wall and rubbed her fingers together, feeling no residue, as though the tunnel was well-traveled. She became disoriented, however, without grounding herself to the wall and quickly reached back to anchor herself to it.

After walking a long distance, Caia felt she could risk whispering. "I knew you'd come for me," she thanked her sister, pulling her into an embrace.

Dhara didn't want to tell Caia just how lucky they were to be alive – her sister's faith in her was absolute.

"Nina?" Caia asked worriedly.

"She's with Zara," Dhara replied, reassuring Caia that her young daughter was safe.

"Thank the Goddess," Caia declared and pulled Dhara back into a hug.

"We should probably keep moving," Dhara reminded her.

"Have you noticed that the air isn't getting staler as we descend?" Caia asked.

Dhara hadn't.

"There has to be some airflow, even if we can't feel it. That means the tunnel must connect to the surface at both ends. We should keep descending."

Dhara didn't like the idea of going deeper underground, but Caia's inference made sense, and it gave purpose to their progress, so they continued. Dhara had torches in her pack but feared that the way wouldn't always remain this easy to follow, so she resisted the urge to pull one out and light it.

As they advanced farther, the tunnel widened slightly, pulling them a little farther apart. Dhara felt the wall give way to open air at the exact moment her foot failed to find purchase. She and her sister pitched forward.

They landed on their hands and knees, but aside from some scrapes, they were no worse for wear. Dhara reached around her but didn't feel the wall. She pulled her pack from her back, rooted through it until she found her flint, and struck the pieces together to illumine their surroundings with a spark. It was only by gradations in the darkness that they could tell that they'd fallen into a circular depression surrounded by six branching tunnels.

"Which one did we come through?" Caia asked.

"I'm not sure, but I think it's one of those three."

"Which one should we take, now?"

"I don't know."

They sat in darkness, contemplating their options, when a thought struck Caia. "I have an idea, but we'll need light."

Dhara pulled out a torch and lit it.

"On the count of three, point to an entryway that *feels* right. Don't think about it. Just use your intuition," Caia suggested. "One, two, three…"

They looked at each other but found that they were each pointing to different tunnels.

"Let's try again. One, two, three…"

Again, they pointed to different tunnels. Caia sighed, but her failed experiment gave Dhara an idea. "From the moment I first entered this place, I've felt repelled," she recounted. "It's as if it's warded by strong magic. On the count of three, point to an entryway that feels *wrong*. Okay?"

Caia nodded her understanding.

"One, two, three…"

The girls looked at each other and found that they were pointing at the same tunnel.

"Does that mean we should take any route except that one?" Caia asked.

"No. Just the opposite. That's the one we should take because it's the one we're not supposed to take."

Caia was confused, but she'd never doubted her sister before, and this hardly seemed like the time to start, so she shrugged and gestured her to lead on.

Dhara stepped into the warded tunnel, which appeared identical to the others. It was the same width, and the walls felt as smooth. "I think we can extinguish the torch and save it for when we really need it," she concluded.

Caia agreed and moved to stand beside her sister as she put out the light. Once the torch had cooled, she wrapped it in leather and placed it back in her pack. Caia felt in the dark for her sister's hand. Holding it tightly, she squeezed it to say, "Let's go," and they set off again. The tunnel rose slightly as if it were a mirror image of the one they'd descended. It could even be the same tunnel for all they knew. In fact, at the edge of their hearing was the same skittering sound they'd heard before and the same feeling of being watched. It didn't unsettle Dhara much, however, because she knew that if a spirit were going to consume her, there wasn't much she could do about it, so what was the point of worrying?

The distance they'd walked since leaving the nexus seemed farther than they'd walked before arriving at it, and given that they hadn't re-emerged into the arms of murderous villagers, they concluded that it must be a different tunnel.

Caia thought she saw flickers of light ahead but assumed it was probably just her vision playing tricks on her again. Several times earlier, she'd begun to see vivid images as her brain, denied sensory input, concluded that she was asleep and filled the dark void with dreams.

The wall fell away again beneath Dhara's hand, and she tensed for a fall, but her foot struck the ground as it always had. She and her sister stopped.

"Do you see a faint glow ahead?" Dhara whispered.

"I thought I was imagining it, but yes."

They edged forward slightly into what appeared to be an enormous cavern and found themselves on a ledge, high above its floor. Below, at the cavern's center, was a crystal lit from within by flickering sparks. The intermittent crimson flashes were the faint source of light they'd seen. As their eyes adjusted to the dim and inconsistent light, they noticed dozens of metallic spiders moving in and out of fissures in the ground around the crystal. The girls' blood froze.

It's the home of a demon, Dhara concluded. They looked about for any manner of escape other than the tunnel they'd just exited, but all they could see was the ledge they were standing on ringing the cavern. Deciding that moving onward was preferable to backward, Dhara motioned to her sister that they should proceed along the ledge. Caia didn't like the idea and hoped they wouldn't wake the sleeping demon.

Dhara led the way across the narrow ledge. She and her sister edged along, holding hands with their backs to the wall. They'd made it halfway around when they noticed that the spiders had ceased moving and watched them with unblinking eyes, making Caia's skin crawl. She disliked spiders at the best of times, and devil-spiders with razor legs took her fear to a whole new level. But they were halfway around and committed, so they kept moving. They braced themselves for the spiders to surge toward them, but mercifully, they simply watched them with soulless eyes.

Arriving at the cavern's far side, they found another tunnel, identical to the one they'd entered from, ducked into it, and fled. No sound followed them, but they didn't slow down until fatigue forced them to.

Over time, the tunnel wall began to feel faintly damp, then increasingly wet. *Perhaps we're nearing the river*, Dhara thought hopefully. Accounting for the faster progress they'd made underground rather than through dense jungle, it was possible, she concluded. Her sense of direction had always served her well in the labyrinth of the jungle, and despite the sensory deprivation underground, some part of her felt that they'd been traveling in the direction of home.

Caia was the first to notice that she could make out the faint outline of her sister beside her. Advancing farther, the pitch dark gradually gave way to gloom, which in turn gave way to soft light. Eventually, they pushed through a vine-covered opening into the jungle, where they gulped in deep breaths of humid air. There were no black pillars in sight, and Dhara said a silent prayer thanking the Goddess. She and Caia both heard but didn't yet see flowing water. They moved toward the sound and soon found themselves at the river's edge.

"We'll have to wait for the sun to set and rise again for me to be sure whether we're upstream or downstream from where I hid the canoe," Dhara told her sister. "If we can find it, it'll make the trip home that much faster."

Caia noticed for the first time just how exhausted her sister looked, so she suggested, "Why don't you light a fire while I look around for something to eat?"

Dhara agreed and handed her knife to her sister. "No bow or spear, sorry."

Caia shrugged and took the knife, turning it over in her hand to judge its weight and balance. "I'll see what I can do," she said and ventured out, keeping her eyes on the trees. It didn't take long for her to spot a tree rat munching on leaves. She snuck closer and let fly her sister's knife. The rat fell to the jungle floor, impaled. Caia raced to finish it off, but it had already succumbed to its injuries. It was a good omen, she concluded.

She returned to her sister, who had a small fire going, and they feasted on roast rat. As the sun set, Dhara used it to get a sense of their position, which the morning would hopefully confirm. The girls fell into a deep sleep holding each other.

Dhara woke before dawn and was careful not to disturb her sister as she rose to watch the direction in which the sun rose, concluding that they were upstream from where she'd hidden the canoe. Dhara let Caia sleep, and once she eventually woke, they walked along the water's edge, which the sparse undergrowth thankfully permitted. Several times Dhara thought she spotted the tree that she'd used to mark the canoe's hiding place, but it was only at the fourth such tree that she finally found it. They pulled the canoe into the water and paddled downriver, staying far from the shore and possible attack. The jungle gradually began to look familiar.

At the point where the river came closest to their village, they steered for shore and pulled the canoe out of the water, placing it alongside the others that the village stored there. A guard observed their approach as she cleaned her nails with the tip of her knife. She addressed Dhara, "Your mother says that you're not welcome to return."

"It's my sister who returns. I'm merely escorting her."

The guard considered this. "I guess she never said that Caia wasn't welcome. Do as you please. It's your funeral," she shrugged and didn't bar their way.

The girls walked the well-worn paths until they came across a rope ladder that would take them up to their village in the trees. Climbing off the ground, Dhara felt liberated. She despised treading the earth unless she was hunting. Reaching the first of many crisscrossing catwalks, they began the elevated trek back to their family's dwellings, which were built on platforms suspended high in the trees.

They passed many surprised villagers, none of whom addressed them until they spotted their sister Zara running across a swaying rope bridge to pick Caia up in an embrace. She pulled Dhara in as well, and the three of them hugged. Dhara was the first to break away, feeling self-conscious.

"Mother knows you're back," Zara informed them.

"That figures. She has eyes everywhere," Dhara replied.

"She wants to see you both at the family tree immediately."

"We just saw her deep underground," Caia joked, recalling the devil crystal.

Dhara laughed, but Zara looked confused.

"I'll explain later," Caia told her. "Where's Nina?"

"Playing, but the longer we make mother wait, the more hell there'll be to pay," Zara replied, unable to outrightly suggest that her sister wait to see her daughter but advising against it.

Caia hated to put off their reunion but knew her mother's temperament and agreed to meet with her first. As the tribe's matriarch, their mother's chambers ringed a towering Sumaumeira tree, around which her family members lived in adjacent trees while their servants dwelt on the ground. The sisters traversed paths that took them straight to the room in which their mother held court.

Walking into its antechamber, several servants looked up as they passed. One of them stepped clumsily into Dhara's way, and she shoved the man aside. "Remember your place," she told him angrily, pushing past. It burdened her to know that her father had been a slave, and the entire tribe knew it. It lessened her in their eyes.

Dhara's mother had first married Zara's father to form an alliance between their families, but she could barely stand the man, and when a servant in his household caught her eye, she took him as a lover. When she became pregnant with Dhara, however, she had her lover executed to guard her secret, despite it being the worst kept in the tribe. But, if anyone spoke of it, they risked having their tongue cut out, or worse. Zara's father had since died as well, the victim of some intrigue or other, but Dhara's parentage was still never spoken of.

After Dhara's father's death, her mother married again, to a widower whose family she absorbed when she birthed Caia. With his family assimilated, Caia no longer served any purpose to her, so her mother callously wrote her off. When Caia was raped at twelve, her mother was ambivalent, and it was Zara who hunted the man down. His body was discovered tied to his family's tree, less the majority of his skin. When his kin were predictably outraged, Dhara's mother was ready and had them slaughtered. Dhara suspected that she'd likely engineered Caia's mistreatment to consolidate her power. Caia probably thought so, too, because she refused to give up the resulting baby to spite her mother.

The sisters entered their mother's chamber, where she sat on her throne, ironically carved from the heartwood of an ancient tree. Her eyes spat fire. "Why did you come back?" she snapped.

"Happy to see you too, mother," Dhara quipped.

Zara glared at her sister to mind her tongue, but Dhara lacked the patience to feign subservience.

"You disobeyed me by leaving," her mother declared.

"No one forbade it," Dhara pointed out.

"You interfered with the sacrifice."

"Unsuccessfully," Dhara reminded her. "Caia was still sent away. I just brought her back."

"And risked angering the gods."

"If the gods are angry, it's with the tribe downwind. We met their obligation to send someone in the balloon. What happened later is not on us."

"Do not speak as though you know the gods' will."

Dhara knew her mother wasn't the least bit superstitious, only self-serving. "I thought you'd be happy to see your daughter back," she goaded her.

"That useless girl? I sent her away to strengthen our bloodline, and you have the audacity to bring her back?"

"I'm not useless," Caia protested.

Her mother rolled her eyes dismissively and called for her personal maid, who entered nervously. Caia's mother pulled a dagger from her belt and handed it to the girl to bring to Caia. She crossed the room apprehensively and gave it to her.

"Kill her," her mother commanded Caia, gesturing to the maid. The confused girl's eyes went wide with fear, but the matriarch's stare pinned her to where she stood shaking.

Caia hesitated, then strode over to her mother's throne and stuck the dagger into the armrest. "Kill her yourself."

"Useless," her mother concluded. Then, turning to Dhara, said, "And what's that outfit? You insult your family by wearing it."

"Its owner had no use for it in the afterlife," she shrugged.

"You two disappoint me. Leave my chambers. You too, Zara."

The girls withdrew and returned to the dwelling they all shared. Caia held her breath as she pushed open the door, surprising her daughter.

"Mommy!" she shrieked and raced into her arms. "Where have you been?" she asked accusatorily.

"On an adventure, darling. I'll tell you all about it tomorrow."

Nina looked none too pleased to have to wait.

"There were airships, devils, and daggers," Caia teased.

"I want to know now!" her daughter demanded.

"Mommy's tired and needs to wash. Tomorrow, I promise."

Dhara ordered the servants to prepare a bath. They hesitated to take orders from someone the matriarch had effectively excommunicated until Zara put a hand on the hilt of her knife, prompting them to scramble for water and wood. Dhara and Caia bathed and only began to feel like themselves once they'd washed the dark underground off their bodies. Everyone climbed into their beds, Caia holding her daughter tightly, and they all fell into a deep sleep.

Dhara woke to the feeling of something amiss. She opened an eye to see a blade falling on her. She grabbed the assassin's wrist and barely kept the knife from piercing her chest. Zara was roused by the struggle and leaped up to grab the man from behind. While he fought to free himself from Zara's grip, Dhara slowly turned his blade around and drove it into his chest. He stopped struggling, and Zara threw him off her sister.

"Great," Dhara said, wiping the man's blood off of herself, "Now I'll have to wash again."

Caia put Nina back to bed, who didn't seem terribly bothered by the assassination attempt, and the sisters spent the remainder of the night alternating who kept watch for further attempts on their lives. In the morning, they were again summoned to their mother's chambers.

Caia left her daughter with a servant, reminding her that it would be no fun for her at her grandmother's court.

"She's mean," Nina agreed.

"She sure is," Caia replied, "but we only say that in our heads, never out loud."

When they arrived, they saw that their mother was flanked by the matriarchs of the next two largest families. This did not bode well.

Her mother stood, pointed an accusatory finger at Dhara, and addressed all those present, "Last night, my daughter returned, against my wishes. If this weren't insulting enough, she took a slave to her bed, and when she was finished with him, brutally murdered him."

Dhara opened her mouth to speak the truth of the night's events, but her mother's guards raised their crossbows, and she knew it was futile to set the record straight.

Her mother continued, "While I don't care what my daughter does in her bed, this slave was my property, and I'll not brook this final insult. Dhara, you are hereby banished from the village. If you're seen again after the rising of tomorrow's sun, you will be put to death." She looked to the crones on either side of her, "Has this decree been duly witnessed?"

"It has," they replied.

"And will you uphold it?"

"As you would ours."

Settled as it was, two of her mother's guards advanced to escort Dhara from the room. Caia started to protest, but Zara silenced her. The guards reached to grab Dhara by the arms, but she shrugged away from them.

"I know the way," she spat.

They wouldn't let her return to her dwelling and instead shadowed her as she walked directly to the edge of the village, then watched her descend the rope ladder to the ground. Dhara winced when her feet touched the earth, but she walked to the canoes. The guard there smirked and shrugged.

"Told you," she said sarcastically.

Dhara resisted punching her in the face and dragged a canoe toward the water instead.

"Wait!" Caia's voice rang out as she raced down the path toward her sister.

Dhara stopped what she was doing but resisted hugging her sister goodbye. She needed to leave with her dignity intact. "You know that if I return, you're sworn to kill me?" she reminded Caia.

"Of course. That's why we're going with you."

"We?"

"Yes, we," Zara added, emerging from the path carrying Nina in one arm and three packs in the other.

Dhara could no longer resist hugging them.

"Sisters," Caia declared.

"Sisters," Dhara and Zara replied in unison.

They each grabbed a canoe and dragged it into the river. Caia positioned Nina at her feet, sat down, and joined her sisters in steering toward the northlands.

5
Kala

Skye, Celeste, Petr, and Twill all stared at Kala in shock. "What do you mean, 'We have to steal one of the Church's airships?'" Skye asked her. "And where do you imagine it keeps its private stock?"

"I'm not sure, but if we follow the Priestess, I'm sure she'll lead us straight to them. I saw her walk up to the temple, so it stands to reason that the ship she took to get here isn't inside, but we've got to hurry – she could leave anytime, and I have to be there to follow her when she does." She grabbed her leathers, pulled her top over her head, and tossed it aside.

"Whoa!" Petr declared, and he, Twill, and Skye spun around to face away.

"No time for modesty," Kala explained as she hurriedly changed. Letting them know that she was done, the boys turned back around. She pulled a tin of black ointment out of her pack and spread it over her exposed skin before pulling the hood of her tunic over her head. Lastly, she strapped on her daggers but left her swords behind.

Skye gawked at her transformation.

"This is what I do," she told him gently. "It's what I'm good at." She squeezed his arm and raced out the door into the gathering dusk. She made her way among the shadows to the temple gates and took a position as far away as she dared. Soon after, several monks slipped out the gate and made their way into the night. *Scouts*, Kala surmised. *Prudent.* She melted deeper into the shadows and kept watch.

The debate she'd overheard at the temple kept intruding into her thoughts, distracting her. *The old woman called me "the Church's champion,"* she recalled. It couldn't feel further from the truth to Kala as she hid, alone, in the shadows. *If I'm who they expect to counter the army of that Soren-fellow, Goddess help us all!*

Before long, the Priestess exited the temple, flanked by a couple more monks. *I wonder if Brother Grey is one of them,* Kala thought, surprising herself that she missed him despite his standoffishness.

The party turned left and made their way down the street with Kala following at a distance, constantly wary of crossing paths with a member of the Priestess's advance party, who were out in the night somewhere. She followed the Priestess halfway across the city, then abruptly lost her trail in an out-of-the-way alley. Kala traced and retraced her steps but couldn't figure out where the Priestess had gone. She stood in the lane, trying to stay calm and think, when she caught the faint smell of lilac. *Still using the same soap?* she thought and smiled. She followed the scent to a grate, but the fragrance went no farther. She bent down and attempted to lift the grate up and out of her way. It gave way grudgingly, but with some effort, she managed to push it aside far enough for her to climb into the shaft it covered. It was even harder to drag the grate back into position from beneath it, but she succeeded.

Kala descended the ladder into darkness. The tunnel at the bottom of the shaft was pitch black, but she didn't dare light a torch for fear of announcing her presence. She felt her way along in the dark instead, following the scent of lilac. It was slow going, but she was able to follow the Priestess's trail. At first, she tried to keep track of the turns she took but following the Priestess's faint scent took all of her attention. *There is no way I'm going to remember this later,* she thought ruefully but continued to follow the tunnels blindly until they disgorged her into the night through an exit covered with vines. She breathed in the fresh air hungrily after the stale air of the tunnels.

The wind had dispersed the Priestess's scent, but Kala saw a lone torch flit in and out of the trees in the distance. She followed at a comfortable distance, although she struggled not to trip over the uneven ground. The Priestess's party walked for what felt like an eternity until strange forms began to poke up from the ground, and Kala started to feel a powerful sense of unease. Had she not made up her mind to follow the Priestess, she would have turned back. Finally, the torch stopped its steady advance. Whatever her destination, the Priestess had arrived at it. Kala crept forward with all the stealth she'd honed over her long years in the forest, then positioned herself in some brush close enough to see what the Priestess was doing. As she peered through the branches, the sense of foreboding continued to gnaw at her.

The Priestess's party grew to five, and Kala thanked the Goddess that she hadn't stumbled into one of the scouts. The Priestess was standing in a stone circle, much like the dais outside Kala's village where airships landed, except that this one was surrounded by a ring of unevenly spaced onyx cenotaphs. Three of the monks had established a perimeter, and the fourth was speaking with the Priestess in low tones. After what seemed like an eternity, one of the monks signaled the others, and the Priestess and her counsel moved outside the circle as an airship slowly drifted down. Kala could only make out the matte-black ship because it eclipsed the stars. The ship drew closer to the center of the stone circle as it approached. How it adjusted course was unclear because it descended utterly silently. When it finally reached the ground, Kala heard a low metallic thump, and the ship held still without the usual small army of people holding it down with ropes. *That's new*, Kala remarked.

The Priestess and her counsel approached the ship and boarded it. The departing monk handed one of his colleagues his torch, waved them away, and closed the door behind him. Two of the monks walked over to one of the creepy cenotaphs, and while it was hard to make out what they were doing, it looked like they rolled a large stone a short distance away from where it had been resting against the pillar. Kala heard the same low metallic thud she'd heard earlier, but this time the ship rose.

The monks left behind turned and headed back toward the city, passing nerve-wrackingly close to where she lay but not detecting her. Once she judged them safely gone, she rushed out to mark which cenotaph she thought the stone had rested against, but she didn't need to, as the stone still lay closer to it than any of the others. Kala then scrambled to mark the direction she believed the ship had headed when it departed. It was hard to gauge as it was only by gradations of darkness that she'd been able to infer where the ship went at all.

Kala decided that she needed to spend the night near this spot so she could better infer the mechanics of directing an airship in the light of day. However, she needed somewhere to overnight off the ground, and the surrounding trees weren't tall enough to provide security. She scanned the horizon and spotted the ruins of some ancient structure. She shivered as she looked at it but decided that staying alive outweighed her trepidation and trudged in its direction. Arriving, she discovered that it was the framework of some multi-level structure that had canted over as the ground beneath it had given way. *What type of structure outlasts the earth itself?* she wondered. *Something ancient and best forgotten*, she concluded. She pulled herself up and shimmed up the cold obsidian pillars until she was several levels above the ground. Only a predator that could jump great heights had any chance of following her to where she lay panting in the dark. She slept fitfully and was awoken several times by the sound of nails on stone below her. She pulled her tunic tighter and huddled against a pillar.

The dawning light gradually illumined her surroundings and revealed nothing overtly frightening, but the sense of dread persisted. *This place reeks of ancient death*, she thought and climbed down. The ground below her didn't appear disturbed, making her wonder if she'd imagined the sounds in the night. She oriented herself toward the direction in which she believed the airship landing area lay and walked back to it, finding it easily enough. She walked around the stone circle on which the airship had landed. In the daylight, the cenotaphs ringing it rose skyward like the legs of a dead spider on its back. The thought made her irrationally afraid that it would spring to life and rend her apart. With an effort, she pushed the image aside.

Several small, round stones surrounded the dais, but she was able to identify the one that the monks had moved by the fresh tracks that moving it had made. Kala placed a pebble on top of it to mark it, just in case she forgot which one it was later. There was no rhyme or reason to the stones or cenotaphs, but Kala vaguely recalled that the airship had left in the general direction of the cenotaph against which the stone had rested, more or less. The margin of error included almost half of the cenotaphs, however, so she concluded that she shouldn't put too much stock in that theory.

Satisfied that staring at the stones any longer wouldn't reveal any more secrets, she turned and headed back toward the city. She knew she'd never find the entrance to the tunnel that would take her back inside the city walls but assumed she could enter through its main gate. As expected, the tunnel entrance eluded her, but she could see in the distance that the city's great gate lay open to farmers streaming in with the day's harvest. *I don't look like much of a farmer in my leathers*, she thought but decided to improvise when she got closer. She noticed several men and women wearing little in the heat, so she turned down her leather top, exposing her undershirt. She rubbed the black ointment off her face with handfuls of grass. *That's as good as it's going to get*, she concluded, her skin raw. She walked up to an ox-drawn wagon and mimicked a woman picking up potatoes that fell off it and returning them to the wagon. This kept her busy until she entered the city walls and a bit beyond. When the wagons veered in the direction of the city stores, she slunk away and pulled her top back up.

There were more guards out than usual, she noted, and parents hustling their children off the streets. As she neared Celeste's hideout, she heard sounds of a struggle. She raced toward them, rounding a corner to see Celeste struggling between two guards, Skye with a sword to his throat, Petr on the ground with a guard bent over him, and Twill surrounded by the younger children clinging to him in fear.

Twill was the first to spot Kala. "They've got Celeste! Help her!" he yelled, beside himself with panic.

Something in Kala snapped – she'd seen too much thuggery in her short life already. "Take your hands off of her," she commanded coolly as she walked down the alley. They responded by tightening their grip instead. *Wrong move*, Kala thought. The guard that had been standing over Petr advanced toward her.

Skye moved to intercept him, but the guard with the sword at his throat prevented him.

"I was going to go easy on you because you're just doing your job," Kala began as she stalked closer, "but it's an evil job, and you do it anyway. So, it's no excuse, and I don't excuse you."

"Are you done, little girl?" the guard that had beat up Petr sneered and pulled a heavy wooden mace from behind his back.

"I haven't even started, but I can already tell that I'm going to enjoy this," she replied, cracking her knuckles.

The man charged at her, swinging, but Kala deftly side-stepped him as he reached up to where his throat had formerly been intact. Kala wiped her bloody dagger on a pant leg and turned to face the two men holding Celeste while her assailant collapsed, gurgling on his blood. The men released Celeste, and each pulled out a knife. Kala smiled an evil smile and returned her own dagger to its sheath, gesturing the men forward empty-handed. The men looked at each other and attacked. Kala ducked under the first man's blade and guided his momentum in an arc that took the point of his knife under and into the other man's armpit. She then yanked the knife free, bent the man's arm at the elbow, and drove his blade deep into his stomach. She pulled it upward, and both men fell to the ground trying in vain to stop their lifeblood from escaping them.

The guard holding Skye at sword-point moved behind him and warned her, "One step closer and…" He never finished, however, as Kala's dagger lodged in his forehead. His grip turned to jelly, and his sword clattered to the ground before he did.

In less time than it took to draw three breaths, four men lay dead in the street, and everyone stared at Kala in shock.

She moved to Celeste's side, who was visibly shaken, and told her, "You've got to get yourself and the kids out of here before this is discovered."

Celeste recovered her composure and nodded, then called to Twill, "Have the kids gather their things," then asked him, "Can we hide at your studio tonight until we figure ourselves out in the morning?"

"Of course," he replied and sent the kids inside.

Skye moved to help Petr up.

"They smashed my guitar," he said, wincing. "Why would they do that?"

Kala suggested to Celeste that they all hide out for a while.

"Like hell," she replied. "I'm going to live my life, and these bastards aren't going to stop me."

Kala understood and turned to Skye. "We should leave now. I may have found our way home."

"Take whatever supplies you need," Celeste offered.

Kala found tears springing to her eyes at Celeste's kindness and the prospect of leaving someone she'd just begun to regard as a friend and kindred spirit. "How can I ever repay you?"

"By fulfilling your destiny," Celeste replied.

"Oh, you don't want that," Kala shuddered. "My destiny is to plunge the world into fire."

"Not someone else's version of your destiny – I mean the one you choose for yourself. Besides, in case you haven't noticed, the world is already on fire… people just haven't noticed yet."

Kala pulled Celeste into a hug. "I should very much like to see you again," she said through her tears.

"I'd like that too," Celeste replied and pulled away to lead Twill, Petr, and the children off into the night.

Kala and Skye quickly fetched their belongings. He rooted through the kitchen for food to bring with them while she hunted about for anything useful, like twine. She had just finished strapping her swords to her back when Skye emerged similarly ready to depart.

"I don't suppose you know a way out of the city that isn't through the main gate? I'm sure it's closed at this hour," Kala asked.

"I do indeed," Skye replied, happy to be helpful for a change. "Follow me."

Before they left, Kala grabbed him and looked into his eyes pleadingly. "I'm sorry you had to see that side of me. Do you think I'm a monster?"

"You're not a monster. You're the most beautiful weapon I've ever seen."

"I don't want to be a weapon," she choked. "I just want to be a girl."

"You're both, and you're the best of both," he replied and held her in an embrace. "Now, are you going to let me lead us out of here?"

She nodded weakly and held his hand as they walked around the guards' bodies and out of the alley. He led them to a grate in a quiet side street and pointed to it.

"Oh, no. I don't remember the way the monks took," Kala said.

"I have no idea what you're talking about, but I know the way out the seaward side of the city, as long as you have enough torches for me to hunt around a bit."

"I have a few," she confirmed.

"Good, then help me lift this damn grate."

They wandered around the sewers for a while until Skye finally found the broken grate that let them escape the city. They then fumbled their way over the rocky coast in the dark, hoping not to be seen by the guards on the walls. They'd made their way around the city and past the fields by the time the sun rose in earnest. They were both dead tired.

"I think we should find a spot to stop and light a fire so we can rest," Kala suggested. "I have a feeling that the Church's airships only come under cover of darkness anyway; otherwise, we'd have seen one before."

Skye nodded. "This is your world out here. I defer to you."

Kala found a hollow they could rest in with stone at their backs and a fire in front of them. She got a smokeless fire going, but they still took turns keeping watch while the other slept. By late afternoon, Kala judged that they were rested enough to travel, and she wanted daylight to find the ruins in which the airship landed. They headed out.

Entering the edge of the ruins, Skye remarked, "I've been this way once before when I jumped off the boat."

"It sounds like you have stories of your own to tell," Kala remarked.

"That I have, but I'll save them for when you don't need to concentrate so hard on keeping us alive."

"You noticed that, did you?"

"You get a cute little crease in your forehead when you're concentrating."

"Shut up," she laughed and guided them to the circle of cenotaphs.

"This place is creepy as hell," Skye noted.

"Tell me about it," Kala agreed as she stalked about the stone circle, thinking. "Okay – I have theories," she began.

"We're standing on the belly of a questionably-dead spider, and you have theories?"

"You thought it looked like that too?"

"More like it feels that way. This place unnerves me," he replied.

"Okay, back to my theories." She gestured southward. "I think the Priestess's airship headed that way, which makes sense if she wanted to make her way west again eventually. I also think that she used some properties of the stones lying around here to hail the airship." Kala bent down to touch one of the stones, but besides its curious lack of moss, it seemed like a regular stone. "I think the placement of the stones might also serve to give the ship rough directions. See how there are more cenotaphs on the west side of the dais than the east side?" She gestured to the spider legs.

"Well, there's just the one on the far side, so I assume that's east?"

"Really? And you're the map guy?" she asked, shocked.

"Maps are easy. West is left, and east is right."

"Well, I think we should take our chances and go right."

"So, east over the ocean?" he asked.

"Yup. Like Celeste said, the world is on fire, and we don't have the luxury of time to play it safe." She decided not to tell him about the danger Soren's advance posed to his mother's village unless it was absolutely necessary – Skye was already plagued with enough worry. Luckily, he agreed with her about heading east, so she kept the information to herself.

"I'm always up for dying in your arms," he told her.

"That's the spirit!" she laughed.

"How do we call our ride?"

"Roll this stone over to that far cenotaph," she instructed, "the one all on its own."

"That's random. Is that so we get some exercise while you figure out how we're actually supposed to call an airship?"

"Very funny. It's all I have to work with at the moment," she explained.

Skye shrugged and helped her move the stone. Then they waited. Once it got well and dark, Kala spotted a ship descending, nudging Skye. "Our ship is here." He struggled to see it himself and wound up just taking her word for it.

The ship touched down, and its door slid open.

"How's that for service?" Kala asked.

"Not bad," Skye congratulated her.

They entered the airship and noted that all of the compartments lay open and empty, providing more space than they'd had in the past, although it was still fairly tight. They closed the door behind them, but the ship refused to leave. They opened and closed it a few more times but were clearly missing something.

"I think we have to roll that stone away from the cenotaph to release the ship," Kala guessed.

"That means one of us will be outside. I'm not so sure I like the idea of that."

"Got any better ones?"

"I suppose not, but hold the door open for me, just in case," he said and walked over to the stone they'd moved. He braced himself against the cenotaph, rolled it away several rotations, then sprinted back to the airship door. He needn't have rushed, however, as the ship rose at a glacial pace. They closed the door a final time and were pleased to see that a few panels slid aside to reveal windows.

"We're flying in style now!" Skye declared as they drifted upward. "I guess the fact that I can smell the ocean means that we're heading east as planned?"

"We'll know at first light," Kala responded and pulled him down to the floor to snuggle against him.

Several days later, they were still huddling together, cold, hungry, and still flying over the ocean. Kala's teeth were chattering, and Skye was starting to turn blue. She made a joke about her "blue sky," but he was so preoccupied with trying to generate body heat that he didn't catch it. He got up to move about.

"Does the water look like it's getting closer?" he asked, looking out a window.

Kala rose and replaced him at the window. "It sort of does," she replied.

A gust of wind caught the airship and spun it slowly until an island swung into view. As they neared it, Kala could make out a volcano spewing lava into the air.

"That doesn't look good," she concluded.

6
Dhara

Dhara, her sisters, and her niece paddled north along the slow-moving, muddy river. They kept close to shore to keep an eye out for game but moved farther out at the tell-tale splash of an alligator sliding into the water. Those devils were hard enough to kill on land and even more formidable in the water.

Zara helped look after Nina as her way of making up for not trying to stop their mother from sending Caia away. Caia didn't need her sister to prove her love, but Zara was hounded by guilt. Had Dhara not saved Caia, she was sure that Zara's guilt would eventually have consumed her. As it was, Zara thanked the Goddess for Dhara's brashness. Somewhere along the way, in serving their tyrant mother, Zara had lost sight of a fundamental truth – her sisters came first.

They paddled in silence, each wrapped in their own thoughts. They'd each given up different things when they left their village, but none of them regretted it. Their bond was all that mattered. The river narrowed and became swifter, allowing them to make good progress with the stronger current. They were aware of the risks posed by rapids and stayed nearer to shore, portaging around unsafe waters several times. Given the unfamiliar terrain, it was an uncertain business lugging their canoes over the rocky shoreline, especially with little Nina in tow.

None of them was a particularly good swimmer, if they could swim at all. Near their village, the river was too dangerous to learn in. If you were unskilled enough in a canoe to find yourself needing to swim, you either figured it out quickly or drowned – that's it, that's all. None of them had yet needed to test their swimming ability, but there was always a first time for everything.

They were progressing along near shore when an enormous alligator slid into the water near Zara, prompting her to steer away from it but with the misfortune of doing so just as the current picked up, carrying her swiftly into churning water that she couldn't escape.

Caia glanced at Dhara to see her paddling like hell straight into the raging water after Zara. *Damn it,* Caia thought. "Hold on tight," she commanded Nina, steeled her nerves, and steered away from shore.

Zara held on for dear life as her canoe spun about. Dhara paddled straight at her, fighting the current's attempts to pull her off course. Caia paddled as hard as she could downriver, hoping to outrace them both, but trying to avoid the worst of the turbulence.

Zara's canoe hit a submerged boulder, and she was pitched into the frothing water. Dhara yelled for her to grab hold, then almost sailed over her before Zara spotted her. Zara fought to hang on to Dhara's canoe as submerged rocks battered her legs. Dhara struggled to counterbalance her weight and keep the canoe from overturning. The current swept them toward a fallen tree, which Dhara tried to duck but failed, causing the canoe to flip.

Both of them had their grips torn from the canoe, which sped downstream without them. They struggled to keep their heads above water and fought for breath every time they surfaced.

Caia got ahead of them, dug in, and spun her canoe around. She steadied it and steered to intersect her sisters, yelling to them over the roar of the water. Dhara heard her and reached for the canoe, angry at herself for needing to be rescued. Zara only noticed Caia's canoe when she smashed into it and barely grabbed hold before she was pulled past. Caia balanced the canoe with a sister on each side as they drifted downstream and out of the rapids.

When the water calmed, Caia steered them toward the shore, where Dhara and Zara dragged themselves onto the grass and nursed their scrapes and bruises.

"That was fun!" Nina exclaimed. "Can we do it again?"

"Let's not," Zara replied.

Caia left them to search for the capsized canoes, eventually finding both and towing them back. Caia still had her pack, and Dhara was able to recover hers because she'd tied it to her canoe, but they'd lost Zara's and both their paddles. They fashioned crude replacements from branches.

Zara sulked for days for getting them into the mess they were in. Dhara had been the brave one who'd saved her when she fell in, and Caia was the smart one who'd saved them both after that. *What was she?*

"Cheer up, sis," Caia told her, but Zara continued to brood.

The jungle slowly thinned out, and the ground around the river began to undulate. Eventually, the river wound its way into a wide canyon. They were nervous about the prospect of encountering rapids where the canyon walls hemmed them in, and there was no option to portage, but they decided to take their chances. *The Goddess favors the bold*, Dhara thought.

As the river flowed placidly through the canyon, it seemed as though their fears had indeed been unfounded. The sun glinted off the vibrant blue river had become, and they soaked in its beauty. Nina dragged a finger in the water and watched the ripples recede. Caia pointed out caves set high on the cliffs, but before she could conclude that they had the look of dwellings, an arrow whizzed past her into the water.

"Get low!" she shouted, and they all lay flat in their canoes.

More arrows rained down, and one landed a hair's breadth from Dhara's head. "It's not good enough; they've got too much height on us

– flip over!" she yelled and rolled her canoe, popping up in the cavity of air beneath it. The sunlight filtering through the water was enough for her to see that her sisters had followed suit and overturned their canoes. Caia held Nina around the waist and struggled to help her stay afloat.

Dhara pulled her canoe toward Caia's, and when she came alongside, she ducked underwater and resurfaced under hers, pulling her own snug against it. She used her free hand to help Caia hold Nina while the thudding of arrows continued above their heads. Dhara peeked underwater for any sign of Zara, making out the faint outline of her legs and steering toward them. She popped up under Zara's canoe. "Come join us," she told her and returned to her position under Caia's canoe. Zara joined them, and the sound of arrows stopped.

"Well, that was fun," Zara said sarcastically before a boulder heaved down from high up the cliff shattered her canoe with a deafening crash.

"Push right!" Caia commanded, and they kicked their legs to move the surviving canoes out of range.

Zara was struck on the leg by another rock, and while the worst of the impact was absorbed by the water, it still hurt like hell.

"Perfectly good rocks... and they're just throwing them away," Caia joked.

Dhara cast her a withering glance.

"Might have been a good idea to have learned to swim before now," Zara pointed out.

"Really, Zara?" Caia replied.

Rocks continued to splash around them, and one glanced off their canoe, sounding thunderously loud beneath it before the next impact shattered the nose of Caia's canoe.

"Switch!" Dhara shouted, and they dove underwater to pop up again under her canoe. They released Caia's mangled one, and it drifted away.

Rocks continued to splash to their left, then stopped altogether, and they drifted in silence.

"Want to flip the canoe back over?" Caia asked.

"Might as well," Dhara replied.

Zara just grunted, and the two of them hefted it up and over while Caia held on to Nina, struggling to keep their heads above water. Zara shifted to the opposite side of the canoe and surfaced. They all grabbed a side, careful not to flip the canoe over again. They looked back up the canyon but didn't see their attackers.

"Damn savages," Zara complained, her leg still smarting.

Dhara stared at the cliffs as they receded, judging the cave dwellers inferior even to ground dwellers as they chose to live *in* the ground. Dhara cringed at the thought.

"Swim for shore?" Caia suggested. They all nodded and kicked toward it, dragging themselves out of the water with Zara favoring her good leg before laying down and staring at the sky, exhausted.

"That was scary," Nina observed.

Caia nodded and pushed wet hair out of her daughter's face.

"Anyone want to rub my leg?" Zara joked.

Caia laughed, and Dhara punched Zara's uninjured leg. "Now you're even."

Zara rolled onto her, and she and Dhara wrestled, laughing.

"Done yet?" Caia asked, although she was as amused by their roughhousing as they were.

They took stock of their situation. "Down another pack," Caia informed them, stating what they already knew.

"We've still got mine, luckily," Dhara pointed out.

"Thank the Goddess for small mercies," Zara said.

"No point in carrying on by river now," Caia observed.

"Yup, we're on foot now," Zara agreed unhappily.

"I hate walking," Dhara said, saying what they were all thinking. She looked around at the grasslands stretching out before them. "Is anyone else creeped out by open spaces?" she asked.

Caia and Zara raised their hands.

"Good," Dhara said. "I'd hate to be alone in that." She grabbed her soaking pack, and they started off on foot parallel to the river.

"There's nothing to eat in this Goddess-forsaken wasteland," Dhara complained, her stomach rumbling. They'd walked for days and struggled to hunt. The few animals they spotted on the plains either hid in their burrows or seemed to be possessed of unnatural speed and reflexes.

They resorted to digging up earthworms and frying them on rocks beside their nightly fire. Dhara began to despair that they'd never eat real food again as she chewed on what felt like her millionth worm. *At least we have ample water*, she thought, gazing over the river just as five large canoes rounded the bend and came into view.

"Look at that," she said, pointing them out to her sisters. "Turns out we're not alone in the world after all."

A man in the lead canoe spotted them and waved.

Caia waved back tentatively. "What do they want?" she asked her sisters, who shrugged in response.

The canoes altered course and headed for them. Dhara placed her knife in her belt behind her back while Caia and Zara placed rocks on the ground within easy reach.

"Stay behind me," Caia instructed her daughter.

"Hello," the man from the lead canoe hailed as it neared, his accent pronounced but understandable.

"Hello," Caia replied uncertainly.

The man jumped into the water and pulled his canoe toward shore, prompting his companions to do the same. Once they were all secure, he turned to address the sisters.

"Sorry about that," he said.

"Sorry about what?" Dhara asked, confused.

"My lack of manners. Had to attend to the canoes first – don't want them floating away," he replied.

"Of course," Dhara replied.

"I'm Kieran," he said, holding out his hand.

"Dhara," she replied, staring at his hand, then taking it while bracing herself just in case he tried to throw her off balance.

He shook her hand instead and turned to introduce the rest of his party, rhyming off their names while each of them waved in response.

Caia and Zara introduced themselves, and Caia introduced Nina.

"I hope we're not intruding," Kieran said.

Dhara felt a pang of shame, remembering that he'd interrupted them eating worms. She looked over her shoulder at the fire to see if any evidence remained. Her stomach rumbled loud enough for everyone to hear, and she cursed it.

"We were just thinking of stopping for dinner and probably the night when we saw you. Do you mind if we join you?" he asked.

Dhara looked around at the infinite expanse that surrounded them and wondered why he felt compelled to share their little corner of it. "We won't stop you," she replied.

Kieran thought her response hilarious and motioned for a young man to bring food to cook. "Can we use your fire?" he asked, hastily adding, "We'll share our dinner in exchange. We have more than enough."

Dhara's pride said, "Hell no," but her stomach said, "Hell yes," so she grudgingly accepted his offer. The cook got busy, and soon, the air was filled with savory smells. Dhara had to fight not to drool and cursed her weakness. Caia visited with the cook, while Nina ran around with Zara keeping a watchful eye on her. Dhara studied the cooking, puzzling over how they'd arrange to poison only them if the food was being prepared communally. *They're an artful troop of assassins*, she surmised and maintained her vigilance.

Time came for dinner, and everyone grabbed a dish and queued up so the cook could ladle out what he'd prepared. Dhara, Zara, Caia, and Nina hung back, but Kieran refused to line up before them, and the stalemate was only broken when Caia relented, and she and Nina joined the line. Dhara still couldn't figure out how they were to be poisoned, so she accepted her meal and returned to sit with her sisters, waiting until everyone else was well into eating before hazarding the food herself. After days without proper nourishment, the simple fare felt like the richest she'd ever eaten. Dhara thought that if she were murdered that evening, at least she'd die happy with a full stomach.

"This is *way* better than worms," Nina declared, to Dhara's mortification and that of the cook as well, apparently. Caia shushed her and smiled an apology to the cook.

Their meal concluded, Kieran asked the sisters, "Where are you headed?"

"North," Dhara replied.

"Anywhere specific?" he asked.

"Never been there, so no," Dhara admitted.

"Well, there is a settlement about five or six days' walk from here, but I warn you – the northlands are a mess these days. That's why we're plying our trade farther south than we have before."

"What's your trade?" Dhara asked.

"Our trade is trading," he replied, chuckling at his play on words.

"There's no one to trade with for quite a distance upstream," Dhara supplied. "And, if you find yourself in a narrow canyon, beware of being stoned by the savages that live on the cliff faces."

"Good to know. Your advice is worth its weight in gold."

Dhara wondered about the value he attributed to advice. It seemed freely enough given – if not overly freely, in her opinion.

Kieran got up to check on his group and bid her good night. Dhara wandered over to Caia and Zara, who were chatting while Nina slept soundly in Caia's lap.

Dhara patted Zara on the shoulder. "Keep an eye out tonight," she said. "They don't seem to have poisoned us, so they're probably planning on killing us in our sleep."

"What would they have to gain by that?" Caia asked skeptically. "We have absolutely *nothing* worth killing over. I think they're just being nice."

"What would they have to gain from that?" Dhara challenged.

"Nothing. That's the point – they're just nice."

"Well, I'm sleeping with a knife in my hand," Dhara declared.

"Don't stab yourself then, you idiot," Caia replied. "I'm just sleeping."

Zara wisely kept her opinion to herself.

Dhara stayed up half the night listening for signs of attack, but all she heard was loud snoring. *These are the most inept assassins ever*, she changed her mind and eventually succumbed to fatigue and slept. She awoke to an "*I told you so*" look from Caia, which she promptly brushed off.

Kieran and his crew prepared a hearty breakfast of eggs and dried bacon, which they shared with Dhara and her sisters. Dhara's pride was wounded from twice receiving charity from strangers, and she bristled, but Caia was more than appreciative for the both of them.

Kieran and his crew finished preparing to head out, and he walked over to say goodbye to the sisters.

"It was a pleasure sharing your company," he said.

Dhara couldn't imagine how that had been the case.

He continued, "I noticed that you seem a little under-provisioned for your trek north – can we give you anything to help you out?"

"We have nothing to trade," Dhara replied, "and I refuse to pay with my body."

Kieran choked. "What? No. Why would you…?" he stammered. "I wouldn't dream of it!"

"Why not? I'm quite skilled," Dhara huffed.

"By the gods, woman – I don't want anything from you – I'm just trying to help."

"Why would you do that?" she challenged.

"Because it is the right thing to do," he replied, flustered.

Caia, who had stayed on the periphery of the exchange, finding it hugely entertaining, stepped in front of her sister. "That would be very kind of you and very much appreciated."

"Come with me, and we'll get you sorted out," he told her and walked away with her, still shaking his head.

Kieran and his party pushed off shortly after that, leaving the sisters watching from the shore. Nina waved at them, and Kieran waved back before taking his seat and paddling off.

"I don't understand that one," Dhara thought out loud.

"I like him," Zara declared. "I'd mate with him."

"You two have all the charm of an alligator," Caia declared and threw the pack over her shoulder that Kieran had given her. "Come on, Nina," she called to her daughter, and they resumed their journey north.

"I wonder what he meant by 'the northlands are a mess,'" Zara mused. "I can't imagine they're worse than home."

"What if it's all open spaces like this without high enough trees to build a city in? They'd have to live on the ground," Dhara pointed out, making them all shudder.

Five days later, just as Kieran promised, they came upon a small city with an encampment outside its walls for new arrivals, brimming with refugees from Soren's advancing army. It was a place of misery, violence, and strife, and Dhara took it all in.

Now this, I can relate to, she thought.

7
Kala

Kala and Skye's airship drifted toward the volcanic island through an ash cloud that rose from the crater to swirl around them. The updraft caused the ship to pitch wildly, the heat palpable through the walls.

The island was intermittently visible through the windows and was covered in fine black sand that reflected the sanguine glow of the magma that the volcano belched into the air. The island was trapped in an endless war with the ocean, its waves eroding it as steadily as the lava replenished it. The two met in a wall of billowing steam.

It was as foreign and unwelcoming a hellscape as they could imagine, and they were descending toward it. Kala reached for Skye's hand and held it firmly as they gazed out the window.

Through the drifting fog created by the lava's assault on the sea, Kala saw row upon row of airships stretching across the plain in the lee of the volcano. Their own made its way toward a gap in the nearest row, touching down equidistant from the ones surrounding it. A low metallic thud signaled that their ship had somehow anchored itself.

Skye opened the door, and a warm wind blew past, swirling the fine black sand into eddies. The grains quickly worked their way into the folds of his clothing and grated on him almost immediately.

"Is it safe to go outside?" Kala asked.

"We gain nothing by staying in here," Skye pointed out, and she had to agree. At least color was seeping back into his cheeks after the days they'd spent in the frigid airship crossing the ocean at high altitude. The air felt thick and syrupy by comparison this close to the ground. It was cloying.

Skye took a tentative step outside, finding that the sand thinly covered hard basalt. Kala joined him, scanning the vicinity but finding no stones or cenotaphs to direct the ships. She pushed hard against theirs, but it didn't budge. "How do we get this thing back in the air? And how do we tell it where to go?" she asked, even though she knew that Skye had no more notion than she did.

"Your guess is as good as mine," he confirmed, "But I'm not sure if I'd survive another stint like that over the ocean, anyway. I almost froze to death. Besides, we're out of food and water, and I haven't seen a source of either.

Kala kicked up a cloud of sand. "I guess we might as well explore," she suggested fatalistically, "but let's stick together."

Skye looked at the rows of identical airships. "Let's bring our things. I wouldn't remember which one of these things is ours if we tried to return to it."

"I'm not overly attached to it, anyway," Kala replied and went inside to fetch her things while he did similarly. She strapped on her weapons, even though the island seemed devoid of life, let alone any that could pose a threat.

Skye joined her outside a moment later. "Which way?" he mused.

"Toward the volcano," Kala replied.

Skye looked at her like she had three heads.

"There's nothing else here," she explained. "If we're going to find anything, it'll probably be there. Besides, there has to be a reason why a fleet of airships is on this gods-forsaken island."

"Good point," he conceded and started walking.

Kala placed a hand on his shoulder and angled him ninety degrees. "That way," she pointed.

"I knew that," he said while she suppressed an eye roll. They walked out of the airfield, passing perhaps a hundred airships in their row alone. Kala noted that there were subtle differences between them. While they were all generally the same shape, some were larger and others smaller. In places where the sand had been blown clear of the stone, she saw markings in a strange alphabet on the ground in front of each airship but couldn't decipher a pattern and went back to ignoring them.

The volcano towered in front of them, the only feature on the desolate island. *At least getting lost is impossible,* Kala thought. "We can't circumnavigate the volcano because of the lava flows on the far side," she mused aloud.

"Thank the gods," Skye replied. "That would take forever, and it would probably be as unremarkable on that side as it is on this one." He scratched his head.

"I guess up it is, then," Kala decided.

"Wait, what? No! That's worse," he pouted.

"Stop complaining. It's a gradual slope, and we might spot something from higher up."

"Just my weary corpse," he grumbled.

"Corpses aren't weary; they're dead," Kala needled.

"Well, mine will be both after this gods-damned climb," he replied but headed in the direction she pointed. They trudged upward for a while, and the slope gradually steepened. The exertion sapped what little energy they had, and they paused frequently to rest.

"Shelter, water, fire, food…" she muttered. "I think we're screwed on all four fronts, except maybe that we could shelter in an airship if we walked back. I haven't seen any freshwater, and all the saltwater in the world is useless to us. No vegetation means no wood, and no wood means no fire, although I doubt we'll freeze to death with all this lava flowing about, and there sure don't seem to be any predators to keep at bay. On the downside, though, the lack of predators is probably because of a lack of prey, which means no food for us. This is looking bleaker every moment," she concluded.

Skye fought to stay positive. "It's not an option for us to be trapped here until we expire. My mother needs me. This can't be the end."

Kala placed a hand on his arm. "It's never the end until it's the end. We'll climb to that ledge, at least," motioning to an outcropping a bit higher up. "Then we'll regroup and devise a plan."

Skye had no better idea of what to do, so he went along with Kala's suggestion and trudged upward. Cresting the ledge, they collapsed from exhaustion on it.

"I'll be fine in a moment," Skye assured Kala while she surveyed the island from their vantage point. Nothing caught her eye, but she kept looking. Skye noticed a glow emanating from a recess and rose to his feet to check it out, pointing out the fissure to Kala.

"That doesn't look particularly welcoming," he declared, "Sort of like the gates of hell."

Kala nodded. "True, but I've seen nothing better to investigate."

Skye stared out across the island, hoping she'd missed something, but spotted nothing himself.

Kala walked over to the crevasse, peered in, and reported that it looked as though it led all the way to the caldera. "It's hot as hell, but it looks passable," she added. "I'm going to roast dressed like this," she decided and stripped down to her undergarments, her skin glistening with sweat. She piled her belongings neatly and strapped a couple of daggers to her thighs while Skye stripped off his clothes as well. When he finished, he just stared at Kala.

"What are we waiting for?" she asked.

"Nothing. Just thinking that you make hell look sexy."

She smiled. "If I didn't know that you were as sticky and smelly as I feel, I'd say you don't look so bad yourself."

"Thanks. I think."

Kala led the way as they gingerly squeezed through the opening. The heat was stifling, but they pushed through it. Kala caught a glimpse of movement halfway through and stopped, motioning for Skye to wait where he was. He shook his head emphatically, so Kala gestured that he could follow if he wished, then turned and continued winding her way forward. She finally peeked out the far opening and saw metallic spiders roaming around the inside of the caldera. She blinked hard to make sure she wasn't hallucinating, but they were still there when she opened her eyes. Her skin crawled. She was about to motion Skye backward until she spotted one of the creatures suspended from the wall behind him. It stared at her with unblinking black eyes.

Skye hadn't seen the spiders yet and looked quizzically at her, turning to see what kept her transfixed. She stopped him by pulling him to her. "There's something behind you that, trust me, you don't want to see," she told him. "Move forward with me slowly. Oh, and ready yourself."

He followed her cryptic instructions, and as they stepped out of the opening, freezing as soon as he noticed the spiders. He paled. "There's one of those things behind me, isn't there?" he asked.

Kala nodded meekly but held his hands tight. His knees turned to jelly, and she helped him stay upright. Recovering after a moment, he confided with a whisper, "I hate spiders."

"I'm not much of a fan either," Kala remarked but noted that the spiders hadn't yet done anything to bother them. She noticed that the ones in the caldera had ceased moving and were staring at them en masse. That was somehow much worse. She raised her hands in surrender, but the unblinking monsters gave no sign of comprehension.

Then, just as suddenly, they resumed moving about, ignoring her and Skye again. Kala glanced over Skye's shoulder, but the spider in the fissure was nowhere to be seen. "I don't know if it's creepier to be noticed by devil-spiders or ignored by them," she quipped.

"I'll go with whatever option that doesn't have one of those things anywhere near me," he replied.

Kala watched the spiders' movements for a while. "They're coming in and out of a myriad of caves, it seems. I think we should check one out."

"Hell no!" Skye countered.

"Our only other option is to leave and waste away on the empty plain."

"I vote for wasting away."

"Do as you will, but I want answers," she told him and turned toward the caves.

"Gods-damn it," he complained and followed her.

Peeking into the first cave, Kala saw spiders crawling over an expanse of the fabric that covered the balloons. *Curious*, she thought, but when nothing else seemed to be going on, she moved on to peer into the next cave. This one was gigantic and filled with the frames of several airships. Spiders crawled over them, trailing sparks that were too bright to look at. Kala covered her eyes and moved back out of it. Skye had stayed close enough to her to avoid the spiders but not close enough to see what she'd seen. "Nothing interesting," she reported and moved to a third cave, which turned out to be more of a tunnel, and devoid of any spiders.

Skye peeked over her shoulder. "This one seems promising," he said. She sighed but gestured for him to follow her into it. He looked back at the spiders moving about the caldera and scooted closer to her. It was, at least, cooler in the tunnel. They followed it until it opened into a large room dimly lit by the same fluorescent moss that Kala had seen in the catacombs of the ancients. *Why doesn't it surprise me that the only plant growing here is the eeriest one I've ever seen?* she thought. The floor of the room was littered with glistening gemstones of different colors.

"Pretty," Skye remarked, but something about it struck him as familiar. He stepped in and noted that while the floor was pretty level, it wasn't perfectly flat. He walked around, careful not to trip over the bumpy parts or winding cracks. Suddenly, it occurred to him why it looked familiar. "It's a map," he declared, awed. "In relief," he added, marveling at how the bumps and cracks along the floor depicted elevation." He stared at it, wishing he had his journal.

Just then, a spider entered from across the room, ignoring them and skittering across the map. It stopped at a red gemstone and worked it out, replacing it with a black one. Its work apparently done, it skittered back out the way it came.

Kala wandered over to the stone that the spider had replaced. "There's a band of black stones here and a few red ones, but the rest are mostly blue, with some green ones thrown in for good measure. Any guesses what the colors represent?"

Skye wasn't listening. He was staring at one gemstone in particular. Kala tried to read the expression on his face.

"See the mountains crossing the black stones?" he asked her.

She oriented herself based on where he was staring. "Okay. Yes, I see them."

"See the red one in the middle?" he asked.

"The one surrounded by all the black ones?" she asked back.

"Yes. That's my village. I recognize its place in the mountains." He was silent for a moment wondering why it was surrounded by black stones. Something about it felt ominous, like erasure or death. "I need to get home," he decided in a panic. "We need to get off this island!"

93

Kala did her best to calm him. "We will, I promise... we just need to figure out how." She oriented herself to figure out which gemstone represented her village. The best she could tell was that it was one of the ones in the band of red stones bordered by black ones.

"I think I found my village," she relayed, pointing it out. "It's also red."

"I think red means 'under threat,'" Skye surmised, agitated. "The black area is spreading south, and our homes are in its path."

Skye stood in the doorway, barely restraining himself. His mother was in more imminent danger than he thought.

Kala worried about her grandfather, too, and hated the feeling of helplessness. *There must be something here*, she thought. She scanned the room and spied a bank of amulets hanging from pegs set in the far wall. *What have we here?* she thought. "I need a moment," she told Skye and pulled one off its peg. It was made of two concentric rings and displayed a level of craftsmanship that she doubted still existed in the world. She spun the outer ring, and a light on the ceiling illuminated one of the gemstones on the floor. She turned the ring slowly, and the light moved sideways to shine on a series of stones in sequence. She spun the inner ring, and the light moved in the perpendicular direction, lighting different gemstones as it went. She adjusted the rings until the light shone on the stone marking Skye's village. "For whatever purpose," she said, "this is the setting for your village. I wonder if these amulets are connected to the airships. Everything else seems to be." She was struck with inspiration. "We need my journal. I have to write down some of these settings on my map."

They turned at the same time, and their bare arms touched. A bolt of electricity coursed through her. *Was it hope or was it Skye?* she wondered.

They made their way back out to the ledge where they'd left their things and found them undisturbed by spiders or anything else. Kala scooped up her journal, and they hurried back inside. In the map room, she annotated her journal with the amulet settings for all of the locations they recognized. Kala noticed that Bayre was marked by a blue stone with a green one beside it. "I think the green stones might be 'dead spiders,'" she told Skye, "beacons from which you can call an airship." She made sure to add all of their locations to her map.

Skye made his own discovery. "I think I found our island," he announced, standing in a region that would be off the far west side of the continent. "The stone is black, which is why it was so hard to find." He'd used the amulet to illuminate it by spinning its outer ring as far in one direction as it would go. "There's nothing else this far west. That means it's closer to the west coast than the east coast, though, thank the gods. If we can coax an airship to leave this place, we should go to this place on the coast," he suggested, walking across the map to point out a blue gemstone. "Then, on to my village. We'd only stop to gather supplies. Besides, it looks too far to make it to my village in one hop. To be honest, I'm not even sure we'll make it to the coast in the state we're in."

"We've got to try," Kala agreed and finished updating her journal.

Having gotten as much information as they could from the map room, they each grabbed an amulet and headed back to the caldera, then through the fissure to the ledge. It had grown dark, but the glow of the lava bathed their surroundings in a red light that was eerie but sufficient to see by.

They collected their belongings, including their clothes, but they were still too hot to even think about putting them back on, so they just carried them as they descended the mountain. They walked in silence, as neither wanted to comment on their slim odds of making it to the coast alive.

"I'm only suggesting we go to my village first because it's closer," Skye explained.

"It's okay," Kala assured him. Part of her feared going home. She'd left it a murderer and had only been forced further down that path since. Perhaps helping Skye would redeem her, so she could look her grandfather in the eye with something other than shame. *If I can just do one good thing first,* she thought, then pushed the unpleasant thoughts deep down and continued trudging down the mountain.

They arrived at the airfield dead tired. Skye walked up to the first ship, sizing it up and declaring, "This one will do," then set about finding the door by the faint light of the lava flows. Once they were on board, Skye consulted Kala's journal and dialed the amulet around his neck. Nothing happened. He tried again with the same result. Turning it over, he pressed its center, and they heard the familiar thud of the ship's anchor releasing. The ship began to rise, and they slumped to the floor, relieved beyond measure.

Not sure if they'd live to see landfall, Skye prayed silently for their loved ones in their besieged villages. Kala wondered who she should pray to – her patron was Death.

8
Forest

Forest led her tiny party out the village gates, praying it wasn't too late for them to escape Soren's advancing forces. She hoped that the damn fools who stayed behind would come to their senses and follow her, but there was nothing more she could say to convince them that she hadn't said already. She looked over her motley band, and while she doubted she could do much to protect them, she felt that she had to at least try, so she pulled her bow from across her back and held it handy.

She led them across the fields surrounding their village toward the southern tree line, a barrier that only she'd ever meaningfully crossed. The predators in the woods terrified the villagers, and with good reason, Forest accepted.

Kala's grandfather walked closely behind her, dressed suitably in ranging attire and sturdy boots and trying to look brave for the rest of them. He held little Abdi's hand, who was still dead tired from his and Forest's long trek from Soren's camp. She felt bad for him but judged that they couldn't risk resting for even a moment until they'd put some distance between themselves and the village.

Lily and Cera followed, walking side by side. Lily wore gardening attire and a tunic, which would have to do, Forest thought. Cera's outfit was well-fitting but not particularly suited to a long journey. She kept up a steady stream of cheery conversation to distract Lily from the terror the woods evoked in her. Lily and Forest's mother had walked into the woods to die years earlier, and Lily was reliving that memory with every step she took. Forest worried about them both.

Councilor Fayre and Councilor Sayer's former scribe came next, talking to each other. It struck Forest that if there were no longer a village, and therefore no longer a village council, would Fayre still be Councilor

Fayre or just Fayre? She couldn't imagine her as just Fayre. Worse, she'd always thought of Sayer's scribe as just an extension of him – she'd never thought of him as his own person, with his own name. She dredged her memory to recall it – Will. Fayre and Will looked like they'd never left the village walls, let alone ventured into the woods. They put up a brave face, but Forest could tell that they both assumed they were only postponing their demise rather than averting it.

Calix, Oriel, and his young wife, Allie, followed at the rear, the men pulling the cart of supplies that Calix had hastily assembled from the village stores. As a hunter, Oriel was appropriately dressed in leathers and armed with a bow and knife. After Forest, he knew the most about surviving in the wilderness, but because he'd never overnighted in it and always hunted as part of a group, she wasn't sure how deep his knowledge really went. Allie stuck close to his side and looked fearful of her shadow. Forest surmised that they'd only joined her because Oriel's commitment to keeping Allie safe overrode their shared terror at the prospect of leaving the village.

Calix had his grandfather's rusty sword strapped to his belt, but Forest knew from their play swordfights that he had no idea how to wield it; but in a crisis, it was comforting to have another person who might be able to help out. He and Oriel were their defensive flank, and she was their tiny party's vanguard. The responsibility weighed heavily on her.

They entered the trees, and all talking ceased. They knew, with good reason, that the forest was fraught with danger. Forest guided them along a path that permitted the cart to be more easily pulled after them, even if there were safer ones. Enough light filtered through the trees that Forest judged they had about a third of the day left before the light failed them, and they'd have to stop for the night. They did their best to move quickly, but the cart slowed them down. They tried to be quiet, too, but the inexperienced among them were prone to stepping on twigs and snapping branches. *They're trying*, Forest thought, and that's the most anyone could ask.

Cera pointed out some flowers, bent to pick one, and put it in her hair. *Trust Cera to make fleeing for her life look good*, Forest thought. In contrast, Allie jumped at every rustling in the underbrush. Only Forest grasped that if a sound were truly to be feared, you wouldn't hear it until it was too late. She sighed.

After walking a fair distance, Forest judged that Abdi and Kala's grandfather needed to rest, so she signaled a halt at the next clearing. Even the fittest among them collapsed to the ground. Forest judged it would do more for their morale to let them talk than it would for their safety to have them sit quietly, so she encouraged them to do so. They passed around waterskins, and Forest advised them to drink only a little, lest they run out. "Water is our most precious resource," she informed them.

Fayre sat down beside Forest to ask her questions, and the others quieted to hear her answers.

"How big is the force that threatens our village?" she asked.

"A thousand fighters, maybe more," Forest replied. "Plus, that many again following them."

Fayre couldn't believe so many people existed. "Where did such a force come from?"

"Soren's been growing his army with every conquered village as he moves south."

"Who is this Soren?"

"Their leader."

"What does he want?"

"To destroy the airships to stop communities from being dependent on them."

"How can destruction be an improvement?" Fayre asked uncomprehendingly.

"I don't think he's thought it through. He just believes he needs to wipe the table clear to set it again."

"How do you know what he believes?"

"He told me."

The silence that followed was palpable.

Lily asked the question that everyone was thinking, "You talked to him?"

Forest shrugged. "I spent time in his camp. I hunted airships with him."

Lily couldn't comprehend how Forest could be so cavalier about it.

Fayre pressed on with more questions. "Why would anyone follow such a madman?"

"He's very persuasive, and the freedom to decide one's fate is a powerful message to rally people around. Besides, the northern clans were pretty violent to begin with."

"But why is he doing it?"

"It's personal for him. Soren calls himself a 'child of the winds,' having been sent away from his family in an airship. That's why he hates them so much."

Fayre thought that over but still couldn't believe that one man's vendetta could galvanize such a force. "How do we avoid his army?"

"We stay ahead of it."

"So, where are we headed?"

"I have no idea – just *away* at this point. We need to keep moving until we find somewhere safe, if such a place even exists."

Fayre had no more questions, so Forest signaled everyone to prepare to resume walking. They rose wearily and continued south until the light filtering through the trees dimmed, and Forest declared that they'd need to make camp soon.

A rustling in a nearby tree startled Allie, and she shrieked. Forest spun, bow at the ready, only to see a squirrel perched on the branch beside Allie's head.

"It's just a squirrel," Oriel pointed out just before Forest's arrow struck it. Allie's eyes went wide.

"Waste want, want not," Forest pointed out, reslinging her bow. Allie looked shocked as Forest walked over to recover the squirrel, secured it to her belt, and resumed walking.

Forest stopped them at the next clearing, directing Calix, Oriel, and Will to haul their food high into the trees, which was time-consuming and backbreaking. Meanwhile, she rounded up Fayre, Lily, and Cera and led them in collecting firewood. She let Abdi and Kala's grandfather rest, and Allie was still too petrified to leave Oriel's side.

They sat around the fire that night, making small talk. Forest skinned the squirrel, cooked it, and passed it around. Everyone cut off a morsel, except Allie, who shunned it like poison.

Lily massaged Cera's sore feet, her footwear being less than ideal for hiking. Lily asked Forest more about Soren's camp, and she obliged her, with Abdi adding details where he could. Forest told Lily about meeting a kindly fighter named Jarom and his family but stopped short of revealing that he was her and Lily's step-uncle. *Too much, too soon*, Forest thought. *I'll tell her when she's not already overwhelmed.*

Despite the protection their fire offered, Forest strung a perimeter wire with bells, the way Kala had shown her. She also set up a watch rotation among her, Oriel and Calix. Kala's grandfather insisted that he join in, so Forest assigned him the early morning shift. When Calix woke Forest for her turn, she could tell by everyone's breathing that they struggled to sleep. They had so much to process, and it was the first time that most of them had slept on hard ground rather than a soft bed, never mind in a place replete with things that could kill them. Still, they didn't complain, and Forest respected them more for it. She watched Cera hold Lily as she slept and wished she had someone to look after her.

In the morning, as they prepared to decamp, Oriel shouted, and everyone turned to see why. He pointed to the sky through the trees in the direction they'd come. Smoke was rising from where their village lay. The implication sunk in, to everyone's horror – they'd all left loved ones behind.

Calix drew his sword. "We have to go back," he said, looking about desperately for support.

Fayre walked over and bade him lower his weapon. "There's nothing we can do," she told him gently.

"My father," he pleaded.

"Pray he made it out safely."

"We should wait here in case he did – in case anyone did."

"We can't," Forest said resignedly. "We have to keep moving and hope they follow us."

"They can't survive this," Calix despaired, knowing that it was only because of Forest's experience in the woods that they had any chance themselves.

"Honor him by living, and we'll pray for his safety," Fayre said, placing a consoling hand on his shoulder.

They packed in silence, each of them consumed with grief. Forest secretly hoped that the sacking of the village might slow Soren's advance and buy her party a little time, and she hated herself for thinking it.

They continued south, and it clouded over by afternoon, with a light drizzle adding to their misery. Near evening, they came across a rock outcropping that overhung the mouth of a shallow cave. Fayre suggested they shelter from the rain beneath it.

"I don't like it," Forest replied. She hated caves – things lived in caves – unpleasant things. Taking in the sorry state of her companions, however, she concluded that the risk might be necessary and reluctantly agreed. She and Oriel drew their knives and investigated the opening. It narrowed into a tunnel at the back, but it was too dark to explore deeply. There was no sign, however, that the ground inside the cave or the tunnel had been disturbed recently, but it still made her uneasy. Despite Forest's reservations, they decided that it was safe enough to chance overnighting in the cave mouth and pulled the cart out of the rain.

A fire would be difficult to light after an afternoon of rain, but they needed it to ward off predators, so Forest explained to everyone how to find wood that was hopefully either still dry or at least not totally soaked and sent them out to find some. They finally got a fire going and set about drying their clothes and preparing for sleep. Those not on watch slept more soundly that night from sheer exhaustion.

Forest was deep asleep when Oriel roused her. "There's something out there," he told her.

She rose and pulled out her knife, concluding that her bow would be useless in the dark. She stood still and listened, concluding that there was definitely something prowling around in the rain. She caught sight of a pair of red eyes reflecting the firelight. "Wake the others," she instructed Oriel and kept watch while he did. The creature moved closer.

"Torches!" Forest shouted as a gigantic bear reared into view. It stood twice her height, shook its wet fur, and roared at her. Forest felt pitifully small before it but stood her ground. The beast dropped to all fours and closed on her, tearing the ground with clawed paws. Oriel rushed to her side with two torches, and the bear halted and reared, gnashing its teeth. Oriel handed Forest one of the torches, and together they waved them at the beast, shouting. The bear swung at them, and they alternated between pressing the torches forward at it and dodging backward from its swipes. It was a stalemate that Forest feared they'd eventually lose.

Realizing the uselessness of the knife she still held in her hand against such a creature, Forest sheathed it and grabbed Oriel's torch. "Get more," she commanded and turned back to face the bear alone. The bear, emboldened, advanced, and Forest did her best to hold it back, waving the torches in front of it and yelling a string of obscenities. Everyone joined her in yelling at the beast, or screaming, at least. It disoriented the beast, which bellowed at her and clawed the ground.

Oriel reappeared at her side, with Calix on the other, and the three of them moved closer to the bear, fanning out to push it back. It glared from one of them to another, waving its claw-tipped paws. Oriel got close enough to shake a torch in its face, and the bear swatted him off his feet. He lay groaning while Forest and Calix continued to push forward. The bear finally turned and crashed away into the woods, leaving Forest shaking and Calix rushing to Oriel's side.

Forest stood watch with her torches in case the bear came back while the others pulled Oriel close to the fire to tend to his injuries. He likely had broken ribs, but there was nothing they could do for him except keep him still and comfortable.

The morning came with no return of the bear, and Forest collapsed in a heap beside Lily.

Fayre approached to inform her, "We can't press on with Oriel in his condition. We need to wait at least a day."

We can't risk it, Forest thought, but one look at Oriel confirmed the truth of what Fayre said, and there was no way they could abandon him. She nodded her agreement, and Fayre went to let everyone know they'd be staying put for the day.

"I need a moment," Forest told Lily and wandered a little way into the woods. When she was far enough away, she collapsed to a mossy patch of ground and sobbed from the stress.

She looked up to see that her sister had followed her. Lily bent down beside her and placed a soothing hand on her back. "You don't have to be so strong all the time," Lily said.

"Someone has to," Forest replied between sobs.

"No, you don't."

"I'm not Kala," Forest despaired.

"No one expects you to be," Lily assured her.

"They need me to be."

"We're scared. You can be scared, too. We can be scared together. We have each other."

Forest leaned into her and surrendered to her fear.

9

Emrys

Wilm sat hidden high in the branches just like Councilor Janus had instructed him to do. It was the first night he'd ever spent outside the village walls, hell, the first night anyone had except that strange girl, Forest, and Kala before her. He'd been on edge all night, but he supposed that was the point. He was assigned to look out for anything unusual, just in case Forest had been telling the truth about marauders heading toward the village. He thought about how fearful his girlfriend had been at his assignment but relished the bragging he'd be able to do when it was over – and the rising light indicated that it soon would be. *Dawn can't come fast enough*, he thought ruefully. *This gods-damned branch is killing my behind.*

A hint of motion distracted him from his self-pity, then another, and another. He peered down into the dim forest to see a wave of warriors moving silently through the trees. *I must be dreaming*, he thought and shifted his weight to see if he could feel his body. The sharp stab of pain as his legs protested being woken from their slumber confirmed that he was indeed awake. He slowly lifted the horn to his lips, as he'd been told to, and blew a deep, sustained note.

The warriors disregarded him and didn't even speed up their advance. After three more blasts of the horn, one man turned, annoyed, and fired an arrow through Wilm's throat.

As he choked his last breath, he thought, *Please let that have been enough warning*, then Death collected him.

The sound of the horn jolted Emrys awake. *Gods, no!* he thought. *Forest spoke the truth.* He jumped out of bed, fully clothed, grabbed his pack, and raced out the door for the southern gate. The streets were filled with panicked villagers streaming out of their homes, bleary-eyed and in various states of wakefulness and readiness. He smelled the smoke from the grass fires that Janus had lit at the northern gate to obscure the village and hopefully make their attackers warier.

Janus and his men were already at the southern gate by the time Emrys and the rest of the villagers arrived. Janus spotted him, nodded, and signaled to his men, who advanced out the gate as a phalanx. They'd fashioned makeshift shields from tables and anything else they could find. Emrys stayed close behind Janus, noticing that the man had no pack – nor did any of his men. *They didn't expect to leave this place*, he realized and felt a pang of guilt.

Arrows pelted their makeshift shields, and the villagers huddled at the center of the formation, advancing slowly. Several men were struck by arrows, but they grimaced and did their best to continue shielding the women and children. They'd made it halfway across the field toward the safety of the trees when a line of advancing warriors blocked their escape. Janus and Torin were at the tip of the phalanx, and they dropped their shields to engage them.

"Run for the trees!" Emrys yelled at the frightened villagers behind him. Janus and Torin swung hand axes in wide arcs to create an opening for the villagers, who surged toward the tree line, heading for the ribbon that Emrys had tied to the tree nearest where he'd watched Forest lead her party into the woods.

A woman in front of Emrys, carrying a small girl, was struck by an arrow, fell, and didn't get up. The girl she'd been carrying pressed herself against the woman's body as people ran past. Emrys scooped the girl into his arms, despite her protests at leaving her mother. "We've got to go," he told her. "We'll come back for your mommy later," he lied and raced toward the trees with her, dodging the fighting.

Arriving, he paused briefly to look back. Janus struggled against two men, and Torin kept a circle of others at bay. Most of their comrades had fallen. Torin looked back to see his nephew, Cade, hesitating near Emrys, unsure whether to desert his uncle.

"Flee, boy!" Torin yelled, and Cade turned for the woods. Only Emrys saw Torin mouth the words, "I love you," and turn his attention back to his foes.

"Surrender, and we'll spare the boy," one of the warriors offered Torin. "You two can join us."

"I'm sparing the boy from having to join you," Torin spat and swung his axes.

Emrys looked down at the frightened girl in his arms and ran after Cade, leaving Torin to his fate and the village in flames. He crashed through the trees away from the din, catching up with the rest of the survivors. They'd stopped, and Emrys blundered through them to the front. Arrayed in front of them was a row of warriors standing with swords drawn. Emrys felt the jaws of the trap close. Their leader took a step forward.

Emrys held the girl tightly to his chest and demanded as bravely as he could, "At least let the children go."

"I will do no such thing," the man replied and pulled off his helmet to reveal a head of shockingly red hair. "Allow me to introduce myself – I'm Jarom," Forest's uncle informed him.

10

Forest

Oriel was too injured to walk, but everyone knew they had to resume their flight, so room was made for him in the cart by everyone's carrying what they could. They took turns pulling the cart in pairs and advanced slowly, ever nervous that the forces that had destroyed their village would overtake them.

After several days' walk, consumption of their supplies lightened the cart, which pleased most people but worried Forest that they'd need to find a new home soon or starve. Oriel recovered enough to walk but not enough to help pull the cart or hunt. Allie fawned over him, and this at least distracted her from her fear.

After almost a moon of walking, the forest thinned and gave way to fields and scents they hadn't smelled in ages. In the distance lay a town tenfold the size of their tiny village.

Allie collapsed crying for joy, and Oriel knelt to hold her. Cera limped forward, her footwear in rough shape after so long a trek. Lily put an arm around her sister. "This was all you," she told her. "We're only alive because of you."

Farmers working in the fields eyed them suspiciously. Forest's party stared dumbly – their first contact with people they hadn't grown up with. It didn't feel quite real to them, and they struggled to rethink their place in the world. Forest patiently gave them the time to come to terms with their new reality, sharing a knowing look with Kala's grandfather.

"What are we waiting for?" little Abdi asked, and it pulled everyone out of their thoughts and back to their present circumstance.

Fayre recovered quickest and pointed to the town. "That's where we should go," she concluded unnecessarily but signaling that they should resume walking toward it. They were ashamed of their sorry state and struggled to hold their heads high under the unwelcoming stares of the people working in the fields.

They made it halfway to the town when they were spotted by a guard, who moved to intercept them. "Follow me," he commanded. They complied, but their weary pace slowed him, so he added charitably, "At least you're in better shape than most refugees." They didn't feel in particularly good shape and immediately felt sorry for the people he was referring to.

The guard led them to a makeshift settlement outside the city walls that had sprung up to accommodate people fleeing the violence in the north. A pall of despair hung over the camp. It was crowded, and few people had proper shelter. The inhabitants looked at the new arrivals with morbid curiosity. Children ran barefoot through the muddy pathways that wound between plots claimed by various groups. Cera's heart broke for them.

The guard cleared his throat to get their attention and guided them to a table, at which an official sat waiting. He thanked the guard and waved him away.

"You're not from here, I gather," he said, stating the obvious but going through his script.

"That's correct," Fayre responded, speaking for their party.

"Just checking," he muttered and opened a ledger. "Okay, what do we have here?" he said to himself, looking them over. "Three men, four women..." He paused to examine Forest and Abdi, then continued, "and two children – condition 'fair.'"

Forest bristled, and Lily squeezed her shoulder.

The man made some quick notes and closed the ledger. "This camp is for refugees from the north. You're not to leave its confines or enter the town without my express permission. Is that clear?"

Fayre nodded. "Crystal."

"We don't have much to spare, but townspeople will bring food out to the camp from time to time. You'll figure it out. Everybody does," he concluded. "Any questions?"

"What are you doing to ready the city's defenses?" Forest piped up, observing a lack of them.

The official just stared at her like she had two heads.

Fayre explained, "We're fleeing forces pushing southward. I imagine that's the story for everyone here."

The man nodded uncomprehendingly.

"So, when those forces make it here, what's your plan?"

"Not my department," he replied. "Now, if there are no more questions, I suggest you find yourself a place somewhere." He gestured vaguely in the direction of the camp. "It grows more crowded by the day." They were clearly dismissed, so they turned and headed into the camp.

The guard was correct that most of the inhabitants were in desperate condition. Most were dirty, emaciated, and wholly dispirited. Many simply lay on the ground, preserving what little strength remained in them. Fayre led their party through the camp until they found an empty spot large enough to accommodate them. People eyed their cart hungrily, despite no food remaining in it. Calix tightened his grip on it as he wheeled it along.

"This place is so sad," Cera thought out loud.

"These people are alive," Fayre countered, reminding everyone how many weren't.

They settled in, and as logistics became the focus again, Fayre deferred to Forest. "What can I do?" she asked. Forest had her help construct a firepit and sent Will and Kala's grandfather back to the woods to collect firewood.

Sketchy characters sauntered by to check out the new arrivals. Calix puffed out his chest, prompting them to chuckle but move on. Allie grabbed Oriel's arm. "I don't like it here," she told him.

"It's okay – it's only temporary," he replied and put an arm around her.

Forest cringed, thinking that he was right, but not in a good way. Eventually, Soren's forces would find them here, and they'd have to flee anew, likely to worse places.

Once organized, they sat by their fire and wondered what would become of them.

Forest spent the following days hunting and foraging in the woods. Luckily for her party, very few of the other refugees had any skill or comfort in the woods, so she found that they hadn't been entirely cleared of game and other edibles the way she feared they might have been. Most refugees seemed to content themselves with the meager staples provided by the townsfolk or braved the guards patrolling the fields to steal what they could under cover of darkness, straining the already tense relations with the townsfolk.

Soon enough, Oriel healed enough to join Forest hunting, and together they were able to provide enough game for their party to supplement what the townsfolk provided. When Forest brought down a deer, Cera and Calix moved through the camp, giving meat to the people who looked to be in the sorriest condition, more often than not children, and it broke Cera's heart.

She organized a makeshift school with Kala's grandfather's help, giving the camp children something to look forward to.

Lily found an old woman from town tending a tiny garden outside its walls. The woman was suspicious of her at first, as she was of all foreigners, but Lily offered her help and slowly won her over, receiving a few vegetables every day as payment. Forest had also shown Lily how to forage for edibles in the woods, but she was still too fearful of them, their mother's death there years before continuing to haunt her.

Calix guarded their party's plot against the camp's unsavory tenants while keeping watch over the tree line, clinging to the faint hope that his father hadn't perished with the village. People emerged from time to time, but never his father – until the day he did. Calix spotted a ragtag group emerge from the trees, and something about them caught his eye. They were led by a burly redhead with a thin man at his side carrying a small child. Calix abandoned his post to make his way toward them. Something about the man holding the child made him speed up. As he got closer, the man began to resemble his father more and more until Calix threw pride to the wind and sprinted for him. He stopped in front of him and couldn't quite believe that it was indeed his father, Emrys.

"You're alive," was all he could manage to say and embraced his father fiercely.

"Don't crush the child," Emrys said but held his son equally tightly.

The remainder of their party emerged from the woods: thirty people from their village and twenty warriors from the north. Calix regarded them nervously.

Emrys noticed his son's unease. "It's okay; they're with us. We wouldn't be alive were it not for them," he said.

Calix turned to the redheaded leader. "I'm in your debt, then."

"It was my pleasure," the man replied. "I'm Jarom," he introduced himself, offering his hand.

"Calix," he replied, taking it. "Let me show you the way to our spot."

"Is Forest with you?" Jarom asked hopefully.

"Yes," Calix replied warily. "You could say that we wouldn't be alive were it not for her."

"Good girl," Jarom replied, smiling wide. "Is her sister with her?"

Calix raised an eyebrow suspiciously, protective of his friends. "Yes, Lily is with us, too – why?"

"It's just good to have family together," he replied, clasping Calix's shoulder. "Wouldn't you say?" he said, looking to Emrys, who smiled his agreement but didn't shed any light on why the warrior wanted to know about Forest and Lily.

"Let me show you the way," Calix said, taking the young girl from his father's arms.

"Lead on," Jarom replied good-naturedly and turned to have a word with his kin.

Calix led them to the official at the check-in table. The man looked even more nonplussed than usual with this large influx, but when Jarom laid his axe on the table, he swallowed hard and remained silent, just taking his census and waving them on under Calix's direction.

Calix escorted Emrys, Jarom, and their companions to their place in camp. Everyone happened to be present, even Forest. Calix walked up with his father in tow, prompting a moment of shocked silence, then a flurry of tears and hugs.

"We thought you were..." Fayre began. "How?" she asked Emrys.

"This gentleman here," Emrys replied, calling Jarom over.

"You overstate our role," he deflected but only had eyes for Forest.

Hers went wide at the sight of her uncle, and her heart leaped, but she glanced nervously at her sister. Jarom picked up on her signal and nodded to her.

"Hardly," Emrys continued. "Jarom and his people fought to cover our retreat from the village, then kept us alive on the way here."

"Happy to help," Jarom replied humbly, then begged his leave to organize his people.

Forest took her sister by the arm. "We need to talk," she told her.

"Now?" Lily asked. "Everyone just got here."

"Yes, now."

"Okay," Lily replied, waiting.

"Not here. Come with me," Forest said cryptically.

Cera looked up, concerned.

"We won't be long," Forest assured her, and Cera nodded her assent.

Forest led Lily to where Jarom was setting up camp. Nara spotted Forest and jumped to her feet, but Jarom shot her a stern look, and she restrained herself, albeit barely.

"Do you have a moment?" Forest asked Jarom.

"For you, I have all the time in the world," he replied warmly.

"Sit down, Lily," Forest ordered her sister gently but firmly.

Lily sat down, confused, and Forest and Jarom joined her. Nara hovered.

"Lily…" Forest began. "I don't know how to say this, so I'm just going to say it. I'd like you to meet your uncle," she said, gesturing to an expectant Jarom.

Lily didn't grasp what her sister was saying. "Our parents didn't have siblings," she said, struggling to find some reasoning that would explain Forest's bizarre declaration.

"Not from before," Forest said. "From after. Mother didn't die when she left us. She lived, and she met Jarom's brother, who took her in."

"That's not possible," Lily replied, stunned. "Mother's alive?" she asked, hopefully.

Forest hated to crush that hope. "Not any longer – I'm sorry."

"You saw her?"

"No. Jarom told me about her."

"Then I don't believe it," Lily concluded. "If you'll excuse me," she said, getting up uncertainly. "I need a moment." She struggled with her warring emotions.

"Now?" Nara asked Jarom, peeking over his shoulder.

He sighed. "Okay."

She exploded forward and enveloped Forest in a hug, jumping up and down. "Cousin!" she exclaimed. "I missed you."

Forest hugged her back, a little reluctantly in front of her sister. "I missed you, too." Nara eyed Lily, but Forest cautioned her. "Too soon," she said.

"Okay," replied Nara, disappointed. "I have *so* much to tell you. Thorvyn's here."

"Thorvyn – your crush?" Forest asked.

"Yes," she replied, positively vibrating.

Lily interjected, "Pardon me, but I need to get back."

"Of course," Forest replied, detaching herself from Nara. "We'll catch up later," she promised Nara.

Nara was disappointed but let her go.

Forest and Lily walked back to their campsite in silence.

Cera looked up at their return, reading Lily's agitation and shooting to her feet. "Are you okay?"

Lily ignored her and turned to Forest. "You knew. You knew, and you didn't tell me." She stared down her sister. Forest had no reply, which only heightened the tension.

"I'll leave you two alone," Cera said, stepping back to give them space, then looking around. "I'll go for a walk," she said to herself and wandered off.

"I couldn't find the words," Forest finally replied.

"How about – 'Hey Lily, mum's not dead?'" Lily asked, furious.

"Can't you hear how harsh that sounds?"

"You can stop shielding me. I'm your *older* sister, for the gods' sakes!" She held up a hand, stopping Forest from responding. "Don't even. I need to be alone."

"Fine," Forest replied. "I'll go find Cera." She stalked off in the direction she'd headed.

Cera was wandering through camp, consumed with worry for Lily. She'd never seen her so agitated since her mother's death and then Claudius's. She didn't notice the attention she was attracting from a pack of rough-looking men that began following her.

"Where are you going, beautiful?" one of them asked her.

Cera looked up. "None of your business – now, if you'll excuse me."

"Don't be so mean. We'll treat you right," the man said, edging closer.

Forest stumbled upon them at that moment. "There you are," she declared.

"Piss off, little girl – we're busy here," the leader of the pack said.

"Go to hell," Forest said and gripped the hilt of the knife at her belt, catching the attention of a woman lounging nearby.

The men sneered and moved to surround Cera and Forest.

"Get out of here, Forest," Cera pleaded. "I'll handle this."

"I'm not leaving," Forest declared and stepped in front of her, brandishing her knife. She wasn't a fighter, but she'd be damned if she was going to leave Cera to these animals.

The men laughed and moved closer.

"Brave girl," the approaching woman concluded. "Leave them alone," she ordered the men.

"Make us," the leader said belligerently.

"I was *so* hoping you'd say that. Girls," she called over her shoulder and was joined by two companions.

The man looked at the two approaching women and was leveled by a bone-crushing punch to his jaw from the first.

The woman's companions surged forward, and the three of them made short work of the men.

Forest just surveyed the carnage, wondering whether some of the men would ever rise again.

"That was fun," the first woman said and turned to introduce herself. "I'm Dhara, and I run this camp."

11
Kala

Kala woke in a strange bed, bolted upright, and reached for a dagger, only to discover it was no longer strapped to her thigh. She looked about in a panic.

"There, there dear – you're all right," an elderly woman's voice soothed.

Kala homed in on the source of the voice and found a woman reclining in an upholstered chair, cup in one hand and saucer in the other. She put them down on the cluttered table beside her chair and pulled off the heavy blankets that covered her, which pooled in a heap on the floor. She picked up a candle balanced precariously on a pile of books. "Let's have a look at you," she said, rose with an effort, and ambled over. "This old body isn't what it used to be," she sighed and lifted the candle to illumine Kala's face. "Oh – you're pretty," she exclaimed. "Couldn't tell by the state you were in when we found you, pale as you were... but your color is returning, and it suits you," she concluded, satisfied.

"Is my...," Kala began but paused, unsure of what to call Skye. *Her boyfriend?*

"Your friend?" the woman finished for her.

Kala nodded.

"He's on the sofa in the front room. I can't say what condition he's in, other than he looked worse off than you did when we brought you both here – but he was breathing regularly when I checked on him a moment ago."

Kala relaxed, then realized she was wearing an enormous flannel nightgown.

The woman chuckled at her confusion. "That's mine. I had to pin it in places – you being skin and bones and all. It wasn't easy getting you out of that leather outfit of yours, though. I mean, really – how could you ever be comfortable in a thing like that?" She stared at Kala in amazement. "But I did my best to wash it. It's drying on the line outside. The neighbors worked themselves into a tizzy when they saw it," she chuckled. "That alone is more scandal than we've had in years, never mind your unusual arrival." The woman headed for the door. "I'll fetch you some soup – then you'll have quite the story to tell, I imagine." She paused at the doorway and added, "I'll check on your friend on my way past," then sauntered out of the room.

Kala looked around at the cozy bedroom lit by flickering candlelight. The bed filled most of the space, but there was a comfortable reading nook in which the woman had been sitting and a tiny wood-burning stove in the corner. Paintings and sketches of smiling faces filled the walls. Heavy floral drapes were pulled closed in front of the windows, and a collection of well-worn carpets covered the floor. Quilts spilled off the bed, clothes were scattered about the floor, and piles of books surrounded the woman's chair. Order was obviously not a priority, but it radiated comfort. Kala felt a pang of longing for her old cottage.

A yellow tabby startled her by jumping up onto the bed. It strolled over and lay down on her lap, then butted her hand with its head until she scratched behind its ears.

"Well, hello there," Kala greeted it.

"I see you've met Tiberius," the old woman noted, returning with a steaming bowl of broth and shooing the cat off Kala's lap. "Let's start you off slowly," she advised, "Then we'll work you up to something more substantial." The smell wafted over to Kala, and she realized she was ravenous.

"Can you sit up without help, dear?" the woman asked, puzzling over where to put the soup down if the answer were 'no.'

"Yes, I can, thank you," Kala replied, rearranging the mountain of pillows surrounding her into a tidy pile behind her and propping herself against them.

The woman handed her the bowl and a spoon. "Careful now – it's hot," she fussed. "Oh, and your friend still breathes," she added happily.

Kala blew on a spoonful of broth. She only noticed how chapped her lips were as she closed them over the spoon. The soup tasted heavenly after so long without eating, but her stomach revolted, nonetheless. She sat stock-still for a moment, wondering if she was going to be sick.

"There, there – just take your time, and you'll be fine," the woman coached. She walked back to drag her chair across the floor to Kala's bedside while Kala sipped her soup. The screeching it made as the back legs scraped against the bare wood floor could have woken the dead, and Kala peeked out the doorway to see if it had, in fact, woken Skye. It didn't appear to have done so, making her worry for him despite the woman's assurances.

The woman positioned the chair beside Kala and collapsed into it, breathing hard. "I'll need a moment," she wheezed. Once she'd recovered, she started again, "Allow me to introduce myself properly. I'm Edith. Welcome to my humble home." She looked at Kala for her to respond in kind.

Kala put her soup down. "Pardon my manners. The soup is delicious, and I was finding that distracting," she apologized. She collected her thoughts and decided that here in this tiny bedroom, she wanted to be Kala, a girl woefully far from home, rather than Raven, Angel of Death. "I'm Kala," she said and marveled at how right it felt.

Edith beamed. "I knew a Kala once when I was a young girl." She leaned back in her chair. "Now, tell me how you and your friend came to us on death's door in an airship from across the sea. We've never had a ship arrive from the west, only south along the coast, and never with two such intriguing passengers, or two at all. Imagine our surprise." She folded her blankets back over herself, readying herself for a lengthy tale.

"There's not much to the story, I'm afraid. My friend and I are from villages east of here, and we stowed away aboard an airship trying to get back home."

"I can't say I blame you," Edith declared. "I'm quite attached to mine as well, simple though it may be." She mulled over something that puzzled her. "You say you're from the east – but you arrived from the west. Our fishermen tell us that there's no land west of here. And it was the damnedest thing – pardon my language – but your airship drifted in out of the fog and landed squarely with nary a soul tugging it down. It's sitting there still – not even tied to the ground – just sitting there," Edith marveled.

"I don't know about any of that," Kala replied truthfully. "I don't think I was conscious when the ship landed."

"I'll say," Edith replied. "We had to check you for a heartbeat, which was complicated mightily by those confounded leather clothes of yours. At least your friend wears regular clothes. And what were you doing with so many weapons? Are you two weapons traders?"

"No, they're mine." Kala blushed. "I'm a bit protective of my well-being and a hunter by training."

Edith looked skeptical. "You hunt with swords?"

Kala giggled at the image of her chasing rabbits, waving swords. "No. I don't think that'd be very successful. They're for my protection."

"From what?"

"It's a dangerous world out there."

"Not this little corner of it," the woman sighed contentedly. "I'd say it's pretty sleepy here, but then you two fall out of the sky. That's enough excitement for years," she concluded.

A wave of tiredness overcame Kala that Edith noticed and tucked her back in. "You're going to need some time to get your energy back," she said and blew out the candle.

Kala woke later to find Skye snoring in the chair beside her bed, barely visible under a mountain of blankets, sweat beading on his forehead. Kala rose to pull a few off of him but was shooed back into bed by Edith.

"My word – first him, then you. The boy woke and refused to be separated from you. He dragged himself in here and almost crawled into bed with you. Well, that wouldn't do – you two without wedding bracelets and all – unless that's something your matching necklaces signify. Darn – it didn't occur to me to ask. Oh well, he was content to plant himself in that chair there and just be close to you."

"Can we wake him?" Kala asked. "I'd feel more at ease knowing that he's okay."

"Well, my mother used to say that if we didn't wake sleeping men, there'd be no men awake." She chuckled to herself and made her way over to Skye's chair, gently shaking him until he roused from his slumber.

His eyes focused, and he saw Kala watching him. "Thank the gods," he exclaimed, "I had such terrible dreams. You turned into a bird and flew away. I was chasing you, but I couldn't catch you." He sighed and reached for her hand. Kala extended it, and he held it tightly.

"My mistake," Edith stammered. "I can see that you're betrothed. Sorry about that. Well, no harm was done."

Skye turned to Edith. "You've been very kind to nurse us back to health."

Edith snorted, "I wouldn't say that either of you is anywhere near healthy."

"Be that as it may," Skye continued. "We have to be on our way as quickly as possible. There are people in worse condition than us. People we care about deeply."

Edith objected firmly, "Neither of you is in any condition to go anywhere. You have to recover your strength first. Yesterday, you struggled with soup," she reminded Kala.

They hated to admit it, but she was right. "Are you sure we wouldn't be imposing?" Kala asked.

"Hardly. I so rarely get company. It's a pleasure," she assured them. "Now, who are these people that you say are in dire straits?"

"The people of my village," Skye replied. "It's high in the mountains, and with the airship disruptions of late, we fear that they lack the means to survive. We have to find food and bring it to them immediately. That's why we commandeered a large airship."

"Commandeered? I thought you stowed away."

"He's just exaggerating," Kala covered.

Edith thought out loud, "We'd noticed that the airships weren't coming as often as they used to. We don't need much from the outside world, though – although it's always nice to see a young face disembark – our numbers have been shrinking for generations. The youth rejuvenate us – although I can't say they're happy about it, given how few other young people there are here." She realized that her thoughts had strayed a bit. "Right, food. With the dearth of airships coming to take it away, our stores are overstocked with fish. The village elders will probably let you take some with you if you like."

Skye jumped from his chair and hugged Edith tightly. "You're gods-sent," he exclaimed.

"Oh, my," she exclaimed. "People are really affectionate where you come from, I see." She patted him on the back uncomfortably until Skye sat back down. She reflected a little longer, and a thought struck her, "Wait a moment – you can't very well make an airship go where you want it to. You're at the mercy of the winds."

Kala leaned closer. "I'll tell you a secret – we can. It's a bit of magic we've learned."

"Do you control the winds or the airship?" Edith asked without skepticism.

"The airship, I think, but the 'how' of it is lost on me. I'm surprised you believe me."

"You don't come from a long line of fisherfolk without a healthy acceptance of magic," she said.

"We really must leave quickly, though," Skye interjected. "Who do we see about the fish?"

"I'll put the word out, but not until tomorrow. You spend at least one day resting, and we'll see what we can do then. I warn you, though – not everyone is as accepting of magic as I am. They'll likely be resistant."

"Then I'll just have to show them," Kala resolved.

Edith left to prepare dinner, and Skye offered his help, leaving Kala alone to explore. He found her later wrapped in a blanket in a chair on the porch, watching the sea. She had a cup of kai in one hand and stroked the cat with her other.

"You look comfy," he said as he approached.

She smiled up at him. "This is paradise," she said contentedly. "I'd love to live here."

"I don't know about that," Skye replied, pulling up a chair of his own, "Too much fish for my liking."

Kala chuckled. "We could have goats. You'd feel right at home."

Skye thought about his home in the mountains and worried about his mother.

"Have you ever just stared at the sea?" Kala asked to distract him from her gaffe.

"Yes. It's very calming," he replied, relaxing slightly.

"Exactly, it's like watching a fire," Kala agreed, taking his hand in hers. They spent the rest of the afternoon enjoying the view and recovering their strength.

The next morning, Skye helped Edith walk over to her neighbor's, where she asked the young boy who lived there to run around the town, telling everyone to bring as much food from the stores as they could spare and meet them at the airship.

Kala made her way to the airship before anyone arrived. She looked out over the quaint cottages huddled together in a semi-circle along the water's edge, then over the brightly colored fishing vessels bobbing in the harbor, and finally at the waves lapping against the shore. A gust of wind stirred her hair, and Kala tied it back. It was as charming a place as she'd ever seen.

Several village elders wound their way up the path from the village, arguing amongst themselves. It didn't look like a good sign to Kala.

"We're giving up valuable food to these crazy kids," one was saying as they came without earshot.

"We can't eat all that we have, so what's the harm?" another countered. "It'll benefit someone downwind," she added. "It always has."

They continued arguing until Skye and Edith arrived with villagers pulling cartloads of dried fish and preserved vegetables. The skeptical elders seemed to be in the majority, and they put a halt to the proceedings before the supplies could be loaded into the airship. Skye looked desperate and helpless.

Kala motioned for everyone's attention, which was easy to obtain, given how many people were eyeing her form-fitting leathers. She'd at least had the foresight to stow her visible weapons onboard the ship. "I know you're skeptical that we can ensure that this precious food of yours makes its way into the mouths of the desperate people of my friend's village, so let me prove to you that we can."

The crowd murmured its doubts.

Kala raised her hands to the heavens. "I implore the gods to help us in our mission of mercy. If the hearts of these kind people be true, bring me back to them." She stepped back into the ship and slammed the door closed.

What is she doing? Skye wondered.

There was a resonating thud, and the ship lifted off the ground. Skye ran over and pounded on the door. "Don't go!" he yelled, but it spiraled upward and away to the east. Skye slumped to his knees until the villagers' shouts got his attention. He looked up to see them pointing at the airship high in the sky. It had ceased drifting east and miraculously swung in a huge arc back around to the west. People watched it descend, adjusting course as it drifted lower. The men of the village looked about for ropes to haul it down, but there were none. The airship just shifted until it touched down with a thud, centered on the landing pad. The door opened, and Kala stepped out to stunned silence.

"The gods thank you," she declared.

Kala and Skye sat on the floor of the airship under a pile of blankets furnished by Edith.

"Edith was so kind to us," Kala said, tugging a blanket snugly around her.

"Yes, she was," Skye agreed, slipping an arm under the blanket and wrapping it around her. "You gambled a bit with your stunt with the airship, though," he added.

"Fortune favors the bold," she replied and snuggled closer.

He kissed her tenderly. "You could have warned me."

"I didn't plan it. I was inspired."

"That's what worried me, and I hate it when you disappear, but it worked, so I guess I have to accept the gods' thanks."

Kala chuckled and kissed him back reassuringly.

The airship drifted high in the sky toward the distant mountains, and they were incredibly grateful for the blankets as the temperature fell to frigid levels.

Skye's nerves forced him up to look out the windows. Sunlight glinted off the peaks like a diamond necklace, but its beauty did nothing to calm him.

Kala looked up at him from her nest of blankets. "Come back here. You can't will the ship to the ground any faster by staring at it."

"What if she's not okay?" he asked, thinking of his mother, growing terrified at the thought.

"Of course she is. We wouldn't be here if she weren't – it's fate," Kala reassured him.

"Fate hasn't exactly been a friend to either of us," Skye grumbled.

The airship seemed to descend faster, so Kala rose and strapped on her weapons.

Skye eyed her from across the compartment.

"What? You can never be too careful," she defended herself.

Skye turned to look out the window again. He spied a collection of dots that grew to become people awaiting the ship. "That's fewer people than I'd expect, but at least there are people down there." It gnawed at him whether his mother would be among them.

"Remember that they don't need to haul us down. We've got magic," Kala said, waggling her fingers as if casting a spell, then clapping her hands together to warm them. That proved fruitless, so she rewrapped herself in blankets while standing.

She caught Skye raising an eyebrow at her. "You can never be too warm!" she said, and he rolled his eyes.

The airship completed its descent onto a promontory jutting from the steep mountainside and anchored itself to its landing pad. Skye took a deep breath, swung the door open, and a blast of cold mountain air entered the compartment, carrying with it flakes of snow. He readied himself and stepped out, followed by Kala.

The Chief stood before them, surrounded by a collection of armed men loyal to him. His recognition of Skye was followed by shock. "What the hell are you doing back here?" he asked.

"Surprised?" Skye asked in reply.

"*I* am," a beautiful blond of eighteen years replied, stepping out from behind her father.

Kala looked from the girl to Skye and back again.

"Hi, Ashlyn," he greeted her sheepishly.

"You came back for me?" she asked hopefully.

Kala leaned forward and whispered, "Awkward."

Skye shushed her. "It's good to see you, Ashlyn, but I've come back for my mother." Ashlyn looked crestfallen, so he added, "You've grown more beautiful since I left."

Kala made quiet gagging noises behind him, and Skye made an obscene gesture behind his back.

"Where is my mother – I don't see her?" Skye asked those present loudly.

"She fled to the mines with the others," the Chief replied coldly.

"And why would she do that?" Skye asked, his anger rising.

"They refused to leave as they were ordered to. There's not enough food for everyone. We can't all starve."

"So, they can starve so you can live?" Skye replied and took a step forward. Kala restrained him with a fistful of his tunic.

"Tough choices go with the job," the Chief replied indifferently.

"I tried to change his mind," Ashlyn interjected.

"Shut up, Ashlyn," her father barked.

"If she's dead, you'll be fast on her heels," Skye threatened.

The Chief smirked at the threat. "I doubt she's starved to death by now. They barricaded themselves in the mushroom farms," he replied.

Skye clenched his fists. "Then, that's where I'm going."

"Suit yourself," the Chief replied. "Now, what have you brought us in that ship of yours?"

"Nothing for you and your thugs, I assure you," Skye replied, already pushing past them on his way to the mines.

"And how would you stop me if I just took it?" the Chief smirked.

"I wouldn't lift a finger," Skye replied. "That's what she's here for," he added, gesturing to Kala.

"Hi there," she said innocently, waving at the man.

Skye returned before the sun had crossed a quarter of the sky, carrying his mother in his arms with thirty emaciated villagers following him.

Kala rose. "Is she…?"

"No," Skye replied, "just weak." He threaded his way among the bodies of men lying on the ground groaning from their injuries. "You've been busy, I see," he observed.

"I needed the exercise, and these men were kind enough to oblige me," Kala shrugged.

Skye motioned to the people following him and tilted his head toward the airship. "Onboard, you'll find enough food to help you regain your strength. Unload it and store it somewhere safe. If any of this lot even looks at it…," he gestured to the men strewn about the ground, "my friend will be less merciful with them." With that, he turned toward his old home carrying his mother.

Kala stayed with the ship to supervise its orderly unloading, and once that had been accomplished, asked for directions to Skye's home. A young girl offered to bring her there, and Kala gratefully accepted. The girl gestured to an archway cut into the stone of the cliff. "Do you want to take the inside way or the outside way?"

It was uncomfortably cold in the open air, but Kala didn't like the idea of threading through tunnels with the weight of the mountain on top of her. It was irrational, but she gestured in the direction of the outdoor route.

The girl pivoted and led Kala along a path that wound around clustered dwellings. The girl seemed oblivious to the frigid wind and the perilous drop off the cliff.

Kala stopped on a landing of a winding stair and paused for a moment to admire the view of the sun glinting off the snowy peaks. The girl waited patiently for her.

"What's your name?" Kala asked her.

"Opal," the girl replied.

"That's a pretty name," Kala replied, noting as the wind blew the girl's wild hair out of her face that she had iridescent eyes. "Mine is Kala."

"Did you really beat up all of the Chief's men?" Opal asked, brushing her hair behind her ears as it swirled in the wind.

Kala smiled self-consciously.

"Cool," Opal replied and turned to bound up the rest of the stairs. She waited for Kala outside a door to a dwelling on the higher level. "This is it," Opal announced.

"Thank you," Kala told her.

Opal smiled and rested her hand briefly on Kala's arm before scampering back down the way they'd come.

Kala watched the girl descend, then turned and knocked quietly on the door so as not to disturb Skye and his mother, then let herself in.

Skye was cradling his mother in front of a roaring fire, giving her sips of water from his waterskin.

His mother looked up at Kala and took her time to digest what she saw. "So, you're my son's savior," she managed in a small voice.

"I wouldn't say that," Kala blushed.

"He does," she replied but lacked the strength to say anything more. She rolled toward her son, and he stroked her hair.

"We're getting her out of here as soon as she's well enough to travel," Skye told Kala, not looking up from his mother.

"Of course. We'll take her to Edith. She says her village needs people."

Skye nodded, and she left him to care for his mother in peace. She found a modest sofa and brought some blankets out from the bedroom. Skye was still sitting with his mother when she fell asleep.

Kala woke at dawn and looked about the tiny cottage. It was constructed of stone rather than timber, and while it was spare, it was comfortable now that it had been warmed up. She spied Skye's mother in her bed with a freshly tended fire crackling in the bedroom fireplace. Skye was nowhere to be seen. She checked each room until she heard heated voices outside. She cracked open the door to see Skye arguing with an older man, saying, "Get the hell out of here, and I don't ever want to see your face darken my mother's door again. If you do, so help the gods, I'll darken it further with your blood."

Kala had never seen Skye so angry. She poked her head out. "Morning, honey. Want me to kill him?"

The man blanched, but Skye replied, "Tempting, but no, thank you. Not unless he returns." The man bolted down the narrow path, and Skye came back inside.

"My mother's onetime 'boyfriend,'" he explained, directing Kala to the table and beginning to prepare her morning kai.

"Thank you," she said as he handed it to her and kissed her cheek.

He looked in on his mother, then returned to sit across from Kala. He ran a hand through his hair. "I can't believe we did it. We're home," he said incredulously.

Kala put her cup down, reached out, and put a hand on his. "*You're* home. I need to go check on mine."

He squeezed her hand as if to hold her there but released her reluctantly. "Of course. I understand. You'll come back?" he asked hopefully.

"We'll work that out. I know we'll be together in the end, but first, I have to do right by those I love, as you have by those you do."

Skye rose, circled the table, and enveloped her from behind. She held his arms tightly. "This is not goodbye," she reminded him.

"I know," he said, but his breath caught. "I'm going to check on my mother," he told her as an excuse so she wouldn't see him lose his composure.

Kala released her hold on him, and he went into the bedroom. She finished her kai and got dressed for travel. She was securing her pack when a knock on the door interrupted her. Skye was still with his mother, so she answered it for him, finding Ashlyn on the step. Her white furs framed her cheeks, pink from the cold, and her green eyes sparkled as she looked uncertainly into Kala's.

"May I come in?" she asked timidly.

Kala hesitated but stepped back out of her way.

Ashlyn assumed that meant she could, so she did.

Kala closed the door behind her.

"I wanted to thank you for bringing food to the village," Ashlyn told her. "Things were looking grim."

"You're welcome," Kala replied, feeling uncomfortable for being thanked just for being a decent person.

Ashlyn looked her over. "So, you're my boyfriend's girlfriend?" she asked.

"We're many things to each other," Kala replied cautiously.

"I'm happy for you," Ashlyn assured her. "Skye's a great guy."

Kala began to feel a little guilty.

Ashlyn could tell she was making Kala uncomfortable, so she changed the topic. "So, you're getting out of here?"

"That's the plan. Why?"

"Take me with you when you go – please!" she begged.

"I'm sure there'll be room for you, and you're welcome to come with us."

Ashlyn breathed a deep sigh of relief. "Thank you. I thought you'd hate me and punish me by leaving me in this hell-hole."

"Skye has never said anything but the nicest things about you, so I couldn't hate you even if I wanted to."

"That's a relief. I wouldn't want to be on your bad side."

Kala laughed. "No, I suppose not."

Ashlyn stuck out her hand tentatively. "Friends?"

Kala hesitated, feeling it was too early to tell, but accepted her offer. "Friends." She looked through the bedroom door. "If you'll excuse me, I have to talk to Skye before leaving."

"You're leaving?"

Kala couldn't decipher whether it was concern or hope in Ashlyn's voice. "I have business to attend to, but you'll see me again." She walked Ashlyn to the door, wished her well, and stepped back inside.

Skye exited the bedroom, closing the door quietly behind him.

"That was Ashlyn," Kala told him. "She's nice... I hate that. Why can't she be a bitch?"

Skye chuckled and hugged her.

She looked up at him. "Do you still love me, even though I'm a terrible person?"

"Warts and all, my little tree frog."

"Tree frog? That is *so* not sexy," she said and snuggled into his embrace. "Can I borrow your amulet, please? I'm going to take the airship to my village. If I can't come back immediately, I'll send it back to you with your amulet in it and use mine to hail myself another to meet up with you later."

Skye agreed and handed it over.

"Thank you. Oh, and by the way, I agreed to bring your girlfriend with us when we leave here," Kala told him.

Skye bristled. "*Ex*-girlfriend."

"Just teasing, but I did agree to her coming."

"It's the right thing to do, so thank you."

"Someone has to look out for all of your exes."

Skye swatted her, then kissed her deeply. "I won't be whole until you return to me."

"Then I'd better get going," she replied, then hesitated. "In a moment," she added and kissed him back.

Kala felt the ship land outside her village. She hadn't noticed that it had been descending, it had been so gradual. She readied herself. *Would she be greeted as a murderer? Would Lily forgive her? Would her grandfather recoil from the person she'd become?* She steeled herself for every possibility and opened the door.

She hadn't prepared herself for what she saw – the ruins of her village. Nothing was left except charred foundations; nothing was left of her grandfather's cottage at all. She stared out in disbelief at the burned-out buildings. Her heart convulsed with pain.

She pulled out Skye's amulet, dialed the setting for his village and threw it inside, slamming the door closed as the ship began to rise. She turned to face the swirling ash.

The ones she loved were gone – her grandfather, Lily, Cera, Forest, Calix... She'd failed them, waited too long to try in earnest to return home in the futile hope that she could rehabilitate herself first, to free herself from Death's hold. The folly of it was plain to her now.

They want a weapon – I'll be a weapon.

PART II
REUNION

12

Soren

Soren stood in the entrance of his tent, staring at the town across the river. He imagined its inhabitants cowering behind its stone walls, walls which would never hold him back, regardless of their height or thickness.

He closed the flap and returned to his place at the table, where his war council sat impatiently. General Trax drummed his fingers, making plain his annoyance at being made to wait. He was a hulking man, a warrior chieftain from the north, born into a life of violence. He'd learned how to wield it to his ends and was brutally efficient as Soren's hammer.

To Trax's right sat Seline, who Soren had come across early in his conquest. He and Trax had razed a village that was more advanced than any other they'd seen – it even had running water. Soren had discovered that Seline was the talented engineer behind it and had her spared. Now that his war was bringing him up against walled cities and not just isolated villages, he needed her expertise to design siege equipment. She had a knack for creatively solving any problem, even with limited resources, and she was taking advantage of the respite in their meeting to perform calculations. She scribbled and couldn't have cared less how long the recess lasted.

On Trax's other side sat Lennox. He was as slippery as they came, having run a criminal enterprise in a town they'd recently overrun. When captured, he calmly informed his captors that their leader wanted to see him. His boldness had piqued Soren's curiosity and won him an audience. Lennox pointed out no less than twenty things that would make Soren's advance unsustainable and promised to help him if he made him a captain. Soren was intelligent enough to recognize an asset when he saw one, and Lennox became one of his inner circle, despite his distastefulness.

Soren surveyed each member of his council. Trax had been with him the longest, having ruled the tribe into which Soren found himself transplanted as a youth. Despite lounging in his chair, Trax stared back with an intense gaze and furrowed brow as if barely restraining his anger. His unruly, dark hair fell to his shoulders, around which he wore furs, despite the warm climate. His enormous broadsword was forever strapped to his back, and Soren wondered if the man slept with it. Trax flexed his giant hands as if adjusting his sword grip. The muscles of his arms and chest bulged, and scars crisscrossed his exposed skin. Soren disliked the man and was sure the feeling was mutual, but they needed each other – Soren articulated the vision that Trax could rally men behind to further his desire for conquest, but Trax's cruelty bothered Soren. Soren wanted to see the world torn down so that it could be rebuilt; Trax just seemed to relish tearing it down. He enjoyed the suffering he caused. Soren wondered, *What would he do with him at the end of the conquest, or would Trax overthrow him before then and lord over the ashes of the world?* Soren shuddered. *But how to eliminate him? The man had a talent for survival.*

He turned his attention to Seline. She wore trousers and a tunic, with her unadorned hair tied back in a loose braid, betraying a shock of premature grey hair, despite being middle-aged. Soren liked her – he admired how her mind worked. *She could be pretty if she wanted to, too*, he thought, *but she was uninterested in anyone or anything beyond her thoughts.* She was an ally, but neither companion nor friend, if Soren were honest with himself.

Lennox squirmed in his chair and brushed his thin, greasy hair back over his head. Soren found him almost as distasteful as Trax, mostly because he was rumored to fancy children, whom he did not treat well. Soren sought evidence and would have happily punished him severely at the first sign of any such transgression of Soren's values, but Lennox was so devious that only rumors escaped his black hole.

Soren sighed. "Where were we?" he asked.

"The townsfolk fleeing," Trax reminded him testily. "Do we hunt them down?"

Soren thought for a moment. "There's no reason to. If we destroy their town, we destroy them. In the wild, they're nothing and certainly no threat to us. Let them flee."

This did not sit well with Trax, who hated missing an opportunity for bloodshed.

Soren could tell what he was thinking. "Our focus is the town," he pointed out. "There'll be plenty of people to kill inside its walls." That seemed to appease him.

"If I may…" Lennox began, and upon confirmation from Soren to proceed, continued, "Could we *not* kill all the farmers? It's in our best interests to have some remain alive to harvest the crops we need to sustain our army's advance."

Trax shrugged, "They all look alike – peasant, farmer, merchant. Hard to be particular when you're killing people."

"Can you at least try?" Lennox requested.

"Of course," Trax replied, having no such intention.

"Oh…" Lennox added, "And how about not torching the fields or killing the livestock. That's your own dinner you're destroying."

Trax shrugged, bored when the conversation veered away from murder.

Lennox knew he was wasting his time with Trax but trying ingratiated himself with Soren, to whom he turned. "My interviews continue to bear fruit," he began.

Soren knew that by "interviews," the man actually meant "interrogations." Lennox thought it would be valuable to learn more about the world they were aiming to conquer, so he had rounded up anyone who had been displaced as a youth in an airship and extracted information from them about the wider world. It bothered Soren that Lennox preyed on those carried away from their homes by the airships, as he felt a connection to them, but the information he gathered was valuable enough for Soren to look the other way. It was fragmented, but a picture of the world was beginning to emerge.

"We have large expanses of territory still before us and cities far larger than any we've seen. An army marches on its stomach, and if we keep destroying food sources, we cripple our ability to push forward."

"That's sensible," Soren agreed, risking taking Lennox's side over Trax's. He turned to Trax. "Tell your men not to destroy crops or livestock. They're ours. I want them."

Trax grumbled but indicated his consent.

Soren turned to Seline. "How goes your siege equipment?"

She looked up. "Hmm? Oh, right – yes," she said, shifting gears from thinker to speaker. "Two towers are being built to my specifications right now. That's not a lot, but we just need to breach the walls in one place to have the town fall. I'm having a battering ram built too. The towers are mostly to provide cover for the men wielding it."

Trax found the length of time it was taking to complete her projects infuriating. "How much longer?" he asked, annoyed. "My men grow restless."

"Just a few more days," she assured him. "Oh – and there's something else I've been experimenting with," she continued in her briefing to Soren. "It's a white powder I acquired from merchants who say they got it from somewhere in the far west. It burns hotter than any forge. Would you care to see a demonstration?"

"No, that's all right. I believe you," Soren replied, losing interest when Seline's science bordered on sorcery.

"I have several ideas for its application," she continued. "I think it'll come in handy in torching the town gates and weakening them for the battering ram."

"Sounds good," Soren concluded, trusting her judgment in the matter. "Keep at it."

Soren got up again and moved back to the door, where he lifted the flap and looked out over the town. The townsfolk would provide minimal resistance to Trax's hardened warriors. "We attack in three days," he told his council, "And yes, Trax, you can kill everyone except the farmers."

13
Kala

Kala moved among the charred buildings of her village in a daze. *This isn't real*, she thought. She couldn't reconcile the images of her village etched in her memory with the devastation around her. She could navigate these streets with her eyes closed, and so she did, retreating to the world she remembered rather than the one that was. People she'd known her whole life came into view in her mind, carrying out their mundane tasks. Calix popped his head out of the smithy, smiled, and waved. She caught a glimpse of Cera and followed her across the village square and through the door of Lily's house. She heard Lily singing contently in the kitchen, despite burning whatever she was baking. Forest sat cross-legged on the living room floor, gazing forward, so Kala sat down to face her. Forest registered Kala's presence and stared deeply into her eyes.

"It won't bring us back," Forest told her.

"What won't?" Kala asked.

"Vengeance."

"It's all I have," Kala countered.

"It's not enough," Forest replied and began to fade.

"Don't go," Kala begged, hot tears flowing down her cheeks. "Please, don't leave me," she pleaded – but Forest's apparition dissolved. Kala reached forward but found only empty air. She opened her eyes, screaming at the skies. There was no house; Forest had never been. Kala wrapped her arms around her knees and curled into a ball. She lay alone on the ashen ground, sobbing piteously.

She cried until her tears ran dry, and she lay still and hollow. Her heart had turned to stone, and if it still beat at all, it was without her knowledge or blessing. The wind blew across her prone form, and an ember of anger glowed briefly in her heart, then expired. Desperate to feel anything, Kala fanned at it until it relit. She cradled it and blew on it until it sparked into flame. Kala warmed herself by the flame as the fire rose and rose until it consumed her. The fire coursed through her veins, cleansing her of every emotion she'd ever felt until nothing was left but vengeance. The fire cried out for blood, urging Kala to her feet. If Death wanted her so badly, she would give Her what she demanded – she'd bring Her death. She rose like a predator, the fire thrumming in her veins.

She walked to the tree line and scouted along it for signs of her prey. She found traces of a small party heading south and a larger party heading east. Her need to punish decided for her – she'd head east. Forest's ghost appeared before her, blocking her path.

"This is not the way," Forest told her, but Kala walked through her. Forest's spirit turned and followed, and together they stalked together into the gloom of the trees. Kala advanced with no concern other than the need to find someone to punish. She felt no fear, for what use had Death for fear? Death could not be killed. Kala walked until she was tired, or it was dark, and then she'd simply lie down where she was and sleep, haunted by dark spirits. Forest's ghost would greet her when she woke, staring at her with baleful, disapproving eyes. Kala disregarded her and continued her hunt. The trail was cold, but Kala's predatorial instincts drove her, and she was rewarded by the occasional confirmation that a force of men had indeed passed this way.

In a dream, Kala strode into a misty clearing in which a pack of dire wolves reposed. An enormous beast with midnight-black fur rose to face her. A pair of greys appeared at its sides and advanced past it toward her. Kala halted and waited impatiently. The grey on her left came to her and sniffed around her chest, its breath hot on her neck. Kala knew what it was drawn to and brought out the wolf's tooth necklace from inside her tunic. The wolf sniffed at it while the second wolf breathed in the scent of her hair. Satisfied, they lay down deferentially before her. She took a step forward and patted their heads. The black wolf lay down facing her, and one by one, the others did the same. Kala strode between the greys toward the black wolf and held out her hand for it to sniff. It nuzzled her hand, and she scratched behind its ears. She gave it a final pat and walked past. The wolves turned their heads to watch her go but did not rise as she walked out of the misty clearing. They paid no attention at all to Forest's ghost trailing after her.

In the days that followed, Kala would sometimes glimpse a wolf through the trees, but only fleetingly. They were kindred spirits, and she felt their companionship despite the distance they kept. One day, it rained all day, and Kala collapsed cold and shivering that night on a bed of moss. Kala felt more than heard the dark wolf stride out of the inky night and curl up against her back. The rest of the pack joined in, huddling together in a mass of wet fur. The heat from their bodies warmed Kala through the night. In the morning, when she woke, they got up and returned silently to the forest.

Kala tasted smoke on the air, this time more real than a memory. She breathed in its acrid smell, and by gradation of scent and the direction of the wind, she followed it to its source. Emerging from the trees into open fields, not unlike those that surrounded her village, Kala beheld a smoldering settlement and rough-looking men prodding through its still-smoking ruins. *Finally, I will have retribution*, she thought. She unslung her bow and quiver and lay them on the ground. She pulled off her pack and placed it beside them. She drew her short swords from the scabbards at her back and waved them in lazy circles to reacquaint her hands with them. Satisfied, she slid them back into their scabbards and advanced purposefully toward the men.

One of them spotted her and signaled the others. They moved to the edge of the village nearest her until they stood twenty-strong between her and the village.

The leader called to her, "Come to meet the same fate, young one?"

Kala's smile twitched upward. *Yes, I've come to mete the same fate.* She pulled a pair of daggers from sheaths on her thighs and centered herself. She quickened her pace toward their ranks until it was a run. The men stood their ground, unsure what to make of her. She bellowed and hurled the daggers in her hands, then the pair from her belt. She pulled two more from behind her and slashed the throats of the men she passed between, spun, and hurled them at two others.

She turned, pulling her swords from their scabbards and racing at a man, dodging his blade but wrapping her arm in his cloak. She launched herself in the air, using him for leverage, spinning him around and cutting open his neck in the process as she slashed at a second man, and flew into a third from an angle he'd not thought possible.

She rolled and rose between three men. She stabbed one cruelly in the knee, then vaulted him as he collapsed, stabbing downward and outward at the other two. She landed in a roll, cutting crimson lines into the thighs of the men she passed, finally rising to plant a sword in the chest of the two men in front of her. Fifteen men lay dead or dying behind her. Two of the three remaining men turned and ran. She spun to gain momentum and threw her swords, impaling both of them in the back.

She strolled up to the final man, the one who had challenged her initially, hands empty of weapons. He stood transfixed. She sidled up to him, close enough for a lover's embrace, drawing her final pair of daggers from her thighs, and drove them between his ribs. His eyes rolled back, and she drank in his death.

It was over too quickly. Kala tensed in frustration. She moved like a wraith from body to body, collecting her weapons and dispatching those slow to expire. Forest's ghost watched her from a nearby, overturned wagon.

"It doesn't satiate you, does it?" Forest asked her.

"It's not enough," Kala agreed.

"It never will be," Forest told her, shook her head, and wandered off.

Kala scanned her surroundings for anyone she might have missed. She caught sight of the wolves watching her from the trees.

"Be my guest," she called to them, gesturing to the field of battle, and followed Forest into the remains of the village.

The wolves emerged and unhurriedly advanced toward the bodies of the freshly fallen men. Kala heard the sound of gnashing teeth behind her, and it pleased her.

She studied the ruins. The townsfolk's bodies had been piled into what would have been a pyre had Kala not interrupted the men's work. Forest bent to stare into the unseeing eyes of a boy about her age. Kala picked up an apple that had spilled from a basket dropped in someone's haste. She sat down at the table of a house that had burned down around it, somehow sparing the table. She ate her lunch while the wolves ate theirs.

As Forest continued her inventory of the dead, Kala pulled out her journal and laid it in front of her. She examined her maps and tried to piece together the direction of the closest settlement. Kala guessed that continuing southeast gave her the best odds of coming across another village, and gods willing, the men who preyed on them. She rose from the table and went to collect the possessions she'd left by the tree line.

Kala, Forest's ghost, and her entourage of wolves continued southeast on her quest for blood. She encountered the ruins of more villages and occasionally the marauders that had laid waste to them, whom she dispatched with calm fury.

Kala emerged from the trees to a sight she hadn't beheld in several moons – a village still standing. There was a sizable force of armed men before it – forty or fifty – and a frightened collection of townsfolk hunkering behind overturned tables and brandishing farm tools as weapons. They stood no chance whatsoever, and the men were toying with them, relishing their hopelessness and fear.

A middle-aged woman stepped from among the huddled villagers and raised her hands toward the marauders to show that she only wanted to talk. The men leaned on their weapons, in no hurry to commence their dark business.

They'll neither negotiate nor show mercy, Kala thought dispassionately.

The men let the woman approach and say her peace. Then, the leader lifted his sword, considered it, and ran it through her stomach. The others laughed – a wound like that was an excruciatingly painful way to die.

Kala finished depositing the possessions that she didn't need to deal death and advanced toward the jovial murderers. She bade Forest's judgmental ghost to piss off.

The men noticed her approach, and one of them called to her, bored, "There'll be no parlay."

"Suits me fine," Kala replied and halted her advance, facing the men.

One of them looked to the cowering villagers and back to her. "Seems you're all alone," he snickered.

"I'm never alone," she replied, glancing at Forest's ghost as it walked up beside her.

The men struggled to see what she was looking at, but one of them caught sight of the dire wolves in the trees and paled.

Kala noted his discomfort and looked over her shoulder at the advancing pack. "My friends," she said sardonically as they emerged from the trees licking their chops.

The men stood their ground, assessing what to make of this young woman and her pack of wolves.

"Shall we?" Kala asked them, drawing her swords, and snarling. She charged, cueing the wolves to do the same. She gave herself over to the bloodlust and crashed into their ranks in a whirlwind of steel, dispatching men in any manner that brought them down. Kala was merciless in her onslaught – she didn't care how they died, as long as they did. Their blood spattered her, and perhaps her own, although she couldn't tell and wouldn't have cared even if she could.

Kala ran through the man in front of her and searched for another foe but found that she and her pack had won the field. The remaining men fled for the tree line, chased by the wolves. Kala was left alone on the field with the dead. Screams echoed through the trees as Kala wiped the blood off her swords and resheathed them.

The townsfolk remained cowering behind their makeshift embattlements, now more afraid of her than they had been of the marauders. *Better a death you understand than one you don't*, she mused.

She spotted the woman who had tried to negotiate with the marauders. She lay on the ground in unbearable pain. Kala pulled out a dagger and approached her to see if she wished to be released from the pain. A small child ran to intercept her. "Don't hurt her!" she cried.

She was too young to know that no greater harm could be done to the woman, and Kala only meant to ease her suffering. She sheathed her dagger.

The woman on the ground gestured weakly to the young girl, who ran to her side and flung her arms around her, not realizing the additional pain she caused.

"Mommy – you'll be okay, right?" the girl asked her desperately.

The woman shook her head gently.

The girl turned to Kala and pleaded, "Help her!"

"I can't hold back death, child, only hasten it," she replied.

The girl's eyes opened wide in horror, and she clutched her mother tighter to protect her from Kala.

"It's okay," the woman whispered to her daughter and used the last of her strength to stroke her hair. "Thank you…" she said to Kala. "For her," she continued, inclining her head toward her daughter. "And for them," she added, glancing at the still-terrified villagers.

"They're not safe here," Kala replied.

"I think they understand that now," she replied, her voice drifting off. Her hand stopped stroking the girl's hair, and Kala looked into her eyes to see that they no longer contained sight. The girl picked up her mother's hand and guided it back to her hair. It fell back to the earth. She picked it up and stroked her own hair with it, releasing a pitiful wail that Kala could not bear to hear. She turned her back on the girl.

Forest's ghost stared at her accusingly. "Do something for her," she demanded.

"There is nothing I can do," Kala replied.

Movement on the field caught Kala's eye, and she noted that one of the marauders was not yet dead, but judging by the way blood spurted through his fingers, he soon would be. Kala walked up to him, toying with the idea of making his last few moments a little more unpleasant.

He looked up at her as she approached and spat blood at her feet. "I hope you're proud of yourself," he said. "We're nothing – just an offshoot of an offshoot of the main host, cleaning up the countryside while they advance south. There's nothing you and your pack of dogs can do to stop them." He choked and spat more blood. Kala had no more time for him and strode away to collect her belongings.

She pulled out her journal as she walked and tried to find her position on the map, then traced a finger south. It intersected a city that she'd circled on her map. She moved her finger out of the way to see how she'd labeled it. She'd written below it with evident care – *Amber*.

14
Kala

Kala looked at her journal for the hundredth time. No matter how many times she wished it were otherwise, nothing changed the fact that Soren's forces were bearing down on Amber's town. She hadn't been there to protect her friends and family when her village was overrun, so she vowed that she'd at least be there for her dear friend, Amber. Kala examined her journal a final time to find the nearest beacon from which she could hail an airship. She looked up to confirm that she was heading in the right direction, due east, then returned her journal to her pack and resumed walking. The wolves trailed her, flitting in and out of view.

Two days later, she arrived at the forest's edge as it gave way to rolling plains. She paused at the tree line and whistled shrilly. A dark shape emerged from the depths of the woods. She placed her arms around the black wolf's neck and scratched behind its ears. "Goodbye, my friend," she said, and it dipped its head in recognition of their parting. Kala turned sadly and walked out of the woods into the bright light of day. The wolves howled plaintively behind her, tugging on her already-heavy heart.

The plains were vast, and the horizon an impossible distance away. Despite her steady pace, it never drew closer. The only clue that she was advancing at all was that the plains grew subtly rockier. Strange and forbidding formations began to jut from the ground. *This feels about right*, she mused. *Now, where can a girl find a dead spider?* She sheltered beneath a twisted rock formation as lightning lit the sky. *Great, rain*, she grumbled and rolled to face the stone. She was awakened by a barrage of droplets blown sideways by the howling wind into her shelter. She'd get no rest tonight. *Might as well keep going*, she decided and rose wearily. Lightning flashed steadily enough to provide light for her to see by. She pulled her collar tight against her neck and leaned into the driving rain.

She crested rise after rise, hunting for signs of the beacon and was beginning to despair when a flash of lightning illumined a formation of rocks that made her shudder. The structure resembled a dead spider on its back. *So inviting*, she thought sarcastically and trudged toward it. She arrived to find it greatly overgrown and hunted about but couldn't find any signal boulders. She sat down on a mound to think and was struck by inspiration, getting up to dig at the wet earth. It yielded easily beneath her hands, and she dug until her fingers grazed something hard beneath the soil. She cleared away the dirt to reveal the top of a roundish rock, long covered by the passage of time. She struggled to free it and had to dig around it before she was able to pry it out of the ground. She leaned her shoulder into it and, pushing hard against her heels, rolled it toward one of the pillars that jutted skyward around the dais. She struggled until it would move no farther and looked up to see that it rested against the pillar.

She rolled onto her back and lay on the soft ground, closing her eyes for a moment's rest despite the rain pelting her face. She awoke with a start sometime later to find that she'd slept through the rain stopping. An airship sat waiting on the dais. She felt inside her tunic for her amulet, relieved when her fingers grasped it. She rose and walked toward the ship, stretching her stiff legs. She opened the door and sat down in a heap on the floor inside. She dialed the amulet to the coordinates she'd written down for Amber's city, but nothing happened. *The signal stone*, she thought and forced herself to stand. She returned to the signal rock and pushed it away from the pillar, hearing it release the airship. She hopped back in, closed the door, then lay on the floor as the ship rose skyward.

Soren's forces crossed the river under the cover of darkness and regrouped on the opposite shore. Seline's siege equipment was moved across the river on barges in pieces and reassembled once across. As the sun rose, the drums of war began, and Soren's army advanced on the town. The blaring of horns went up from within the walls, and archers assembled atop them. Trax halted the advance just out of their range and waited for the siege towers to roll to the front lines, pushed by a large number of captives. The two towers flanked the battering ram, which was shielded from above by timber planking. Trax gave the signal, and the towers rolled forward with the ram between them.

The town's archers fired on the towers, but the occupants were well shielded within, and the men behind them were largely blocked from view. Occasionally an angled arrow would fell one of the men pushing the towers, but he'd be quickly replaced, and the advance didn't slow. Flaming arrows flew toward the towers, but Seline had soaked the wood with river water, so it did not catch fire, despite the barrage. The towers advanced right to the town walls, their arrival signaled by a loud clunk as they contacted stone. Hatches burst open on their tops, and armored warriors streamed toward the parapets atop the town walls. The town's archers kept up a withering fire, but their arrows were largely deflected by the warriors' shields. Any of Trax's warriors that fell was replaced by two more rushing forward. Very quickly, hand-to-hand combat ensued.

Under cover of the battle on the walls above, Seline's white powder was thrown on the massive wooden gates and ignited in a brilliant flash. Blinded men stumbled about and fell to the archers above, but the damage had been done. The fire burned the thick wood of the gate with unnatural intensity. Water was brought up from inside the gate to douse the fire, but it proved useless against the chemical.

The signal was given for the battering ram, which swung forward under the cover of its timber shield. A rhythmic knocking reverberated through the town as the ram commenced its assault on the weakened gates. The archers gave up, and rocks were hauled up and thrown down on the ram's shield. This slowed its hammering on the gates until Trax's men who'd battled their way onto the walls beat back the rock-throwers. The gate began to splinter. The bulk of Trax's forces amassed behind the towers and readied themselves for the gate to be breached.

No one paid any attention to the airship drifting overhead except Soren, who watched it while tightening his grip on the reins of his horse. The ship landed on a rise near the city just as the gates were sundered. Warriors poured into the city and were met with what resistance had been readied in anticipation of the breach. Kala stepped out of the ship and moved quickly to the tunnels that Baron had once used to move undetected between the airship landing pad and the city. She found the entrance and hurried inside, emerging within the city walls to chaos. People were screaming and running in all directions in terror. She fought her way through the crowds until a familiar voice stopped her dead in her tracks.

"Raven? What are you doing here?" it asked.

Kala wheeled to see Hawke staring at her from across the busy street, his girlfriend Emilie holding on tightly to his arm. Kala pushed her way through the tide of people to get to him. "I'm here for Amber," she told him.

"It's too late – the city's fallen," he replied.

"I don't care. I'm not leaving without her."

Hawke looked from Kala to Emilie and back and hesitated. "Gods damn it, Raven," he protested, but she stared at him resolutely. "Tell me you have a way out of here."

"I'll get us out," she confirmed, "but not without Amber."

He paused as he weighed their chances. "Okay, I'll help you," he decided, "but then we get the hell out of here."

"All right. The city can burn to the ground for all I care, just not with Amber in it," she declared and turned to face the direction from which everyone was running.

"Stay close behind me," Hawke told Emilie. "Don't lose sight of me. If you do, or if anything happens to me, go to where I told you — understood?"

"Yes," she nodded, terrified.

"Let's do this," Hawke declared and pulled short swords from his belt.

Kala drew hers from her back. "Just like old times," she said, and they surged forward.

The crowds thinned as they ran forward, the sour smell of smoke filling the air. Kala guided them toward the bakery where Amber worked and lived above, praying that she'd find her there. An invader leaped into her path, and she cut him down. More and more surged toward them down the streets, and Kala and Hawke battled their way through them, leaving a trail of bodies in their wake.

Rounding a corner, Kala spotted the bakery. Two invaders had kicked open its door and were looking around inside. Kala raced forward, taking the legs out from under a marauder who barred her path and opening up the neck of another. She flew through the shattered doorway, swords raised. The two men turned, but Kala drove through them like a wraith.

When Hawke entered the bakery, hustling Emilie out of the street, Kala was standing over the bodies of the two men. He looked around the empty store. "She's not here. We have to go."

Kala hesitated, then turned reluctantly to leave, but the faint sound of crying stopped her. She spun and raced to the back of the store, tearing through the kitchens, shouting for Amber. Kala ripped cupboard doors off their hinges, looking everywhere. She finally found Amber cowering behind the ovens. She placed a hand gently on her back. "Amber, it's me – please come out," she told her.

Amber looked up, frightened and unsure, but emerged, covered in dust and flour.

"Well, don't you look like a proper ghost?" Kala teased her.

Recognition dawned on Amber, and she burst into tears. "You came for me," she bawled.

"Of course, I came for you," Kala said, pulling her into an embrace. "But we've got to get out of here. Can you do that?"

Amber nodded, despite her uncertainty, and Kala led her out to the storefront. Hawke was finishing running through an intruder and looked over his shoulder. "Hi, Amber," he said, pulling his sword out of the man's chest.

Amber flinched at the carnage.

"We're done here," Kala told Hawke, and they stepped out onto the street, shepherding Amber and Emilie behind them.

"You lead," Hawke suggested to Kala. "I'll guard our rear."

Kala nodded and looked down the street.

Hawke grabbed Emilie and Amber by their arms. "You follow her and do *not* look back, understood?"

They nodded, and Kala took off like a shot, swords at the ready. She tore down the street, weaving past overturned carts and other obstacles. Any invader unlucky enough to bar her path was cut down mercilessly. Amber and Emilie were left to step over their bodies.

An invader jumped out of a doorway at Kala, and a sweep of her sword made him fall back into it, but another smashed through a window and grabbed for Emilie. She shrieked, and Kala spun in time to see one of Hawke's daggers sail into the man's chest. She turned back around and charged ahead, cutting down a side street past the temple, hoping for some support from the monks defending it. She raced up to its gates, but the grounds were eerily silent.

"Don't waste your time," Hawke shouted, catching up, blood dripping from a wound to his arm. "They're long gone. They left in the night before the invaders showed up. Cleaned the place out. There isn't even a single book left in the library."

"You're hurt," Emilie noticed, panic in her voice.

"It's nothing," he assured her, but Kala could tell it was anything but.

"Pardon me, I need to borrow this," she said and roughly tore a sleeve off Emilie's blouse. She grabbed Hawke's arm and used the fabric to bandage his wound.

"We don't have time for this," he protested, looking through the smoke back down the street from which they'd come.

"Shut up," Kala hushed him. "You're no use to us dead."

He relented for the briefest of moments, then spun and buried two daggers in the chests of onrushing men. He grabbed his arm and winced. "Gods damn, that hurt."

Finished bandaging Hawke, Kala raced off again, the girls in tow, with him covering their backs. She guided them toward the tunnels she'd used to sneak into the city. Kala passed people paralyzed with fear. "Run, you idiots," she yelled at them, but they stayed rooted to the spot, and she abandoned them to their fate.

She kicked in the door of the building that housed the entrance to the tunnels and hurried Emilie and Amber inside.

Hawke followed and closed the door behind them. "It's no use using the tunnels – they have the city surrounded. We'll never make it past them."

"By air, we will," Kala replied and led them onward. She pushed aside the crates and barrels that hid the tunnel entrance, not caring if it were discovered after they'd exited it. If someone else could use it to escape, so much the better. She lit a torch to help the girls see and guided them down the tunnel, squeezing through its twists and turns but not slowing down. Seeing faint light at its far end, she dropped the torch and pushed through the vines that covered the exit to emerge into the bright light of day. Smoke billowed into the sky over the city walls at their backs.

The airship still rested on the hill, but a party of invaders milled around it. Kala looked back at Hawke, noting that he was pale from blood loss. "Watch the girls," she ordered him and advanced toward the men. Hawke shook his head but realized that he lacked the strength to fight her on the matter and moved to stand between the invaders and Amber and Emilie.

Kala advanced toward the men. "Are we going to do this the easy way or the hard way?" she asked them.

They drew their weapons in response.

"Always the hard way," she sighed.

The first man brought his axe down on her, which she sidestepped and cut open the length of his arm. She pivoted around him, and the nearest men swung at her with their swords. She dropped to the ground, and their blows connected with the man whose arm she'd just sliced open. They pulled their swords from his body, but not before she'd stabbed one in the thigh, then rotated on her knees to run a sword through the other. They fell to the ground howling as she rose to her feet and advanced toward the remaining five men.

The next two advanced with spears, and she had to contort herself to avoid being impaled. She deepened her focus, dodged, and parried. One of the men finally overreached, and she swept his spear aside, pivoted close to him, and ran the two of them through with the same stroke. She turned to face the final three.

They just raised their hands and backed away slowly.

"Finally... the easy way," she muttered and waved Hawke forward with the girls. The men had fled by the time the four of them stepped into the airship.

Hawke looked out the door at the forces arrayed around the city. "We can't hide in here forever," he told her.

"Not planning to," she replied, pulling the amulet from around her neck and pressing the button in its center. The airship was released and began to rise. Kala pushed Hawke gently out of the way to close the door. She caught the eye of a man on horseback, watching her intently. She paused, ensnared by his gaze, then shook it off and slammed the door.

When the realization sunk in that they were going to survive, Emilie broke down and collapsed to the floor sobbing. Hawke slid down beside her and put his good arm around her, whispering reassurances as he held her tightly.

Amber looked down at her hands, trying and failing to will them to stop shaking. She looked up helplessly at Kala, tears filling her eyes. Kala stepped forward and enveloped her in a hug. "You're going to be okay – *we're* going to be okay," she assured her. Relief washed over both of them.

Kala lifted the amulet and stared at the setting that her fingers had traced subconsciously a hundred times whenever she found herself holding it at night. She let herself breathe and slumped to the floor with Amber. "We're going somewhere safe," she told her.

15

Forest

Forest and Cera walked back to their spot in the refugee camp, followed by Dhara and her sisters. Forest spotted Lily and called to her as they walked up, "Cera and I made some friends."

Lily looked up and glanced at the sisters. "Hi," she greeted them tentatively.

"Cera was getting hassled by some real lowlifes," Forest told her.

Lily looked Cera over, concerned.

"It's okay," Cera reassured her. "Dhara and her sisters rescued me."

"It was epic," Forest chimed in. "They beat up five guys!"

"Six," Dhara corrected.

"I got one," Caia announced, somewhat disappointed.

"I got two," Zara added.

"I got three," Dhara gloated, flexing her sore hand.

"You had a head start," Zara complained. "Totally unfair."

Lily watched in awed silence as the sisters squabbled.

Dhara turned to Lily. "We were getting pretty restless, cooped up in this Goddess-forsaken camp. It was refreshing."

Lily couldn't comprehend how beating people up, even lowlifes, was refreshing. "Thank you for looking out for Cera," she said sincerely and sat her down, fussing over her.

"I have an idea," Dhara announced.

Everyone swiveled to hear it.

"Girls' night out."

Lily began to shake her head, but Cera looked at her beseechingly. "It could be fun," she said, then added earnestly, "We could use some fun."

"Go ahead," Forest encouraged them, "Enjoy yourselves."

"Oh, no," Dhara declared. "Don't think you're not coming," she said to Forest. Lily objected, but Dhara waved it away. "The girl's got heart," she said, daring Lily to say otherwise, which of course, she couldn't.

"Nina will be fine on her own for one night," Caia confirmed.

"Who's Nina?" Lily asked.

"My daughter," she replied, which confused Lily, given that Caia looked younger than her.

"Great – it's settled," Dhara concluded. "We'll meet back here at dusk."

"Can Nara come?" Forest asked. "She'll be pissed if she finds out that we left her out."

"Friend?" Dhara asked.

"Cousin," Forest replied.

"Well, then, of course, she can come," she said, and with that, she and her sisters turned and strode off.

"Wow," said Lily. "Could this day get any stranger?"

Cera smiled and examined her. "We'll need to see which of the clothes you brought are best suited to going out."

"Nothing's appropriate," Lily frowned.

"Then we'll have to find you something inappropriate," Cera winked.

"Oh gods," Forest said, rolling her eyes. "I'm going to go tell Nara."

Cera waved her off jovially and rummaged through her and Lily's bags.

Forest walked over to where Nara was camped. Nara spied her coming and rushed over.

"Girls' night out," Forest informed her.

Nara almost exploded for joy. She turned to her father. "Can I?" she asked.

"I guess so," Jarom replied, "Just don't make Thorvyn jealous."

"You're brilliant, Dad," Nara declared. "Of course, I have to make him jealous. What would I do without you?"

"Oh, gods," Jarom muttered. "Be normal, maybe." He turned his attention back to getting a fire going, and Nara turned hers to selecting an outfit.

"Which one would be more risqué?" she asked Forest, showing her two options.

"That one," Forest replied, pointing.

"That one it is then. You're the best cousin ever."

Forest frowned over her own lack of options for an outfit. She'd never "gone out" before, ever.

"Oh, don't worry about you," Nara told her gleefully, noticing her consternation. "We'll work on you next."

Forest reluctantly placed herself under Nara's care, which made her cousin ecstatic. Nara had to borrow items from several of her kin but eventually assembled an outfit for Forest.

Nara put the finishing touches on their makeup, and they wandered back together to meet Lily and Cera a little before dusk.

Lily did a double-take when she saw her little sister. "You look so… mature," she said uncomfortably.

"I know!" Nara burst in. "Isn't she gorgeous?"

Lily smiled wanly. Cera had done her up, and she looked radiant. Cera looked like an angel descended to earth, but she always looked that way, so Forest and Lily didn't blink. Only Nara stared. "Wow," she mouthed.

Lily turned to Nara. "I apologize for my manners when we met. I was a bit stunned, to say the least. I still am, to be truthful."

Nara took it with good grace. "I understand," she said, then added with a wink, "Cousin." She rubbed her hands together. "When are the sisters getting here?" she asked Forest.

"Already here," Dhara announced, walking up.

Lily's mouth fell open. "That… is a lot of skin," she stammered.

Dhara looked herself over. She and her sisters wore short skirts and cloth strips that barely contained their breasts. She looked down and hiked them up, asking, "There'll be boys there, won't there?"

"Probably," Cera replied.

"So, there might be sex," she concluded.

Lily choked.

"What? Boys like skin." Dhara muttered, confused.

"I think you look great," Cera intervened. "We make quite the spectacle, we seven," she said, smiling.

"That we do," agreed Dhara. "Time's wasting. Let's go," she said and strode toward the town gates.

"We don't have any coin," Lily admitted.

"No problem – we do – from our 'business dealings' in the camp," Dhara said, jingling a purse tied to her waist. She didn't elaborate on what those business dealings were, and Lily didn't press her.

"You're twice over gods-sent," Cera thanked Dhara, taking Lily's arm and nestling her head on her shoulder as they walked.

Nara nudged Forest and whispered, "Cera is a puzzle. If I had a tenth of her beauty, I'd be queen. She seems so oblivious to it."

"She's not, but she finds it more of a burden than a boon."

"Only beautiful people say that," Nara replied dismissively. "I'm gorgeous... poor me."

Forest stopped her. "Let me tell you about Cera. I owe her my sister. When our mother walked out on us, Lily fell to pieces, and Cera helped put her back together. When our father became increasingly abusive, Cera shielded her. When we trekked through woods that terrified Lily, Cera cheered her, despite her own fears. Never a thought for herself – my sister her entire world. So, if living in the shadow of her radiance is the price we all have to pay for that, I'd pay it a thousand times over." Having said her peace, Forest turned to catch up with the girls.

"Sheesh," Nara called after her. "I just said, 'I'd be queen' – that's all." She hurried to keep up to Forest.

They caught up at the town gates, only for their party to be stopped by a pair of guards. "You can't come in here," one of them told the girls.

Dhara clenched her fists, but Caia restrained her. "I've got this," she whispered in her sister's ear and stepped forward, sticking one of her long legs forward to ensure the two men had ample time to examine it. She placed a hand above her breast and batted her eyelashes. "We're just looking for a drink," she said demurely. "You're welcome to join us when you finish keeping the bad people out," she added innocently.

The man turned to his colleague. "What could it hurt?" he asked. His companion had no objections. "Fine," he said, "but no wandering about. You stay put until we arrive."

"You're so sweet," Caia cooed and held onto his arm. "Where do you suggest we go?"

The man looked at his colleague. "It's got to be somewhere out of the way, or we'll catch hell," he said.

"I know just the place," his friend replied and gave the girls directions on how to get there.

"Thank you, boys," Caia said with a wink and a wave.

Dhara marveled as they strode off. "Who knew you could be so beguiling?" she said.

"Take notes," Caia replied, smiling. "You're about as subtle as a hammer."

Dhara smacked her but smiled and put an arm around her.

They arrived at the recommended place, and it was far seedier than Lily or Cera imagined it could be. The furniture looked tired, as did the patrons. Even the staff were too bored to clean the dirt off the floor.

"I love it," Dhara declared as she stepped inside. The rest of the girls shook their heads but followed her to a table for eight. Dhara slammed her purse on the table, calling, "Bartender – drinks!"

He rolled his eyes but poured seven glasses of beer. He motioned for a serving girl to bring them to the table, and she put a mug down in front of each of the girls.

Lily pulled the mug away from Forest. "She's only thirteen," she whispered to Dhara.

Dhara looked to Forest for an objection, but Forest knew her sister needed to feel some measure of control and raised her hands in surrender.

"Suit yourself," Dhara declared, grabbed Forest's drink, and drained it.

Lily pulled her own mug closer. "I need a drink. It's been quite a day."

"How's that?" Caia asked.

"I learned that my mother wasn't dead," she replied.

"I wish mine was," Caia replied, stone-faced.

Lily spit out her beer, then wiped her face with a napkin embarrassedly.

"She's an evil bitch," Zara agreed.

"She sent me off to be sacrificed," Caia added, taking a sip of her beer.

"She tried to have me murdered in my sleep," Dhara joined in.

"Wow," was all Lily could think to say as she blotted her blouse with her napkin. "My mother was wonderful," she said wistfully but guiltily after the girls' confession.

"I'll say," Nara piped in. "She used to make cookies for all the village children, and she'd sing while she brushed the horses."

Lily felt a phantom brush pass through her hair, and tears sprang to her eyes. Cera put a hand on hers.

"A toast…" Dhara chimed in to lighten the mood. "…To mothers – were the live ones dead and the dead ones alive." Drinks went up around the table. Dhara looked at Forest's empty hands. "For the Goddess's sake. At least get the girl a small glass."

"I like her," Nara confided, nudging Forest.

They ordered another round, and this time Forest was given a small glass of her own, which she cradled happily.

A handful of townsfolk walked into the bar and sneered at the party of girls. "Go home, foreigners," one of them muttered.

Dhara flexed. "Now the party is really getting started," she said and started to rise.

Lily put a hand on her shoulder to stop her, which annoyed Dhara.

Cera took this as her cue, got up, and walked over, sashaying her hips as she approached. The men watched dumbstruck as she placed her hands on the table, leaned forward, said a few words in quiet tones, then wandered back.

"Can I punch them now?" Dhara asked, a little tipsy.

"That would be impolite," Cera replied. "They're buying us drinks."

Zara hooted. "Now that's more like it!"

The girls lingered until closing time and wandered home well after dark. Calix had stayed up waiting for them, but they pushed past him giggling. He sighed and headed off to bed.

Lily and Cera waved goodnight to Dhara and her sisters. Nara begged Forest to spend the night with her, and she allowed herself to be dragged off toward Nara's campsite.

"I forgive you," Lily called after her.

"I know," Forest called back as Nara tugged her away.

16
Kala

Kala looked out the airship window as she thought about the distance to their destination. "We'll have to stop for food and water," she concluded and informed Hawke, Emilie and Amber. "I didn't bring enough provisions for four."

Hawke looked a little guilty.

"I didn't mean anything by that," Kala added hastily. "I'm beyond happy to have run into you." She turned to Emilie, "And I'm happy to see you again, although the circumstances never seem ideal."

Emilie smiled. "You can say that again."

Hawke touched the makeshift bandage across his arm and winced. "We place ourselves in your capable hands."

Kala replied, "I'm bringing us somewhere where I know the hunting well. We'll be okay."

The airship drifted for a long while, then began its slow descent, finally landing with a thud.

"It's not pretty out there," Kala warned them, "but it's home." She swung open the door to reveal the remains of her burnt-out village. The four of them disembarked, taking in the devastation. It smelled like wet charcoal.

"This was your home?" Amber asked in shock.

"A long time ago," Kala replied distantly. "Another lifetime."

"I'm so sorry," Amber said.

"Thank you," Kala replied genuinely and paused to collect her thoughts. "Shelter, water, fire, food," she rhymed off. "Let's see what we can do."

The airship was the safest place to shelter, but they all needed space to stretch and to feel unconfined for a time. No building in the village had been left unscathed, and even the least damaged of them was filled with charred timber and ash. Most of the wall that had ringed the village had been pushed in or fallen over, but they found a section that still stood to provide protection at their backs. The sky was clear, so they didn't rue the absence of a roof.

Kala helped prop up Hawke with his back to the wall and ordered him to rest. She gathered wood for a fire, and Amber and Emilie joined her once she brought the first load back, and they figured out what she was up to. Kala got a fire going, and the girls helped stock a good supply of wood beside it. Kala walked to the village well and confirmed from the smell that the water didn't seem to have been poisoned. She pulled up a bucketful and carried it over to the fire, boiling the water while taking a closer look at Hawke's wound. It was deep and ugly but showed no signs of infection. Hawke bit down hard against the pain as she washed it. He was sweating from the effort when Kala applied salve and a fresh bandage and declared him good.

She gave the girls instructions to keep the fire going and keep an eye out for any unwelcome visitors while she headed into the woods to hunt. Not much light remained, but the absence of villagers had emboldened the smaller animals that once lived in its shadow. Kala returned before nightfall with a brace of rabbits and some grouse. She cooked them and passed the meat around.

"It's delicious," Amber said. "Ever think of opening a restaurant?"

The absurdity of it struck Kala, and she began to laugh, and once she started, she couldn't stop. "Maybe once the world stops burning, we can open one together," she replied once she'd regained some composure.

"You laugh," Amber replied, "but I'd like that."

Kala patted her leg. "Me too. Let's hope our story turns out that way." She turned to face Hawke. "What did I miss after I left? How did your story turn out?"

"You're looking at it," he replied.

"I mean before, you idiot."

"I know… you're so easy to rile," he chuckled and shifted his weight. "I more or less dismantled Baron's criminal empire, such as it was. I gave the brothel to Marija with the understanding that the girls would keep an even share of their earnings. I thought I was doing right by them, but I guess that's all gone now."

"Some of them will have survived," Amber pointed out. "We're survivors," she trailed off, remembering her former profession.

"What happened to your baker beau?" Kala asked.

"Dead," Amber replied wistfully.

"I'm sorry," Kala replied, sorry she'd asked.

"It was an accident. He was kicked by a horse in the street outside the bakery. I ran it after he died. I think I got pretty good at it," she mused.

"I'll expect proof-by-pastry at your earliest convenience, madame," Kala mocked.

Amber laughed, the sound of tinkling glass, surprising herself. "I guess I haven't laughed in a while," she said and laughed at laughing.

Emilie had scrounged up some unlooted blankets that were mercifully dry and pest-free. She cradled Hawke in her arms, and Kala lay beside Amber for warmth. They fell asleep, almost feeling at peace.

Amber woke in the night to Kala calling her name. Kala was dreaming that she was still searching for her at the bakery but couldn't find her. She looked frantically, but no matter how thoroughly she searched, there was always another room. Kala thrashed in her sleep.

"Shh, I'm right here," Amber soothed, rolling over and pulling Kala closer. She held her until she stilled, stroking her hair and whispering calmingly in her ear. Kala never woke, and Amber gradually fell back asleep herself.

They stayed at the village another two days while Hawke recovered. Kala continued to provide them with game, and Emilie miraculously found some turnips and potatoes that hadn't been pulled from the ground or trampled into oblivion. It reminded Kala of Lily's garden, and she thanked Emilie with teary eyes.

"She's a keeper," Kala told Hawke as they dined that night on baked potatoes and rabbit.

"I know," he said, pulling Emilie close. She looked at him lovingly, and Kala wondered if Skye would still love her, broken as she was.

Kala excused herself and wandered into the remains of the village to be alone. She made her way to Lily's house and sat down on what had been the living room floor. Forest's ghost joined her.

"Haven't seen you in a while," Kala remarked.

"I haven't gone anywhere," Forest replied, staring at Kala with soulful eyes. "I was right, wasn't I?"

"About what?" Kala asked.

"That no amount of blood can heal a heart."

"I suppose so." Kala stirred her thoughts like embers. "You're one hell of a preachy ghost – you know that?"

"I know," she replied, smiled sadly, and faded from view, leaving Kala alone in the dark.

She got up stiffly and returned to the fireside.

"There you are," said Amber, worried.

"Here I am," Kala replied and realized that a part of herself had actually returned. *Here I am*, she thought, mulling over the truth of it.

They loaded the food they had left, some water, and Emilie's blankets, and relaunched the airship.

"Where are we going?" asked Hawke.

"I hope you like fish," Kala replied.

The airship touched down, and Kala took a deep breath behind the door before opening it slowly to find Skye standing before her, expectantly. She stepped out hesitantly, allowing herself to be wrapped in his embrace, and burst into tears. "They're gone," she cried. "Grandfather, Lily, Cera, Forest, Calix – all gone – ash."

"I'm sorry," he comforted her and held her tight. *What can you say in the face of that magnitude of loss?* he wondered and cursed his inability to find words that would heal her. She clung to him, sobbing, as he stroked her hair.

Hawke, Emilie, and Amber emerged awkwardly behind her.

"Sorry," Kala said, wiping away her tears. "Skye, this is Hawke, Emilie, and Amber," she introduced each in turn.

"This is your beau?" Amber asked.

Kala looked up into Skye's eyes uncertainly. "Still my beau?" she asked.

He pulled her in for a passionate kiss.

Amber jokingly cleared her throat. "Hello… standing right here."

Kala pulled back from Skye's kiss. "Yup – this is my beau," she replied, feeling relieved.

"He's cute," Amber assessed, making Skye blush.

"Edith has tea ready," he reported. "She'll be waiting for us. And Tiberius will be happy to see you too. Apparently, I don't rub him the way you do," he said and held up a hand covered in scratches as proof.

"He's a tyrant," Kala agreed and placed an arm tightly around Skye's waist.

They walked down the path to Edith's tiny house, where she was waiting for them on the porch with hot tea and warm cookies.

"Kala, so good to see you, child," she greeted her.

"Kala?" Hawke asked, raising an eyebrow at the name he'd never heard before.

"I'm Kala here," she admitted. "It's a different world."

He nodded his understanding.

They all took a seat, a cup of tea, and a cookie or two, or in Hawke's case, three or four.

"Sweet tooth?" Kala teased.

"There's a lot you don't know about me," he smiled.

"How did you come to know each other?" Skye asked.

"Hawke used to torture me," Kala replied, straight-faced.

Skye froze.

"Technically, I patched you up *after* the torture," Hawke corrected her.

"Well, you have to admit, you did hit me with sticks."

"You got me there," he admitted, "but only because you were slow."

"I'm not slow now. Maybe I should hit you with sticks," Kala joked.

Skye watched their easy banter in shock.

Kala caught his expression. "It's okay, Skye. It's water under the bridge," she said and tossed Hawke another cookie.

"See, you do care," he joked.

Emilie looked a little put-off by her boyfriend's familiarity with Kala. Noticing this, he pulled Emilie onto his lap and tickled her until she relaxed.

"I did *not* need to see that," Kala said, jokingly putting her cup of tea down.

"And where did you meet Kala?" Edith asked Amber.

"At the brothel," she replied. "The one she burned down, then the other one too, I guess. She's my guardian angel." She smiled broadly, and Kala's heart leaped.

Edith, to her credit, just nodded and sipped her tea. "So, what brings you to our quiet hamlet? Escaping the strife inland?"

Before she could answer, Tiberius jumped onto Kala's lap and padded around until he deemed himself comfortable enough to lie down. Kala rubbed his tummy.

Skye pointed warningly to his scratched hand, which only made Kala laugh when Tiberius began to purr.

"Sorry for the interruption," Kala continued, glancing down at the cat. "Yes, we've come fleeing the conflict. But sadly, we can't just hide out here. Someone has to put an end to it."

Forest's ghost nodded her assent from where she sat on the railing.

"But we just got here," Amber protested.

"Oh, you're staying," Kala said, patting her leg, "but I have to return."

"Please, don't go," Amber pleaded.

"I'll be back before you know it," Kala replied with confidence that she didn't feel. "We'll get you set up here in the meantime." She turned to Edith. "Does the town have a baker?"

"Of course,"

"Does the baker need help?"

"I imagine she'd welcome it."

"Well, that's settled, then. We just need somewhere for you to stay."

"She's dear to you, isn't she?" Edith asked gently.

"More than you could possibly know," Kala replied, a lump forming in her throat.

Edith turned to Amber. "I have a spare room here. You're welcome to keep me company if you'd like. Would that be okay?"

"That would be lovely," Amber replied.

Edith turned to Hawke and Emilie. "Tomorrow, I'll take you two lovebirds into town, and we'll get you squared away too."

Hawke nodded his thanks.

Skye turned to Kala. "I can be packed and ready to leave when you are."

"But your mother…" she began.

"Is doing well and expecting us for dinner," he finished for her, smiling broadly. With that, he stood up and held out his hand.

She took it tentatively, shooed the cat off her lap, and rose.

"Edith, thank you for your hospitality," Skye told her. "Can we leave these three in your care?" he asked.

"Anytime," she replied amicably.

"Thank you. My mother will be waiting. Good night," he said and led Kala off toward the village.

"I'm really in no condition," she protested, still feeling like a collection of jagged pieces that didn't fit together.

"My mother doesn't care."

She pulled him to a stop. "You don't understand… I'm not quite… whole," she finally got out.

"She'll welcome whatever parts of you there are."

"Some parts are pretty dark," Kala said apprehensively.

"So they are," he said, wrapping his arm around her reassuringly and guiding her the rest of the way in comfortable silence.

Kala looked to Forest's ghost for help, but she just shrugged. Kala felt the darkness flowing in her veins just below her skin and prayed to the Goddess to grant her a reprieve. The darkness moved deeper in response, and she had to content herself with that.

She looked up to see that they'd arrived at a tiny cottage on the edge of the village. She tensed in apprehension as Skye swung open the door. "We're home, mother," he announced.

Mouth-watering smells enveloped them as they stepped inside, and Skye's mother stepped out of the kitchen to greet them. Her health and color had returned, and she was beautiful. Kala could tell in an instant where Skye got his good looks.

"Perfect timing, dear," she said and gestured for them to sit at the places she'd set for them. Once they had, she brought out an array of terra-cotta bowls containing steaming dishes. "I made lamb," she told Kala. "Skye hates fish."

Skye leaned over and kissed his mother's cheek, then served them all dinner. They ate in silence while Skye's mother studied Kala with kind eyes.

Kala prayed she couldn't see the darkness swirling below the surface and shifted uncomfortably. "You're looking well," she said as a distraction.

"Thank you," Skye's mother replied. "I owe it to the two of you."

Kala blushed. "It was nothing."

"It was *everything* to me," she replied seriously and placed her hand over Kala's.

Kala looked around the cozy cottage. "I'm sorry I can't stay," she announced guiltily.

"I know, dear. Destiny calls. Hell, even I can hear it calling you," she laughed. "It's okay. It really is. Just bring my Skye back to me if you can."

Kala felt a lump in her throat, and all she could do was nod.

"Thank you," Skye's mother said, patting Kala's hand. "Now eat up; I have a cobbler in the oven."

After dinner, Skye cleaned up and made Kala a bed on the oversized sofa in the front room. He made one for himself on the floor in front of it. "It's small, but it's home," he apologized.

She gripped his hand. "Thank you for waiting for me," she said.

"To the end of time," he mumbled and drifted off to sleep.

They woke in the morning, breakfasted, and said goodbye to Skye's mother, who stood in the doorway, watching them depart.

"She's happier here than she's ever been," Skye confided.

"You know what?" Kala admitted guiltily. "I never asked her name."

"Evelyn," Skye replied.

"It suits her," Kala mused, and they trudged up the path to the airship.

Hawke, Emilie, and Amber were waiting for them.

Kala gave Amber a big hug, and both their eyes filled with tears.

Hawke gave Emilie an equally big hug.

Kala looked over at him, confused. "What are you doing?" she asked him.

"Coming with you," he replied.

"But… Emilie?" she stammered.

"If I can't make the world safer for her, what kind of boyfriend would I be?" he asked her back.

She didn't have an answer for that. "Fair enough," she replied finally and turned to Emilie. "I'll get him back to you in one piece," she promised.

"You'd better," she said, wiping away tears.

Kala, Skye, and Hawke boarded the airship. Hawke closed the door, and Kala dialed in their destination. The ship lifted off.

"Where are we headed?" Skye asked.

"Into the path of the storm," Kala answered, and the darkness in her stirred in anticipation.

17
Forest

Fayre sat down beside Jarom, who was running a whetstone over the edge of his axe. "You were with Soren, were you not?" she asked him.

"For a time, yes," he replied, pausing his sharpening.

"Is what Forest says about him wanting to destroy the world true?"

"Completely."

She mulled this over, then gestured toward the city, "They're doing nothing here to prepare for him."

"People can be stupid that way," he replied, shrugging.

"We can't just sit by," she said frustratedly.

"People are pretty persistent in their stupidity in my experience," he said but saw that his response didn't satisfy her. He sighed and put his axe down. "What were you thinking?" he asked.

"We should meet with the city officials and let them know the danger they're in. They clearly don't fully grasp it."

"By 'we,' you mean 'you and me'?" he asked.

"Yes."

He sighed again. "Okay. I'll join you – but if they had the sense to listen, they'd already be preparing a defense or an evacuation."

"We'll just need to be convincing," Fayre concluded, and Jarom joined her in making her way to the officiant's table.

"We need to see your town's council," Fayre informed the man.

"They're busy," he replied dismissively.

Jarom slammed his fist on the table, scattering the man's papers and getting his full attention. "We weren't asking," he said with cold menace.

The man swallowed hard. "Why didn't you say so?" he said nervously. "Follow me."

He led them past the gates, waving the guards aside, and through the town to the council hall. Arriving outside the doors to the council chambers, he told them, "I'll let them know you're here."

"No need," Jarom replied. "We'll let them know ourselves." He pushed past the officiant and swung open the doors to the council chambers as the man howled his objections.

Fayre walked past the apoplectic man. "What's done is done," she soothed and joined Jarom inside.

Jarom took in the room with a sweep of his gaze. Four women and three men sat around a semi-circular table, papers strewn in front of them. He cleared his throat. "We've come to inquire about the city's defenses or lack thereof."

"Who pray-tell is this gentleman?" the man seated at the center of the table inquired.

"They're from the camp," the officiant replied, rushing into the room. "I told them you were busy," he added lamely.

Jarom ignored them both. "I've spent time in the camp outside your gates, yes, and before that, I spent time in Soren's camp." He paused to let that sink in. "I can tell you that he'll raze this place to the ground and everyone in it."

"We appreciate your candor – thank you," the Councilor said cavalierly.

Jarom stood firm, staring him down.

The man sighed and asked Jarom the way one might a child, "Do you think we could beat this Soren fellow in battle?"

"Of course not," Jarom responded.

"Then, fighting isn't an option, so we'll negotiate our surrender instead."

"He doesn't want your surrender. Don't you see? He doesn't want to *conquer* you. He wants to *destroy* you and build a new world of his own design out of the ashes. There will be no negotiation – there will only be bloodshed."

"We will take what you say under advisement," the man concluded, shuffling his papers and glancing about at his colleagues.

Jarom clenched his fists, then spun toward the door. "I told you this was pointless," he said to Fayre, stomping past her.

She joined him in exiting but stopped in the doorway to address the council. "I know it's hard to fathom the situation you find yourselves in, I really do – I've been in your shoes. If there's anyone you care about in this city, I pray you don't let your short-sightedness doom them with you." She strode out before they could reply, the doors slamming closed behind her.

The officiant motioned to show them the way back to camp.

"I remember the way," Jarom snarled, and the man slunk away. "That went about as well as expected," he said to Fayre.

"We had to try," she replied. She placed a hand on his arm and looked at him earnestly. "Thank you. You're a good man."

They walked back to the camp in silence only to find it abuzz with rumors of a girl in the northlands they were calling Soren's Scourge.

"She faced down his entire army alone," a young man claimed.

"She travels with a pack of dire wolves," a woman added.

"I hear she's a shape-shifter," another joined in.

"She killed fifty men without breaking a sweat."

Fantastic as it sounded, it kindled hope in the camp that maybe all was not lost.

Forest heard the rumors and was skeptical. "We can't wait for some made-up girl from the north to save our skins," she told Lily. "We've got to save ourselves." She got up. "I'm tired of sitting around – I've got an idea," she said without elaborating. Lily looked at her worriedly, so Forest added, "It's not *all* that dangerous," which didn't reassure Lily in the slightest.

Forest walked out of the camp and stared at the town walls. She needed to scout around inside, but camp dwellers were not permitted beyond the walls unless escorted by the official in charge, and she couldn't very well ask the pompous ass, "Excuse me – could you show me around your town so I can advance my nefarious plans?" All the reasons she could come up with for having to enter the town would likely raise his suspicions, so she decided on a different approach. She sat down cross-legged and studied the comings and goings of the townsfolk through the gates, mostly farming families heading to and from the fields. She spied a family with a daughter about her age, who looked unhappy but resigned to be dragged out to the fields. *Perfect*, thought Forest.

Forest walked back to camp and changed into clothes suitable for a day in the fields. She put her hair into ponytails and did her best to look girlish.

Lily eyed her dubiously.

"Just thought I'd change my look," Forest told her, which only raised Lily's suspicions further.

Forest walked out to the fields and located the girl she'd seen. "Hi there," she said, approaching her.

"Hi," the girl responded, surprised.

"It's pretty boring in the camp," Forest told her, looking back at it over her shoulder. "Want some help?" she asked, then added, "It beats sitting around all day."

"That would be nice," the girl replied, and Forest spent the day chatting with her as they pulled weeds. That evening, she walked back to town with her and, as she thought would be the case, walked right past the guards without their taking any notice. The girl asked her parents if Forest could join them for dinner, and they accepted, happy that she had a new friend. The girl walked Forest back to the gate after dinner.

Forest repeated this routine for a few days to ensure that the guards became habituated to seeing her come and go. Soon enough, she was able to enter and exit the gate on her own without their batting an eye.

Once she'd accomplished that feat, she spent her days strolling around the town, marking the location of key buildings, the routine of the guards, and, most importantly, the placement of the armory.

Forest returned to camp and sought out Dhara and her sisters, finding them organizing some black-market trade in hard-to-get foods that refugees from the most northerly villages craved but couldn't procure.

"Can I ask you for some help?" Forest asked Dhara.

Dhara looked skeptical. "You can ask."

"I'm planning on raiding the armory – but I can't do it alone."

Dhara continued to look skeptical.

"There will most likely be violence," Forest suggested, then added, "and maybe a little nudity."

"Two of my favorite things!" Dhara exclaimed, halfway won over. "Tell me this plan of yours."

On the day of the raid, Forest dressed as she would if she were going to school and brushed out her hair. She walked through the gates, smiling pleasantly at the guards, who smiled back absentmindedly but didn't really notice her.

Zara met her inside the city, having snuck in through some means that she and her sisters had established to further their black-market dealings. Together they bided their time until dark.

Forest waited for the armory guards to change to the night shift and gave them a little extra time to settle in and become bored. She wandered up with as much innocence as she could muster. "Excuse me," she said shyly. "Can you help me?"

The gruffer-looking guard replied. "You can't be here. Go ask someone else."

Forest looked crestfallen and wiped away fake tears.

"Oh, for the gods' sake," the second man exclaimed and nudged his companion. He turned back to Forest. "What do you want?"

"Just a moment of your attention," she replied.

They puzzled briefly over her meaning until Zara slammed their heads together, having crept up behind them while Forest provided the distraction.

Forest walked up and surveyed the unconscious men. "Should we tie them up, in case they come to?" she asked Zara.

"I could slam their heads together again, only harder," Zara suggested and bent down toward the men.

"No, no – I think it's okay," Forest stopped her. "We'll take our chances." Forest walked up to the armory doors, only to find them padlocked. "Oh no," she said. "I should've assumed they'd be locked."

"I did," Zara replied and pulled a hairpin from her hair.

Forest looked at her, confused.

"My mother taught me how to pick locks. No daughter of hers was going to be barred entry anywhere." She leaned over the padlock and made short work of opening it. She repeated it on the door lock, and it creaked open equally quickly. Zara slid the hairpin back into her hair and smiled over her shoulder to Forest.

"Figure out what's most worth stealing," she told Zara. "I'll go grab a cart from the family of the girl I play with, so we can wheel it out of here." She stepped over the bodies of the guards and hurried down the street, returning a few moments later, pulling the empty cart. She noticed with alarm that the guards' bodies had changed position.

Zara poked her head out of the armory door and noticed her concern. "I thought I'd slam their heads together again anyway, just in case," she declared.

Forest sighed and pulled the cart up to the door where Zara had made a pile of bows, arrows, and shields, with a few daggers thrown in. Forest looked at the pile and raised an eyebrow about her choices.

"Up against trained fighters, we need missile weapons. If they get close enough to engage us in hand-to-hand combat, we've already lost."

Forest nodded her understanding, and together they loaded the cart. Forest laid a blanket over the top and secured it.

Zara moved toward the two prone guards.

"I think they're all right," Forest intervened, and Zara shrugged and joined her. *Getting back out of the town gates was always going to be the hardest part*, Forest thought as they pulled the cart toward them.

Just outside the gates, Dhara and Caia had lit a campfire and were passing around a bottle of wine. They'd persuaded Calix, Lily, and Cera to join them, and Lily had invited Oriel and Allie. Dhara was more than a little tipsy, and she put an arm around Calix.

"You're cute," she declared, slurring her words slightly.

Calix smiled wanly but uncertainly.

Caia got up and sauntered over to the guards at the gate. "Come join us!" she suggested.

"Look, miss – we've already told you we can't," one of them replied wearily.

"You're no fun," Caia protested, pouting.

Dhara leaned over and gave Calix a peck on the cheek, then winked at him and rose unsteadily to her feet while he stared up at her, confused. She started unbuttoning her top.

"Dhara," Calix began. "I really don't think that's appropriate."

Dhara ignored him and removed her top, revealing a tight-fitting brassiere. She waved her blouse over her head and shrieked while she ran over to her sister at the gate, sloshing the contents of the wine bottle in her other hand. She stopped beside her sister and looked down unhappily at the wine that had spilled over her hand.

Forest chose that moment to appear out of the shadows on the other side of the guards, looking the picture of innocence, but out incongruously late. "Excuse me," she called to the guards.

Dhara shrieked louder and chased Caia in a circle.

The guards just stared, bewildered at their antics.

"Excuse me!" Forest called out more insistently.

The guards turned around, confused and annoyed. "What?!" one of them asked Forest.

"That woman is following me," Forest said, pointing out Zara lurking in the shadows.

The guards peered into the darkness, trying to fathom Zara's intentions.

Dhara and Caia each struck a guard hard in the side of the neck, and their eyes rolled back as they lost consciousness and slumped to the ground. Caia pulled the unconscious men off to the side while Dhara wiped the wine off her hand and buttoned up her top. Dhara joined her sister and poured a little wine into both men's mouths, then left the bottle propped between them. "Sweet dreams," she said, looking down on them.

Zara pulled the cart up to the gate. "Some help?" she grunted. Caia and Dhara gave her a hand while Forest led them back toward the camp, past the fire.

"Hi, Lily," she said to her bewildered sister as she passed.

18
Kala

Kala pulled out her journal to show Skye and Hawke a map while their airship drifted southeast. She pointed out a circle and told Hawke, "Here's your town," then slid her finger southward. "And here is the next sizable town in Soren's path. We'll land there and warn people to either prepare a defense or flee." She closed the journal and put it away, then looked out the window, thinking that people would eventually run out of places to flee to. *They had to fight. But how and where?* Soren had amassed an army, while the settlements he preyed upon were spread out and isolated from each other. The impossibility of her task gnawed at her.

Skye could tell that she was unsettled and put an arm around her. "Whatever we face, we'll face it together," he told her.

It didn't comfort her, but she leaned into him anyway and readied herself for the coming storm.

The airship descended slowly toward the city. Skye watched out the window and let them know that it still stood. Kala said a silent prayer of thanks that they'd not arrived too late, then secured her swords to her back and checked the placement of her daggers around her body. Hawke did the same, and Skye felt a little useless off to the side. *Perhaps I should start arming myself*, he thought as the ship touched down with a gentle thud just outside the city walls.

Kala breathed in deeply and centered herself. She opened the door and stepped out into the bright daylight. A small crowd of hungry-looking people had arrived to check out the airship that had curiously landed itself. A silence fell over them when Kala stepped out.

"It's her," a murmur went up.

Kala disregarded the chatter. If they knew anything about who she'd become and what she'd done, she didn't want to be reminded of it. Hawke and Skye emerged from the airship and stood behind her. "Who's in charge?" she asked the crowd.

They parted instead of answering and pointed to an official sitting at a distant table, flanked by a pair of guards. *Great*, thought Kala. *The world burns, and administrators keep administering.* She marched toward the man, with Hawke and Skye at her sides. The crowd followed at their heels, gossiping wildly.

The man looked up from his papers. "Name?" he asked, bored.

Kala stared at him intensely. "Death," she replied.

His pen hovered over his book, and he looked up at her, confused.

Kala gripped the table and threw it aside, stepping menacingly closer.

He blanched, terrified, and his guards took a step forward, placing their hands on the hilts of their swords.

"I wouldn't do that if I were you," Hawke informed them. "Not if you value your life," he added conversationally.

Forest's ghost pushed through to the front of the crowd and confronted her. "Kala?" she asked uncertainly.

"I wasn't going to kill him," she replied, annoyed.

"Meadow?" Skye asked, turning around.

Kala glanced over at him. "Forest," she corrected, then stopped herself. "Wait, you can see her?" she asked him.

Skye narrowed his eyes in confusion. "Of course, I can see her," he replied, unsure of what Kala was getting at.

Kala turned back to Forest, who still looked unsure. "Forest, is that you?" she asked.

A dam burst in Forest, and she surged forward into Kala's confused arms, hugging her fiercely and burying her head against Kala's chest. Kala hugged her back, still too shocked to register the truth of Forest's being alive.

Lily made her way to the front of the crowd and stopped, staring at Kala in stunned disbelief. Their eyes met, and the crowd quieted at the newly risen tension. Images of Lily screaming as Kala hurled her dagger into her father's throat flashed in Kala's memory. Lily advanced purposefully toward Kala, and Forest detached herself. Lily stopped in front of Kala and stared at her accusingly.

"Lily…" Kala began but was interrupted by a hard slap across her face.

"You took him from me," Lily accused her, shaking with anger.

Kala could find no words to apologize for killing her father.

"He was all I had left of her, and you took him from me."

Kala realized that Lily was talking about her mother. She looked at Forest, who was standing beside them. "You have Forest," she countered cautiously.

"You stole her from me, too," Lily replied. "She becomes more like you every day. I miss my sister. I miss Meadow," she declared and burst into tears.

Cera strode up and put an arm around Lily, who surrendered to her embrace. "It's good to see you, Kala," Cera said, slowly turning Lily around to lead her off. "Give her time," she added over her shoulder and guided a sobbing Lily away.

Kala stood in stunned silence while Skye placed a comforting hand on her shoulder.

Calix raced up, wide-eyed, but stopped abruptly when he registered Skye's presence. He stood there briefly, then turned away. *Not you too,*

Kala thought, and her heart broke. *Calix, who'd always been there for me, who'd always helped me up when I'd been knocked down.*

A hand wormed its way into hers, and she looked down at Forest. "Don't mind my sister," Forest said. "She didn't mean it. She loves you."

"Thank you, Forest," Kala replied, but her heart was shattered into a million pieces, and she didn't know what to believe or feel.

Forest looked up at her and brightened. "Let me take you to someone who will be thrilled to see you... your grandfather."

Kala's breath caught, and she simply nodded.

"We'll be here when you need us," Skye told her, gesturing to himself and Hawke.

Kala let Forest lead her off, arriving to find her grandfather washing dishes in a bucket. He stopped and stared in disbelief, dropping the plate he was holding.

"Please tell me I'm not dreaming this," he said.

Kala rushed up and threw her arms around him. For a moment, she was a little girl – she wasn't the Angel of Death. She wasn't Soren's Scourge. She was just a girl, wrapped in the comforting arms of her grandfather. She sobbed.

"You're home," he said, hugging her tightly.

"I'm home," she replied.

At Kala's request, Forest went to collect Skye and Hawke and bring them back to Kala and her grandfather. Her grandfather made dinner with Skye's help, and they chatted about everything that had gone on since Skye and Kala had left the village. Kala offered very little about what she'd done since leaving and what had happened to her. As was his way, her grandfather took this in his stride and gave her the space to tell him what she wanted when she was ready.

Kala's grandfather laughed at Skye's stories of his battle against the plains bandits armed with nothing but sacks and fistfuls of sand and his fight against the pirates, armed with nothing but a bucket of potatoes. Kala laughed, too, not having heard either story before.

Kala's grandfather asked Hawke how he'd come to know his granddaughter. Kala sobered when Hawke told him that she'd rescued him from a life of servitude, and more importantly, saved his girlfriend from Soren's invasion. "I am forever in her debt," he concluded. "My life is hers," he added matter-of-factly, and Kala was stunned by his conviction and terrified by the responsibility.

"My granddaughter couldn't ask for more upstanding companions," Kala's grandfather concluded, and they settled in around the fire, too energized to sleep once darkness fell. Sleep did claim each of them eventually.

The next morning, Kala woke and told Skye that there was something she had to do.

"I'll rustle up some kai for you when you return," he replied, bleary-eyed.

"That's why I love you," she told him.

"The kai?"

"Mostly," she replied and hugged him.

She decided to give Lily more time to process, but she felt that Calix had no excuse, so she tracked him down, finding him at the edge of camp.

"What's your problem?" she asked.

"I have no problem," he replied defensively.

"Well, you sure don't seem happy to see me."

"I *am* happy."

"Bullshit. What's going on?"

He hesitated, then made up his mind to tell her. "Okay," he started. "I've always been there for you – I've always had your back. But then Skye breezes in, and you fall for him. He leaves you, and you were crushed. Do you know how hard that was for me to watch?"

Kala just looked at him, shocked, and opened her mouth to answer.

"Don't," he stopped her. "I'm not done. Then Skye waltzes back into your life, apparently, and you throw yourself at him like he didn't break your heart. Me, I've never hurt you, and I never would, but that doesn't seem to matter to you. I'm invisible."

Kala reached out and took his hands. "I see you," she said. "You're not invisible – and you matter the world to me. You've always had my back, and I love you for that. But I don't want to *not* be hurt. I want to love, and that means I'm going to get hurt."

"Why can't you love me the way I love you?" he asked her directly.

Kala sighed. "The girl you love is dead. She died a dozen times – throat ripped out by a wolf – torn apart, alone and cowering in a tree – dangling in a cage, spirit broken. Every time she died, the path forked, and I'm on the one that should not have been. Can you just join me in mourning that girl? I loved her too."

Kala sat down on the ground and pulled Calix down with her. She grabbed his hand, laced her fingers through it, and leaned her head on his shoulder. They watched the sunrise together.

"I *am* happy to see you," he whispered in her ear. "It just hurts."

"I know," she replied and held him tighter.

19

Priestess

The Priestess was greeted by a blast of frigid air as the airship door opened. She looked out over the frozen wastes appreciatively. *Things were unchanging here – they didn't require constant oversight and guidance – they just were.*

Howling winds lifted snow off the ground, carrying it skyward like a snowstorm in reverse. She pulled her collar tight around her neck and stepped out into the wind, orienting herself toward the lone structure on the otherwise featureless tundra and trudging toward it.

The entrance was set in the side of the building that was typically leeward to the wind, so it abated somewhat as she got closer and was shielded from the worst of it. The walls were constructed of centuries-old blocks of ice – shaped by people long forgotten but whose mission she carried on. The walls jutted skyward at sharp angles in stark contrast to the surrounding landscape, which had been smoothed by eons of unrelenting wind. Even the distant hills were uniformly rounded.

The entry was recessed at the end of a long, slightly inclined ramp. The Priestess trudged up it to a pair of giant wooden doors that had been transported here in some manner that was no longer conceivable. She unstuck the knocker and banged loudly on the door. Moments later, it swung open, and she stepped inside.

An old monk, swaddled in furs, greeted her nervously. "Priestess, please accept my apologies – we weren't expecting you."

"No need to apologize, brother – this visit was unplanned."

"Would you like to eat and rest first after your long trip?" he asked.

"No, thank you. I'd like to examine the Vaults, but afterward, dinner would be appreciated."

"As you wish, Priestess. I believe you know the way."

She nodded, and he scurried off. She released her grip on her collar but still shuddered from the cold. The building was kept unheated; even when it was occupied, the only heat came from the bodies of its inhabitants. She turned in the opposite direction that the old monk had taken and walked deeper into the building, descending several levels. She lit a torch as the dim light from the skylights did not extend to the depths of the building.

She followed the labyrinthian path from memory until she arrived at the door to the Vaults, then took a key from around her neck, one of very few in existence, and placed it in the keyhole. Turning it, a series of clicks and whirs told her that the door had been unsealed. She swung it open and stepped inside, then closed and relocked it. If something befell her inside, the Vaults would remain sealed.

She lit a torch on the wall, in case the one she held went out unexpectedly, then switched hers to the other hand and set off across the antechamber. The flickering light revealed a long corridor that stretched on into the darkness. She passed the first of several rooms that contained seed stock for some of the more useful strains of plants that grew across the planet. These rooms were located near the Vault's entrance as they were the most frequently accessed.

She next passed rooms containing biological weapons that the Church used to regulate the population. These rooms were accessed moderately frequently, but what she sought lay in the deepest recesses of the Vaults and was something she'd only learned about by poring through the Church's oldest texts. She continued to the farthest rooms, passing rooms that hadn't been inventoried in generations – she'd have to consult ledgers to recall what they contained.

She arrived at the farthest rooms and counted doorways until she found the one she sought. It hadn't been disturbed in ages, so she brushed the cobwebs away from the keyhole and inserted a second key, of which she was presently the sole owner, and opened the door. She stepped inside and found a room full of crates extending into the distance. She pried the lid off the nearest one and beheld items created by chemists in times so ancient that even those who remembered them were long dead. It was a fearsome technology that the Church hadn't had to employ in recorded history. Just touching it comforted her to know that it existed and was at her disposal.

Satisfied with what she'd come to verify, she retraced her steps out of the Vaults, walking back to the building's entrance, then on to the dining area. The old monk had been expecting her and didn't comment on the length of time she'd spent in the building's recesses. He simply motioned her toward a small room off the main dining room.

Closing the door behind her, he apologized. "It's easier to heat this small room." He bade her sit down at a table sized for two. A cold soup, small salad, and roll were set at her place. "Please start with this while I fetch your meal."

"Thank you, brother," she replied, and he scurried off through an open door.

He returned a moment later with a plate of roast lamb and vegetables and set it before her.

"You're not eating?" she asked.

"I've eaten earlier – thank you. I don't need much at my age," he added.

"Please sit regardless and tell me of your progress in readying this place."

He sat down, slightly uncomfortable, whether because of the infrequency of visitors in general or her in particular, she couldn't tell.

"We've tested the system that extracts heat from deep in the ground. It still works, and we can turn it on at a moment's notice."

"Why don't you have it on now?" she asked, not accusingly, just curious.

"We don't really need it, and it would be wasteful – but as I said, it's ready when needed." He went on. "The quarters are in good repair – we can accommodate several hundred souls. We walked through the dining hall, and the kitchens behind me can serve several hundred as well."

She ate her lamb and nodded at him to continue.

"We keep the subterranean farms running constantly. They do not yield very much, and they do so slowly, but we preserve what they produce and place it in cold storage. We also have a fair number of livestock housed here as well. All in all, we have sufficient provisions for a full complement for about two moons," he concluded.

"Impressive," she responded.

He looked relieved to have passed inspection, then blanched when he noticed that she'd been finished with her meal for a little while and was just reclining in her chair. He jumped to his feet and grabbed her dishes. "I have a bread pudding just coming out of the oven," he reported and ducked out of the room. He returned a moment later with the steaming dish, then cringed. "Perhaps it needs to cool off a bit."

"I'm sure it's fine," she said and smiled warmly. "I commend you on your hospitality in such a difficult place."

He smiled back, uncertainly. "May I take my leave, Priestess? I have to attend to the animals."

"By all means. Your company has been very informative."

"You have your pick of sleeping quarters. I will have your breakfast ready at dawn."

She thanked him and waved him away. She lifted a forkful of pudding to her lips and blew on it, then spent the evening mulling over what she'd found in the Vaults.

The Priestess was happy to have returned to the land of warmth. She passed through the gardens surrounding the temple, breathing the scents of flowers transported from around the globe, and wondered how long it would be before they were trampled beneath Soren's boots. She entered the building that led to the catacombs and descended in darkness, finally positioning herself on a stone bench across from the scintillating crystal and opening her mind to anything the Ancients wanted to tell her. Her breathing slowed, and the visions started.

She saw through the eyes of a raven flying high above an army camped on a vast plane. She looked in all directions, but the host stretched on as far as she could see. The vision dimmed, and she found herself looking out to sea. Two mighty waves reared and crashed into each other, obliterating each other. She tasted saltwater and found herself floating on the sea's calm surface. The tide changed direction, and she felt its tug shift from pushing her inland to pulling her out to sea.

She opened her eyes, exhausted. The entire day had passed, she hadn't moved, and her body ached. She sat pondering the meaning of her visions – the Ancients communicated obtusely, and it was mentally exhausting to interpret their messages. Her stomach protested having missed lunch, so she decided to unravel their meaning later. She'd need to consult with the other oracles and compare visions.

She was so familiar with the space that she navigated her way back in the dark, not bothering to light a torch, her thoughts consumed by the visions.

The Priestess lay in bed, watching the moon hanging low in the sky outside her window, the cool night air wafting over her bare shoulders.

"Brother Grey?" she asked.

"Yes, milady," he replied. He reserved this term of familiarity for within her chambers.

"Our weapon...," she began and rolled over to place her head on his chest and drum her nails on his stomach. "You built a rapport with her, did you not?"

"I trained her. She progressed," he replied.

"She's been developing well," the Priestess conceded, "and loss has been instrumental in that growth, but time is slipping away. We need to push her harder. Her consort – the boy named Skye – I want you to kill him."

"As you wish, milady," he replied.

20
Kala

With the weapons that she'd "liberated" from the armory, Forest enlisted Kala's help teaching the refugees archery. If they were to defend themselves against Soren's army, they had to learn quickly. Calix set up hay bale targets to be helpful and as a peace offering to Kala. She lined up her makeshift army, and she and Forest moved among them, correcting their form and urging them to keep practicing despite their fatigue. Kala picked up a young girl's bow to show her how to pull it back and release it without its string hitting her forearm. Kala wondered how many of these bows had been built by her and carried here by the winds.

The townsfolk watched from a distance. The guards had been too afraid to inform the council about Forest's successful raid on the armory, so there had been no repercussions.

Kala watched Hawke teaching people how to defend themselves with a dagger, including children as young as eight. Something about it broke her heart and infuriated her. These children should be playing, not learning to kill or be killed.

Skye walked over to Kala with a skin of cold water, some cheese, and apples, urging her to take a break from her instruction and join him as he laid a blanket on the ground.

"You spoil me," she told him.

"Only the best for Soren's Scourge," he joked.

Kala winced. "You heard that, too, did you?"

"I did – but to be honest, I prefer the 'unkillable killing machine.'"

"Stop it," she said. "It's not funny. These people are pinning their hopes on me, but I'm just a girl."

"You've never been 'just a girl,'" Skye corrected her. She frowned at him, so he relented. "I know it's a lot of pressure. But just do what you can. No one can ask any more of you than that."

"But they do," she sighed.

Skye decided to lighten the mood by changing topics. "You'll never guess who I saw here."

"I'll bite… who?" Kala replied, curious.

"Kira."

"Your one-time girlfriend, from the village?" she asked incredulously.

"Don't be too hard on her," he replied. "She's scarred from her home being torched and the difficult journey here. She's not tough like you."

Kala softened. "You're right. She didn't deserve any of that. No one did." She thought about it in silence, then smiled a mischievous smile. "Ashlyn, Kira, Eden… we should start a club for all your exes."

Skye raised an eyebrow, and Kala laughed at him. "Where did you see Kira?" she asked.

"Near the firewood pile with her grandfather."

"That weasel Sayer made it out? There is no justice," she said bitterly.

"I heard that Calix's dad found him in the woods. He said he was hiding the village archives to protect them, but that sounds fishy to me."

"That's Sayer, alright. He must be at a loss here with no paperwork to fill out."

"I'm sure he'll find some," Skye chuckled.

They continued their lunch in comfortable silence until Kala saw Cera marching Lily over. She rose to her feet hesitantly, and Skye withdrew to give them privacy.

Lily looked down at her feet. "I'm sorry about the other day," she began. "Cera has been reminding me constantly since then what an asshole my father was. She's right, of course, but I can't bring myself to hate him."

"That's messed up," Cera muttered.

"*I'm* messed up," Lily replied. "But I wouldn't even be here to be messed up if you hadn't rescued me from that airship."

The image of the airship landing and Lily being the one to be hauled out to face Baron flashed before Kala, and she found herself crying.

"I'm sorry," Lily repeated and stepped forward to embrace a limp Kala in a hug. "Don't cry," she soothed and started bawling herself. "I'm sorry I slapped you," she wailed. "Cera tells me that slapping the Angel of Death isn't so smart."

Kala laughed through her tears.

"I don't know what possessed me. It's been so stressful, and it all came barreling back to me when I saw you. I just snapped."

"It's okay," Kala replied. "I know how that feels. I sort of lost it when I thought you were dead. Forest's ghost haunted me."

Lily pulled back and said soberly, "About that… I was *so* out-of-line for what I said to you about her. You've been nothing but great with Forest, and you have a special connection – I guess I'm just jealous, to be honest." She paused. "I do miss Meadow, though. I miss scones. I miss the way it was before."

"I miss that too," Kala replied and pulled Lily back into a hug. She reached out her hand to Cera and pulled her in too. *Thank you*, she mouthed silently to her.

Cera wiped away a tear and nodded.

"Remind me to tell Forest that she was a terrible ghost," Kala said. "She was so pushy."

"Sounds about right," Lily laughed, and things began to feel right between them again.

Forest approached Kala just before dinner. "There's someone I'd like you to meet," she said.

Kala reached out tentatively and pinched her.

"Oww! What was that for?" Forest asked.

"Nothing. Just checking," Kala replied. "Who would you like me to meet?"

"My uncle," she replied.

"I didn't know you had an uncle."

"Neither did I, until recently."

"Show me the way, then."

Forest led Kala to where Jarom and his family were camped. Nara spotted Forest approaching and greeted her with a shriek and a hug. Forest looked at Kala, silently voicing her apologies for the spectacle, and pulled back the flap of Jarom's tent so they could enter. Kala, Forest, and Nara ducked inside.

Jarom noticed them and rose. "Niece," he called to Forest. "Come join us. Your sister and her girlfriend are here."

Kala looked past Jarom to see Lily and Cera sitting by the fireside. She walked over to join them and held out her hand to greet Jarom. "Pleased to meet you, sir," she said.

"Sir? Now that's a first." He chuckled and shook his head. "Call me Jarom." He gestured for her to sit beside him.

Kala sat down, and Forest and Nara took spots across from her.

"Forest tells me that you met my brother," Jarom said to Kala.

Kala glanced nervously at Lily.

"It's okay," Lily assured her. "I understand why you didn't tell me."

Kala relaxed and turned back to Jarom. "We shared very few words, but from what little I gleaned, he was a man of honor."

"That he was," Jarom agreed, and his eyes momentarily fogged.

"I met him when he was trying to get to Lily and Forest. He was beset by dire wolves, and while he fought them off admirably, he succumbed to his injuries. He made me swear to look out for Lily and Forest."

A look of understanding registered in Lily's eyes, and she reddened with guilt.

"We miss him, and Bria too," Jarom said.

"Mercy," Forest clarified for Kala. "My mother changed her name from Mercy to Bria when she met Jarom's people."

"Speaking of 'my people,'" Jarom added, pointing to Cera's auburn hair, then twirling his own bright red locks around a finger. "We must share a distant cousin."

"A *really* distant cousin," Nara piped in. "Seeing how you don't share Cera's good looks," she laughed.

"Hey – I'd watch what you say – you're *my* daughter," Jarom reminded her, chuckling.

"Thorvyn appreciates my inner beauty," Nara replied with mock indignation.

Forest turned to her. "I've been dying to ask you about him. You say that he's here."

"I rescued him, so to speak," Nara replied proudly.

"How's that?" Forest asked.

"Well, the horses in Thorvyn's care got out, and Soren got so angry that he had him tied to a post for days."

Forest's eyes widened with guilt at having been the one to free the horses, but Nara didn't notice and carried on, "When my father declared that we were leaving to follow you, I couldn't leave him like that, so I cut him down in the night and brought him with us. He's around here somewhere."

"I'm glad he's okay," Forest said sheepishly.

"More than okay," Nara replied. "The horses' escaping was the best thing that ever happened to me."

"Thank the gods for small mercies then," Forest replied.

Jarom waited for them to finish and turned back to Kala. "Thank you for fulfilling your promise to my brother. I'm in your debt."

"You really aren't," Kala replied.

"Good luck telling an old fool what he is or isn't," he chuckled. "Now, let's see about dinner."

Jarom, Nara, Forest, Kala, Dhara, and her sisters assembled the next day at dawn to go hunting. Ravi and Oriel wanted to join them, but Kala had them take over the refugees' archery training. Their students were improving, but they were still woefully far from being able to defend themselves. Kala put Hawke in charge of the training overall but admonished him, "No whacking anyone with sticks."

"Just you," he laughed and had things running smoothly in no time. A few of the town's off-duty guards came to help with the instruction. Hawke thanked them and put them to good use.

Kala rejoined the hunting party at the northern tree line. They discussed strategy quickly, then fanned out to advance in a line. Kala was in the middle, with Forest to her right, then Jarom and Nara. Dhara was on her left, then Caia and Zara.

Kala felt good to be in the forest again. She breathed in the smell of wet, cool earth and an array of mosses. She kept a keen eye out for sizable game and caught glimpses of Forest and Dhara through the trees from time to time.

The sounds of the forest altered slightly as she advanced, and it put her on sudden alert. She surveyed around her and crept forward. Motion caught her eye high up in a tree, and she notched an arrow. She shifted slowly around a trunk, pulling back the bowstring and sighting down the arrow. She found herself looking at a gangly youth, sitting on a crudely constructed seat, looking wholly unthreatening. She sighed and returned her arrow to her quiver. Stepping from around the tree, she called up, "What are you doing?"

The youth almost fell out of the tree, he was so startled. Once he regained his wits, he called down, "I almost crapped my pants – thanks for that!" Then he answered her question, "Emrys told me to watch the ridgeline for movement, and that's what I'm doing."

"You're wasting your time," Kala told him. "No self-respecting marauder would cross a ridge in plain view. They'll stick to low places or move under the cover of darkness."

"I'm just doing as I was told," he replied.

"Fair enough. Stay vigilant," she called and shook her head. *I'll have to explain a few things to Emrys, apparently*, Kala thought and returned to her slow advance. She was growing frustrated by the lack of game and took a break to lean against a tree and drink from her waterskin. *Maybe we need to venture farther away from town. Have they already emptied the woods of game nearer to it?* The distant sound of metal striking metal stopped her cold. She strained her ears, and the unmistakable sound occurred again to her left from the direction she'd last seen Dhara. Kala turned and whistled shrilly to her right, where she'd last seen Forest. Forest returned the whistle, and Kala picked up her bow in one hand and a handful of arrows in the other and tore through the trees toward Dhara.

She ran past where she judged Dhara should have been but found no trace of her. The sound of fighting grew louder ahead, and she raced toward it, scanning the trees for movement. She crested a rise to see Dhara and her sisters surrounded by a party of four lightly armored warriors. Caia lay on the ground, with an arrow in her side, wincing at the pain but holding her bow up, looking for a shot. Zara stood over top of her, spear outstretched, holding off two burly men that slashed at her with swords. Dhara was off to their right, nearer to Kala, fighting fiercely with the other pair, two more dead on the ground behind her. She fought low as arrows sailed over her from archers positioned farther back.

Kala dropped to her knees and jammed her fistful of arrows into the earth. She notched one and lined up a shot. Dhara and her assailants moved so rapidly that Kala couldn't get a clear shot. *Damn it, Kala*, she told herself. *Breathe.* She centered herself and stared farther down the path of the melee. She aimed her arrow squarely at Dhara's back, closed her eyes, and let fly.

Dhara wheeled to parry a thrust from the man on her right and pulled herself back to narrowly avoid a sweep by the one on her left just as Kala's arrow sailed over her shoulder and embedded itself in his chest. He clutched it and collapsed, and Dhara seized her chance to throw herself at the remaining man, dodging two blows before burying her knife in the underside of his chin. He crumpled, and she yanked her blade free and spun toward her sisters. Arrows flew around her, but she disregarded them and rushed to their aid.

Kala couldn't see the archers through the trees and dropped her bow in frustration. She shrugged off her quiver and pack, pulled out a pair of daggers, and raced around in a wide arc to where she assumed they were hiding. She could hear the sounds of Zara and Dhara fighting staunchly against the elite fighters of Soren's vanguard. Her boots bit harder into the soft earth as she ran.

She tore between trees and spotted a crouching archer before he heard her approach. She slashed through both him and his bow without slowing. She vaulted a fallen log and came upon a party of three more men hidden in low bushes. She let sail her daggers, catching two of the men off guard. The third whirled and fired an arrow at her. She brushed it aside and hurled herself at him, grabbing both ends of his bow as she leaped over him, twisting it around his neck as she went. She turned and garroted the man with his own bowstring.

Instinct told her to duck, and an arrow buried itself in the tree where her head had just been. She spun the struggling man in front of her as a shield, and two more arrows embedded themselves in his chest. She dropped him and pulled a second pair of daggers from behind her back. The two men facing her dropped their bows and pulled out wicked-looking swords. *Have it your way*, she thought and closed the distance. The men were skilled swordsmen, but their skill only made their path shine more clearly to her, and she followed it until her daggers dripped with their blood.

As the men around her fell, she looked up to see an archer standing perpendicular to her, drawing back an arrow. He smiled, and she recognized the look of a clear shot. She screamed and hurled her daggers as hard as she could but not before he'd loosed his arrow. She turned to follow its path and watched it in slow motion as it flew toward Zara and buried itself in her left breast. She staggered, stunned, and dropped to her knees beside Caia.

Caia screamed, and Dhara turned to see her older sister slump to the ground. She let loose a sound of inhuman fury and tore apart the man she was fighting. She turned again to find Caia cradling Zara, who was struggling to stay conscious.

"I'm sorry," Zara whispered to Caia and closed her eyes.

"Don't go," Caia pleaded, shaking her sister's limp body.

Dhara knelt and held her sister. A piteous moan escaped her lips as Kala rushed over.

"I'm sorry," Kala repeated, over and over. "I tried. I really did."

Forest, Jarom, and Nara arrived a moment later. Jarom surveyed the scene and snarled. "Nara, Forest, Kala – help Caia back to camp and bring Zara back with you."

Nara hesitated, and Jarom yelled at her, "Do not make me ask again, girl! Dhara and I have some hunting to do."

Nara hurried to Forest's side and helped her tend to Caia's wound. Kala picked up one of the fallen men's swords and began hacking down saplings to make a travois for Zara's body.

Dhara rose with murder in her eyes.

"We won't leave these woods until we've cleared it of vermin," Jarom assured her.

Dhara picked up Zara's spear and stalked past him. He turned and followed her.

It was late that night when Forest and Nara emerged from the tree line, holding Caia between them, barely conscious from blood loss. Kala followed closely behind, pulling the travois that carried Zara's body.

Calix had been watching for them and ran up, shooing Forest aside and taking her place under Caia's arm. "Jarom and Dhara?" he asked.

"Hunting survivors," Nara spat.

"Forest, run ahead and get help for Caia," Kala ordered but added, "Please."

Forest ran as fast as she could, weary as she was. The rest followed slowly as they made their way toward the camp.

"What happened?" Calix asked.

"The sisters came upon one of Soren's scouting parties. Caia was wounded, and Zara didn't survive," Kala replied.

"So, it's begun," Calix said.

"It has," Kala replied grimly.

Dhara and Jarom emerged from the forest near dawn. Dhara was bloody but strode purposefully. Jarom walked at her side.

Nara ran to them and hugged her father.

"Caia?" Dhara asked numbly.

"Alive and resting," Nara replied.

"Take me to her," Dhara commanded.

"Of course," Nara replied, and Jarom released her to lead Dhara off. He went to speak with Fayre and Emrys.

Nara guided Dhara to Caia's bedside. She was unconscious, and her daughter, Nina, slept soundly beside her. Her wound had been tended to, and she was breathing deeply and evenly.

Dhara collapsed onto the ground at her sister's side, picking up her hand and cradling it. "Leave us," she told Nara, and Nara backed out of the tent, glancing back to see Dhara bury her head on Caia's chest and sob. She felt guilty for the intrusion and hurried abashedly back to her father's side.

21
Kala

Zara's body had been laid on a bed of dry timber. Dhara placed her spear on top of her, bent over, and kissed her eyelids. Caia watched from a nearby chair with Nina on her lap. Dhara straightened, reached for the torch that Forest held out to her, and lit the pyre in several places. The flames rose quickly to surround Zara, and smoke billowed upward into the clear sky. Dhara walked over to Caia's side and placed a hand on her shoulder. Caia reached up and held it. Together, they witnessed their sister cross over to the home of their ancestors.

Nina looked up at her mother, tears in her eyes. "Why?" she demanded to know.

How could she tell her daughter that there was no good reason? That the world was a terrible place? Instead, Caia simply told her, "Your aunt died standing over me – protecting me. In this family, there is no greater honor."

Calix looked up at the flames from the defensive preparations he was readying. He led a small party hammering stakes into the ground, then sharpening them. Another group was constructing low walls to shelter archers, and several farmers were digging a wide trench to hamper the advance of any war machines. Carpenters were reinforcing the city gates. Everywhere there was work to be done, and Calix hadn't slept since the skirmish with Soren's scouting party. His muscles ached, but he felt he couldn't afford to give them a rest.

Jarom, Fayre and Emrys met in Jarom's tent to discuss strategy. Fayre briefed them on the progress she'd made in preparing for the evacuation of the children and the elderly. Emrys tried again to advocate that they all flee, but Jarom argued him down, saying that the longer they ran, the stronger Soren would become and that this would continue until there was nowhere left to run. They had to start fighting back. Emrys wasn't happy with the conclusion, but he had to accept Jarom's logic. Waiting would never improve the situation.

Elsewhere, Kala sat surrounded by a pile of branches that she was transforming into arrows. She'd tried to help Hawke train the refugees earlier but was reminded that she was a terrible team player, especially when she was in a foul mood, which she definitely was as she brooded over Zara's death. *Had I been a hair quicker, I could have saved her.* Her self-recriminations gnawed at her and dragged her into a tight spiral of self-loathing. She and Skye had had a brief fight about it. He'd tried to make her feel better by telling her that she'd tried her best, but it had the opposite effect.

"Did I?" she'd replied bitterly.

"Of course you did. I know you, and you know no other way."

"Well, my best just isn't good enough then," she concluded grimly.

"Your best is more than the world deserves," he'd said, but on that point, he was wrong. *Lily and Cera were part of the world, and they deserved a quiet life together. Forest deserved to be a kid. Dhara deserved to terrorize the world or whatever she did, with both her sisters at her side. It wasn't just about Zara – it was about all of them.* Kala felt the weight of their futures on her shoulders. *And what about her – what kind of life did she deserve? Would she and Skye ever have a normal life? Was she allowed to be happy, or was that what she bartered away with every death wrought by her hands?*

Skye could tell that she'd descended into a profoundly dark place and gently raised his hands in surrender. "I'm going to go help Calix," he told her and withdrew. Kala didn't notice his departure, she was so wrapped in her thoughts.

She stood up abruptly, scattering the branches. *This is stupid*, she thought. *We need allies – we can't do this alone.* She marched toward the town gates. The guards had long since given up on restricting access to people from the camp, or if their orders were to limit their access, they disregarded them entirely. Either way, they let Kala pass.

She sought out the temple that had to be located somewhere within the city walls, stopping a delivery boy to ask for directions, which he provided before hurrying off.

Kala walked in the direction he'd indicated and passed through an open-air market. She was amazed at the number of people just going about their day as though nothing were amiss. They drank wine, sipped kai, and sat chatting. It was surreal. *Maybe denying the reality of their plight was the only way they could cope*, Kala thought. She followed the boy's instructions until she found herself at the closed gates of the temple. They would typically be open during the day, albeit guarded, so she looked around for the guards. Looking up at the walls, she spotted a man on the parapet and called up to him.

"Go away," he called back down. "We've claimed the temple for ourselves."

"What do you mean, 'you've claimed it?'" Kala asked. "Where are the monks?"

"They left… now piss off," he concluded and returned to whatever preparation he was up to.

Kala briefly considered skewering him, but the thought passed. *He likely won't live out the moon*, she concluded and stalked back to camp. *Where did you go?* she asked herself about the monks' disappearance.

Back at camp, she started packing. There was someone she needed to go see. She changed into clothing more suitable for a journey and went to tell Skye her plans. She found him helping dig the trench. Of course he had his shirt off, and Kala had to admit that his lean body looked good, glistening with sweat. She watched him appreciatively until he spotted her.

Taking in her outfit, he climbed out of the trench. "You look like you're going somewhere," he observed.

"We need allies," she replied. "I'm going to ask for some."

"I assume they're nowhere near here."

"Right. I need to hitch a ride."

"And you know where to find an airship."

"Yup – northwest of here – in the hills."

"That direction isn't safe," he reminded her.

"No direction is anymore. I'll keep a low profile."

"I guess you wouldn't listen to me if I told you that I'm still not comfortable with it," he said.

She just looked at him apologetically.

"All right. I know you know how to look after yourself, but gods-damn it, I worry."

"And that's why I love you."

"I thought it was because of my cooking."

"Okay, mostly the cooking, but a teensy bit because of the worry."

He sighed. "I guess you want me to let everyone know what you're up to so they don't fret."

"Could you?"

"Of course – just give me a kiss before you leave," he said and extended his arms.

"No way – you're filthy," she said but leaned in and gave him a peck on the lips.

She strode toward the tree line, consulting her journal one more time as she headed across the fields, careful to weave around the defenses being constructed. She got her bearings from distant hills and proceeded into the woods.

She was alert to the possibility of running into more of Soren's scouts, but her attention only revealed that she wasn't the first to follow the path she took. The monks had likely also headed in this direction when they'd abandoned the city. They'd taken pains to minimize the evidence of their passing, but Kala could see the signs, nevertheless. It made reaching her destination that much easier.

The way became more uneven as she progressed until the forest yielded to rocky hills. She had to scramble up and down their steep sides to continue in the right direction. There were numerous caves, and some may have held shortcuts if she had time to explore them, but she didn't, so she continued clambering up the steep rock faces. The landscape was wholly uninviting.

She squeezed through a chimney in the rock and emerged to face a formation that was too regularly shaped to have occurred naturally but too large to have been built. Its sheer unnaturalness marked it as her destination. She slid down a rockface, spraying loose stones until she found herself at the base of the towering structure. She decided to scale it, despite the late hour, as something about the place warned her against spending the night exposed. She passed caves, but they radiated danger rather than shelter, so she climbed past them quickly. A rock pulled loose in her hand, and she swung to her other handhold to avoid falling after it. It made a terrible crashing sound as it tumbled down. *That'll wake the dead*, Kala thought grimly.

The last rays of the sun faded as she hauled herself up to the top of the structure. Her hands were scraped raw from the sharp rock, and she was exhausted. In the descending dusk, she could make out the familiar shape of a circle of pillared rocks pointing skyward. Its familiarity made it no less disturbing, and she hurried to find a signal stone to hail an airship.

She found one that looked recently moved and rolled it close to one of the spires on the east side of the circle and waited.

She couldn't shake the feeling of having been followed up the rock by something sinister. She pulled her knees into a ball with her back to one of the stone spires and pulled out a pair of daggers. She felt she couldn't risk a fire and hadn't in any case seen fuel for one since she'd entered the rocky hills. She could do nothing other than wait for the airship to arrive or whatever was stalking her in the dark, whichever appeared first.

She swore that she saw the faint reflection of the last remaining light shining in the eyes of some gigantic beast, and it chilled her to the bone. She pulled out her pack and decided to chance lighting a torch. She lit it and waved it in front of her, wreaking havoc with her night vision. She couldn't see what was watching her from the inky blackness and sensed more than saw movement in the shadows created by the lit torch. She prayed that the fire would dissuade the creature from attacking, but over time, the torch consumed its fuel and began to gutter. She had one more in her pack and began to reach for it when she heard the thump of an airship making landfall.

She stumbled toward the ship in the failing light of her torch and felt oily tendrils touch her skin. She spun and waved the dying torch, which made it glow brighter but revealed nothing in the dark. She waved it back and forth as she backed toward the airship. Bumping into it, she knew that she'd have to expose her back to whatever was prowling in order to find the door. She spun and frantically searched for the wheel that opened the door. She found it, spun it madly, and dove through the opening that appeared. As she turned to close it, something wrenched the remains of her torch from her grasp, and she barely had time to slam the door before it grabbed her too.

She collapsed onto the floor of the ship, shaking uncontrollably with fear. Something began to hammer against the door, and the airship shook with each blow. She realized in a panic that she hadn't rolled the stone away from the pillar to release the ship. She'd have to go back outside and face the monster, which she couldn't bring herself to do. She spun the dial on the amulet around her neck and prayed it would somehow override the signaling stone. She depressed the center of the amulet, and nothing happened. She pushed it again and again and again, and still, nothing happened. The hammering grew louder and more insistent. She pressed and held the amulet, praying to any goddess that would listen.

The airship released itself from its mooring and rose. An unnatural wail split the night as the ship rose up and away.

When the light of day peeked through the ship's windows and Kala could finally see, she adjusted the settings on the amulet to the city where she'd met the High Priestess. *If she wanted Soren stopped, then she'd better help*, Kala thought. *This is too much for me to accomplish on my own.* The airship drifted toward its destination while Kala rested and rehearsed her plea.

The ship landed, and she stepped out, unsure whether she'd find the temple occupied or deserted. But she was greeted by the sight of monks, priestesses, and workers going about their business, and she breathed a sigh of relief. No one paid her any attention, and she relaxed further. She strode off in search of the Priestess.

She didn't know too many places to check, so she started with the catacombs. A different woman was seated before the scintillating crystal. Kala felt a faint tug on her mind that made her shudder and hurry out. She checked the building with the auditorium and then the dining hall but came up empty-handed. She had no idea where the Priestess's quarters were and finally accepted that she needed to ask someone. *How do I ask where 'the' Priestess is when everyone is a priestess?* she wondered but saw no other option. She stopped a young monk and asked, "Do you know where I can find the Priestess?"

"Try the gardens," he replied and carried on when it was clear that Kala had no further questions for him.

She entered the flower gardens, assuming that the young monk hadn't meant the vegetable gardens, and wandered the paths until she spotted the Priestess sitting quietly on a bench before a calm pool. Kala sat beside her but didn't want to interrupt her thoughts, so she waited to be acknowledged.

The Priestess continued to stare out over the water's surface but greeted Kala amiably. "It's nice to see you," she said.

Kala felt awkward replying in kind, so she just decided to jump right in. "I need your help," she said.

"With what, dear girl?"

"Stopping Soren."

"You have that well in hand," the Priestess replied serenely.

"I do not. He has an army. I only have my friends, and they're not warriors."

"Do not sell short the power of friendship."

"They're going to get killed," Kala objected.

"Everybody dies in some way or another."

"How can you be so uncaring?"

"I'm not. I care deeply about the world. I care enough about it to sacrifice what needs be sacrificed for it."

"I would rather not sacrifice my friends. They matter too much to me."

"And that is precisely why they'll sacrifice themselves for you."

That only made Kala feel worse about it. "Can't you spare some monks to help us? They train their whole lives to fight. Wouldn't they want the opportunity to put that training to good use?"

"We watch. We don't interfere."

"Then what's the point of the training?" Kala asked bitterly.

"They train because sometimes the world cannot restore balance on its own, and we have to do it. We don't want to do that – it is absolutely the last option."

Kala sat there frustrated, struggling to come up with anything she could say that might sway the Priestess.

The Priestess tried to reassure her. "Has it ever struck you as odd that villages, towns, and cities have walls when they have almost no interaction with the outside world?"

"I assumed it was to keep out predators."

"That may have been true for your tiny village, set deep in the forest, but do you really think it necessary for large cities to have such towering walls just to keep wolves out?"

"I guess not."

"Cities have walls because they get invaded. No one alive remembers the last time or has any record of it, but we do, and it's a cycle that has repeated for millennia. The world will survive this. It always has."

This did not reassure Kala in the slightest. "I don't want the world to survive. I want my friends to survive."

"We can't choose our fate any more than we can choose the era we're born into. At least you were born to matter – to make a difference. Content yourself with that. The Ancients have faith in you. You should too."

What some glowing rock thought mattered nothing to Kala. "Can I at least ask Brother Grey for advice?" she asked.

"He's not here, I'm afraid," the Priestess replied. "I sent him on an errand, and I believe he attends to it now."

Kala just sat deflated, feeling like she'd utterly failed her friends.

22

Forest

Jarom called his kin together. Nara fetched Forest but told her that it would be best not to bring Lily. Once they'd all gathered, Jarom began.

"If we fight Soren on the fields surrounding the city, we'll be overwhelmed. If we fight him from the city walls or in its streets, we'll have the advantage, but only briefly. We have to take the fight to him, on our terms, on terrain we're familiar with. We have to fight him in the forest."

His kin nodded their assent.

"By eliminating his scouting party, we've only alerted Soren to our location and probably hastened his descent upon us. We'll slow his advance by attacking his supply lines. That's where he'll be most vulnerable."

"Wouldn't his supply lines trail his forces?" Ravi asked.

"That's what I saw," Forest agreed.

"We'll sneak past his main force and attack from behind," Jarom pointed out. "It won't be easy, of course, but the forest is *our* home, not that of the barbarians from the northern plains. We leave immediately, so gather your gear for a long excursion and dress for stealth," he said and dismissed them.

As Nara and Forest turned to go, he called them over. "Stick close to me, girls."

"How come Ravi doesn't have to?" Nara protested.

"Because I love him less," Jarom replied.

"Father!" Nara exclaimed.

"Just humor an old man and do as I ask," he requested.

Forest replied for her. "Of course, Uncle," she said and spun Nara, who was still pouting, toward the flap of the tent. "I know what it feels like to want to protect those you love," Forest told her. "Let him have that."

Nara sighed. "Meet you back here?" she asked.

"I won't be long," Forest replied and headed back to collect her things. She let Lily know that she'd be out in the woods with Jarom for a while but gave her no specifics that would only serve to worry her. She returned to Nara, and they joined Jarom's party heading out.

Forest asked Jarom as they walked, "Shouldn't we invite Dhara to join us? She's as capable a fighter as anyone, more so in fact."

"Her sister's loss is still too raw. I fear it may cloud her judgment. We need to be stealthy, not vengeful. Best to let her tend to her sister Caia and grieve Zara."

Forest mulled this over as they moved through the trees. After walking for a long while, they took a break and sat drinking from their waterskins. Someone passed around small pots of paints that served as camouflage. When they were given to her, Forest stared at them, trying to figure out how best to apply them, but Nara snatched them from her.

"Let me do it," she said and began applying paint to Forest's face. When she'd finished dabbing and rubbing, she leaned back and took in her work. "Perfect," she declared. "You have a rugged beauty about you."

"Right — because you've made me up to look like a rock," Forest replied.

"Well — more like a bush," Nara admitted. "But an attractive bush," she reassured her.

Forest rolled her eyes, and Nara passed the pots to the next person. They waited until everyone had applied the paint before they moved out. They proceeded cautiously with Jarom in the lead, and he grew more cautious the farther north they ventured. He led them over challenging terrain so they wouldn't find themselves in the path of any advancing forces. It made the going slower but safer.

They'd walked for days when Jarom signaled a sudden halt. He motioned for everyone to drop to the ground and pointed ahead and left. Forest and Nara lay down and crawled to some scrub for cover. Having stayed close to Jarom, they could see what had caused him to signal the halt – an enemy scout was moving through the trees in the distance toward them. Forest feared that he'd stumble upon them and alert others. She was less concerned about any ensuing fight and more worried that this chance encounter would undo their mission. She willed herself flatter to the ground. Nara reached for her hand and held it tight.

She watched as Jarom hid behind a thick tree trunk and pulled a throwing axe from his belt. He looked back over the party and glared at anyone he could make out until they hid better. He locked eyes with Forest and looked to her to prompt him. She used her eyes to tell him to hold his position and tracked the advancing scout. The man moved closer and closer, then angled off slightly to the left toward lower ground. Forest looked right insistently, and Jarom edged a little around the tree in that direction. She continued guiding him around the tree to enable him to remain hidden, despite his not being able to see the scout himself.

When the man drew too close for comfort, Forest dipped her head and pressed her cheek into the cool earth beneath her. She breathed in the pungent aroma of moss and willed her heart to stop beating. She could hear the man's steps and held her breath until they seemed to recede. Eventually, she risked peeking up, then worried when she couldn't see her uncle. She stared at the tree that she'd seen him edge around until he peeked back around it. He cautiously moved back into view and between the trees until he arrived at the girls' position and knelt beside them.

"Here's where it gets tricky," he said, his voice barely audible. "We don't know if that scout leads the main force or if it's somewhere off to the side, or which side. We don't want to be in front of the host when it arrives. I'm going to climb this rise and look for it. Be ready to move quickly when I signal you."

"No," said Forest.

"No?" he asked.

"I'm smaller than you and less likely to be noticed. I'm also used to being on my own in the woods – I can read its signals. Let me do it."

To her surprise, he did.

She rose and moved like a phantom through the trees to the top of the rise. She lay down in a depression and stilled her breathing, listening for the sounds of the forest – crickets, birds, squirrels – anything that moved or made noise. She closed her eyes and extended her senses farther and farther around her. She heard a distant bird burst into the air, and she opened her eyes to track it. Far to the right, she caught sight of another bird taking wing. A squirrel froze on a branch overhead. She peered toward where the birds had left their perches and was rewarded with a glimpse of movement, although she didn't take the time to confirm what moved. It had spooked the birds, and that was good enough for her. She edged back down the ridge to Jarom's position.

"We need to move off to the left and fast," she reported.

Jarom signaled the others, and their party moved quickly in the direction that Forest instructed. Jarom searched for a vantage point, spotted a slight rise, and headed straight for it. He waved everyone past to the other side and bade them hide. As Forest made to move past him, he reached out his arm to stop her. "Not you. Stay with me," he told her and lay down in a pile of leaves.

Forest lay down nearby and pushed the leaves out of the way of her view. She waited patiently and caught sight of a scout cresting the rise she'd just vacated. With time, more and more men appeared, silently moving southward. If she weren't watching them, she wouldn't have believed that so large a force could move so quietly, so near to her.

Jarom motioned to her to move, and they crept down the back of the rise, staying low until they reunited with the party. "We'll move away," he commanded, "then swing back in due course." The party moved perpendicular to the direction of advance of Soren's forces, then slowly turned northward again. "We need to stay out of sight of any scouts that Soren might have spread out around his forces," Jarom explained to her when she was beginning to wonder if they'd moved off too far.

They headed due north for two more days before risking returning toward Soren's forces. "By my reckoning, we should be even with his supply lines by now if his host has continued to grow as I expect it has," Jarom told the party as they rested briefly. "Here's the plan," he said. "Our aim is not to kill – it's to slow them down. We want to be as disruptive as possible but don't take unnecessary chances. Use the element of surprise, hit hard, then get out. We'll move westward after our attack, and regroup in the woods far off, so don't get disoriented. Got it?" he finished.

Everyone nodded their assent.

"Let's do this then," he said. "I've timed our approach so that we'll meet back up with Soren's forces late in the day. They'll be less inclined to pursue us at night. That should work in our favor."

Jarom led them due east until they heard creaking wagons and bleating livestock.

"Fan out," he motioned, then pointed at Forest and Nara. "Stay back," he ordered, "cover us."

Forest pulled out her bow, and Jarom handed her the arrows from his quiver, which she and Nara split between them.

They waited until dusk fell, and the convoy stopped for the night, then crept forward until stealth was no longer possible, rose, and sprinted for the wagons.

Forest notched an arrow and waited. Jarom hefted his battle axe and smashed the wheel of the nearest wagon, then moved on the next, and the next. Ravi ran for the livestock and hurled a throwing axe that caught their handler off guard and split his skull. Ravi made quick work of cutting the animals loose and shooing them off into the forest while his cousin smashed water barrels nearby.

The people leading the wagons and animals were not warriors and fled into the woods in a panic. The few guards that traveled among them rushed to engage their ambushers, and Jarom's kin turned their attention to fighting them in between their wanton destruction.

Forest took her time to make every arrow count and felled several men before they engaged Jarom's party. Two guards rushed at Jarom from both sides of a wagon. Jarom turned to face the closer one, and Forest barely took down the second before he reached her uncle. Jarom waved his thanks and continued his attack.

A trio of guards noticed Nara and Forest and rushed at them. Nara took down one and Forest another, but they'd moved swiftly, and the third man swung his sword down on Forest. She tensed and closed her eyes, awaiting the blow. When it didn't come, she opened an eye to see Nara pulling her dagger from the man's side. His sword was still upraised, and she flinched as he collapsed to the ground.

"I've got your back, cousin," Nara told her.

Forest spotted a large force of men cresting a distant hill, racing toward them. She raised her bow and fired an arrow into a barrel beside Jarom's head. He spun around and saw her motioning frantically toward the advancing forces.

"Fall back!" Jarom yelled, and his kin broke off their attack. One of their party had just smashed a barrel that he discovered contained oil. He took the time to pull out a flint and strike it until the fuel ignited. Forest covered him and took down two approaching guards to buy him time. He raced away as flames exploded into the air.

Everyone melted into the forest. Nara and Forest pulled back last, harrying their pursuers with arrows until they ran out. With everyone fleeing ahead of them, they turned and raced after them.

Darkness fell rapidly, and they stumbled on in the descending gloom until they caught up to the rest of their party.

"Anyone injured?" Jarom asked. When no one spoke, he added, "We keep moving. Stay near me." He began to sing a low song that they were able to follow in the dark. They walked for a long time before he called a halt. "We rest here," he announced, and everyone collapsed where they were.

Nara mussed up her brother's hair, and Ravi shoved her away playfully. Forest crawled closer to her. "Thank you," she told her.

"I'm just making sure I have a bridesmaid for Thorvyn and my wedding," Nara replied.

"Aren't you getting a little ahead of yourself?" Forest asked.

"I sure hope not," she replied and snuggled into Forest. She was asleep before Forest could think how to respond, and Forest joined her in slumber not long after.

Forest bolted upright at dawn, having slept so soundly that she felt vulnerable on waking. Nara had snored in her ear all night, but even that hadn't disturbed her. She looked about and saw Jarom sitting with his back to a tree, watching her. She rose and moved to sit down beside him.

"You're a credit to your kin," he told her. "I'll have you at my back any day."

It meant a lot to her, and she blushed with pride.

"We haven't bought ourselves much time, sadly. Hopefully, we've slowed them down by a day or two and given the city more time to prepare or evacuate. Maybe we've made them divert some forces to protect their rear better. We can only hope that we've accomplished something here," he said, but his eyes didn't convey enthusiasm.

Forest nodded and headed back to rouse Nara.

"Too soon," she mumbled and rolled over.

Forest shook her until she opened a groggy eye. "Wake up. We're heading out."

Nara grumbled but rose, and they moved out as a party, heading back toward the town and the certainty that the fight would come to them before long.

23
Soren

Lennox was growing annoyed. "Why are you smiling?" he asked Soren. "I just told you that our supply lines were ambushed last night."

"Finally, we're meeting resistance. It means we're ruffling the feathers of our real foes. Did you think it would stay easy forever?"

"I suppose not, but it sets us back several days."

"A trifling matter."

"I have a guard in for questioning who was present during the attack. Is there anything you want to ask him?"

Much as Soren detested Lennox's methods of extracting information, there were questions he wanted answered, so he nodded.

Lennox led Soren to his tent. Inside, a man was tied to a chair, bruised and bloody. Soren disregarded the discomfort he felt and approached the man, who couldn't decide whether he should be hopeful or terrified at the sight of Soren.

"I understand you witnessed the ambush on our supply lines," Soren began.

"Yes, sir," the man croaked through split lips.

"Describe what you saw."

"It was getting dark, but I believe there were about twenty of them." The man initially claimed they'd met with a more significant force, but Lennox was persuasive at extracting the truth, and he'd abandoned any tack other than recounting exactly what he knew.

"Go on," Soren coached, "I want details."

"I didn't see everyone, but their leader was a burly man who wielded an axe."

"What else?"

"There was a girl. She was petite but accurate with a bow. She provided cover fire and took out many of our men."

"Forest," Soren mused out loud. "Brave girl."

"Sorry, sir?" Lennox inquired, but Soren disregarded him.

"I have no further questions," Soren concluded. "You're welcome to do what you will with him," he added and stalked out of Lennox's tent. He called over his shoulder, "Council at dawn."

"Yes, sir," Lennox replied and turned his attention back to the man. The screaming resumed before Soren had even made it ten paces.

"Barbarian," Soren muttered and headed back to his tent. He lay awake for a long time feeling alone and isolated among his host, despite its size. Sleep came grudgingly.

At dawn, Lennox, Trax and Seline met at Soren's tent. Soren felt haggard and nursed a cup of kai as he sat down. "Status?" he asked his council.

Seline looked at the other two, and judging it opportune to begin, did so. "We've had no detailed reports from our scouts ever since we lost a party days ago. We've dispatched another, but they haven't reported back yet."

Lennox added, "I've interviewed people familiar with the area, and I'm told there's a sizable city ahead, but nothing better defended than any we've encountered so far."

"We can't assume anything," Seline countered.

"Bah," Trax dismissed her concerns, leaned back, and rested his boots on the table. "They all fall easily enough."

"This may be different," Seline pointed out. "We've lost a scouting party, and we've been attacked strategically. They're getting smarter."

"Smart doesn't matter against steel," Trax deflected.

Seline bristled, obviously disagreeing with Trax's assessment of the value of intelligence. Soren leaned toward Seline's position but judged it not the time to push Trax back into submission.

"I've told my men to push on," Trax informed them.

Not your call, Soren thought, annoyed, but said nothing. *I'm losing control of him*, he realized. "I don't see why not," Soren lied, seeing a multitude of reasons for caution.

Seline looked at Soren with unveiled disapproval, but he gave her a look that said, "Patience," and she pursed her lips.

"What condition are our siege machines in?" he asked her.

"Disassembled and moving forward with the main host," she replied. "We don't know what we're up against yet. I'm inclined to wait to hear from our scouts."

"Waste of time," Trax declared. "We're going to find a city filled with cowering people and surrounded by a breachable wall. What else do we need to know?"

Seline also knew when to pick her battles, so she didn't reply. Patience came naturally to Lennox as well, who just took everything in and bided his time. He was most comfortable operating in the shadows, which unnerved Soren the most. Trax, at least, was utterly transparent.

"How much longer until we arrive?" Soren asked.

"No more than a few days," Lennox replied.

Soren smiled. *At least it's beginning to get interesting*, he thought.

24

Kala

Kala's airship drifted westward on a high-altitude wind. It was too high for her to see anything below, and she shivered, partly from the cold but more from her despair at returning without allies. She paced back and forth despondently, trying to keep warm and wracking her brain for some way out of their impending disaster. The ship descended toward the city where her friends awaited their doom.

Soren spotted Kala's airship high in the sky. He signaled the men around him to stop their advance and pointed at it through the trees. "We're getting closer to the masters of those infernal things, and when we find them, we'll make sure they never control us again!" he shouted. His men roared back, and he gave the signal to resume their march.

Kala's ship landed, and she stepped out to find Skye waiting for her. Her shoulders slumped, and she shook her head to let him know she'd failed in her mission. He held out his arms, and she collapsed into them. "I tried," she told him, crushed.

"I know," he said, rubbing her back. "It wasn't meant to be."

A distant horn blew, then another closer, and another. Everyone in the fields stopped what they were doing and stared northward. Kala looked to Skye for an explanation.

"Jarom sent his nephews far afield to sound the alarm when they spotted Soren's vanguard. It means that it should be here sometime tomorrow. They know they have no element of surprise, so they'll take their time and attack when they're good and ready."

"You should get ready to leave," Kala told him.

"Are *you* leaving?" he challenged her.

"No. We make our stand."

"Then, here is where I'll be. I'm not leaving you."

"You know what we're up against. We're not walking off the battlefield."

"Then I'll be just where I want to be – at your side."

Kala had no words and just held him tight.

Lily and Cera walked over. "You're back," Lily observed.

Kala looked up in shock at her voice. "What are you still doing here?" she asked, panicked. "At least go inside the city walls," she begged.

Lily shook her head. "We'll see this through together, come what may."

"There's no 'come what may.' It's death coming our way."

Lily and Cera stood their ground.

Kala stood stunned, replaying the Priestess's words in her head – "They love you enough to die for you." The guilt crushed her. No matter how vehemently she vowed to protect her friends, her best was never enough, could never be enough. She held out her arms, and the three of them embraced for a long time.

"I should see my grandfather off," Kala said, pulling away. "Has anyone seen him?"

"On the archery range," Cera volunteered.

"Thanks," Kala replied and gave them a final hug before detaching herself and heading toward the range. She passed Fayre and Emrys, who were organizing the evacuation of everyone unable to fight, mostly the very young and the very old. Kala's grandfather wasn't among them, so she continued on to the range.

She arrived to find him squinting at a hay bale, bow in hand. Kala glanced at the target, and arrows seemed to be everywhere but in it. She looked inquiringly at him.

He noted her approach. "I'm getting better," he told her, looking down the shaft of an arrow and firing it over the hay bale entirely.

"This is better?" Kala asked jokingly. "You know you can't see a damned thing at that distance."

"I'll just aim for the center of the blur. How hard is that?"

Kala took his hand gently. "It's time to leave."

He stood firm. "We need everyone we can get."

Kala gestured at the children surrounding Fayre. "They need you more."

Her grandfather looked long and hard at the faces of his former students, wavered, then slumped his shoulders in grudging acceptance.

Kala leaned in and hugged him tightly. She pressed her head into his chest, and he placed his chin on it. "Let me help you get your things together," she said, pulling away reluctantly and walking with him toward the camp.

They passed Dhara working with Caia to rehabilitate her wound. She winced with pain as she stabbed and parried Dhara's spear. Nina mimicked her mother with a staff of her own.

"Give me a moment, grandpa," Kala requested. He nodded and carried on toward the camp while she altered course toward Dhara and Caia. "Hi, girls," she greeted them.

They paused and wiped the sweat off their brows. Nina kept up her assault against her imaginary foe.

"Can I have a word with Caia for a moment?" Kala asked Dhara.

"Sure," Dhara replied for her sister but didn't move. "Whatever you have to say, you can say in front of me – we're family."

Kala looked to Caia for support, but she obviously agreed with her sister, so Kala steeled herself. "You should leave with Nina," Kala suggested.

"Zara must be avenged," Caia replied flatly.

"But your daughter?" Kala protested.

"She's family."

"Surely you're not suggesting that Nina stay and fight?" Kala asked incredulously.

"No. Her spear-work needs practice," Caia admitted. "Besides, if I fall in battle, she'll need to avenge me."

Kala looked hard at Caia to see if there were a way of changing her mind about joining her daughter, but she stared back resolutely. "Okay," Kala conceded. "Let me find someone to look after Nina."

Caia accepted this, and Kala called Allie over. "Can you look after Nina?" Kala asked her, gesturing to Caia's daughter.

"Of course," Allie replied, "but please talk to Oriel. He says he's not coming with us."

"I will," Kala agreed, then turned to Caia. "Caia, this is Allie. She'll keep an eye on Nina, if that's okay with you."

Caia nodded her agreement and called Nina over. "Nina, honey, go with this woman. Her name is Allie."

Nina looked Allie over skeptically.

"She needs your protection, honey," Caia told her, and Nina seemed to accept her mother's logic. "I'll join you as soon as I can," Caia added.

"How long?" Nina wanted to know.

"Soon," Caia reassured her and kissed her forehead.

Allie offered Nina her hand, and she took it reluctantly. Allie chatted with Nina as she led her away, looking over her shoulder at Kala to remind her to talk to her husband.

Caia and Dhara resumed their sparring, leaving Kala to hunt down Oriel. She found him talking with Hawke. At a glance, she could tell that he hadn't fully recovered from the bear attack and possibly never would.

"Grab your things, Oriel," Kala ordered him. "The evacuees need you."

"I'm staying," he replied.

Kala couldn't take it anymore. "I'm getting tired of being told 'no,'" she said and pulled out a sword. "Draw your blade, Oriel."

"Why?"

"Don't make me ask again," she replied and advanced.

He pulled out his sword, and she swung at him. He blocked her blow, but pain exploded down his side. She struck at him again and again until he was forced to drop his guard because of the pain. She pointed her sword at him as he clutched his side. "I get that you want to help, but you're more help alive than dead. They need you," she said, gesturing to the assembling evacuees. "Allie needs you. Now, go."

Oriel limped off.

"A bit harsh," Hawke observed.

"I only did what needed to be done," she replied, watching Oriel as he headed back toward camp. She turned to Hawke and looked intensely into his eyes, "Leave while you still can. Go back to Emilie and use your skills to protect her and live out this gods-damned war," she implored him. She pulled the amulet out from under her tunic and pressed it on him. "Take this."

He placed a hand on her arm, surprisingly gently, to stop her. "You know I can't do that," he said. "I made a vow to make the world a better place for her, and that's what I'm going to do... even if I don't live to see it." He didn't give her time to respond and walked away as she struggled to come up with words that would change his mind.

That evening, Kala found herself drifting between campfires, imparting words of encouragement, or sharing a drink or a hug. The camp had thinned out considerably. The evacuees took little with them, so much of the camp still stood – it was simply deserted.

Kala eventually found herself at Jarom's campfire, where she found Forest sitting between Nara and Ravi. Forest had also begged Lily and Cera to leave, but they'd refused her too. "I can't have my little sister fight all our battles alone," Lily had told her.

"But you're not a fighter," Forest had pleaded, but Lily was adamant that she could help, and Cera refused to leave Lily's side. Forest watched them sullenly from afar. Nara looked at Forest, followed her gaze to Lily and Cera, and sighed.

"I want what she has," she told Forest, referring to Lily. "I want Thorvyn to be my Cera. Her eyes light up when Lily appears. I want Thorvyn's to light up when I appear."

"There'll be plenty of time for that," Forest lied. "I've seen how he looks at you."

"That's just because I cut him down from a stake," Nara countered.

"He looks at you with affection, not gratitude," Forest corrected her.

"You think?" she asked hopefully.

"I'm certain of it."

Nara shifted closer and hugged her cousin.

Jarom looked up from the axe that he was sharpening. "We leave when the moon is at its highest."

Solemn nods went around the fire.

"You're leaving?" Kala asked, surprised.

"Only into the woods," he clarified. "We'll fight them on our terms."

"Shall I join you?" Kala asked.

"No – but thank you. You're too important here as a symbol. You need to remain visible."

"I'm hardly a symbol," Kala replied dismissively.

"Don't say that," he countered. "You don't see what people see in you. You're the hope they cling to. If they have nothing else, at least let them have that."

Kala was about to respond that people were fools, but she looked around the fire at the eyes upon her and realized that it would be cruel to take away what little hope anyone had, misplaced though it may be. "You're right," she conceded. "Pass me that whetstone," she requested and pulled out her already razor-sharp swords to sharpen them a bit more.

Calix was sitting around a fire with Lily and Cera when Dhara walked up.

"You – come with me," she said, gesturing to him.

Calix looked at Lily and Cera, and realizing that he should probably give them what could be their last night together alone, got up and followed Dhara.

"Is there something that needs attention?" he asked.

"You could say that," she replied and kept walking until they arrived at her tent.

I don't understand," he said, but she shut him up with a deep kiss, pulling him inside.

Forest sat crouched beside a leafy tree, camouflaged accordingly. Dawn was only slowly starting to filter through the trees. She was able to make out Jarom's outline nearby and Nara's a little farther off. The sounds of the night gradually gave way to the sounds of the day, then abruptly quieted. Forest pulled an arrow from her quiver and notched it to her bow. A scout emerged from around a tree, and she patiently lined up her shot. There was no signal. Her instructions were simply to take any clean shot she could. She pulled back and loosed the arrow into the man's throat. He staggered backward and fell.

Forest heard the twang of bows around her and knew that her target wasn't the only one. She readied another arrow and waited. Another man appeared and stopped in his tracks when he came across the fallen man. It allowed Forest time to line up her shot and send an arrow through his eye. He was dead before he hit the ground, but the third man was near enough to see him fall, and he brought a horn to his lips and blew a strong note. It was followed by the sound of many men crashing forward through the brush.

Forest glanced down at the row of arrows she'd stuck into the earth, burning their placement into her mind, just as the woods erupted with charging soldiers. She fired arrow after arrow, felling several men even as they grew close enough to swing at her. Forest quickly exhausted her arrows, but the men kept coming. She rose and bolted back through the brush toward the fields surrounding the city.

Men with swords, axes, and spears pursued her, but they were heavier-set and more bulkily armored, so Forest was able to stay out of their reach as she ran. She dodged around trees, denying any straight shot for an enemy archer or spear thrower. Arrows still sailed past her nevertheless, but none found their mark. She burst through the trees in time to see Nara and Jarom dive behind one of the battlements that Calix had helped construct. Forest followed suit.

Soldiers burst through the trees after her and were met with withering fire from the archers waiting behind the battlements. None made it very far onto the field until enemy archers made their way forward, and soon, the two sides were trading fire from behind trees and the battlements. They were quickly joined by a row of warriors with long shields, who advanced toward the positions held by the defenders.

"Fall back!" Jarom bellowed, realizing they'd be quickly overrun if they didn't retreat immediately.

Forest had thrown her empty quiver aside and picked up another that lay at the ready. She caught a man in the shin and ricocheted a few shots off angled shields that found their mark in the sides of adjacent men. Several dropped their shields, and Forest took out one or two more men behind them. She couldn't hold out any longer and ran serpentine for the next row of battlements. Arrows whizzed past her, but her luck held. One became tangled up in the folds of the cloak that she'd worn for camouflage, so she simply tore it off and discarded it on the run.

The placement of stakes funneled the soldiers so that they became easier targets for the defending archers, but their shields proved to be sufficient protection. Forest and the other defenders were forced to retreat to the next ring of battlements. This placed the tree line out of bow range, and Soren's forces profited from it to pour out onto the open fields at their leisure. Their archers took up positions and advanced with shield men to suppress any defending fire. Soon, the field filled with Soren's soldiers, and their sheer number was dispiriting.

Forest watched as a handler led a horse out of the woods, and a man stepped forward to climb astride it. Soren himself had arrived on the field of battle. Forest swallowed hard as his cold gaze swept past her. He moved past row after row of men, with a giant of a man beside him barking orders at the soldiers they passed. A woman appeared at their side, gesturing expansively to the field. Soren nodded to her.

A horn sounded from the city walls, and all heads turned toward it. The gates cracked open, and a man in white robes emerged, holding his hands high, the gates closing swiftly behind him. Forest watched as Soren sat in his saddle and watched the man approach. He spurred his horse forward, and his men made way for him to meet the man at the front ranks of his forces. Soren's giant general stalked forward with him.

Forest couldn't make out what was said but could tell by Soren's relaxed demeanor that he was letting the man say his peace. When he'd made his case, Soren gestured casually to his general, who advanced, sword in hand. The emissary froze with fear and pleaded for his life but was quickly relieved of his head. The general bent to collect it and threw it high in the air back toward the city gates.

There's your answer, Forest thought bitterly. She looked behind her and scanned the defensive forces until she spied Kala standing exposed, staring defiantly at the swelling number of the enemy. The majority of the defenders, few though they were, stood near her. Forest felt time drag on as she waited in limbo – too far away to engage the enemy, but near enough to watch as they organized.

Two enormous siege machines were assembled at the forest's edge under the instruction of the woman that Forest had seen briefly at Soren's side. The towers took shape and eventually began to move toward the city gates, one in front of the other. They advanced quickly on the hard-packed ground, then suddenly, the lead tower lurched sideways as it rolled into soil that had been dug up and replaced, but much more loosely. The tower canted further over and, reaching some critical angle, toppled altogether. The woman in charge swore, and

Forest could hear her colorful tirade from where she awaited the advancing forces.

The second tower was redirected around the first and continued its advance until it arrived at the trench dug around the city and became stuck. The woman yelled for planking to be brought forward, but in the time that the tower was immobilized, Forest and her kin lit arrows and launched them at it. Several struck it, but the wood had been wetted and did not catch fire. However, the longer it stayed stuck, the more quickly it dried, and eventually, it would succumb to the flame.

Forest watched as Soren made a gesture, and a wave of captive children rushed forward with buckets of water to douse the immobilized tower.

"Don't hit the children," Jarom yelled, and they did their best to keep peppering the tower with burning arrows without hurting the children who were doing their best to put out the flames. Smoke eventually rose from it, but Forest, Jarom, and the others were forced back to the final ring of battlements where Kala and the others waited. Forest dove behind a barrier, but not before seeing Kala flash her a tight smile.

Forest could see Soren's general arguing with the woman in charge of the siege machinery while Soren looked on without intervening. The general eventually waved the woman aside and commanded the soldiers to begin their advance. *This is it,* Forest thought, *the endgame.* Thousands of hardened warriors closed in on their paltry defense. She made her peace and readied her bow.

Kala drew her swords. A wind blew across the field, bringing with it the smell of steel, the taste of ash, and the promise of ruin. A solitary raven watched the proceedings. Kala could feel its anticipation as she drew deeply on the darkness inside herself, straining against invisible restraints as the enemy closed. As soon as their front ranks occluded the archers' view, she loosed a battle cry and ran forward, spurring those around her to rush forward with her. They met the enemy in a clash of steel. Kala slashed and rent, and men fell, but more always took their place. Hawke guarded her back, and anyone unlucky enough to make a move on her from behind was quickly dispatched.

Dhara and Caia held the tide of attackers at bay at the end of their spears and capitalized on openings to puncture lungs and pierce guts. Jarom fought nearby, cutting broad swaths through the enemy with his enormous axe. Ravi, Nara and Thorvyn fought near him and did their best to give him a safe flank as Soren's forces inexorably surrounded them. The rest of Jarom's kin and the remaining fighting men from the camp were arrayed in a ragged line, trying to hold back the advancing soldiers. Lily and Cera stayed back unless they saw an opening to rush in and tend to a wounded defender. Calix and Skye tried to protect them, but they were not skilled fighters and barely succeeded in keeping themselves alive. Archers from the city walls did their best to pepper the enemy, but they were terrible marksmen and easily thwarted by helmets and shields.

The battle wore on, and both attackers and defenders fell. Dhara found herself fending off a skilled fighter while her sister struggled against a colossus of a man. Out of the corner of her eye, she saw the man bat Caia's spear aside and raise a killing stroke. Dhara leaped to parry it for her sister, exposing her back to the man she was battling. Calix saw all of this in slow motion and dove between them. He was facing her when the man's sword went through his right shoulder. He blinked, looked down at the blade protruding from his chest, and locked eyes with Dhara.

"No!" she screamed as she ran her spear through Caia's assailant's chin and out the top of his skull. Calix's attacker pulled his sword from his back, and Calix slumped to his knees.

"Tend to him," Dhara ordered her sister. "This one's mine," she seethed and dove at him in a berserk fury, slashing until his armor and flesh were ribbons.

Caia pulled Calix back to Lily and Cera, left him with them, and returned to her sister's side.

A deep pile of corpses surrounded Kala, but soldiers kept pressing her. She panted from exhaustion.

"Kala!" Hawke called to get her attention.

A distant part of her registered, and she spared him a glance.

"It's no use," he told her. "We have to retreat."

Kala nodded grimly, and they moved slowly back toward the gate, collecting any surviving defenders as they went. They finally neared the gate, and Hawke turned to pound on it. "Open up!" he yelled to the men on the walls. "The field is lost."

The guards controlling the gate shook their heads and adamantly refused to open it. Hawke shook his fist at them, but they were more terrified of the army before them than Hawke's anger. "I guess this is it, then," he said to Kala as he returned to her side. The two of them held the center as they were slowly pushed back. An exhausted Jarom held the left with a small number of his kin, including Nara and Forest, who now wielded daggers. Dhara and Caia held the right, but collectively, they could barely stand. Lily and Cera huddled behind over Calix, with Skye trying to protect them.

A horn blast split the air, and Soren's men paused and pulled back slightly out of the defenders' sword range. Kala looked up to see a man on horseback trotting toward her. She wiped the blood and sweat out of her eyes and studied him. Soren stopped out of bow range of the city walls, and his men moved back to form a corridor with him at one end and Kala and her allies at the other.

Soren leaned back in his saddle and surveyed the field of the dead. "Impressive," he concluded, then looked Kala up and down. "So, you must be my Scourge," he said conversationally.

Kala judged the distance and decided it was worth a try. She dropped her swords and hurled a dagger with as much force as she had left.

Soren's general Trax stepped forward and casually batted it out of the air.

Soren leaned forward. "You'll have to do better than that," he declared and studied her. "I won't insult you by offering you a chance to switch sides, but I do have a proposition for you. I'll negotiate the terms of your survival..." He paused to let that register. "...If you can best my champion."

Trax looked up at Soren, angry at the interruption in the bloodshed.

"Humor me," Soren told the man, and Trax clenched his fists in barely contained restraint.

Kala highly doubted that Soren would honor any arrangement he made, but she judged that she had little choice and even fewer options. She looked around her at her loved ones and decided that any chance of their survival was worth taking. "I accept," she replied.

Soren looked pleased and turned to Trax. "Do you think you can handle this little girl?" he asked.

Trax was infuriated by the insult but had to accept the challenge, framed as it was. He swallowed his curses and turned to face Kala. "Let's get this over with," he said, drawing his enormous broadsword.

"This should be interesting," Soren declared and leaned back in his saddle, amused at the thought that whatever the outcome, he will have rid himself of a problem.

Trax looked at the bodies on the ground with disgust. "Clear some space, damn it," he growled, and men rushed forward to drag the dead out of his way. Quickly, a circle of open but blood-stained ground lay around Trax and Kala.

Trax swung his sword around him to loosen his muscles. Kala, beyond exhaustion, simply watched him, her own swords recovered and hanging limply in her hands. He approached her slowly like a predator playing with its prey, then, without warning, he swung, blindingly fast for a man his size. Kala barely managed to fall to the ground to avoid being cleft in two. She looked up at him, uncertain whether she had the strength to rise. He swung down, and Kala rolled aside in the nick of time. She backed up while he turned to face her. "Get over here and die with some dignity," he spat at her.

She watched him from the ground and studied his movements. He swung his sword from side to side and advanced again with a flurry of strokes. How she found the space to evade them was a miracle, but he again found himself facing her, unscathed but lying prone. She rose slowly to her feet with apparent effort.

"That's more like it," he declared, smirking. He raised his sword and rushed at her.

Kala closed her eyes and counted two heartbeats. She opened them and stepped into his downstroke. In one swift motion, she ran a sword through his foot, making him stiffen in pain, and used the momentum of his swing to sweep herself upward and onto his back. She spun around his neck, using her second sword as leverage, and landed in a crouch. As Trax's body wavered and fell, she lifted his severed head and tossed it toward Soren.

"Satisfied?" she asked.

"Bravo," he replied. "You've prevailed, so you've earned some consideration, but, seeing how you're also a viper…" he looked her party over, nodding to Forest with respect. His eyes settled on Cera, and he stared at her for a moment. "Her," he said, pointing at Cera. "I'll speak with her."

"That wasn't the deal," Kala replied defiantly.

Soren looked at the legions of men surrounding them. "You're not in a position to negotiate," he observed flatly.

Cera placed a hand on Kala's shoulder. "It's okay," she said and walked past her before she could object.

Kala stepped after her, and a hundred men pointed their swords at her. She paused, not wanting to imperil her friends more than they already were.

Cera strode up to Soren's horse and inclined her head toward him. He bent down and spoke quietly to her. She nodded, lowered her head, and came back to Kala.

"We have a deal," she said resignedly. "You're free to walk out of here," she added, gesturing to their entire party.

"And?" Kala asked, understanding that there had to be a catch.

"And…," Cera replied, "I'm not. I'm the barter for your lives."

"No!" Kala and Lily cried out simultaneously.

Cera looked Kala square in the eye. "It's my decision," she said and strode past her to hug Lily. "I do this for you," she whispered in her ear.

"You can't," Lily sobbed.

"You have to let me," she replied and kissed her forehead. She released Lily, steeled herself, and walked back toward Soren.

Kala raised a hand but stopped short of grabbing her. "Please, Cera. A friend once told me that when you sell your soul, it can still return to you – but it's not true. It fades with every compromise you make until it's gone forever. Please don't do this."

"I already have," she said and continued to Soren's side.

"You have until sundown," Soren announced to Kala's party. "After that, I will hunt you, and when I find you, I will kill you."

Lennox had stood quietly by but could stand it no longer. "What are you doing? Kill her now."

Soren turned to him and said quietly, "I don't have to kill her to destroy her," then turned back to Kala. "Go. You have until sundown." He waved, and his men cleared a path all the way to the southern edge of the woods.

Skye collected Kala. "The battle is lost," he told her, "but not the war. Let's go." She hesitated, but he guided her through the corridor of soldiers and off the field of battle.

Kala hazarded a final look over her shoulder to catch a glimpse of Soren, smug on his horse, and Cera standing stoically at his side.

Her soul shriveled.

PART III
ALLIES

25

Kala

Kala and her party filed silently toward the woods through the corridor created for them by Soren's soldiers. They limped along like a funeral procession, each of them consumed with their individual grief. The soldiers watched wordlessly as they passed, then closed ranks behind them. As they approached the trees, Soren's forces turned their attention back to the sack of the city.

Kala was bone-weary. It was all she could do to put one foot in front of the other. Skye kept up a steady stream of reassurances, but she didn't hear any of it. All she could think about was the waste of life and the futility of fighting so large an army. Kala spiraled downward into a dark and familiar place. Skye had to guide her as her feet trod a different world from the one she now inhabited deep within herself.

Lily followed in a daze, led by Forest, who had to keep pulling her forward when she'd stop and try to return to Cera. Lily kept up an anguished mantra of, "No, no, no."

Hawke and Jarom followed, carrying Calix between them. They were so exhausted that it was only through sheer willpower that they found the strength to transport his limp body. Calix drifted in and out of consciousness as they shifted their holds. His shirt was soaked with his blood, and his skin had a ghostly grey pallor. It was a mercy that he passed out so frequently.

Dhara and Caia came next, Dhara in a foul mood. "Zara was inadequately avenged," she complained.

Jarom shook his head. "You sent tens of men to their grave, girl."

"My sister is worth hundreds," she countered.

"Then content yourself that you live to fight another day. Few enough can say that."

"Now I've got this mess to deal with," she complained, gesturing at Calix.

Caia shushed her, given that Calix looked like he'd probably not survive the day. It was bad manners to speak ill of the dead or dying.

Nara followed next, guiding Thorvyn, who was having trouble seeing through swollen eyes, the result of a mace blow to the head. He staggered, and one of her cousins took hold of his other side and helped prop him up. Nara looked through the small number of surviving relatives for her brother. "Ravi?" she asked her father, who shook his head sadly. Nara burst into tears.

The sad procession continued until they arrived at the first clearing that was big enough for them all to stop and rest. Skye sat Kala down, and Hawke and Jarom propped Calix against a tree. Dhara moved to examine his wound.

"It's stopped bleeding," she observed, but likely only because he had so little blood left. "Prepare a poultice, Caia," she instructed her sister, who got up and started examining the bases of nearby trees for mosses.

"We don't have time for that," one of Jarom's cousins objected. "Soren said he'd start hunting us at sundown."

Dhara reached for a dagger, but Jarom stepped in to pacify the man. "Soren has more pressing matters to attend to with the sack of the city, and I hardly think he'll start chasing us at sundown, just as night descends. If he pursues us at all, he'll do it at his leisure, more likely tomorrow. Besides, if we move Calix in the state he's in, he'll die for sure."

The man looked at Jarom as if to say, "He's dead anyway – surely we should accept that and press on."

Jarom sighed wearily. "There's been too much death already. Let's try to prevent any more if we can." His word was final, and the man dropped his objection and began preparing a fire.

These men are unfailingly loyal, Hawke marveled, never having seen such bonds. He got up to help the man collect firewood.

Nara did her best to clean Thorvyn's wounds but could only do so much before the fire would allow her to boil water. Thorvyn reached out and took her free hand while she dabbed his face. "I'm sorry about your brother," he said, and she leaned into him.

Lily stayed standing, staring back toward the city. Forest had to turn her around and guide her to where the fire was being prepared. "There's nothing we can do for Cera now," Forest told her, "but we *will* do something... we just need time to figure out what and when." Lily was inconsolable, so Forest continued. "*She's* safe. *We're* safe. And we're only safe because of the bargain she made."

"*I* don't accept it," Lily objected, knowing full-well that what she did or did not accept was irrelevant, only that she was unable to carry on without Cera.

Forest sat beside her. "I know," she said and held her older sister while she cried.

Skye hated feeling so powerless. He guided Kala to her feet and led her outside the clearing, where he held her tight. She just stared over his shoulder into the woods and oblivion. He waited until he could feel their hearts beating in sync. "We need you," he whispered in her ear. "We need you here. Wherever you've gone, come back to us." She stirred slightly, so he continued. "I know it's unfair to lay this on you, but these people look to you for guidance. You don't have to have a plan. You don't need to believe that any plan will work, but they need you to act as if you do."

She slowly returned to herself and looked into his eyes. "It was awful," she said, tearing up.

"I know," he replied and squeezed her tighter.

"So much death, and for what?"

Skye had no answer and simply stroked her back.

Kala slowly collected her wits.

"Thank you for coming back," Skye told her.

Kala breathed in deeply, turned slowly, and walked back to the clearing, with Skye following close behind. People watched her return and sit down by the fire, and they waited for her to speak.

"We failed," she said quietly. "There's no shame in admitting it. We did our best, but we failed. It was a lesson that cost us many loved ones." She looked into everyone's eyes, acknowledging their loss. She couldn't hold Lily's forlorn gaze. "We can't fight Soren's army without one of our own. We need allies to rival his. That's our only hope." She looked at Dhara and Nara, who were tending to Calix and Thorvyn. "We'll deal with our wounded. Then, we'll pick ourselves up, dust ourselves off, and find allies."

Everyone nodded their understanding. How exactly they would accomplish this task was unknown, but the logic was irrefutable. They nursed their injuries and looked after their comrades. Dhara and Caia prepared a poultice for Calix's wound and scrounged some fabric to bandage it.

"He won't die from infection, at least," Dhara concluded and collapsed onto the ground beside him.

Forest wanted to search for water, but Jarom wouldn't let her, telling her it was too dangerous. Soren had granted them a brief reprieve, but it wasn't certain that his men patrolling the woods knew of it or would honor it if they did.

They rested fitfully at their makeshift camp until dawn's early light chased away the dark. The smell of smoke permeated the air, and it was accepted, although never stated, that the city had fallen. It took little time to ready themselves to move out. Thorvyn had recovered enough vision to walk unaided, but a sled was constructed for Calix.

Skye handed Kala her journal, which he'd kept with him, refusing to leave it at the refugee camp. She thanked him and consulted it. The closest place to hail an airship was northwest of where they were, but they were cut off from it by Soren's forces. They could try to circle around to it, but that likely wasn't a good idea. The next closest place was marked on her map to the southeast on the plains. That was where they'd head. She told Jarom what she was thinking, and he deferred to her in the matter, so she guided their party south.

They had no provisions, so Kala and Forest hunted game every night with borrowed bows when they paused to rest, and they were adept enough that the party didn't starve. It didn't seem that they were being chased by Soren's forces, mercifully, given that with the slow progress they made, if they were, they'd probably have been caught by now.

Skye spent time walking with Hawke. Hawke kept glancing at Jarom.

"It's not right for a father to outlive a son," Hawke muttered.

Nothing about this is right, Skye thought and kept walking.

The forest gradually gave way to plains, and Calix stubbornly clung to life, although he looked more gaunt every day. They kept up as steady a pace as their strength would allow and got closer to the airship beacon. Cross-referencing what they'd learned on the volcanic island with Eden's maps, Kala and Skye concluded that it lay in the ruins of an ancient city located at what had once been the confluence of two great rivers. They walked until they reached one of them, then followed along its bank.

After a short break, they rose to continue, but Lily refused to get up. Forest walked back to her.

"Leave me here," Lily told her despairingly. "I can't keep this up. I'm not rugged like the rest of you. The farther I get from Cera, the more stretched I feel, and right now, I'm stretched so thin that there's nothing left of me. I belong here in the middle of nowhere."

"Not an option," Forest told her flatly and held out her hand to help her up. Lily ignored her, so Forest added, "Is that what Cera would want?"

"That's not fair," Lily complained.

"She gave you a chance at life, and I'll be damned if you're going to throw it away in a fit of self-pity. It's disrespectful of Cera's sacrifice." She held out her hand again more firmly, and Lily reluctantly took it.

"I hate you," Lily said.

"As long as you're around to hate me, I'll take it," Forest replied and helped her sister to her feet. Then she added bitterly, "I know you love her, but you don't exactly have a monopoly on that – we all do, and we're hurting too."

Lily had nothing to say but a quiet "sorry" under her breath. Forest didn't need to hear it to know that her sister was aware that they all mourned Cera's loss.

Nara kicked at a loose pile of dirt while they trudged along. "The earth here is fertile," she noted, looking around. "So why has no one settled here?"

Kala replied over her shoulder. "No airships. If a settlement couldn't be entirely self-sufficient here, they couldn't survive without the ships. They dictate where and how we live."

"You sound like Soren," Lily accused her meanly.

"I don't agree with his methods, but he has a point," Kala replied. The wind picked up and blew her hair in her face. She tied it back, but it always found some way to get loose and bother her. Eventually, she gave up and just squinted through the strands that flailed her face.

The tell-tale ruins of the Ancients' buildings began to poke through the soil as they advanced until they finally stood before the confluence of the two rivers.

"Gods-damn it," Kala cursed.

"What is it?" Skye asked. "We're here."

"You didn't happen to see a circle of rocks pointing skyward?"

"I don't think so," he replied uncertainly.

"That's what we're looking for, and if it isn't on this side of the river, it must be on the other side, one of three other sides."

Skye looked out over the wide expanse of the river. "Oh," he said. "That's not good."

"You've got that right," she replied unhappily, "and I didn't see any easy way to cross back along the way we came, so we might as well continue and hope we come across one."

No one was happy about it, but they accepted that no other option seemed to exist and resumed walking. As they proceeded away from the intersection of the rivers, the frequency and scale of the Ancients' structures increased.

"Wouldn't you center the city *around* the intersection of the rivers?" Skye wondered out loud.

"Originally, they probably did," Jarom replied.

"So, what gives?" Skye pressed him.

"Rivers meander over time. I think that's what we're seeing here."

"How long does that take?" Skye wondered, then added as it occurred to him, "What if the circle of stones we're looking for has been washed away?"

Jarom placed a hand on his shoulder. "That's always a possibility, so let's hope they built it on stable ground."

Ahead, they spotted the frame of one of the Ancients' gigantic buildings that had toppled into the river, spanning it. It didn't look particularly sturdy, but they looked farther downriver and saw no other way across.

"This is how we get to the other side," Kala decided.

"But we haven't fully explored this side of the river for the circle of stones," Skye countered.

"The bulk of the city seems to lie on the other side," Kala replied. "I'd bet that what we seek is on that side as well."

"We can't carry Calix across that," Skye declared, gesturing to the collapsed building.

"You're right – we'll have to tow him across."

"Gods-damn!"

"Got a better idea?"

"No."

"Okay then – find a rope, and let's get going."

Someone procured some, and they tied it to Calix's sled, which they brought down to the riverbank.

Dhara began to strip down.

"What are you doing?" Skye asked her.

"Someone has to keep him upright in the water," she replied.

It was murky, and no one liked the idea of Dhara and Calix being in it, but carrying him across the uneven "bridge" wasn't an option, nor was leaving him behind. The current looked treacherous, but they'd just have to deal with it.

Forest moved to take the lead in guiding them across the fallen structure, but Kala challenged her.

"I'm the lightest," Forest explained. "We don't even know if this thing is stable. I should be the first to cross it."

"Fair enough," Kala relented. "We'll wait for you to cross, then follow you." She chose not to add, "unless it collapses under you, and you're swept away."

Forest clambered over the structure, and except for a few harrowing moments, made it across. Kala began leading the remainder of their party across, with Jarom and Hawke holding the rope that was attached to Calix's sled. Dhara slipped into the water and held it steady as they towed it across. It was awkward, but they made slow and steady progress. Nara helped Lily with her footing on the uneven structure.

They'd made it halfway across when Forest began shouting. Everyone swiveled their heads to see her pointing agitatedly downstream at the shore from which they'd just crossed. Some massive creature had slid into the water and was bearing down on Calix.

"Hurry!" Jarom shouted, and he and Hawke moved faster and less cautiously across the bridge. Caia jumped into the water to join her sister in swimming with the sled.

"Get out of here!" Dhara barked at her sister.

"Fat chance," she replied and kicked harder.

Skye shouted, "It's getting closer," and pointed to a spot halfway across. Kala whipped out her bow and buried an arrow in the beast's back, but if it noticed, it didn't show it and kept moving toward Calix and the girls.

"You're not going to make it," Skye shouted in warning.

Dhara released her grip on the sled and turned to face the monster bearing down on them, pulling a dagger from the sheath secured to her leg.

"What are you doing?" Caia called back to her.

"Debts need to be paid," she replied. "Swim," she ordered her sister and kicked off toward the beast.

Caia kicked harder while Jarom and Hawke pulled the sled closer to the far shore. Skye and Kala watched as Dhara took a deep breath and dove beneath the surface. The creature swam through where she'd been, and the water roiled when they collided. Water sprayed into the air as they tangled, and the beast thrashed. Finally, the water went deathly still, and blood floated to the surface.

"It's swimming off," Skye reported after a moment.

"Come on, Dhara," Caia prayed, looking over her shoulder as she swam.

An eternity passed before Dhara's head burst through the surface and took a deep breath.

"Damn it, Dhara, you had me worried," Caia called to her.

"*You* were worried? How do you think *I* felt?" Dhara replied between gulps of air.

"I don't know… annoyed, inconvenienced… whatever it is you feel when you dive into the thick of things without thinking."

Dhara laughed a rare laugh and swam back to her sister to continue helping guide Calix's sled to the far shore.

They assembled onshore, and Jarom started a fire. "We've got to warm Calix up, or he'll catch his death of cold," he explained.

Dhara looked at him like he'd made a terrible joke, but he kept a straight face, so she threw up her hands and looked around for firewood.

"I might as well have a look around before dusk," Kala declared, observing that they seemed to be setting up camp for the night.

"I'll join you," Forest offered.

"I'm fine on my own," Kala refused gently. "See if you can find any game. It's been scarce on the plains."

"Can I come?" Skye asked Kala.

"Sure," she replied.

Forest looked scandalized, so Skye smiled and quipped, "Sometimes, it pays to be useless."

Forest grabbed her bow and tramped off.

"I'll keep watch in case that thing comes back," Hawke told Kala. She nodded and gestured for Skye to follow her.

She headed toward the densest ruins, looking for signs of the rock formation from which they could hail an airship. Skye tapped her on the shoulder.

"Is that what we're looking for?" he asked, pointing to a low-flying airship in the distance.

"No," she replied, then paused. "Wait a moment... what's it doing here? Let's follow it."

"It's heading right for us," he pointed out.

"I meant intercept it," she said, shaking her head.

"Oh, sure – we can do that," he replied bashfully and joined her in running toward it.

It drifted lower, and Kala sped up to be there when it landed. Skye could barely keep up with her as she raced through the ruins. It moved out of sight behind a massive structure that had toppled onto its side. Kala spotted an opening underneath it and ducked through. She came to a sudden halt on the other side, facing the airship as it touched down in the middle of an enormous circle, surrounded by the familiar stone pillars. Skye skidded to a stop behind her and watched as the ship moored itself.

"There has to be someone on board," Kala observed, pulling out a sword.

The door slid open, and a monk emerged, flanked by two priestesses carrying crossbows. The monk stared at Kala, disregarding Skye completely.

"Brother Grey?" Kala asked incredulously.

The monk smiled and drew his sword.

26

Soren

Soren paced among the ruins of the smoldering city, with Cera at his side and an entourage of guards surrounding them. Tendrils of smoke drifted skyward from all corners of the city as they stepped over the rubble that lay in the street. Soren strode through it, oblivious to the carnage. Soldiers rounded up survivors and pressed them into service, dragging the dead into huge piles to be burned. Cera did her best not to retch.

Lennox poked his head out a doorway and called Soren over. "This used to be the council hall," he told Soren as they entered. The main room appeared to have been the scene of intense fighting. The council table was overturned and peppered with arrows. Mercifully for Cera, the bodies of the dead had been removed, although blood stained the carpets that littered the floor.

Soren strode over to a chair, righted it, and sat down wearily. Cera stood near the overturned table and brushed her fingers along the feathers of the arrows protruding from it, wondering if each arrow counted for a life lost in this room.

"Leave us," Soren ordered his men. "I wish to talk with my new companion."

His men filed out dutifully and took up positions outside the room's entrances and exits, still within hearing distance, but this was what served for privacy in Soren's world.

Cera turned and stared at her captor, who sat casually in a city that lay burning by his hand. "Why me?" she asked.

"Easy," he replied. "I'm surrounded by people who would sell their soul for the right price and then double-cross you to avoid paying the debt. When I first saw you outside the city gates, I can't lie that it was your beauty that I first noticed, but on closer inspection, I saw you cradling a wounded man and shielding a young woman, both of whom you obviously care for deeply. Call me foolish, but it reminded me that there is still good in the world, and I intend to rebuild it on that."

"But not before torching it," she countered.

"Sometimes, you have to shit in the fields to make the plants grow."

Cera looked appalled.

"So, you're not a farmer," he mused. "And you've clearly never eked out an existence on the barren soil of the northlands."

"So, you had a hard life," she challenged him. "That's more than can be said for the people of this city, whose lives you took entirely."

"In my defense, it's not easy to reign in the northerners when they're sacking a city."

"That's no excuse," she said flatly. She surreptitiously snapped the shaft of an arrow, pulled the arrowhead out of the wood, and slid it into her pocket, emerging from behind the table to walk over to Soren.

"What if I refuse to keep your company as you set the world on fire?" she asked.

"That's your right, but I'd be greatly pleased if you would. I don't want to be your jailer." He paused and thought. "You care about the girl at the gate, do you not? The blonde?"

Cera thought of Lily and bristled. "Leave her out of this."

"I intend to. Stay with me, and I'll make sure that no harm befalls her. Refuse, and I won't guarantee her safety. That's the deal I'm offering you."

"You can protect her?"

"You say that I'm the one she needs protection from, so yes."

Cera thought about it a moment before deciding. "Okay, I'll stay, but I will not give myself to you willingly."

"It is enough that you brighten the darkness that surrounds me," he replied exhaustedly, then called, "Guard." One of his men returned to the room, and Soren instructed him to show Cera to his tent. "See to it that she has a cot and is well fed."

The guard nodded to Soren and gestured for Cera to follow the man. As she was escorted out of the room, Soren called after her, "You can throw away the arrowhead. You're not an assassin."

She reached into her pocket, pulled it out, and handed it to the waiting guard. He tossed it aside and guided her away.

Lennox poked his head in the doorway.

"Gods-damn it, Lennox – you elevate lurking to an art form."

"Thank you, sir," he said.

"That wasn't a compliment."

Lennox simply smiled through yellowed teeth. "I have a captive with information that might interest you."

"I don't have the stomach for one of your interrogations tonight. Can you just summarize the good parts?"

"Of course, sir," Lennox replied, miffed at not being able to share his interrogation skills with someone who, while he might disapprove of them, at least appreciated them. "The man says that he comes from a city on the east coast called Bayre. He says that it has an airfield with a hundred airships. We might have found their source at last."

"That is good news," Soren replied, unaccustomed to it. "Can we reward the bearer of this good news with his life?"

Lennox looked uncertain. "I'll see what I can do," he replied hesitantly.

"Damn it, Lennox – do you have to kill everyone you question?"

Lennox simply shrugged, and Soren shook his head.

"While I have you here, I have an assignment for you," Soren told him. "The girl we let go, my so-called Scourge – I want her dead."

"Then why didn't we just kill her when we had her in our hands?"

"It was more important to kill what she stands for than to kill her."

"I don't follow."

"Letting her live tells the world that I didn't think her enough of a threat to dispatch. By letting her go, I diminished her, and word will spread to this effect. The foolish hope she gave those we haven't yet crushed will be snuffed out. That's more important than her life. But now that that's been accomplished, there's no point in letting her continue to live."

"My thoughts exactly, sir."

"Then we agree. Have her tracked down and executed however you see fit. Feel free to extinguish her entire party. They're irrelevant, so do with them as you wish." Then, remembering his promise to Cera, corrected himself. "Except for the blonde. Don't touch the blonde. Understood?"

Lennox agreed, and Soren wondered if the man could be trusted to practice restraint, but he was the best tool available for the job, despite his crudeness.

"Dismissed," Soren told him and turned to stare out the window at the burning city. *Bayre*, he thought.

Lennox left Soren and made his way across the city to the temple grounds – that would be the most likely place for him to find his assassin. He walked through the shattered gates of the temple and looked for the building in which the monks would perform their devotions. He spied a tall building and judged it a reasonable place to start looking.

Entering, he looked up at the light filtering in through the black and grey stained glass set high in the ceiling. *At least it survived the sack of the city*, he thought. He stared at it for a moment, musing that people thought he only savored destroying things, but that wasn't true – there were other things he appreciated. In particular, he felt that the monks who worshipped death were kindred spirits.

"Are you going to stand there all day?" a voice mocked him.

Lennox looked about for its source and spied a man lounging in a pew. "Roml," he greeted him. "I thought I might find you here."

"At your service," the man replied.

Lennox sat down beside him and looked around at the wreckage of the room. "Weren't you once a monk?" he asked.

"Freelancing pays better," Roml replied. "Besides, a man should have occasion to ply his trade."

"Which is killing people?"

"It sounds so crass when you say it out loud."

"Well, I have a job for a man with your skills."

"Thank the gods – all this butchery lacks subtlety. What do you need?"

Lennox began describing Kala.

Roml sat back, and his eyes glinted darkly as he took it all in.

27
Kala

Brother Grey advanced toward Kala, sword in hand, while the two priestesses casually raised their crossbows.

Kala pulled her second sword from her back and strode toward him. "Not the reunion I'd imagined," she said out loud, raising her swords into a defensive position.

Skye took a step forward, and the priestesses pointed their bolts at his chest.

"Stand down, Skye," Kala called over her shoulder, never taking her eyes off Grey.

Grey didn't break stride as he raised his sword arm and sliced through the air where her head had been, had she not ducked and stepped aside.

"Glad to see you, Kala," she said in her best impression of Grey's voice.

He swung at her again, and she dodged the strike.

"Glad to see you too, Brother Grey," she replied to herself conversationally.

He feinted a slash and instead smashed his pommel into her side.

She wheezed and clutched her side, stepping back out of his range.

"Kala!" Skye called, concerned.

"Stay back," she warned him.

"Ignore him. He's not here," Grey told her.

"He speaks," Kala mocked and raised her swords again, grimacing at the pain in her side.

Grey resumed his attack, and Kala parried, then pressed him with one of her own. He deflected it easily, and when she overextended herself, he shoved her roughly off her feet. "Too slow," he concluded.

"Piss off," she spat as she regained her footing.

He waved her forward, and she answered with a blinding series of slashes.

"Faster," he commanded as he dodged and parried each thrust.

She attacked, and he fell back, then swung unexpectedly and cut open a wound across her thigh. She winced and staggered forward, favoring her other leg, but lifting her swords and waving him forward.

He stepped toward her purposefully and slashed at her repeatedly.

She dodged every blow, despite her wound screaming at her. She tamped down the pain, locked it away deep inside, and resumed her attack.

He spun on a misdirect and smashed her full in the face with his elbow.

She staggered back, spitting blood. "If you ruin my good looks," she smiled through bloody teeth, "I'll never forgive you."

He moved toward her, but she cleared her mind and gave herself over entirely to her anger – every hurt, every defeat – she embraced them all and roared toward him. They met in a clash of steel, and sparks flew off the edge of their blades. They moved so closely and so quickly that Skye couldn't follow their movements; he just stared slack-jawed and helpless.

Kala moved inside Grey's striking range, dropped her swords, grabbed his sword hand, twisted the weapon free of his grip, and held its point to his throat. The world caught up to her, and she came crashing back into her body to find herself holding Grey pinned against a pillar, his own sword at his neck.

He raised his hands in surrender and slowly pushed the sword point away from his throat.

She knew that he was just as dangerous unarmed, but for some reason, she let him.

"Glad to see you, Kala," he said.

"Glad to see you, too, Brother Grey," she replied and lowered his sword, spitting blood. "What the hell was that all about?" she asked, handing him back his sword.

"Kala!" Skye cried. "What are you doing?"

"Thank you," Grey replied and slid the sword back in his scabbard. "Kala, huh?" he asked.

"That's what my friends call me," she replied.

"Okay, Kala," he began, trying out the sound of her name. "I was just testing you."

"What the hell for?" she asked and waved Skye over.

"Just checking to see if you deserved my help."

"If that's your idea of help, I can live without it," she said and turned to pick up her swords.

Skye walked up, and Brother Grey held out his hand. Skye stared at it in disbelief.

"It's okay, Skye. This is Brother Grey. He has questionable ways of expressing his friendship, but he's not the enemy."

"Are you sure?" Skye asked.

"Can anyone be?" Kala replied for Grey.

"You're learning," Brother Grey observed happily.

Kala glanced over at the priestesses, prompting her to tease Grey, "Quite the ladies' man, aren't you?"

He looked at her blankly.

"Come on," she complained. "That was funny. You could stand to loosen up a bit." He didn't look like it was in him, so she asked instead, "What are you doing here?"

"Looking for you – obviously," he replied.

"Obviously," she laughed. "Obviously, I'd be hanging out on this windswept plain, and you just thought you'd pop in for a visit."

"You leave a trail that's pretty easy to follow. Bodies and all."

"Okay, I'll give you that – but why were you looking for me?"

"To offer my help," he repeated.

"What makes you think I need your help?"

"Come on – We both know the force arrayed against you. You can use any and all help."

"All right, I'll give you that too, but I thought the Church was decidedly non-interventionist in these matters."

"It is, but I'm not so sure it should be."

"I thought you were a believer, Grey."

"I am. That's the point. I'm beginning to think that the Priestess's agenda diverges from the Church's." He let her absorb this. "Do you remember your prophecy?" he asked.

She rolled her eyes. "How can I forget it?"

"You never read it too closely, I imagine, or the original for that matter."

"And?"

"The prophecy says that the girl, that's you…"

"I get it, Grey," Kala interjected impatiently.

"The prophecy says the girl will not be beaten. Hence my little test. If I could best you, then you're clearly not her."

"I could have saved you the trouble," Kala replied. "I'm not her."

"I beg to differ."

"Well, everyone's entitled to their opinion, I guess. So, tell me how you can help."

"Everything in time," he replied, annoyingly cryptically, as usual.

"You frustrate the hell out of me, Grey," she concluded.

He smiled a rare smile. "Want to take me to meet your friends?"

She sighed. "Follow me," she said and led him back through the ruins toward the river, favoring her uninjured leg. She looked over her shoulder at the airship.

"It's not going anywhere," he assured her and pulled an amulet from under his collar.

"You look good in jewelry," she teased and led onward.

They arrived back at the shoreline just as the sun was beginning to set. Kala limped forward, with Skye on one side and Grey on the other, the two priestesses following behind.

Hawke took one look at Kala's bloody face and hurled a dagger at Grey's head. He caught it deftly and handed it to Kala.

"It's okay, Hawke," she told him wearily and tossed him his dagger.

"Who are these people?" Hawke asked.

"I'm not sure I can call them friends, but I don't think they're enemies," she replied.

"Well, that doesn't really help, then, does it?" Hawke replied.

"Hawke, this is Brother Grey. Brother Grey, Hawke."

Grey waved a curt greeting, and Kala introduced the rest of her party. She inclined her head toward the two silent priestesses. "Their names?" she asked Grey.

"Priestess," Grey replied.

"Helpful, as always," she commented drily.

Forest returned with a brace of prairie dogs and was stunned to see the newcomers. "We have company?" she observed.

"Yes, we do," Jarom replied. "Can I help you with those?" he asked, gesturing to the prairie dogs.

"Sure," she replied, shrugging them off her shoulder. "They're stupider here," she said, mostly to herself, and Jarom smiled as he took them from her and waved Nara over to help.

Skye looked at the small supply of wood and felt guilty for having gone off with Kala rather than helping. "I'll gather more wood," he suggested.

"Good idea," Jarom replied and tossed him an axe that landed at his feet, making Skye flinch despite himself. "You'll need that," Jarom said and returned his attention to skinning a prairie dog.

Skye picked up the axe and looked about for the nearest woods. Caia pointed over his shoulder, and he smiled his thanks.

"I'll join you," Grey offered. One of Jarom's cousins handed him an axe as well, and Grey walked over to Skye, running his finger along the blade. He noticed Calix and paused. "One of you is hurt."

"Yes," Kala admitted sadly.

Grey waved over the priestesses. "Help him," he ordered and turned back to Skye, hefting his axe. "Ready?" he asked.

Skye nodded, and the two of them headed toward a copse of trees.

The priestesses approached Calix and began removing his bandages.

"Don't," Dhara intervened, but they ignored her.

Caia had to restrain her sister, saying, "Let them see what they can do. They surely can't make things worse at this point."

Dhara relented, and the women continued their examination.

"Heat some water," one of them instructed Caia, judging her the more reasonable of the two sisters. She judged correctly as Caia grabbed Jarom's helmet and carried it to the river, returning and placing it in the fire.

"Do you know how hard it is to clean that thing?" Jarom complained.

"So, bring a bucket next time," Caia replied but did so lightheartedly. Once the water boiled, she brought it over to the waiting priestess, who removed the poultice and cleaned the wound. "This probably saved his life," she said to herself, and Dhara relaxed somewhat.

The second woman pulled jars and vials from the folds of her tunic and applied them to the entry and exit wounds. She pulled a roll of fresh bandages from another pocket and redressed the wound.

"You wouldn't happen to have any spirits with you in those magic pockets of yours, would you?" the man who'd lent Grey an axe joked.

The woman pulled a small flask from inside her tunic and tossed it to him.

"By the gods," he declared, staring at it, then dropping to one knee. "Marry me, fair maiden."

Nara shoved him over, and he rolled away laughing, taking the flask with him.

Forest and Jarom began roasting the prairie dogs and had just thrown the last log on the fire when Grey appeared carrying a fresh armful of wood. He dropped it beside the fire and brought the axe back to the man who'd lent it to him.

"Where's Skye?" Kala asked, concerned.

Grey shrugged as he handed the axe back.

"Here I am," Skye called out, emerging from the dark into the light of the fire. "Grey is inhuman," he said.

Kala laughed, and Grey looked at her critically.

"I mean, I could barely keep up with him," Skye corrected.

"No," Kala corrected, "you were right the first time." She smiled, and Grey rolled his eyes.

Grey conferred with his companions quietly, then sat down beside Kala. "Your friend is not doing well," he said of Calix quietly enough that only she could hear.

"I figured," she replied. "He took a sword clean through the shoulder. We're not giving up on him, though."

"I fear you're wasting your time."

Kala didn't have time to respond before Forest announced that dinner was ready. She just got up and joined the others fireside. One of Grey's companions passed around some cheese and dried fruit, and a little bit of strength returned to each of them. They lay down to sleep that night more content than they'd been in a long while.

Kala balled up her tunic as a pillow and prepared to close her eyes when she noticed Hawke sitting awake, keeping an eye on her. "Get some sleep," she told him.

He looked over at Grey, who had retired with his companions, and replied, "I don't trust him."

"I don't trust him either, but until he gives me a reason not to accept his offer of help, I'm going to take it at face value."

"Forgive me if I don't share your optimism."

Kala laughed. "If only you knew," she replied and closed her eyes.

She woke to find that Hawke had fallen asleep sometime in the night, and she was thankful for it. She joined Grey, who was staring out across the river.

"You're being followed," he told her.

She stared where he was staring. "What do you see?"

"I don't see it – I feel it," he replied and turned back to the fire. "It doesn't matter," he added. "We're not staying."

Kala asked for everyone's attention. "We're leaving by airship to find allies. Think hard about who we can ask. In the meantime, follow me," she said and led them to the ship.

As promised, the airship that Grey had arrived in still sat on the dais, surrounded by rocky pillars.

Dhara placed a hand on Kala's shoulder. "You can make these things go wherever you want?" she asked.

"More or less. Why?"

"I know where to get help for Calix," she replied.

Kala tamped down the hope that rose in her. Dashed hope was crueler than any injustice she'd endured. She looked skeptically at Dhara.

"Doesn't he deserve the attempt?" Dhara asked. All the times he'd offered his hand to help Kala up flashed before her, and she couldn't disagree. Dhara read it in her eyes. "Then trust me," she said to Kala's silence.

"Okay," Kala consented. "Where do you need to go?"

"Home," she replied.

Kala pulled out her journal and opened the page to her well-worn map. "Where's home?"

Dhara stared at it, and Kala pointed out the location of the city they'd just left. Dhara traced her finger over the map. 'I think this was the river we took north, so my village is one of these points," she concluded.

"Okay," Kala replied, pulling out her amulet, explaining how it functioned, and handing it to her.

Dhara took it and embraced Kala firmly. "Where do we meet back up?" she asked.

Kala turned her map around and pointed to the star on the east coast. "Here," she said. "Bayre."

Dhara and Caia pulled Calix's sled to the airship, while Kala explained to Grey that Dhara would take this ship, and they'd hail another one. He nodded his assent as Dhara and Caia helped Calix aboard. Dhara waved from the doorway.

"Good luck and gods' speed," Kala called to her.

Dhara closed the door, and the ship lifted off.

Kala looked around for a signal stone, but Grey waved her off. "Already called one," he told her.

Kala counted the number of people in her party. "Are we all going to fit?" she asked.

"I called a big one," he replied.

"How?" she asked.

He just pointed at the nearest pillar, and Kala noted that he'd placed two signal stones against it.

"Of course," she concluded. "How stupid of me not to have thought of that."

He placed a hand on her shoulder kindly and turned to confer with his colleagues. He stopped and turned back to her. "There's somewhere I must take you, but we've got to drop these people off first."

"I suppose that if I asked you where you wanted to take me, you'd just say, 'All things in time.'"

"I told you that you're smarter than you look," he smiled and walked away.

A large airship drifted into view, and everyone watched it float closer. It landed, and Kala stepped forward to open the door. Jarom's kin seemed uncomfortable boarding it, so he reassured them as he shepherded them inside.

Kala dialed in Bayre, and Grey closed the door.

28

Dhara

Caia looked nervously out the window of the airship. "We're *really* high up," she informed her sister and gripped the window frame a little tighter, despite the coldness of the metal. Her hands smarted, but she felt compelled to brace herself.

"You've been in an airship before," Dhara reminded her.

"And how well did that turn out for me then? Besides, there were no windows in that one."

"It wasn't the height that caused you grief," Dhara said, "It was the woman trying to plunge a dagger into your heart."

"Only because the airship didn't get me first," Caia countered.

Dhara rolled her eyes, annoyed that her sister was arguing with her attempts to reassure her. She looked around at her surroundings instead. The main compartment was more spacious than she thought it would be from the outside, but it still felt confining. The height didn't bother her – she reveled in being off the ground, the higher the better – but the tight space unnerved her. She had to admit that perhaps they were both on edge, and that's why they were arguing.

She looked down at Calix, who lay with his head across her lap. Her sister had raised an eyebrow at this, but she'd told her, "I can't very well lay his head on the cold floor." She grazed the stubble of his chin as she felt for his pulse, which she'd done a hundred times. It felt fainter every time. *Hang in there*, she thought. *I never asked for this*, she reminded herself, *but a debt is a debt.*

Every time she closed her eyes, she saw his expression as he stepped between her and the swordsman that ran him through. She found herself absentmindedly stroking his hair, and it irked her that her subconscious had a gentle side. She looked up to see her sister watching her from the window.

"You like him," Caia stated plainly.

"I do not… I don't dislike him… I just don't like him the way you think I like him," Dhara replied.

"Whatever you say," Caia said and turned back to look out the window.

Dhara thought about the night that she and Calix had spent together before Soren's attack. She'd assumed she just needed the release he'd provided her, but now, staring down at his face, she wondered. *Hang on,* she wished again, this time a little more ardently.

She fiddled with the amulet around her neck. She didn't believe in magic, so she had a hard time believing that the talisman was guiding them home. Dhara blinked at the sun's brightness when it lanced through the window over Caia's shoulder as the airship spun toward it. "This thing had better not plop us down in broad daylight. I don't imagine mother would be happy to see us. Plus, what would we do with him," she added, gesturing to Calix, "if we have to fight our way free of mother's guards?"

"I was thinking about that," Caia replied. "Kala's necklace is bringing us there, right?"

"That's what she said," Dhara confirmed.

"So, if we're not ready to land, maybe you could tell it to go somewhere else for a little while until it gets dark."

"I guess so," Dhara replied skeptically, not wanting to play with the magical device.

"I'm keeping an eye out for any sign that we're nearing home or descending, so I'll let you know if it's too soon."

"And I thought you just liked the view," Dhara teased, remarking on Caia's death-grip on the window frame.

"Funny," she replied and kept up her vigil.

The airship drifted for a long time before Caia reported, "We're running parallel to a river, and I swear the ship is a little closer to the ground, but it's getting darker out, so it's hard to tell."

"If it is home, then at least we'll land at night," Dhara replied, relieved not to have to experiment with the amulet.

A little time went by, and Caia concluded, "We're definitely landing, and the bends in the river look a lot like the ones downstream from our village." She stepped away from the window and rubbed her hands together to warm them up.

Dhara lowered Calix's head gently to the floor, rose, and stretched out her stiff muscles. She looked out the window, but it was pretty dark outside. "How could you see anything out there?"

"It got dark gradually, so I didn't notice," Caia replied, shrugging. "Do you figure there's still just one guard at the landing pad?" she asked.

"I don't see why that would have changed."

"Good," Caia decided as the ship landed with a faint thump that they could feel through the floor. "It'll surprise her when a ship lands at night."

"I'm counting on it," Dhara whispered, listening at the door.

They heard the sound of someone outside.

Dhara waited until the door began to open, then shoved it with all her strength. It flew open, smashing into the person opening it. Dhara jumped out at the ready, only to see the guard lying on her back, out cold, her nose broken and leaking blood.

Caia peeked out. "Isn't that Sari?" she asked.

"Looks like it," Dhara replied, rolling her out of the way. "I never liked her," she added.

"I can see that," Caia replied sarcastically, returning to the airship to help with Calix. Together, they carried him out of the ship. "He weighs so little," Caia declared worriedly.

"Lucky for us," Dhara replied, masking her concern.

Caia paused, midway off the platform.

"What is it?" Dhara asked, annoyed and shifting Calix's weight.

"What do we do about the ship?" Caia asked, gesturing at it with her eyes.

"Good point. It'll draw attention in the morning. Hmm." She lowered Calix to the ground and pulled out the amulet. She spun the outer dial incrementally, but nothing happened. She pressed the center button, and the airship detached and drifted upward. "Problem solved," she declared and bent to pick Calix back up by his shoulders.

They carried him off the dais and onto the surrounding wooden planking, breathing in the muggy jungle air and tasting the sweet scent of tropical flowers. Dhara looked longingly at the stairs leading up to the platforms set high in the trees and sighed. "We should stick to the ground," she concluded.

Caia followed Dhara's lead as they carried Calix toward the far side of their village. They could hear voices and footsteps above them and moved slowly to be as quiet as possible. They froze when they heard their mother's voice. She was speaking to a companion about someone Dhara didn't know, but neither she nor her sister desired to stay and learn more – they hugged the tree trunks and moved off until their mother's voice faded into the sounds of the jungle.

"How much farther?" Caia whispered, her sore muscles crying out.

"Not much," Dhara replied and tried her best to recall the path to the healer's cottage. She wasn't very familiar with the ground below the village, but she remembered her father's taking her there once when she was young and had broken her arm in a fall. Dhara had resisted any care, but he'd overruled her objections and took her to the healer anyway. The way seemed to elude her, but she followed her intuition whenever the path forked.

They were rewarded by the sight of candlelight flickering in a cottage window, and something about it sparked a memory in Dhara. "I think that's it," she declared.

They hefted Calix up for what they hoped would be the final stretch and carried him to the cottage door, where Dhara shifted her weight to knock. The door swung open, and Dhara found herself looking into the eyes of the slave that she'd shoved out of her way so many moons ago. His eyes went wide when he realized who was standing before him.

"What are you doing here?" she asked him rudely, expecting the healer and no one else.

"I live here," he replied indignantly. "What are *you* doing here? Aren't you banished?"

She ignored his impertinent questions. "Get out of the way," she grumbled, pushing past him. "I have business with the healer."

They carried Calix through the doorway and into a room dimly lit by candles and filled with the smell of drying herbs. The small voice of an old woman called from across the room, "Put her down here."

"Her?" Dhara asked, confused. "Our wounded colleague is a man."

"I wasn't expecting that," the voice said. "My vision said it was your sister that was wounded."

"She's dead," Dhara replied bitterly. "As will be this man if we spend all night chatting about the dead."

"The dead deserve to be remembered," the woman brushed off Dhara but continued, "Put *him* down over here."

They carried Calix to the small bed that the crone gestured to from her seated position beside it and laid him down.

"Bad," she concluded after the most cursory glance. "Very bad." Dhara was about to put the woman in her place, but she shushed her. "Quiet," the woman commanded and started unwrapping Calix's bandages. "Daryn, put some water on to boil."

"Yes, grandmum," the man who'd opened the door replied and turned to rummage in the kitchen.

"Do you remember the look of blind wort?" the old woman asked Dhara.

"Of course," Dhara replied.

"Then fetch some," she said, looking back down at Calix. "Your sister can join you or wait outside."

Dhara grumbled but did as she was told. "Stay near him," she said to her sister and headed out into the jungle to look for the plant.

Caia sat down just outside the door while Dhara turned her attention to the search for the pungent smell of blind wort. It smelled of rotting flesh, but that was surprisingly hard to distinguish from the cloying scents of the jungle. She had to hunt quite far afield before she found some. She carried it back to the cottage and through the door.

"Here it is," she announced to the old woman, who was blowing the smoke of some burning herb into Calix's nostrils as he took shallow breaths.

"Put it on the counter," the healer ordered without looking up.

"Don't you need it?" Dhara asked, turning toward the counter to lay it down.

"No. But if I'd let you stay, you wouldn't have given me a moment's peace," she replied.

Dhara slammed the plant down and contemplated punching the woman, but she was busy with Calix, so she reined herself in and stormed outside to join her sister, sitting down beside her while Caia suppressed a laugh.

"Don't," Dhara warned her.

Daryn walked out the door after her and sat down with his back to a tree across from Dhara.

This slave has balls, she thought, staring into arrestingly familiar eyes.

"You don't recognize me, do you?" he declared haughtily.

"Of course I recognize you," Dhara replied, remembering shoving him out of her way outside her mother's quarters before she was banished.

"No, you don't," he concluded, smiling, then added, "Sis."

Caia froze, and Dhara narrowed her eyes, fixing them on his. It finally registered that his eyes were familiar because she saw them every time she looked into a mirror. *If this slave is ribbing me about my part-slave past, he'll be smiling through a throat slit from ear to ear*, Dhara decided, reaching for a dagger, but a flash of memory of the healer's cottage from her childhood stopped her. "You were here," she said in confusion.

"I live here," he reminded her.

"When..." she started.

"You broke your arm," he finished for her.

She couldn't speak. She simply breathed in and out as the information washed over her.

Caia stood up abruptly and walked over to him.

He rose to his feet defiantly as she stopped in his face.

She stared into his eyes, then slowly raised her arms and embraced him, which he bore awkwardly. "Brother," she said.

"How do we know?" Dhara asked skeptically.

"Dhara – you know it's true," Caia declared, releasing their brother and returning to sit beside her.

Daryn and Dhara stared at each other wordlessly until he told her, "I watched you grow up around your mother's chair. Do you know how hard that was, knowing that you were the reason your mother executed our father?"

Dhara had never wondered if the slave that her mother had had an affair with had other children. She felt guilty for never wondering about her father at all, just ruing that he was a slave.

"I'm sorry," Caia inserted for them both.

"*Your* little sister always was the conscience that *my* little sister never had," he concluded ruefully but thanked Caia.

"The healer?" Dhara asked.

"Your grandmother," he answered.

"She doesn't like me much," Dhara concluded.

"No one does," he replied.

"That's not fair," Caia objected on her sister's behalf.

Daryn just shrugged.

"I'm sorry," Dhara said.

"That no one likes you?" he asked.

"That I deserve it," she replied, got up, and stormed off to be alone.

He watched her walk away.

"She just needs time," Caia assured him.

The healer poked her head out of the door. "That's something we don't have," she said.

29

Kala

Once airborne, everyone staked out a spot. Kala and Skye sat down beside each other. Her injured leg still smarted, and her grimace made Skye frown at Brother Grey.

Jarom and his kin claimed the adjacent compartment. Nara poked her head through the opening and asked Forest to join her. "I saved a spot for you," she informed her hopefully.

Forest was torn. She knew that Nara grieved her brother, and Lily suffered from her separation from Cera. Forest desperately wanted to raise both their spirits.

"Go on," Lily shooed her away and sat down alone.

"May I?" Hawke asked, indicating the spot beside her. Lily smiled her assent, and he engaged her in light conversation.

Brother Grey moved closer to Kala and told her that before they headed to Bayre, they needed to stop at the city where the Priestess resides. "She has a book that'll guide us to allies, but she keeps it in a bookcase beside her bed, so we'll have to steal it."

Kala wondered how he knew what the Priestess kept beside her bed, but he didn't volunteer that information, and she didn't press him.

"The problem," he continued, "is that she's the most observant person I've ever met, and she would notice in a heartbeat if the book were missing."

"What if we replaced it with a book that looks just like it?"

"As I said, she'd notice even the most minor difference."

"I know someone who can create a facsimile good enough to fool her."

Skye overheard. "You're not thinking…" he began.

"Oh, yes – we're going to visit Eden," she cut him off.

Skye cringed inwardly at the prospect of being reunited with the girl he'd duped to get access to her maps, but he was man enough to see its necessity and kept quiet.

"We'll land at night, and hopefully, no one will notice that we're in town," Grey added.

"No one would blink at your return," Kala countered.

"The Priestess would want to know if I'd succeeded in my mission."

"And what is it?" Kala asked.

"To kill your boyfriend," he replied.

Skye moved a little closer to Kala.

"Don't worry," Grey reassured him. "I don't share her belief in the utility of killing you."

"Lucky me," Skye replied unconvinced.

Kala changed the setting on her amulet to their new destination, tucked it back inside her tunic, and snuggled into Skye, ostensibly to "protect" him she kidded.

Everyone rested as the airship completed the journey. As it drifted closer to the city that was the seat of the Church, they timed its landing for near midnight. On the ground, Grey peeked out the door. "No one is around," he confirmed, and their party filed out one by one after him. Grey sent his two priestess companions on errands that he didn't explain to the rest of them, then guided everyone else over a wall to a nondescript building beside the winery. "It's not the season for this building to be used, so we should go undiscovered here," he told them.

The room smelled pleasantly of mulled wine, so no one complained. A moment later, the door creaked open, and one of Grey's companions slipped in with an armful of bedrolls.

"Thank you for your thoughtfulness," Forest told Grey.

He nodded to her, and everyone found somewhere to lie down for the night. Skye slept fitfully, wondering if the inscrutable Brother Grey had really decided against killing him.

Kala awoke in the night to the sound of movement and opened an eye in time to catch Jarom slipping out. Curious as to where he might be going, she rose quietly and followed after him. She shadowed him at a distance as he walked purposefully down the deserted streets. He stepped into one of the tiny buildings marked as a shrine to the Goddess of Death that the town's citizens frequented. She hadn't thought him particularly religious, so despite her best judgment, she edged closer and peeked through the open door. She spied him kneeling before a statue of the Goddess, having lit three candles.

"You might as well join me," he said to the air. "She's your Goddess, isn't She?"

Kala was mortified that she'd been caught spying and had no choice but to enter and take a seat beside him. "The Goddess and I have a complicated relationship," she admitted, not understanding it herself.

"She's hard to fathom," he agreed. "She spared Forest's mother but took my brother as payment. She gave me a niece but took my son." Jarom's voice faltered at Ravi's mention. "She demands balance, and I try to accept it. Some days are just harder than others."

Kala thought about what he'd said while they knelt in silence. The Goddess had spared her repeatedly. *What's my price?* she wondered.

Jarom rose, placed a hand on her shoulder, and they walked back together, careful not to wake the others on their return.

In the morning, Kala borrowed the habit of one of Grey's priestess companions so that she could sneak a visit with Eden. She pulled up the hood, lowered her head piously, and headed to Eden's room. She stopped by the dining hall on the way and picked up a basket of fruit and cheese.

Arriving at Eden's apartment, she nodded to the guard stationed outside and knocked.

Eden opened the door a moment later, paint smudges on her fingers and cheeks. Her eyes went wide when she recognized Kala.

"The lunch you requested," Kala said and communicated with her eyes to play along.

"Thank you, but I didn't mean to make you bring it here, only to have it ready for me so I could bring it back with me. Would you like to come in and share it with me?"

"That's kind of you, but not necessary," Kala replied, her eyes communicating otherwise.

"Nonsense. I insist," Eden told her and whisked her inside, smiling at the guard as she did.

Ensuring the door was closed, she turned and hugged Kala fiercely, then guided her to the settee far away from the door. "What are you doing here?" she whispered once they'd sat down, holding hands.

"I'd like to say I'm just here to visit, but I have a favor to ask."

"Anything."

"Can you copy the exterior of a book if I brought it to you?"

"Of course. How close a copy?"

"An exact replica," Kala admitted sheepishly.

"Ooh, okay. That's tougher, but it can be done if I have the right supplies. What can you tell me about the book?"

Kala gave her all the details that Brother Grey had relayed to her.

"I'll have to pick up a blank manuscript from the library, but that would be noticed because the project I just started doesn't require one," Eden told her.

"I might be able to help with that," Kala told her. "I'll stop there and get as close a replica as I can from Tallie."

"You'll have to show her the book you want copied, and she'll know something fishy is going on."

"That's a chance I'll have to take," Kala concluded. "I think Tallie likes me, so I hope that counts for something." She looked at her friend and wiped a smudge of paint off her nose. "By the Goddess, it's good to see you," she said.

Eden leaned in and hugged her again. "I want to know everything about your adventures since you left."

Kala shifted uncomfortably. "I went to Bayre, the city marked as 'capital' on your maps." She paused, not sure how to say the next part. "I met Skye there," she finally confessed.

Eden stiffened but tried to mask it by rolling her shoulder muscles as if to loosen them. "That's good," she lied. "Is he here?" she asked.

"He is," Kala admitted.

"Please don't bring him here. I'd die of embarrassment."

Kala took Eden's hands in hers. "He's *so* sorry, Eden. I think he'd die of embarrassment before you would."

"Well, that makes me feel better," Eden said through a smile. "Although it probably makes me a terrible person."

"Hardly. He was a jerk, and he knows it. You're one of the most wonderful people I know. Sometimes when my life goes to hell, I cling to a picture of you in my mind, and I remind myself why I don't just curl up in a ball and hide from the world."

"You're sweet," Eden gushed and turned to the fruit and cheese. "We can eat this, right? I'm starving."

"I'm famished too," Kala replied, and Eden took that as permission to cut up the fruit. They chatted while they ate their lunch. "I'd better be going," Kala said reluctantly and got up to go.

"I'll walk you out," Eden replied, equally sad to see her go. Eden opened the door for her while Kala flipped up the hood of her habit and stepped into the hallway. Eden stopped her and said loud enough for the guard to hear, "Thank you, priestess, that was a welcome diversion. I'll be illustrating a tricky part tomorrow, and I have precious little vermillion. Can I trouble you to bring breakfast and dinner to my room? I don't want to be a bother, but I don't think I can risk letting the paint dry out while I make the trek to the dining hall."

"It's no bother, miss," Kala replied. "What would you like?"

"Anything, I'm not particular, but something sizable enough that I can skip lunch."

"As you wish, miss," Kala replied, nodded to the guard, and walked away briskly as Eden resumed painting.

Kala returned to the building they were hiding in, but on the way, she was startled to see the Priestess striding across the temple grounds. She tried not to freeze, remembering Grey's warning about the Priestess's observing the slightest details. She continued walking nonchalantly, and soon the Priestess disappeared around a corner. Kala sighed in relief.

Entering the winery building, she told Grey, "I saw her. She's here."

"The Priestess?" Grey asked.

"Yes," she confirmed.

"That's not a problem. I assumed she'd be here. I scouted around, and I saw another of the oracles descend into the catacombs this morning. The Priestess will most likely take her turn at receiving prophecy tomorrow, and that will give us the better part of the day to exchange the book."

Kala filled him in on the details of her visit with Eden and her plan to obtain a blank manuscript from the head librarian tomorrow. He looked unhappy to be involving so many people. "Can't you just steal a blank book?" he asked.

"Probably, but I have no idea where Tallie keeps them, and she'd procure a better match if I asked her than if I did it behind her back."

Grey begrudgingly accepted her plan. They spent most of the day cooped up in the building while Grey's companions brought them things to replace what they'd left behind when they'd fled Soren's forces. Jarom's people were exceedingly grateful, especially when one procured a couple of bottles of wine, unasked.

By evening, despite the glow of a pleasant glass of wine, Kala couldn't stand to be confined any longer and grabbed Skye. "Let me show you the gardens."

Grey pursed his lips but didn't actually tell her it was a bad idea.

Kala led Skye on infrequently traveled paths until they arrived at the otherwise deserted gardens. "There was no one here the last time either," she observed, and led him to an out-of-the-way bench where they sat down, held hands, and took in the beauty around them.

"Eden wasn't too happy to learn that you're here," Kala told him.

"Why did you tell her then?" he complained.

"I'm not going to lie to her. I thought you realized the inappropriateness of that," she chastised him.

"Of course," he replied, "but it doesn't mean we have to tell her everything either."

"We didn't gossip about you like a couple of schoolgirls, if that's what you think."

"I don't think that – I just don't want to remind her of that episode."

"That's big of you."

"I'm serious. I was a heel, and *I* don't want to be reminded of it either."

"I like her," Kala told him. "I'm not going to avoid her just to make you feel better."

"That's not what I was suggesting. Oh gods, never mind. I'll just take my punishment as necessary."

"That's the attitude," Kala told him and leaned her head on his shoulder. "You really were a heel," she concluded, snuggling in.

"Thanks for letting me live it down," he replied, stroking her hair.

He leaned down and kissed her cheek. She shifted her position to meet his lips with hers. He took his time, each kiss an exploration. Her pulse quickened as he moved to kiss her neck. His hot breath in her ear sent a thrill up her spine, and a moan escaped her lips.

She rose quickly and spun to kneel across his lap, straddling him. He shifted under her as she took his head in her hands and kissed him passionately, running her fingers through his thick hair.

The creak of an opening gate made them freeze. Footsteps on gravel followed, and they reluctantly pulled apart and quietly fled the gardens. They returned to the building in the vineyards near dark, still flush and cursing the lack of privacy.

The next day, Kala and Grey woke early and headed to the Priestess's quarters but stayed as far away as they could and still see her leave. They busied themselves while waiting by pretending to prune a row of bushes. They didn't have to wait long before the Priestess left her quarters and headed for the catacombs.

Once she was out of view, they hurried to her room. Kala turned the knob and found it locked as she suspected it would be and pulled out a pin to pick the lock, but Grey pulled a key out of his pocket. "You're really going to have to tell me sometime what you're doing with a key to her chambers," she told him.

"Today is not that day," he told her and turned the key in the lock, opening the door. He moved around her bed to the bookshelf and carefully slid a book from between two others, handing it to Kala, along with the key. "Return the copy exactly as we found it, or she'll notice," he told her unnecessarily.

"Got it," she replied and hurried to the library, leaving Grey to lock up behind her.

She slipped through the main door of the library and headed straight for Tallie's office rather than to the front desk. She peeked her head in and knocked when she saw the head librarian bent over some records.

Tallie looked up, and her eyes widened with recognition. "What brings you by?" she asked warmly.

"I'm on a clandestine mission," Kala confided.

"The best kind," Tallie smiled conspiratorially and leaned back in her chair.

"I need to make an exact copy of a book, at least its exterior. Do you have a blank manuscript that's identical to the original?"

"Hard to say without seeing the book. Show it to me."

Kala handed her the book.

Tallie took it and looked over the spine. She turned it over to examine the front cover, then froze. "It's not possible," she said.

Kala was deflated.

"Oh, no, dear. I didn't mean it wasn't possible to make a copy. I can help you with that. I meant that it's not possible that they exist. They're a myth."

"Who's a myth?" Kala asked.

"You don't know? It's your book. Where did you get it?"

"The less you know, the better, but truth be told, I have no idea what's in that book."

"Then I'm not going to be the one to tell you." Tallie glanced at her supply cabinet, then rose. "I don't have anything here that would pass for the age of this book. Let me see what I've got in the back. Do you mind if I take it with me?"

Kala was nervous about letting the book out of her sight, but her instincts told her that she could trust the librarian. "By all means," she told her.

Tallie carried the book the way one might a priceless treasure or an explosive and headed into the back rooms while Kala waited in her office. Tallie re-emerged a moment later with a second tome that looked to be the same size, color and vintage. "This is the best I've got," Tallie told her.

"It looks perfect," Kala told her.

"I wish I could say that you're right. You're playing with fire with that book. Good luck."

Kala stepped around the desk and hugged her. "You're amazing," she told her and rushed out while Tallie sat back down, muttering to herself.

Kala swung by the dining hall and picked up some convincing breakfast food that she placed carefully on top of the books, which she'd hid under a napkin. She then rushed over to Eden's as quickly as she could without drawing attention.

She greeted the guard outside her door and knocked. Eden opened it quickly. "Just put it down on the table, priestess."

"As you wish, miss," Kala replied and entered her room, peeling the napkin back to reveal the hidden books.

Eden nodded and shooed her out. "Thank you, priestess."

"Would it be okay if I brought your dinner a bit before sundown?"

Eden cringed at the thought of having to do such intricate work in so little time but steeled herself for a demanding day. "That would be fine. Could I trouble you to take away the remains of breakfast when you return?"

"Not a problem, miss," Kala told her and took her leave. She swung past the dining hall again, selected a few foods that she thought her party would appreciate, then headed back to their hideout at the winery.

Kala burst in and seeing Grey sitting on his bedroll, cornered him. "What the hell is in that book?!" she asked.

"Tsk. Language," he chided her.

She looked over at her swords and seriously considered beating an answer out of him.

He sighed and motioned for her to sit close beside him, which she did reluctantly. "It's the history of the anti-Church, an order of fighting priestesses that doesn't share our orthodoxy. They're rumored to intervene in the world, but not the way the Church does when it prunes it back." He said it so cavalierly that Kala cringed. "It's widely believed they're a myth, but I know otherwise," Grey continued.

"How do you know?"

"The Priestess used to be one of them. None were her equal, but she didn't accept their philosophy, so she broke with them and came here. Why do you think she's so fearsome?"

"She doesn't seem so fearsome."

"She is. Don't you remember that I told you she was the one who trained me? Believe me when I say that 'fearsome' is an understatement."

"What have I dragged Eden and Tallie into?" Kala despaired.

"Our only hope, I assure you," he replied, but she was not reassured.

"If any harm befalls them, I'll hold you responsible."

"Without their help, harm will befall us all. It's only a matter of what manner of harm and how far in the future it does. We're trying to remedy that," he reminded her.

She got up and stalked over to the others.

"That didn't look like a friendly conversation," Skye observed.

She handed him some exotic fruit and cheeses. He took some and passed the rest along to the others.

"It's okay," Kala replied. "I just fear that I may have put Eden and Tallie in grave danger."

"That's not good," he agreed.

"Desperate times call for desperate measures," she sighed and took a bite of fruit herself.

Kala waited until near sundown, then headed out to see Eden. She grabbed a plausible dinner from the dining hall and went to her quarters. No sooner had she knocked than an exhausted Eden opened the door.

She nodded at the guard and shepherded Kala inside. "I'm beat," Eden told her. "Can you lay it out for me?" she asked and closed the door on the guard. She pulled Kala over near the balcony.

"Do you know what you brought me?" she asked Kala in terror.

"I'm so sorry, Eden. I wasn't told what it was until after I brought it here."

"If the forgery is discovered, my life is forfeit," Eden told her.

"I know. I'm sorry. Do you want me to take you away from here to safety?"

"I imagine that would raise suspicions."

"Probably," Kala had to admit.

"Then, you can't. I've been worrying about it all day. I'm trusting you with my life," she concluded and handed Kala the basket containing the books that she'd re-wrapped in the napkin and placed under the uneaten fruit and rolls.

Kala hugged her. "I'll do my best to merit that trust."

Eden opened the door for her. "Thank you for dinner, priestess, and for taking away what I didn't have at breakfast."

"My pleasure, miss," Kala replied and turned to go.

"Wait a moment," the guard stopped her.

Kala turned slowly to face him, and he beckoned for the basket. Kala held it out toward him, sliding a hand into the folds of her cloak to grasp a dagger. He reached into the basket and pulled out a pear. "I hope you don't mind, miss," he said to Eden.

"Not at all," she replied, relieved, and retreated into her room to calm her racing heart.

Kala nodded to the guard and withdrew as well. She felt in her pocket for the key to the Priestess's quarters and hurried there. She was crossing the commons when she spied Brother Grey shaking his head and motioning with his eyes toward the academic building. The Priestess was exiting, rubbing her temples.

Kala ducked into the doorway of the building that contained the Priestess's chambers, despite Grey's vehement objections. She raced for her door and opened it with the key as quickly as she could, stepping inside and locking it behind her. Hearing the Priestess's footsteps, Kala pulled the replicated book from the basket and slid it into place between its neighbors. As the Priestess turned the key in the lock, Kala placed the basket in her teeth and swung out the window. She ducked her head below the sill just as the door opened. She stayed deathly still, hanging on for dear life to the stone wall. She heard the Priestess moving about the room while praying she wouldn't be spotted clinging to the wall outside. She heard the Priestess sit down at her desk to transcribe her visions, so Kala shimmied quietly down the wall. Her arms shook from the effort, and she breathed heavily through her nose as she descended into the bushes below. Stepping out onto the grass, she turned to see Brother Grey talking to a pair of young monks, keeping their attention focused away from her.

She smiled at him and crept off toward the winery. Seeing her retreat, he released the young monks and stalked off after her.

Entering the building after her, he cornered her. "What were you thinking?" he demanded.

"Completing the mission," she defended herself.

"It was too dangerous," he seethed.

"What's done is done, and I really had no choice," she reminded him.

He grudgingly accepted, but he was more perturbed than she'd ever seen him, and it heartened her to know that it wasn't just for his sake that he worried.

Kala placed a hand on his arm. "Thank you for caring," she told him and handed him the book from her basket.

He took it and stalked off in a huff.

She smiled at his back.

Grey spent the night studying the book. In the morning, he told her that they needed to head north of Bayre.

"That's as good a place as any to go," she replied. "We'll deposit Lily in the city with a friend of mine." She looked around the room. "Family meeting," she called out good-naturedly, and everyone gathered close around her.

"We're heading to Bayre," she started, then turned to Lily and Forest to add, "I have a friend there that I'd like you to meet."

"I'll go where I'm told," Lily responded. Her resignation since being separated from Cera broke Kala's heart a little more every day.

"I guess this is where we part ways," Jarom announced. In response to Kala's confusion, he clarified. "From what Skye tells me, there are horsemen on the plains northeast of here, and Thorvyn and I are going to go see if we can enlist them to our aid."

"They're brigands," Skye reminded him.

"Who's a brigand and who isn't is always just a matter of perspective," Jarom countered, and Skye rolled his eyes, signaling that it wasn't the first time they'd had that argument.

Forest took the opportunity to chime in. "I'm going with them." Lily pivoted to object, but Forest took her hand gently. "I'm going where I'm useful. Besides, I want to see the lands of the horsemen. Sorry, sis. I won't take any chances," she reassured her.

Lily hugged her. "I imagine that I couldn't stop you any more than I could stop the sun from rising. Promise me that you'll come back to me."

Forest returned her hug and stepped back beside Nara.

"Grey has arranged for horses," Jarom told them. "We'll leave immediately."

Kala shot Grey an accusing look for keeping her in the dark, but he just shrugged.

"I think this is where I get off, too," Skye added. Kala looked mortified, so he quickly explained, "We need allies, and I know people on the coast. I'm going to do my best to convince them to help us."

Kala started to protest, so he pulled her aside and whispered to her, "I can't live out this war in your shadow. Let me do this."

A tear ran down her cheek, and he wiped it away with his thumb and kissed her deeply. "This isn't goodbye," he repeated her words back to her.

She merely nodded, incapable of speech.

"Can I borrow your amulet?" he asked. "Dhara's got mine, and Grey needs his."

"Of course," she said and pulled it from under her collar to hand to him.

Hawke strode up. "I'll keep him safe," he assured her.

"You do that," Kala managed and hugged him.

She stepped back and looked at each person around the room. Their paths were decided, and their futures awaited.

"Gods' speed," Jarom concluded, and the party split up.

The airship in which Brother Grey, Kala, and Lily rode landed safely outside Bayre. "Safer than in the middle of town," Grey concluded. "Even if it is a bit of a hike back to the city."

They headed toward it, and Grey surprised Kala by leading them right to the hidden entrance to the tunnels that lay under the city.

"You've been here before," she observed.

"I've been a great many places," he replied and pushed back the vines for them to enter. He lit a torch once they were inside and led them under the walls of Bayre.

They emerged from a grate into an alley in a quiet part of town, and Grey turned the lead over to Kala.

"The last time I was here," she said, "my friends were relocating, so I'm not sure where they are now, but I have an idea of where to look." She led them to the tavern where she'd seen Celeste perform and asked the doorman, "Is Celeste performing anytime soon?"

"You're in luck," he replied. "She's on tonight."

Kala paid for their entrance, and she, Grey, and Lily sat at a table near the stage.

"Shouldn't we go see your friend backstage?" Grey asked, unsure why they weren't.

"I wouldn't miss hearing her sing for the world. Trust me. This will be magical."

Grey looked skeptical but acquiesced. Lily looked around the lounge, which was lit by a multitude of lanterns. Her inability to share the moment with Cera saddened her further.

They bided their time, sipping their drinks, Grey contenting himself with water. The band changed tempo, and a few lanterns were extinguished to dim the light.

"It's starting," Kala exclaimed, rubbing her hands together gleefully.

Celeste stepped out onto the stage and sat down gracefully on a stool. She canted her head and began to sing low and soulfully. Her voice rose and fell as she sang the story of star-crossed lovers.

Kala's heart swelled in her chest, and she drifted away on the melody until it ended, and she found herself settling back into her body.

"Amazing," Lily said, her cheeks wet with tears.

"Isn't she, though?" Kala agreed, squeezing Lily's hand.

Even Grey looked moved.

Kala rose to greet Celeste, who shrieked a hello, and leaped off the stage to hug her.

"Tell me everything," Kala demanded as Celeste sat down with them.

"Let's see," Celeste began. "Twill sold some paintings and bought Petr a new guitar. He was shaken up by the beating and from seeing you take out those guards, but he's bounced back okay. I don't see him as much since he moved out with his girlfriend."

"He has a girlfriend?"

"Much to Twill's chagrin. I think he was always sweet on Petr, despite their bickering. But he says heartbreak only fuels his art, and I have to admit, he's gotten quite good."

"Never mind them. What about you and your makeshift orphanage? What about the Resistance?"

Celeste chuckled. "It's still going strong, just elsewhere. Frey ran off to become a monk assassin. You had quite an effect on him."

Grey raised an eyebrow in her direction, but Kala didn't elaborate.

Kala took Celeste's hands in hers. "That's all wonderful, but how are *you*?" she asked earnestly.

"I'm well. I miss you and Skye, though," she admitted wistfully. "Can you stay this time?"

Kala shook her head sadly. "I can't, but if my friend Lily could, I'd be grateful."

"Is she an assassin too?" Celeste asked.

Lily spit out her drink "Sorry," she said, wiping her face with a napkin.

"No," Kala replied. "But she makes an impressive scone."

"I'm not sure that's quite equal, but any friend of yours is a friend of mine," Celeste declared magnanimously and reached across the table to hand Lily a second napkin.

Grey and Kala stepped out of the airship, surrounded by marsh as far as the eye could see, and were greeted by a plaintive wail carried on the wind.

"Why does it always have to be so creepy?" Kala asked.

"So we know we're in the right place," Grey replied.

30

Forest

Forest stroked the neck of her steed as they rode north. She loved the feel of the wind in her hair and the sensation when her horse surged forward. *I was made for this*, she thought. She breathed in the smell of the horses and the grasses they trampled. It felt clean and alive, not like the smell of the woods that closed around you and hemmed you in.

She looked beside her at Nara and Thorvyn, who rode side-by-side, then ahead at Jarom, who led them, and behind at the rest of their small party. They rode roughly northeast but occasionally veered off course to hunt for water. They found streams that would appear out of the ground and disappear just as quickly, and pools of water hidden in hollows. Thorvyn had a sense for these things, and he'd ride up alongside Jarom to advise him about the direction in which they should ride.

The plains rolled under their horses' hooves for days on end, and at night they'd shelter under the stars beside any copse of trees that could provide wood for a fire and a place to tie up their horses.

They hadn't seen any trace of the peoples rumored to inhabit the northeastern plains, and Forest began to wonder if they'd joined Soren in marching south or whether they existed at all. Jarom crested a rise in front of them and pulled his horse to a sudden stop. Forest was yanked from her daydreaming as she followed suit and halted beside him. Arrayed before of them was a force of a hundred riders with spears pointed at them. As the rest of Jarom's party crested the rise, the riders circled around until they were surrounded.

Jarom raised his hands in surrender, and the rest of the party followed suit.

One of the riders encircling them urged his mount forward. "Why do you trespass on our lands?" he asked.

Forest leaned over and whispered to Jarom.

"We'd like to talk with your leader," Jarom told the man politely.

"I am the leader," the man declared, "so talk."

"If it's all the same to you, we'd rather talk to your actual leader," Jarom repeated resolutely.

"Stand down, Gerald," a man called from behind the self-declared leader, and Gerald wheeled to rejoin the host. A younger man rode forward. "What makes you think that Gerald here isn't our leader?"

Jarom glanced at Forest, then turned to address the man. "My niece points out that everything about Gerald indicates that he's a man who rides to the right of the host."

"So?" the man asked impatiently.

"A leader rides in the middle. No offense to the man, but Gerald is no leader," Jarom concluded.

"Interesting," the man replied. "You heard him, Gerald," he laughed. "You're no leader." He turned back to Jarom. "I'm Jon, and I'm no more the leader of this bunch than that bush over there, but you pique my curiosity, so I'll take you to the person who actually is." He motioned his men to lower their spears and wheeled his horse toward the east.

Jarom spurred his horse to follow, as did the remainder of his party. The hundred riders spread out to enclose them in a loose circle that made it clear they were still at the horsemen's mercy. Jon guided them between two low hills into an encampment of hundreds more men and women moving around a cluster of tents that filled the hollow.

"We would have ridden right past them," Forest marveled to Jarom. "I wonder how many times we rode past similar groups."

314

Jon led them to a large tent and dismounted while his horse still trotted. He jogged to a stop in front of the tent's opening and called inside, "Cousin, we have visitors."

A moment later, a boy around Forest's age strode out into the daylight. He looked Jarom's party over. "Why shouldn't I have you killed where you sit?" he asked, bored.

Forest urged her mount ahead a pace. "I've got this," she told Jarom, who signaled his deferral. She turned to the speaker and declared, "Because then you'd never hear our stories of distant lands, and you'd go back to being bored."

He perked up. "I'm listening."

Forest shifted in her saddle. "That's piss poor hospitality," she declared. "At least offer me a drink, and we'll chat."

The boy stood shocked, and his riders shifted in their saddles. "This girl has bigger balls than a hundred plainsmen," the boy declared to his riders, then turned to Forest. "You've earned yourself and your friends a drink." He turned to Jon. "See to their mounts." Jon bowed low and strode forward to collect the reins of Forest's party's horses.

Forest, Jarom, Nara, Thorvyn, and the rest of Jarom's kin dismounted and followed the boy into his tent. It was surprisingly spacious, with tall poles supporting the ceiling. Cushions were stacked on pelts that covered the floor. An enormous lantern hung in the center of the tent, its light shining through myriad openings to create the illusion of a star-scape on the tent's ceiling.

He bade them sit down and instructed one of his men to fetch hot cider. He collapsed onto a pile of cushions. "Allow me to introduce myself," he said grandly. "I'm Addis."

"It is our pleasure to make the acquaintance of a horse-lord of the open plains," Forest replied. "I'm Forest, and this is Jarom, my uncle. The rest of our party are his kin or under his protection."

"Forest," Addis mused. "You're out of your element here on the plains."

"Not so much," Forest replied. "I was named Meadow at birth."

"Fancy that," Addis replied. "What brings you so far from your home to my lands?"

"We're seeking allies in the conflict that has embroiled the south. The barbarians of the northwest advance south and east, and we've been battling them."

Addis whistled his appreciation. A man handed Forest a tiny glass of hot cider in an intricately wrought holder, and she took a sip.

"Thank you for this," she lifted her glass to Addis.

"You're welcome," he replied, taking a sip from his own glass. "Why should the riders of the northeast concern themselves with the troubles of strangers to the south?"

"I'd say 'for mutual self-interest,' but I can tell that you feel no threat from the forces south of here, so instead, I'll say, 'for the glory of riding against a host larger than your own and immortalizing your name in song.' Isn't that what men of the plains live for?"

"I would say that you know us fairly well, Forest of the south, but there's plenty of glory right here."

"If you say so," she concluded and put down her glass. "Thank you for the drink, but I think we're done here," she said and strode to the tent flap.

"Wait," he called after her and rose from his seat, bidding Forest's compatriots to stay where they were. "Walk with me," he requested, joining Forest at the opening.

Forest waited as Addis called over his shoulder to his man. "Feed our guests," he ordered and exited with her.

Forest looked at Addis impatiently. "I don't mean to offend, but we need to be on our way. We have allies to find."

"Your friends need to eat. You have at least a little time," he pointed out.

"Every moment we delay, people die." She turned to look him in the eye. "I've seen villages put to the torch, my own among them. I've heard the cries of people I care about being cut down. I will not tolerate this to continue, even if I'm on a fool's errand."

"I admire your passion," he told her. "Please rejoin your friends at my table. I have things to take care of," he told her and strode off, leaving her alone.

She returned to the tent frustrated and sat down glumly beside Jarom. He handed her a terra cotta bowl containing a steaming dish of lamb and chickpeas.

"I think we're wasting our time here," she said bitterly.

"Perhaps, but you followed your instincts well. Do you think Addis will interfere with our leaving?"

"He likes to bluster, but he has no quarrel with us. He'll let us leave," Forest concluded. "But if we can't convince him to help us, I don't think we'll convince anyone. I think we need to return south and explore other options."

Jarom mulled it over. "I'll ask Thorvyn what he thinks, but it's getting late in the day. We wouldn't make it far tonight. I suggest we stay here tonight, if Addis allows it, and in the morning, go wherever we decide." He got up and left Forest chewing ruefully on her lamb.

In the morning, Jarom found Forest brushing her horse. "Thorvyn agrees with you. We ride south." He stalked off to tell the others while Forest saddled her horse.

When she was done, she went to Addis's tent to thank him for his hospitality, but he was nowhere to be found. *Figures*, she thought, and strode back to her horse, joining the others. No one seemed to object to their leaving, so they mounted and rode south.

Near midday, the horses needed a rest, so they stopped and dismounted. Thorvyn glanced north and called their attention to a cloud rolling in and the sound of distant thunder.

"That's not weather," Jarom declared and walked toward the roiling cloud of dust. Forest joined him.

A wall of armed riders crested the hill, chasing them down. Jarom put his arm on Forest's shoulder. Addis rode out of the pack and reared his horse to a halt in front of them. "Which way to glory?" he asked.

31
Kala

Kala and Grey stepped out of the airship onto the marshes. Off the dais, it was hard to spot solid land, so they had to be careful where they stepped to avoid getting sucked into the bog.

"Which direction?" Kala asked.

Grey scanned the horizon. "That way," he said, pointing to distant hills.

"They're so far away," Kala complained.

"So they are," Grey agreed but headed toward them regardless.

They threaded their way through the treacherous terrain, all the while accompanied by wailing on the wind.

"That's creeping me out," Kala admitted.

"Trick of the wind," Grey concluded.

"I'm not so sure," Kala replied, spotting movement beneath the water to their right and moving as far left as the narrow path through the bog allowed.

As they trudged, Kala had a lot of time to think. "Grey, can I ask you a question?"

"When has my permission ever been a prerequisite?" he asked back.

"I'll take that as a 'yes.' You were pretty close with the Priestess, weren't you?"

"We shared a bed," he replied, surprising her with his candor.

Did you love her? Kala wondered. "And yet you broke with her," she noted.

"We disagreed."

"About what?"

"About the only thing that matters."

Kala waited for him to elaborate.

"I can accept that the world is better off with a paring back of the populous, but the Priestess's preoccupation was always with the efficiency of it, not the result. She doesn't care what type of people survive or perish, so long as they are few. The Church's job is to return the world to a garden. You can't do that with weeds, having razed the flowers. She plans to reseed with the faithful, to rebuild the world in her image. In that regard, she's no different than Soren."

Kala marveled at Grey's admission, then realized that she'd been paying inadequate attention to their surroundings. "I think we're being watched," she told him.

"Of course we're being watched," he agreed but seemed unperturbed by it.

As they walked, Kala looked right and was startled to find a woman walking with them a short distance off. Looking back to tell Grey, she noticed a second woman walking to their left.

"It seems we have an escort," he concluded.

As they continued their trek, their escort grew until it numbered four women on either side.

"We're surrounded and outnumbered," Kala observed.

"I think we always were," Grey mused.

Their escort said nothing nor even looked their way but walked alongside them, nevertheless. The hills loomed closer, and the swampy ground gradually receded as they climbed upward toward a break in the hills. The pass they were approaching grew closer, and their escort abandoned them without their noticing.

"I wish I knew how they did that," Kala said to Grey.

"Practice," he concluded as they arrived at the pass. It was flanked by columns of basalt, and the wind howled through the narrow opening. Grey strode forward and passed between the columns, Kala following him closely.

Steaming pools surrounded them, and the smell of sulfur stung their nostrils. Fog rolled down the hillside, obscuring their view. They eventually climbed through the wispy cloud bank and into the midst of a village nestled into the hillside. The villagers watched them unconcernedly and sometimes glanced to an elevated building at the end of the street.

"I guess that's where we're supposed to go," Grey concluded.

On the stairs of the building, a woman stood waiting for them. She wore light armor that suited her chiseled features, which were exposed by her hair tied back in a braid. She was neither young nor old, but somehow both. She stood proudly, and authority radiated from her. She seemed familiar to Kala, but Kala couldn't divine why.

Kala and Grey strode up to the stairs, and with a wave of her hand, the woman bade them enter as she passed between the massive doors, which she left open for them. Inside, she walked around a fire that lit the room and proceeded to the end of the spacious hall, where she sat down in a high-backed chair and waved Kala and Grey to join her. They sat in a pair of chairs facing her, and she studied them for a moment before speaking.

"What brings you to our village?" she asked finally, having taken their measure.

"We come seeking allies," Grey replied bluntly.

"And what makes you think we'd be allies?" the woman asked detachedly.

Kala jumped in. "To be honest, we don't know what to think," she admitted, "but the world is burning, and we aim to put it out."

"We're quite safe from fire in our wet little corner of the world, don't you think?" the woman replied.

"I don't think that's your way," Kala concluded.

The woman raised an eyebrow. "And why might you think that?" she asked.

"Your armor, and the way your scouts pass unseen. If you were truly content to hide from the world, you wouldn't need such things."

"Insightful," the woman concluded, leaning back. "But why would we take your side? Why not the other one? There are always two sides."

"Your reputation."

"And what is our reputation."

"That you prefer to plant than prune."

"I'm not sure you've heard correctly," she replied, "but you're welcome to enjoy our hospitality while we deliberate on your request." The woman looked over Kala's shoulder. "Brinn, escort our guests to their rooms."

Kala looked behind her to see a woman who hadn't been there a moment earlier.

"Follow me," Brinn instructed.

Kala looked back at the woman on the dais to see if they were dismissed, but the chair was already empty.

"A bit over the top," Kala muttered to Grey and got up to follow the woman named Brinn out of the room. She guided them out the doors of the main hall and led them down a side street to a small building. She held open the door, which Kala and Grey entered to find a pleasant interior with a fire already going in a small hearth and a pot of soup bubbling above it.

"Rest," Brinn advised them. "You're welcome to wander around the village as you wish."

"Any restrictions?" Kala asked.

"Why would there be?" she replied over her shoulder and left them.

"Are you sure you weren't raised here?" Kala asked Grey sarcastically. "They're your kind of people."

"I do like it here," Grey replied and bent to stir the soup. "Hungry?"

"Starving."

"Good. It's been simmering for a long time and smells delicious."

"I guess we were expected."

"It was a long walk."

Kala and Grey enjoyed the soup and found themselves overcome with tiredness.

"Do you think we've been drugged?" she asked him.

"No. I think we're just fatigued."

"Well, that makes me feel better," she replied and wandered off in search of a bed, which she found on the second floor. She called over the railing to let Grey know there was another bedroom beside hers but didn't wait for his response before collapsing onto her bed. She was pretty sure she was asleep before her head hit the pillow.

Kala awoke in the morning to the smell of hot kai. She emerged from her bedroom at the same time Grey did and looked over the railing to see Brinn and the woman from the lodge sitting in the main room below.

Two chairs sat across from them with steaming cups of kai resting on the table in front of them.

Kala wasted no time descending, sitting down, and scooping up one of the mugs.

"I'm Tamara," the woman from the lodge introduced herself.

"Pleased to meet you," Kala replied. "I'm Kala, and this is Brother Grey."

"You're from the Church?" Tamara asked.

"No, but we've spent time in its midst – Grey more than I," Kala replied.

"You move like you've been trained," Tamara told Grey.

He sat up. "By a former member of your ranks."

"That's what we assumed. So, you know the woman we called Winter when she lived among us."

"That sounds apt," Grey replied. "Although she goes simply by 'Priestess' now."

"Her path diverged from ours long ago," Brinn noted.

"I think that continues," Grey agreed. "I'm not sure what her agenda is, but she seems to relish destruction a little too much for my liking."

"And what is *your* agenda?" Tamara asked Kala plainly.

"To stop the bloodshed and, gods-willing, to retire to a quiet corner of the world afterward," Kala replied equally plainly.

"Then our agendas align," Tamara concluded. "We'll help you to the extent that we can."

"Thank you," Kala told her, infinitely relieved.

"There is much to do," Brinn concluded, rose from her seat, and strode to the door. "Enjoy our hospitality," she said and left.

Tamara rose and followed Brinn out.

"I'm confused," Kala admitted to Grey when the two women had left. "Who's in charge?"

"I think they both are," he replied and sat back.

"It bothers me that we didn't have to try harder to convince them."

"I think they know more about what's happening in the world than they let on," Grey replied.

Kala finished her kai and got up. "I'm going for a walk," she announced.

Grey simply waved, so she left their dwelling alone and glanced about while deciding which way to go. People moved about purposefully but unhurriedly. She spied motion down the street to her right and wandered over to discover that it was a schoolyard. She sat down on the steps of a building across the street and watched the children as they engaged in a sparring exercise. It seemed to be the opposite of what she'd seen at the temple grounds in the Priestess's city. There, everything was order and repetition. Here, everything was fluid and organic. The children moved with a grace that defied prediction. Kala was mesmerized.

She looked up to see Brinn standing nearby, watching her.

"Beautiful, isn't it?" Brinn asked.

"Amazingly so," Kala admitted. "If Winter grew up here, why doesn't she train her followers the same way you do?"

"I'm sure she does in a way," Brinn conceded, "but she always had a desire for control that ran counter to our teachings, and that's probably why she was so unhappy here."

Tamara strode up. "The preparations have been made," she informed Brinn.

Brinn turned to Kala. "We'll meet you on the field of battle," she told her and walked away.

"Where? When?" Kala called after her.

"We'll find you when it's time," Tamara told her. "I'm sure you'll be wanting to get back," she added. "I took the liberty of calling your ship closer." She gestured uphill rather than down toward the bog.

"Thank you. I didn't think there was a 'closer,'" Kala said, recalling her journal.

"Not everything that exists appears on maps," Tamara replied and strode off.

Kala sought out Grey and found him waiting for her and ready to go.

"We've had success here," he concluded. "Let's hope it makes a difference." And with that, they strode uphill toward their ship.

32

Dhara

"Go get your sister," the healer ordered Caia before returning inside.

Caia got up and chased after Dhara, finding her sitting at the river's edge. "The healer wants you right away," Caia told her.

Dhara threw a stone far out and turned to join her sister as the ripples were swept downstream. "How can you accept him so readily?" she asked Caia of their supposed half-brother Daryn.

"He's family," she replied matter-of-factly.

"He's a slave," Dhara protested.

"And still family," Caia replied as though it had no bearing.

Dhara mulled this over as they walked back to the healer's cottage. Entering, they noticed that Daryn had moved a second bed beside the one in which Calix lay, pale as a ghost.

The healer looked Dhara up and down. "I assume you're willing to do whatever needs be done for this young man," she stated, seeking confirmation.

Dhara nodded, and the old woman instructed her to lie down on the bed beside his. "He needs medicine that his body is too weak to process," the healer told her. "You might be strong enough," she added. "But then again, it might kill you, too."

"Just get on with it," Dhara replied and lay down.

The woman strapped down Dhara's arm and turned to Caia. "Get a wet cloth and sit by your sister's side," she told her, pulling a knife from a pot of boiling water and wiping off the blade.

Caia took a seat as the woman slit Calix's and Dhara's arms, expertly inserted tubing into them, and secured them. Soon, Dhara's heart pumped her blood into Calix's arm, and his heart feebly pumped his back into hers. The healer offered a cup of foul-smelling broth to Dhara. "Drink this," she instructed her.

Dhara raised her head and drank the bitter concoction without complaint, then laid her head back down. Very quickly, she began to sweat as her body fought the medicine coursing through her.

Caia wiped the sweat from Dhara's body, which gave off heat like a furnace.

Dhara closed her eyes and moaned softly.

Daryn passed Caia fresh cloths as she did her best to keep her sister comfortable while her body warred with the medicine. Caia had to hold her sister still as her body trembled and thrashed. She looked beseechingly at the healer, who simply shrugged and said, "What will be will be," and settled into a chair with a cup of tea.

The sun sped across the sky and set. All the while, Dhara's state worsened, and Calix's did not improve noticeably. Daryn had lit a few candles but sat slumped in his chair, sleeping soundly. Caia mopped her sister's brow, allowing herself only the briefest of moments to close her eyes until she also succumbed to fatigue and didn't wake the next time she closed them. Only the old woman kept vigil.

Color slowly returned to Calix's cheeks, and his eyes fluttered open. He looked at Dhara beside him, glowing from the heat that her body generated, and their eyes locked.

"Am I in heaven?" he asked.

"More like hell," Dhara replied with a weak smile. "It's hot as hell."

"So, I am dead, then," he concluded.

"That would *really* suck," Dhara replied, closed her eyes, and fell back asleep.

Calix watched her until he drifted off himself.

Calix opened his eyes to see Dhara watching him from the bed beside him. "So, I'm not dead then, am I?" he asked.

Dhara smiled. "Doesn't look like it."

"Then why do I feel like it?" he grimaced.

"Tell me about it," she replied.

The morning sun peeked in through partly closed drapes, so Calix looked around. Disarray would be a generous way to describe the room that surrounded them. He spotted Caia sitting on a nearby chair, flanked by a handsome young man sitting casually in the chair beside hers.

"How?" Calix asked.

"Cera," Caia replied. "I'll tell you all about it when your strength returns."

"I was wondering the same thing," Daryn mused aloud. "What brings you back from banishment?" he asked Dhara.

She turned to him and propped herself up before responding. "Mostly nursing this guy back to health," she replied, gesturing to Calix, "but also, seeking allies in a conflict that is advancing southward."

"You won't find any support around your mother's tree," Daryn concluded bitterly.

"I didn't expect to," Dhara agreed, "but to be honest, I haven't the faintest idea where we'll find allies."

"Allies against whom?"

"Soren. His forces march south and burn everything in their path. It is only a matter of time before he sets fire to the jungle we call home."

"I doubt even that would worsen our lot in life."

Dhara looked at him, confused.

"Not yours… ours, the slave class. We toil for your mother and her ilk and are put to death for the slightest gaffe, if we're not shipped off in an airship to be sacrificed or marched off at the front lines of some futile power struggle between rival tribes. We toil, and we bleed, and you don't care."

"We care," Caia countered.

"Well, maybe *you* do," Daryn accepted.

"No – *we* care," Dhara interjected. "That's not right."

Daryn looked at her skeptically, but Dhara returned his look so sincerely that he was taken aback. "It doesn't matter," he concluded bitterly. "What you think doesn't matter – no offense – nothing is ever going to change here."

"True," she agreed. "Nothing is going to change *here*… but we're not talking about here."

"What do you mean?"

"Your people have no land of their own. They work the land for my mother's people. Correct?"

"Correct."

"There's ample land in the north that Soren's forces have cleared by their advance. And the land here won't remain free of this conflict for long. Either stay in the service of my mother and be conscripted to defend *her* lands when Soren comes knocking or join us in fighting him and accept your own land in the north as your reward."

"That is tempting, but who are you to make this offer."

"No one, and I am not offering you anything... I'm just speaking the truth of things."

Daryn mulled it over. "I'll bring this to the elders," he concluded and got up to go.

"Thank you," Caia said.

"I'm not doing this for you; I'm doing this for us," he replied.

"Still, thank you for not sitting idly by while the world burns."

He nodded and left the cottage.

He returned later that night. "It didn't take much to convince the elders that taking our chances in the north is preferable to the way things are here. But the distance to there is great."

"True, but the river flows north. We only need boats, and the village has lots of them."

"Your mother guards them."

"Lightly."

"Still, she's not going to sit idly by while we take them."

"We'll have to catch her unaware and move quickly then," Dhara concluded.

"When?"

"How quickly can your people make themselves ready?"

"It'll take three or four days to make all of the necessary arrangements and for the fuss over the guard that was attacked at the landing pad to die down. That was you, I assume?"

"The girl walked into it," Dhara deflected. "We move in four days. Calix will be stronger by then."

Four days went by quickly, and as hoped, Calix regained the ability to move about. Caia hunted to put food on the table, with a little extra set aside for their journey. Dhara spent time with her brother, scouting and planning attacks on the armory, the village stores, and the boat launch.

Daryn was far more influential than he let on and had everyone organized when the day finally came. Dhara had come up with a distraction that she hoped would serve their purposes. She decided to hail an airship in broad daylight, and if it worked, that was the signal to set everything in motion. She wasn't sure how the amulet's magic worked, so she snuck as close to the landing pad with it as she dared.

She spied Sari unhappily on guard at the landing pad, her nose bandaged and her eyes still dark from an ugly bruise. She was being punished with extra guard shifts for having been taken unaware. She looked tired and in pain. Dhara moved silently through the bush behind her until she was close enough to tap on her shoulder. Sari spun around, right into the roundhouse punch that Dhara leveled her with, rebreaking her nose and knocking her unconscious. Dhara looked down at her and felt a twinge of pity for the hell the girl would catch after the dust settled.

Dhara walked to the center of the dais, raised her amulet, and pressed the center button that had released the airship before, hoping the magic worked in reverse. There was no way to know if it had or hadn't, and the slaves waited for her signal. Dhara took the time to truss Sari up as a precaution and waited. She didn't have to wait long before spying a ship high in the sky. *Thank the Goddess*, she thought and pulled the horn from around Sari's neck, blew a sharp blast on it, and ran for the boat launch.

The sound of the horn created mayhem across the village. As guards moved toward the landing pad, slaves were suddenly nowhere to be found. The attacks on the armory and the stores were successful, and soon, slaves were moving swiftly toward the boat launch, some with weapons and others with food. Caia used a stone launched from a sling to take out the woman guarding the canoes, and slaves were heading out into the river in them when Dhara and Daryn arrived with the remainder of his people. Weapons and food were distributed, and the rest of the canoes were pushed away from the shore.

"Mother will figure out quickly that something is wrong and be upon us," Caia told her sister.

"I sure hope so," Dhara replied. "I want to see the look on her face when she sees us leaving."

Caia shook her head and helped Calix into one of the last two-person canoes, getting in behind him and pushing it out into the river.

Daryn stayed on the shore, helping launch the last canoes, while Dhara took a defensive position hidden in the trees. A guard came running past, and Dhara caught her in the neck with a wicked swing of her spear, knocking her clean off her feet. Dhara stood over her with her spear point hovering over the woman's heart. "You have two choices," Dhara informed her. "You lose yourself in the jungle or bleed out here."

The woman rubbed her neck and looked at the jungle.

"Smart choice," Dhara concluded and allowed her to rise and run off into the dense jungle. Dhara turned and raced to the shore.

Daryn was standing astride the last two-person canoe waiting for her.

"Thanks for waiting for me," she said and jumped in. They paddled hard to join the rest.

Dhara heard her mother yelling from the shore and turned to wave.

Her mother saw her with her brother. "You've found your people," her mother called derisively.

Dhara looked at her brother and smiled. "I sure hope so," she said and turned her attention back to paddling.

The flotilla of canoes drew up onto the shore a hard day's paddle downriver, where they set up camp.

Caia, Dhara, Daryn and Calix sat around a fire, watching people revel in the freedom they'd never had before.

Dhara turned to Daryn. "It's a good thing we've done here, but there are enslaved people up and down this river. We can't stop here."

Daryn leaned back and looked at Caia. "Somehow, your conscience has rubbed off on your sister," he joked.

Caia placed a hand on her sister's arm and addressed Daryn sternly. "My sister is the most principled person I've ever known. It is she who rubs off on me."

Dhara blushed and turned to a chastened Daryn. "So, will you help me?"

"It would be my honor," he replied.

Dhara got up and placed a hand on his shoulder. "Thank you, brother."

Caia looked at the mass of canoes drawn up on the shore and the people milling around. "We don't make much of an army. We look more like refugees."

"We're both," Daryn assured her.

"Still, we need a better way of heading north if we're to muster a force to counter Soren," Caia said. She was quiet for a moment, thinking.

"Give me Kala's amulet, Dhara. I'll head to the coast to see if I can find a better way north."

Dhara handed over the amulet, happy to rid herself of it.

"I'll go with you," Calix offered to Caia.

"If you think you're well enough," she replied.

"I'd only slow Dhara and Daryn down if I joined them, and these people aren't my people," he said, gesturing to those around him. "*You're* my people," he said to Caia. "I want to stay with you."

"Then I'd be happy to have your company," she concluded.

"Thank you," Calix replied, relieved.

In the morning, Dhara and Daryn headed back upriver, and Caia and Calix headed downriver, their refugee army following behind.

33

Cera

Cera rode next to Soren on their way to the city called Bayre. They bypassed several settlements on their way, including a town that was rumored to be the seat of a church that worshipped death. Soren had no love for religion and thought it ironic that he could so easily grant them what they worshipped. He marked it on a map in order to return and raze it to the ground later. Cera was thankful that, at least for the moment, there was no killing. There was just the slow advance of Soren's forces, supplied by raiding parties that his man Lennox sent out. Cera detested Lennox, and she had a hunch that if something were ever to happen to Soren, she'd be better off ending her own life than being left to Lennox's mercies.

The countryside rolled past, and she inhaled its scents. They rode past fragrant forests of wild fruit trees, the blossoms providing a stark contrast to the stream of soldiers passing between them. The days were warm and the nights pleasant. In the evenings, Soren moved between campfires to drink and joke with his men. Sometimes he'd request Cera to join him. She didn't like being stared at hungrily by his men, but respect or fear kept them in check. She knew that she was known as his consort, but she didn't care. Her heart had turned to stone the moment she'd been ripped from Lily.

Soren was surprisingly sensitive to her needs and didn't ask her to join him too frequently, although she did whenever he asked. If her compliance guaranteed Lily's safety, she'd follow the man through the gates of hell. He read her moods, however, and didn't push her. She had a separate bed next to his. At nighttime, Soren would move them apart, and in the morning, he'd move them back together. If his men had any inkling that she didn't share his bed, it was never spoken of aloud.

Soren was a pleasant conversationalist and pointed out sights and made observations that she would not have noticed on her own. His piercing blue eyes missed nothing, and he freely shared with her what he saw.

He would often have meetings with his war council as they rode, minus the recently deceased Trax. Cera was pretty sure that Soren had engineered his death at Kala's hands, but it was another of the open secrets not spoken of in the camp. When Lennox or Seline would ride up to talk with Soren, they'd look at Cera as though he should dismiss her, but he never did, telling them that there was no one she could share their secrets with, and Cera bitterly had to agree. She paid little attention to their conversations but still overheard everything.

She learned that Lennox was the source of most of Soren's information about the world they marched through. She wondered what he deigned not to tell his liege, but while he might be selective in what he told Soren, he never seemed to lie to him. Cera had hunches about how he extracted his information that made her stomach turn. Surely men like Lennox would be better left behind than brought into the new world that Soren claimed to want to create.

Lennox briefed him about what he'd learned of their target, Bayre. It was the largest city known to anyone they'd come across, and given Lennox's penchant for targeting anyone who looked out of place, he'd 'extracted' information from people transplanted by airship from all the distant corners of the world. Bayre was home to ten thousand souls behind its towering walls. They were soft from living comfortably, but the city's natural defenses would make it a formidable challenge. In addition to its high walls, it was flanked by the sea. No amount of saltwater would sustain it during a prolonged siege, however, and Soren only needed to surround it in a semi-circle to cut it off from the world.

With Seline, Soren mainly discussed siege strategy. Not that Lennox wasn't eager to participate, but Cera had a suspicion that he wasn't very bright. Of course, even thinking that made her an enemy of the man, who was an eel. Seline, by comparison, was a breath of fresh air. She was intelligent and quick to recognize problems and solve them. She was not, however, warm and engaging, and Cera could understand why her company did nothing to satiate Soren's loneliness.

Seline didn't feel that the city's walls could be breached and didn't suggest trying. She simply advocated starving its inhabitants. Like most of the settlements they'd encountered, its food sources were primarily outside its walls. They could not sustain a long siege. She also had suggestions for ways of delivering diseases inside the city's walls, but Soren dismissed these tactics as beneath the men that followed him, who favored the honor bestowed by cutting a man down with steel. Cera didn't see the difference and noted sadly that honorable men seemed to be in the minority among Soren's host.

The army finally arrived at Bayre on a particularly clear day. The men on the walls could see the ground in the distance ripple and initially mistook it for waves of heat distorting the view, like a mirage. But, to their horror, they slowly realized that it wasn't the ground moving; it was an army so vast that it stretched across the horizon. More and more citizens made their way up the wall to witness their approaching doom until every iota of space was claimed. They stood in rapt silence and watched as the army inexorably advanced. The only sound came from flags snapping in the wind, like the crack, crack, crack of a whip.

The last of the field laborers hurried inside the city's mighty gates, and they were closed a final time, the sound reverberating through the city like the closing of a tomb. The low beating of drums emanated from the trees that ringed the fields surrounding the city. It came from all directions, the only constant its slow increase in volume. The sound grew louder, the tempo more brisk... then it stopped entirely. The citizens stared at the tree line in terrified anticipation.

Soren's army began to pour of the woods, spreading across the fields, filling the space completely. Where the city's lifeblood had grown, boots now trod. The army halted its advance a short distance from the city walls, trapping its inhabitants inside. The siege of Bayre had begun.

Cera felt pity for the city but was grateful for the respite from long days in the saddle. She wasn't sure if she'd ever walk without soreness again. Soren selected the location of his tent to have a commanding view of his army and a pleasant view of the sea. Cera suspected that he'd chosen the site partly to please her, but she resisted feeling any gratitude to the man who orchestrated so much death. He deserved nothing.

During the day, Soren would meet with his council in his tent or sit in front of it, contemplating the city, its conquest, and beyond. Cera would sit behind it, wrapped in blankets, staring out to sea. If she gazed at it long enough, it anesthetized her broken heart.

One day, Soren emerged through the back flap, dragging a chair with him. He placed it beside her, also facing out to sea, then returned to the tent to fetch himself a blanket and cups of tea for them both. He handed her one, which she took graciously, and he sat down beside her.

"It's beautiful, the sea," he said, more to himself than to her.

"It is," she agreed.

"Would you like to settle beside it when this is all over?" he asked her.

"I don't think it matters," she replied flatly. "When the last of the world has been torn asunder, I think it'll take the last of our souls with it. As long as there's some untouched part of the world, there's a chance at redemption, a place to heal. But, when it's 'over,' as you say, even that will be gone." She sat silently, watching the waves locked in an endless battle with the shore.

"Every corner of the world must be set aflame to fully expunge the malady that afflicts it. You can't show disease mercy, or it will roar back. But after a fire, flowers are the first thing to grow back."

"Is it so wrong that people go about their lives, seeking happiness where they can?"

"Yes, it is," he concluded with the force of unshakable conviction. "Complacency allows men like Lennox to fester, and happiness is more and more difficult to obtain in this world. Don't you feel like there's more just beyond our grasp?"

Cera thought of Lily. "Yes," she replied, and silent tears streamed down her face.

Soren calmed himself and stared out to sea. "I wasn't always like this," he admitted to the wind. "I was happy once, or at least as close to it as a person can be. My mother would sing me to sleep, even when I was too old for it, and she had the voice of an angel. My father would stay up with me and point out the constellations on clear nights. He told me that I could be anyone and anything I wanted, although I don't think he meant for me to become what I am now. I even had a dog. He'd follow me everywhere – even sleep beside me. I was oblivious to the true nature of the world. Then, I was ripped from my home and everything I loved to be deposited in a world filled with men like Trax and Lennox. To have nothing is terrible, but to have everything and have it torn from you is so much worse. The airships and their masters perpetuate this injustice. I will end it for all time."

"So, take it up with the airships' masters," Cera countered. "Don't take it out on the world."

"Don't think I haven't tried. They're elusive. I will not waste my time chasing smoke. This world is their creation, and it is through its systems that they keep us enslaved. I will tear it down in a cleansing wave of fire and end our subjugation."

"You'll never build a better world wielding death as a tool. Death only begets more death," she replied.

"Your naïveté is refreshing."

"I am not gods-damn naïve," Cera spat angrily. "It takes more courage to face injustice with open arms than balled fists." She got up. "Thank you for the tea. I need a walk," she told him and strode off. She didn't ask his permission, even though she'd never left his side before, but he didn't stop her.

She walked through the army camp, fists clenched at her sides. Soldiers stared at her as she passed. Her long auburn hair streamed out behind her – she was a sight and clearly in a foul mood, but she was easily recognized as Soren's consort, and soldiers stepped out of her way.

A lone horn blast sounded from the city walls, and everyone turned to its source, Cera included.

34
Lily

Lily moved in with Celeste and Twill and took to her new life, becoming a den-mother to the children that Celeste rounded up off the streets. Lily spent her time in the kitchen or mending broken spirits. Little by little, it helped heal hers as well. Life continued in this manner until rumors spread that Soren's forces were headed toward the city. Suddenly, all her wounds reopened.

The citizens of Bayre convulsed with worry and began hoarding. Food was brought in from outside the walls, crops were harvested prematurely, and markets were converted to livestock pens. Freshwater was carried into the city from outside the walls to top up enormous cisterns. Lily took a place in bucket brigades several times until her arms ached.

The streets became dangerous, and the residents of Celeste's sanctuary stopped going out alone. Crime became more common as people fought over scarce resources, and panic escalated into violence. Petr and his girlfriend moved back in with Celeste, and Lily only ever ventured out with Petr or Twill as an escort.

Everyone viewed Lily as prescient for her rooftop garden and rain barrels. Truth be told, she hadn't been preparing for Soren – she'd just been trying to take her mind off Cera, and gardening and baking were her twin distractions.

Celeste organized the fortification of their dwelling.

"That won't do anything against Soren's forces if the city walls are breached," Lily told her.

"It's not for Soren," Celeste replied. "It's to protect us against the citizens of the city when they get desperate enough."

The children in Celeste's care fanned out across the city, thieving supplies. Celeste chastised them for the risks they took, but the majority had lived most of their lives on the streets, and they'd be damned if they weren't going to increase their odds of surviving a little longer.

When Soren's forces finally arrived and encircled the city, the citizens hunkered down for a long siege. Food became increasingly hard to come by, and Celeste used her connections to keep them supplied. Twill bartered every painting still in his possession for food.

The city council established a curfew and sent guards to patrol the streets and re-establish order. It made them safer, except from the guards who preyed on the weak.

Airships still trickled in, although they became increasingly rare. When a ship landed with an open passenger compartment, the city's wealthiest residents would bid for a chance at sending a loved one temporarily beyond Soren's reach.

Lily volunteered to ferry supplies to the men on the wall that ringed the city. It allowed her to stare out over Soren's forces in the faint hope that someday she'd spot Cera among them. It was an added benefit that she could usually sneak a roll or two back to Celeste's in the folds of her dress.

Soren's soldiers camped within bow range of the walls, but the city's archers conserved their arrows for the inevitable assault and not to provoke their enemy into hastening it. It was a surreal détente between the forces. Lily gazed out at the multitude of warriors arrayed against them. *Where are you, my love?* she repeated to herself as she looked from tent to tent and fire to fire.

A flash of color on the periphery of Soren's army caught her eye, and she tracked it as it progressed through the assembled host. The wind blew up, and a mane of auburn hair trailed out behind the woman Lily was watching. *Please, please, please let it be her,* Lily prayed and looked about anxiously for a way of signaling the woman she hoped was Cera.

She spotted a horn mounted on the wall between two archers and raced to it. "Sorry, I need this," she apologized and snatched it before they could stop her. She ran to the edge of the wall and blew a resounding note.

Silence fell over the city and the army surrounding it. Every head turned to the source of the blast. Even the guards that raced to reclaim the horn from Lily stopped to look out over the army that stared silently up at the wall. A red-haired woman in their midst stopped, turned, and raised a hand to shield her eyes as she joined the army in looking up at the wall. They all beheld the same curious sight – a young blonde woman waving her fool head off.

Cera's heart swelled. *Lily!*

35

Skye

Skye stepped out of the airship, with Hawke following closely behind. The taste of salt in the air announced that they were on the coast, even before the harbor became visible through the shifting fog.

"I hate fish," Skye muttered and headed toward the village.

"You've been here before?" Hawke asked as they walked.

"Briefly. I caught a ride from here on a sailing ship bound for Bayre, but I never really spent time in the town."

"So, what's the plan?"

"Raise a navy."

"Ambitious. How do you propose we start?"

"We go where the sailors are."

"Which is?"

"If they're fogged in, they'll be where you'll find any sailor in port – in a bar." With that, he headed toward the waterfront, where he hoped he'd spot a tavern.

They arrived at the piers to find a fair number of ships tied up, a few sailors moving about on their decks.

He turned back toward the town. *If I were a sailor, flush with coin, where would I go?* Skye asked himself. He picked the most inviting street and walked down it. It was lined with numerous likely establishments, and they stood in the middle of the road, trying to decide where to start, when a drunken sailor stumbled out the door of a tavern called the Mermaid's Tail.

"I have no idea what a mermaid is," Skye confided to Hawke, "but this looks to be as good a place as any."

They stepped inside and were greeted by sounds of laughter over top of a fiddle score. Serving women in low-cut tops circulated among the tables, depositing tankards in front of every man. A sailor slapped the behind of a serving girl, who turned and slapped him hard across the face, then sat on his lap.

"Sailors," Skye muttered.

Surveying the goings-on in the room, Hawke surmised, "I'm guessing a mermaid is a woman of some sort."

Skye looked about the room for a familiar face and spotted the cook for whom he'd peeled potatoes aboard the ship he'd briefly sailed on. He steeled himself and marched over.

"Potatoes, reporting for duty," he told the man.

The cook's eyes focused as he tried to grasp the context, then it hit him like a lightning bolt, and he sloshed his beer.

"Potatoes? Gods-damn it, man – you left me halfway to Bayre. Who does that?"

Skye looked down a little guiltily.

"You're here with your friends, I imagine," the cook said, steadying his precious beer and taking a draught of it.

"They're here?" Skye asked, not having seen them.

"They're in the toilet. Gower looked green."

"Thanks," Skye said and slapped the cook on the arm, making him spill a little more beer. He sped away before the man could take out his annoyance on him.

Skye headed to the back of the building, where he surmised the toilets were, and Hawke followed. He found himself standing in front of two doors. One had a sign with a fish carved on it, and the other a sign inscribed with a hock of ham.

"What the hell?" Skye muttered and pushed open the door marked with a ham, wondering if he was about to get his face slapped. It appeared he'd guessed correctly because he saw the back of his friend Dayl standing outside a stall, surveying another man bent over the toilet, who Skye guessed was Gower. Dayl was telling him, "No, you're not going to die."

Skye hailed his friends from the doorway, and Dayl pivoted at the sound of his name.

"Gower, you'll never guess who just graced us with his presence," Dayl said to his friend, but quickly realizing that Gower was in no position to play guessing games, told him. "It's Skye!"

Gower dragged himself to his feet and wiped his face. His excitement made him forget how terrible he felt.

"By the gods, man, it's good to see you," Gower said to Skye but had the presence of mind not to try and hug him in the condition he was in.

"We've got a table," Dayl announced. "It's far more civilized to talk out there than in here. Come on, Gower, you'll survive."

The four men made their way back to their table, but it'd been taken over by a party of young sailors.

"Push off, lads," Dayl told them, even though he was barely a few years older than they were. "This is Potato – he's a legend."

The sailors vacated the table, leaving it to Dayl, Gower, Skye and Hawke.

"What's with the 'potato' thing?" Hawke asked, his curiosity finally getting the better of him.

347

"Skye here fought off an invasion of pirates with nothing but a bucket of potatoes," Dayl announced.

Hawke looked at Skye skeptically.

"I think I had help," Skye said with embarrassment.

"Plus, he saved my life," Dayl added and rose to his feet for a toast, having stolen the beer of a passed-out sailor nearby. He turned to address the bar.

"Don't, Dayl, you're drunk," Skye said to rein him in before it was too late. It was too late.

"We're all drunk," Dayl countered and rapped his mug on the table to get everyone's attention. "Ladies and gentlemen," he began. "You're attention, please." He looked at the fiddler. "Maurice, a moment, if you will." The fiddler stopped playing, and the bar quieted.

"The conquering hero has returned," Dayl announced. "Behold – Potato!" He turned and lifted his mug in salute.

The bar was silent for the briefest moment, then erupted into cheers.

"Oh gods," Skye said, acknowledging the fanfare but also trying his best to disappear into the upholstery. Soon, drinks started arriving at the table, sent their way by appreciative sailors. Girls came over too, but Hawke waved them off. "He's spoken for, ladies," he told them but thought the whole affair was great fun.

Dayl settled back into his seat. "Pardon Gower. He's just upset that his girlfriend left him for the blacksmith."

Skye patted poor Gower on the shoulder. "There's plenty of other fish in the sea, man. Cheer up."

"That's what I said," Dayl piped in.

"Maybe a mermaid, even," Hawke added, at which Dayl looked at him strangely.

"Not like her," Gower blubbered and hunkered down over his beer.

Skye turned his attention back to Dayl. "Where can I find the Captain?"

"Sure as hell not here," Dayl laughed. "The captains frequent the Admiral's Nook up the road."

"Then that's where I've got to go," Skye concluded and got up. "Care to join me?"

"They'd never let a sail monkey like me in that place, and besides, someone has to stay here and nurse Gower. Do come back, though. We're not shipping out anytime soon, with Bayre under siege and all."

"That I can do," Skye replied and drained his drink for courage. He and Hawke got up and headed out into the street. The air outside was fresh but cold and clammy in contrast to the heat and mugginess of the tavern.

"If Bayre's under siege, we'd better hurry," Skye said to himself.

They turned up the lane looking for the Admiral's Nook, spied it, and entered. The doorman raised an eyebrow at their attire and Hawke's weaponry but otherwise didn't say anything.

Skye spotted his former captain dining with two similarly dressed men that Skye surmised were captains of other vessels. He walked over and stood before their table. "I'm sorry to intrude, gentlemen." he began.

Recognition lit his former Captain's face, despite Skye's thinking the man didn't know him from a plank. "Back from the dead, lad. That alone is worth the intrusion. What's your business?"

"I need a navy, sir," Skye replied seriously.

"Well, that's a tall ask. Why, pray tell, do you need a navy?"

"Soren's forces advance, and we aim to stop them."

"Who's 'we'?"

"Everyone not allied with Soren, led by his Scourge," Skye replied, although he cringed inwardly at calling Kala by that ridiculous title.

"An interesting proposition," the Captain concluded, leaning back in his chair. "The war has been terrible for business, that's for certain," he said, to the nods of his colleagues. "But I can tell you that my men are not fighting men like you."

Hawke kept a straight face, to his credit.

The Captain continued. "I'm happy to ferry supplies if that helps the effort. Hell, I think we'd all be," he added, to the assent of the gentlemen at his table and several around the room who had gone silent to listen in on the curious conversation. "But I can't promise you the lives of my men. You need fighting men, and my men are not that," he concluded flatly.

There was a definite finality to his statement, so Skye bowed his head. "I thank you, gentlemen, and hope to take you up on your offer of support." He turned, dispirited, for the door.

Hawke placed a hand on Skye's shoulder. "The man is being reasonable. We just have to accept that you tried, and it wasn't to be."

A man rose from his seat at a lone table far in the back and intercepted them as they exited into the street. "You need fighting men?" he asked them.

"Yes," Skye replied, unsure of where this was going.

"I know where they are, and I can take you to them," he said. Skye must have looked a little skeptical despite himself, so the man added, "Look, my nephew was aboard your ship when the pirates attacked it. I owe you a favor. Please allow an old man to repay his debts."

Skye's skepticism abated a little. "Where are these men?"

"Pirate's Cove," the man replied.

Skye and Hawke found themselves rowing a skiff into a fog bank with the old man giving them instructions from the prow.

"This is great exercise," Hawke enthused.

Skye looked at him like he was insane and shifted positions to ease his tired muscles and sore bottom. "Is this safe, rowing through the fog?" he asked the old man.

"Of course not," he replied dismissively but kept them at it. "But, if you're going to crash a pirate party unannounced, it's better to do it under cover of darkness or weather."

That did not reassure Skye.

The old man guided them around rocks that drew the small craft to them with a force like gravity. Skye and Hawke had to put their backs into the rowing to prevent the skiff from being sucked into them and smashed to splinters. They rowed over shoals that scraped the underside of the craft. When they finally pulled up onto a short stretch of beach sheltered by two rocky outcroppings, Skye was so relieved he had to resist the urge to kiss the ground.

"The pirate village is that way," the man said, gesturing up the shoreline. "Perhaps a quarter of a day's walk." He started to push the craft back into the waves.

"You're not staying?" Skye asked.

"There's no point. In a short while, you'll either have allies, or you'll be dead. Either way, you don't need me."

"Thank you for your help."

"My pleasure," he said, jumping into the boat and positioning himself between the gunnels. "Don't die," he added and rowed away.

"We'll try," Skye muttered and turned to look up the beach. It wasn't going to be an easy walk along the rocks, but what choice did they have? He sighed and looked at Hawke, who was fresh as a daisy and looking forward to the trek. "You're insufferable," Skye told him and headed out.

They hiked down the beach, over rocks, and in and out of the trees until they spied the pirate village. It was hidden from view of the sea behind a long finger of rock that provided shelter to the vessels tied up alongside a wharf. Skye could see why they'd selected the location as their base. He wondered if airships traveled even here and shuddered to think of any youth transported into the midst of pirates.

Skye and Hawke squatted down behind a pile of rocks within view of the village.

"How should we play this?" Skye asked.

"I don't think there's any other way than bold. There's no point in sneaking up, then announcing that we need their help."

Skye sighed and summoned his courage. "Let's do this, then. No point delaying the inevitable."

They rose and walked toward the town, which looked to have been constructed almost entirely of found wood, even the two-story buildings. Rough-looking characters leaned on railings or hung out of windows and watched their advance with feigned disinterest. Hawke could tell that they were tracking their progress.

A door swung outwards from a building adorned with the flags of captured or sunken vessels. An enormous man emerged from the open door, followed by three equally thuggish-looking compatriots. Two of them carried pool cues, and the third a bottle. They looked miffed at having their entertainment interrupted and walked into the street to intercept Skye and Hawke.

Hawke turned to Skye. "Want to take care of this, Potato?" he joked.

Skye looked a little green, so Hawke patted his shoulder. "Okay. You can have the next one." He strode forward toward the four men. "Shall we?" he asked.

The leader frowned at Hawke's nonchalance and waved his three colleagues forward. They advanced, brandishing their improvised weapons. Hawke stood his ground as the first man swung his pool cue at him, ducking under it and rising quickly to smash his fist into the man's chin, knocking him staggering back. He turned to his next assailant, stepping just out of range of the swung bottle. He awaited the next swing, then punched the man's forearm hard, making him drop the bottle. Hawke flipped it up with his foot and, in one smooth motion, smashed it against the man's temple, sending him crashing to the ground, out cold. He turned to the third man, noting that he'd dropped his pool cue in favor of a knife.

"Smarter, but not that smart," Hawke smirked.

The man rushed forward, and Hawke grabbed his arm, disarmed him of his blade, and peppered his knife arm with four or five stabs. The man howled and held his bleeding arm. Hawke tossed his knife aside and turned to face their leader.

"So, you can fight," the man spat. "Doesn't mean shit. What do you want?"

"Your help, but only if you've got more skilled men than these three louts," Hawke replied.

"Not my call," the man sneered.

"That's right," a voice called out. Hawke turned to face a good-looking man leaning casually against the doorway of the establishment that the four men had just exited. "It's mine." He surveyed Hawke, then waved him and Skye inside after him.

Skye walked up to Hawke and looked at the open doorway. "Is this a good idea?" he asked.

"Probably not," Hawke replied but walked up the steps toward the door regardless.

The man with the bleeding arm took a step forward, and Skye hurried to join Hawke. The man stalked off to bandage his arm while the other two dragged their unconscious colleague out of the street.

Skye and Hawke entered the building and were surprised to find it reasonably tidy. There was even a pool table in a corner and several tables at which men and women lounged, drinking.

The leader returned to his table at the back and gestured for Hawke and Skye to join him. He motioned for the barkeep to bring over three drinks. She nodded and began preparing them.

He turned to face them as they sat. "Ballsy, walking into my town," he observed. "What's this about needing the help of pirates?" he smiled broadly at the absurdity of it.

"You may have noticed a reduction in ships of late," Hawke pointed out.

"I have."

"That's because the siege of Bayre has stalled trade along the coast."

"That's not news," he said and accepted the drinks that arrived. "And how do we figure into this, besides sitting here bored between prizes that too infrequently sail past?"

"We aim to bring the fight back to the forces besieging Bayre, and your men look like they're spoiling for a fight," Hawke replied.

"Why would we trouble ourselves to help in someone else's fight?"

"Soren, who leads the siege, has plundered the continent on his way to Bayre. That treasure should be a good enough incentive."

The man leaned back, insulted. "So, you think plunder is all that motivates us?" he asked.

"Frankly, yes," Hawke replied.

"Okay, that's probably fair," the man admitted, relaxing and leaning forward again. "Why don't I just let you walk out of here without killing you, and you can consider that you came out ahead?"

Hawke whipped out a dagger and slammed it into the table. It sat there, quivering, as the room went silent. "If your preference is to kill us, get it over with. I'd rather die in the thick of battle than in this hidey-hole."

The pirate leader pulled the dagger out of the table and examined it. "Why would I kill you when you amuse me so much?" He handed Hawke back his knife and turned to the barkeep. "We're going to need more beer."

36

Kala

Kala and Grey directed the airship into Bayre during daylight so that they could survey Soren's encircling army from its windows. The force looked to be nearly ten thousand strong. Grey had the ship land at the airfield inside the city. When they opened the door, they simply pushed past the confused guards. One of them reached for his weapon, but a look from Kala and a shake of Grey's head caused him to lift his hands away from it. They headed for Celeste's to wash up and rest after the long flight.

"Let's go past the temple," Grey suggested. "Protocol would dictate that it be abandoned by now, but this might not yet be known by the populous."

Kala agreed, and they walked toward it. Neither of them noticed Lennox's assassin, Roml, watching them from a window that overlooked the airfield. *About time*, the man thought and turned for the door.

Kala and Grey marched up to the closed gates of the temple, on which Kala banged loudly, but they remained unopened.

A shopkeeper from across the road noticed them and called out, "They're not opening up for anyone. Can't say I blame them." He went back to examining the boards he was using to cover his shop's windows and ignored them.

"There are secret ways in," Grey told her, "but they are best used under cover of darkness. Let's go." He turned his back on the temple, and they resumed their walk to Celeste's. The city around them was quiet, but its citizens were on edge. Patrolling guards eyed them but observed their weapons and didn't stop them.

When they arrived at Celeste's, they saw that it had been boarded up, and Kala worried that something had happened or that Celeste had moved again. They made their way around to the side street, and Kala knocked a coded knock on the boarded-up door the way Celeste had instructed her. After a moment, a hinged portion of wall near the door opened, and Celeste peeked out.

Kala and Celeste both sighed deep sighs of relief, and Celeste waved her in furtively before anyone could spot the hidden entrance.

"I hoped it was you," Celeste said. "I changed that code three times since you left."

"It's just us," Kala replied. "We secured allies, but they tell us they'll make their own way here."

"That's welcome news. Speaking of which – Lily has some for you too, but I'll let her tell you herself. She's been here ever since they banned her from the wall. That girl is lucky she's not in prison." True to her word, Celeste didn't elaborate.

Kala and Grey entered the main room, following Celeste. They heard Lily singing in the kitchen, a heartening sound that Kala hadn't heard in moons.

Grey excused himself to go wash up, and Kala made her way into the kitchen on her own. She stood in the doorway, marveling at a reanimated Lily.

Lily felt she was being watched and looked up to see Kala. She dropped the bowl she'd been mixing, raced over, and took Kala by the shoulders. "She's here! Cera's here! I saw her!" she exclaimed excitedly. Even before Kala could acknowledge this information, she added, "We have to rescue her. I know where she is."

"It makes sense that if Soren's here, Cera's here, but so is his army," Kala pointed out.

"They're irrelevant. There's nothing you can't do," Lily declared with a conviction that shook Kala.

She actually believes that, Kala thought in shock. *How can I tell her that there are some things beyond my ability?*

Lily looked into Kala's eyes with an eagerness and unconditional belief that ensnared her.

"Okay. Tell me what you know," Kala capitulated.

"Thank you, thank you!" Lily exclaimed, hugging her and bouncing her around the kitchen.

Kala had to grip a countertop to keep from getting dizzy. "Slow down, Lily. We have the matter of the ten thousand soldiers to work out."

"Of course," Lily sobered. "I saw her leave a tent near the water. It is the biggest one along the shoreline. I'll describe it to you so you can take a look at it from the wall. I sort of got myself banned for life from the parapets," she admitted sheepishly. "Totally worth it, though." She added as she made Kala a cup of kai. "You have time to wash up. You sort of smell."

"Unvarnished as usual, my dear," Kala rolled her eyes and ducked out to see about a shower and a change of clothes. She returned to fresh kai and a hot scone. "I only had enough ingredients to make one," she admitted. "I hope it's okay."

"I'd march through the gates of hell for one of your scones," she replied, scooping it up with her kai and collapsing into a chair tucked in a corner near the pantry.

Lily drew maps in flour on the counter and recounted every detail. A plan began to take shape in Kala's mind. *It could even work*, she thought.

"We need absolute darkness. We'll wait for a moonless or cloudy night. In the meantime, we're moving to a more secure location – tonight."

Grey emerged, and he and Kala found Celeste and told her their plan to relocate to the abandoned temple. "Your reinforcements here are great, but the temple has more space, and it's better fortified. Plus, with any luck, the monks left behind whatever was still in the gardens that wasn't ripe enough to harvest."

Celeste reluctantly agreed to the move. She was attached to her hideout but saw the wisdom in their plan.

That night, well after curfew, they gathered Celeste's wards and headed out. Grey took the lead, followed by Celeste, Petr, his girlfriend, Twill, Lily, and the children, with Kala bringing up the rear. Grey's sixth sense kept them from encountering any patrols. He led them to a quiet street, then down through a grate to the sewers. Kala replaced the grate and hurried to catch up. Grey chanced lighting a torch to guide them. To their credit, the children seemed utterly unperturbed by their surroundings.

Grey led them down a maze of tunnels, and Kala marveled that he either remembered the way or had an impressive sense of direction. He finally led them to a shaft and guided them upward inside the temple walls. As expected, it had been deserted. Grey lit some torches and gave instructions to the children as to where they could find rooms to sleep. They raced to fight over who would get the "best" room. Twill, Petr and his girlfriend, and Celeste followed after the children, leaving Kala, Grey and Lily alone.

"Let's check out the kitchens," Lily suggested.

"Why not?" Kala replied, smiling.

Grey led them through the dining hall to the kitchens at the back. They peeked into the walk-in pantry, but it was sadly and predictably empty. They returned to the kitchens, where Kala picked up a discarded cup, scooped some water from a barrel, and raised it to her lips.

"Don't drink that!" Grey stopped her. "Your path flickered dark for a moment."

Kala lowered the cup slowly to the counter, staring at it.

Roml stepped silently from the shadows behind her, dagger upraised.

Grey shouted a warning, but Kala had sensed his presence too late to evade him and barely turned to face him before he was upon her.

Roml stiffened, a look of surprise on his face.

Kala looked at the point of his dagger pressing against her chest.

The assassin's eyes clouded, his knees buckled, and he collapsed.

Brinn stepped from the shadows behind him, wiping his blood off her blade on his cloak.

"He was good," she said, looking down at his body. "You have formidable enemies."

Kala looked down at his body and felt her chest, relieved that his dagger hadn't pierced it. "I'd say it's good to see you, but that seems like an understatement, considering present circumstances," Kala replied.

"It's good to see you, too," Brinn acknowledged.

"What are you doing here?"

"Scouting a base for our forces. I see we think alike."

"I'm guessing that if you hadn't needed to intervene to save me, you wouldn't have let us know you were here."

"Probably not," she admitted.

"Where's Tamara?"

"Running an errand of her own."

Seemingly at once, Kala, Brinn and Grey noticed Lily standing open-mouthed in the doorway.

"It's okay, Lily. The crisis has passed, thanks to Brinn here, and to Grey earlier, I'll wager," Kala said. "Brinn, this is my dear friend Lily. Lily, Brinn."

The two women acknowledged each other.

Grey looked about. "I'll get rid of the body and dump that barrel before the children rise," he said and set to work.

Kala turned to Brinn. "I'm doubly glad you're here. I could use the help of someone with your talents, if you don't mind."

Brinn shrugged. "What were you thinking?"

Kala filled her in on her plan to rescue Cera, and to her surprise, Brinn agreed to play a part.

A dense bank of cloud rolled in a couple of days later, and Kala decided it was the right time for their gambit. She, Grey and Brinn dressed in dark clothing, and Kala felt good to be back in her black leathers. She and Brinn tied their hair back, and Twill furnished them with black paint for any exposed skin. The three of them were each heavily armed with their preferred weapons.

They headed out under cover of darkness through the tunnels beneath the city, moving by feel with no torchlight to compromise their night vision. They arrived at the broken grate facing the ocean and squeezed through. Grey had some trouble, but he managed with just a few scrapes.

They crept along the rocky shoreline, avoiding sentries and patrols. They all had a sixth sense that told them when to freeze and blend into their surroundings. They continued until they were even with Soren's tent. It was ringed by his most loyal guards, hardened men. Two of them guarded the back entrance, a man stationed on each of the sides, and they assumed at least two more guarded the front. The six or more men were only the closest. The camp never truly slept, and hundreds of soldiers sat around fires or moved about the camp just beyond Soren's tent.

Grey signaled that he'd provide a distraction for Kala and Brinn. They had previously agreed to avoid violence when entering because of the heightened risk of detection but accepted that it might be necessary when the time came to flee.

Kala and Brinn took up positions behind rocks on opposite sides of the tent. Grey whispered something unintelligible, and both men guarding the back flap turned to each other.

"What did you say?" one asked the other.

"I didn't say anything. What did you say?" the man replied.

During this brief exchange, Kala and Brinn slipped silently to the edge of the tent, quickly cut ropes that secured it to stakes, and rolled inside. Grey watched nervously as Kala pulled off the maneuver undetected, but even though he'd been looking for her, he hadn't seen Brinn do the same. He worried that she'd missed the cue but had to have faith that she was a consummate professional. He ducked down, pulled a pair of daggers from their sheaths, and waited for Kala and Brinn to return, hopefully with Cera.

Kala rolled inside the tent and looked around. The interior was faintly lit by coals smoldering in braziers. A large council table and chairs dominated the room. There were two single beds toward the rear of the tent, positioned near each other. Kala rose to her feet and silently approached between the beds. Brinn hung back, ready to deal with any guards that might enter.

Kala could tell from Cera's mane of hair in which bed she slept. She crept closer and looked down at her friend. She looked so peaceful that Kala watched her for several heartbeats before finally putting a hand over Cera's mouth and shaking her shoulder gently. Cera's surprise was muffled by the leather of Kala's glove. She glanced about in a panic, but Kala quickly raised her free hand to her heart and tapped it to send the message of "friend, not foe." Cera relaxed slightly before her eyes went wide with shock when she registered that it was Kala who'd come for her. The look was quickly replaced by one of confusion as she wrestled with whether her rescue would put Lily at risk, and if so, whether she should refuse it. Gradually, she came to accept that Kala would never ask her to trade her safety for Lily's, so she relaxed. Her eyes darted to Soren, sleeping soundly nearby, to confirm that it was okay for her to rise quietly from her bed. Kala nodded that she could.

Cera glanced at the wardrobe, but Brinn shook her head in warning — Cera would have to leave in the clothes she wore to bed. Anything else was too risky. Luckily, her modesty at sleeping near Soren and sharing a tent had accustomed her to wearing more than just undergarments to bed, so she nodded her acceptance.

Kala stared over at Soren, and she wondered how many people had died because of him. She drew a dagger. Brinn shook her head again, and Kala read her meaning. *Better the devil you know than the devil you don't.* There was no telling what manner of monster might succeed Soren if Kala were to kill him in his sleep. She laid the dagger on Cera's pillow instead. *You traded my life for Cera's once; now I return the favor with yours for Cera's.*

Kala led Cera toward the back flap of the tent and paused. Brinn strode forward and pulled two long daggers from her belt. She stood in the doorway, just inside the flap, closed her eyes, and visualized the men standing guard outside. Her hands darted outward, driving her daggers through the canvas and the base of each of the men's skulls. She stood for a moment, with the men impaled on her blades, waiting for the rhythm of the waves to release them. They crumpled to the ground as the next one masked the sound.

Brinn held open the flap, and the three of them ducked through it and outside. They sheltered against the tent, needing to sneak down the rocky shore without being spotted by the men that guarded the tent's sides. Kala opened herself to her surroundings and imagined standing guard outside the tent. In her mind, she looked side-to-side in a steady scan. She heard a sound from inside the camp and turned her head toward it. *Now*, she thought and rushed Cera forward, no attempt at concealment. They raced along the grass and flattened themselves among the rocks that lead down to the water. They lay for a moment to allow their breathing to calm. No alarm was raised, so Kala took Cera's hand and guided her over the rocks toward the broken grate that would grant them admission to Bayre's sewers.

It was much harder to avoid sentries and patrols with Cera in tow, and they made painfully slow progress but eventually arrived at the grate undiscovered. Kala squeezed through and bade Cera follow. Brinn and Grey followed them. They walked the length of the tunnels in silence, with Kala holding Cera's hand. Her feet were cut and scraped from scrambling over rocks, but she didn't complain.

They climbed up the shaft to the temple grounds. Cera didn't know if it was safe to whisper her questions to Kala or not, so she stayed silent.

Kala led her toward a building lit from within by torches. Kala entered first, prompting Lily to rise from her seat, trembling with anticipation. She looked at Kala expectantly, and Kala simply stood aside to let Cera enter. Seeing Cera broke Lily, and she swayed slightly. She stepped forward, bumping into the table that she'd forgotten was there, and skirted it to move toward Cera.

Cera raised her hands slowly, and Lily took them in hers, intertwining their fingers, careful not to spoil the dream. She felt Cera's solidity and drew her into an embrace of silent tears. Kala ducked out to leave them in peace.

37

Soren

Soren woke in the middle of the night to shouting. He jumped out of bed just as his guards burst into his tent, swords drawn.

"You're alive, sir?" one of them asked, surprised.

"Why wouldn't I be?" Soren asked in answer.

"We found guards outside your tent slain," the man replied and searched it for intruders.

Without being aware of it, Soren felt his body for injury and found none. He glanced over to Cera's bed, only to find it empty, save for the dagger on her pillow. "There's why," Soren informed the guards, gesturing to the knife.

"Why didn't they kill you?" the guard asked, then paled and quickly added, "No offense, sir."

"I guess they wanted her alive more than me dead," he replied. *Can't say that I blame them*, he thought, recalling the sunshine that she'd briefly brought into his dark world. He finally noticed the men searching his tent. "They wouldn't have stuck around," he admonished them. "You're dismissed."

"Sorry, sir," one of them said on his way out.

Soren nodded absentmindedly.

The men filed out, and Soren got up to light a candle. He picked up the dagger from Cera's pillow, sat down, and stared at her empty bed, turning the blade over in his hand. *You've stolen my conscience*, he thought ruefully, recalling how Cera would temper the harshest advice of his war council with a look of disdain. *This will not be the victory you believe it to be.* He blew out the candle and lay back down, clutching the dagger to his chest, but sleep did not come.

When hints of daylight peeked through the flap of his tent, at last, he rose, washed, dressed and stepped out into the dawn. His personal guard had been replaced by men he didn't recognize, other than the captain of his former guard, who stood waiting for him.

"This was my failure," he told Soren, handing him the hilt of his sword, his stoicism masking his nervousness.

Soren pushed his sword back to him. "What's done is done. Correct whatever deficiencies made this possible," he told him and waved him away. Soren saw Lennox approaching. *Now there's someone who'll be disappointed that I'm still alive*, he thought.

"Glad to see you alive and well," Lennox called out, looking anything but glad.

"Thank you," Soren replied, feeling obligated to return one falsehood with another.

"Not to worry, I have it all taken care of," Lennox assured him.

"I wasn't worried until now. What do you mean, 'you have it taken care of'?"

"I rounded up everyone with knowledge of what transpired last night and had them executed."

Soren was aghast. "Why would you do that?"

Lennox looked annoyed at having to explain himself but did so anyway. "We couldn't very well have it get out that the enemy spirited your consort away, right under our noses, could we?" He didn't wait for Soren to answer his rhetorical question before continuing. "I've had the rumor spread that she ran away, with help from a guard. Then I made it publicly known that you had the man executed, along with those who should have stopped the plot but failed to. I debated spreading word that you had her killed too, but that wouldn't do if she turns up later," he concluded, proud of himself.

"Lennox, I don't need you to manage my image."

"Apparently, you do," he disagreed.

"Okay, never mind. How did the actual perpetrators do it?"

Lennox scratched his head. "That's what I am trying to figure out. My theory is that they came and went by boat."

Soren looked out to sea and how visible any approaching boat would be. "Doesn't seem likely," he concluded.

"I'm investigating *all* possibilities," Lennox replied, still miffed at not being thanked for his intervention, and stormed off.

Soren watched him recede, wondering how many people Lennox would subject to 'questioning.' He hadn't noticed that Seline had walked up until she cleared her throat. He glanced over at her.

"Hi, Seline. I didn't see you there," he informed her.

"Is this a good time?" she asked.

"Right – status report. Sure, come in," he replied and lifted the tent flap for her. He motioned for the guards to tie it up to let in some light. One of them got to it, and the other moved around to tie up the back flap.

Soren sat down at the table at which he convened his war council. He noticed that he hadn't pushed Cera's bed back against his, but he didn't think that Seline would notice or care, and what was the point of keeping up appearances now that Cera was gone? He got back up and ordered a guard to remove the bed, which was done even before he returned to his seat.

"Sorry about that," he apologized, but Seline just looked blankly at him, so he shook his head and asked, "Status?"

Seline relaxed now that life had returned to its familiar pattern. She consulted some papers, even though she knew by heart the figures she'd scribbled there. "Our food stores are running low, but still not lower than the city's. They'll run out before ours do. And Lennox's foraging parties do add to our supplies somewhat." Her forehead creased when she mentioned Lennox's name, and Soren knew it was because Lennox's 'foraging' was more like 'pillaging.' Seline thought that a solution to a problem that involved less death was more elegant., while Lennox seemed to believe that a solution that involved *more* death was preferable. Soren just wanted solutions to his problems. He rubbed his temples.

Seline continued, "I think it's the right time to break their spirits."

"Refresh my memory as to how… I thought that's what the siege was doing."

"It is… it's just a slow process. We can speed it up."

"Okay, how?"

"We offer amnesty to their fighting men if they switch sides."

"That'll only work for men without families."

"I thought of that. We also offer safe passage for non-combatants wishing to leave the city."

"Lennox isn't going to like that. He's as bloodthirsty as Trax was."

"He needn't worry. They'll wind up as dead in the wilderness as they would if they remain behind their walls. It's just prolonging the inevitable. Our goal is the city. You once said that these people are nothing without the safety of their cities."

"I did, did I? Well, I guess it's as true now as it was then. Okay, I'll make the decree. Is there anything else?"

"No," Seline replied and packed up her papers to leave. She hesitated for a moment at the exit, thinking she should say something about Cera, but couldn't come up with what, and in truth, she didn't care. She just stepped out and walked away.

Returning to his tent, Soren saw Lennox rushing up. *Gods-damn*, he thought, *Can't the man give me a moment's peace*, but as Lennox got closer, Soren could see that he was smiling an evil smile.

Lennox stopped in front of him, breathless. "I found it – the way they got in and out. There's a broken grate. There are tunnels. We can get men inside the city anytime we want."

Soren thought over the new development. "Let Seline know, come up with a plan, and brief me in the morning."

Lennox scurried off, leaving Soren to ponder how to exploit this new information.

38

Forest

Addis moved closer to Forest as they headed south on horseback. "Ride with me?" he asked.

She consented and pulled her mare beside his stallion so they could ride side by side.

"Where are we headed?" he asked.

"A city called Bayre. That's where we're rallying to fight Soren."

"I've heard of Bayre. It's where the land meets the sea, right?"

"So I'm told."

"I will enjoy seeing the ocean."

"Your people are nomadic, and you've got horses, but you've never been to the sea?"

"The grasses on the open plains are their own type of sea. I guess we never really felt the need."

They rode in silence for a while before Forest had to unburden herself. "I appreciate your joining in our fight against Soren, but I should never have implied that there'd be glory in it. There'll be death. Your people will die."

"We all die sometime. Is it so wrong to want your death to count for something? We're not as cavalier as we seem. Every man and woman that rides with me knows exactly what they're getting into. I hold nothing over them. They have all chosen to ride toward their fate."

Forest felt somewhat better but still partly responsible for the lives that would surely be lost.

"We weren't always nomadic," Addis told her. "My people once had a mighty kingdom. No one remembers that, but we ride past the remains of great plains cities that don't exist anymore. At some point, we were brought low, but our nobility was never wrested from us."

"I see that," Forest conceded graciously.

"I've sent riders to rally any other clan that will join with us. My father's influence is still strong, despite his being near death."

"I'm sorry to hear he's not well."

"Thank you. He has a wasting disease, and it's terrible to watch such a proud man decline. I think that's why he sent my brothers, sisters and me away to patrol his lands – so we wouldn't have to see him fail." He was silent for a while. "My sister rides in the direction we're heading. I hope you'll meet her. You remind me very much of her. She's a firebrand like you."

Forest had never thought of herself as such, but she appreciated the compliment.

They rode for the remainder of the day in comfortable silence before stopping for the night. Addis dismounted and handed the reins of his horse to a retainer. "Come," he said to Forest. "I have something for you." He directed his man to take the reins of Forest's mare as well, so she was free to follow him. He led her through the camp that was being set up around them to a collection of horses on long leads staked to the ground to give them room to graze but not wander off.

Forest saw Thorvyn chatting with one of Addis's men near the horses and called out her greetings to him. He waved back. "What was it you wanted to show me?" she asked Addis.

He walked to a beautiful chestnut mare and, calling gently to it, approached it until he could stroke its neck.

"She's gorgeous," Forest told him.

"I want you to have her," he replied.

"That's kind of you, but I already have a horse."

"This horse has ten times the speed of your mount."

"I can see that, but I'm partial to my mare."

"You're loyal to your horse?" he asked incredulously.

Forest blushed. "Is that silly?"

"No. It simply surprises me. You surprise me, Forest-of-the-South."

"Don't call me that. My friend Dhara is from the true south. I'm just from south of here."

"Fair enough, Forest-of-the-Middle."

"That just sounds stupid."

He laughed heartily. "I like you, Forest," he told her and reached for her hand.

She let him take it uncertainly, and he walked her back to the fire that Jarom was preparing, still holding it. He dropped her off and returned to see about his people.

Nara, who'd watched everything, rushed over when he'd left and grabbed Forest by the shoulders. "The young horse-lord is your boyfriend?!" she asked.

"Hardly," Forest replied. "I think he just finds me a welcome distraction from the monotony of the plains."

"Oh no. It's *way* more than that," Nara chided. "He *really* likes you."

"Well, he's not going to be happy when I leave then," Forest concluded ruefully.

Nara was confused. "What do you mean, 'leave?'"

"He said something about family that got me thinking. There's something I have to do."

"Can't it wait?" Nara implored her.

"Absolutely not, sadly," Forest replied.

"Such are the times we live in," Nara said, crushed. "At least kiss him before you leave."

"Nara! I'm thirteen."

"That's never stopped anyone before," Nara countered, "simply follow your heart."

"I will. Now, if we don't help Jarom, he'll disown us," Forest said to end the uncomfortable conversation and hurried to ask Jarom what she could do.

The next day she rode over to Addis. "Can you show me one of the ruined cities?" she asked him.

"An odd request, but yes – we'll be riding near one later today – I can show it to you."

"Thank you. I'll need to gather supplies," Forest told him, riding off.

"It's less than a day's ride," he called after her.

"I fear I may need to journey farther," she called back and rode away.

She returned a short time later with a full pack and blankets tied to her mare.

"Why do you need all that?" he asked.

"It depends on what we find," she replied cryptically, not wanting to tell him she planned on leaving unless she had to.

"Well, aren't you full of mystery!" he concluded and spurred his horse to head perpendicularly to the direction they'd been riding. His cousin

Jon rode after them, but Addis waved him off. "It's okay, Jon. I'll be back before dark." The man reluctantly rejoined the riders.

Forest followed Addis as he led her off on an angle to the east. She hazarded a wave over her shoulder to a despondent Nara.

They rode for a long while, and eventually, twisted shapes rose from the ground, like the ones she'd seen when they'd crossed the river with Kala. A feeling of foreboding came over her, and she shuddered.

"These places are the home of the dead," Addis said, noticing her discomfort.

"That's exactly what I'm looking for," she replied and spurred her reluctant horse forward.

They continued until she spied a formation of twisted spires surrounding a stone circle, with a single one on the east side of the circle. "That is where I need to go," she told Addis, pointing at the lone spire.

He just nodded, and they rode over to it. The wind blowing through the ruins whispered in low tones. They dismounted and tied their reins around the spire. The horses were unsettled, so they stroked their manes.

"They don't like it here," Addis concluded.

"I can't say that I blame them," Forest replied, looking about. Then, spying what she sought, added, "Help me with this." She walked over to a round stone poking through the soil and began clearing it off.

"Redecorating?" Addis asked dryly.

"Just help me," she repeated, and he bent down to help her clear the soil off the stone. Once it was free, she asked him to help her roll it over to the lone spire. He did as she asked without questioning her further.

"Now what?" he asked when she stood up to stare at their handiwork.

"Now, we wait, and we make a fire."

"Homey," he muttered, looking about, but started gathering wood without complaint. They got a fire going, which Forest surrounded with a tight ring of stones.

"The fire's not going to spread," he chided her.

"You're probably right, but I want those stones."

He concluded that she was probably a little insane and sat down beside her. They prepared a simple dinner in silence.

"Are you going to tell me what this is about?" he finally asked, unable to tolerate not knowing any longer.

"That," she said, pointing at the descending airship.

Addis jumped to his feet. "I've seen those things sail overhead but never land."

"We asked it to," Forest informed him and gathered her things. "There's something I have to do that will take me away for a while," she told him, "but I'll meet you in Bayre."

"Can't you at least stay the night?" he asked. "Bayre is more than a moon's ride away, and we have to rendezvous with the rest of my family on the way. What's one night?"

"Everything," she said and kissed him on the cheek as the airship landed. She turned and opened the door to the ship while Addis calmed the spooked horses. She lay her pack inside the door and placed the blankets inside as well. "Help me carry the stones from the fire inside," she asked him.

"You and stones," he muttered but turned to help her.

She lay a small patch of leather near the fire and pushed one onto it with her boot, then motioned for Addis to help her carry it onboard. They repeated this until all the rocks were in a tidy pile inside.

"Why the stones?" he asked.

"Kala says it's freezing on the way to the volcano."

"Forget I asked," he said.

She stepped through the doorway and looked back at him.

"I'll see you in Bayre?" he asked for confirmation.

"Yes," she replied. "Can you do me a final favor and push that stone away from the spire?"

"Push it against the spire, push it away from the spire... the things I do for that girl," he muttered but did as she asked.

"Thank you," she called from the doorway, blew him a final kiss, and closed the door as the airship drifted upward.

Addis watched it until it disappeared from view, then he turned to saddle the horses and ride back to his clan.

The airship drifted lower, and Forest blew into her frozen hands to keep them warm. For the thousandth time, she fumbled with the amulet that she'd acquired on the volcanic island and tucked it back beneath her collar. The ship landed, and she opened the door cautiously.

She found herself outside a sprawling metropolis that looked odd to her for its lack of walls. It was just a guess, but it fit the image in her mind of where Soren might have grown up before being sent away in an airship. If it was such a shock to him to be transplanted to a hard, northern village, he must have come from somewhere entirely the opposite, and this city seemed to be just that.

She left the ship and began the short hike to the city. The warm sea air slowly thawed her, but she wondered if she'd ever not feel the bite of cold metal against her skin.

It was early morning, and she entered the city just as its inhabitants were stirring. She headed to a nearby market and used some of the little coin she had to purchase a hot cup of kai to warm her insides. The shopkeeper eyed her coin suspiciously but shrugged when he concluded that copper was copper. She sipped her drink. *This is disgusting*, she found. *I don't know what Kala sees in it.* But it was warm, so she finished it while scanning the faces of the people frequenting the marketplace. Her mission was a long shot by the most generous odds, but she had to try.

She spent days moving through crowds, scanning faces. She lost weight from eating little and slept anywhere she wouldn't be discovered. The people happily went about their lives, oblivious to the turmoil deeper within the continent. She knew she was failing at her self-appointed task when inspiration struck her. She figured out where the airships landed inside the city, having realized that hers set down apart from where they typically landed. She made her way there and camped out on a street corner with a decent view. A man strode by and tossed a copper in her lap. *This is what I've become?* she wondered as she leaned back against the stone wall and waited.

Airships drifted in occasionally, causing little interest among the people operating the airfield. They'd haul them down, clean them out, fill them back up, and sometimes escort a youth off or onto a ship.

Forest noticed a woman walk up and stare at the airships. She seemed different from the other passersby in that she really watched them rather than merely glancing at them. Forest studied her. Sadness surrounded her, but Forest could tell that she'd been beautiful in her youth. The woman had piercing blue eyes, through which she watched the ships without really seeming to see them. She hung her head and shuffled off. Forest rose to her feet and followed her across town. The woman made no stops along the way as she returned to a small home that appeared empty except for her. Forest watched her through the window from across the street as she collapsed on a sofa and stared across the room.

Forest steadied her courage and crossed the street to the woman's door, where she stood for a moment before knocking. Forest saw the woman rise in the reflection of a mirror that she could see through the window.

The door opened, and Forest studied her face intensely before asking, "Are you Soren's mother?"

The woman's breath caught. "What news have you of my son?"

39

Priestess

The Priestess returned from discussing prophecy with the other oracles and the Council of Elders. She had a pounding headache but walked casually, purposefully even, with her head held high, despite the pain behind her eyes.

The Ancients had burned an image into her mind, and she still wrestled to interpret – a baby girl lying in a charred manger. *Was the baby to be born? Had the baby already been born? Had it been born long ago? Was she a specific person, or was she a symbol of the world that would be reborn from the ruins of this one?* The second oracle had added to the image the bitter taste of ashes on her tongue, and the third had added the feeling of cold. The clues were not contradictory but reinforcing in a way that the Priestess could not yet divine, and her head hurt from trying.

She rounded the corner to her chambers and observed the door wide open – no attempt whatsoever had been made at subterfuge. The Priestess walked through her door to see Tamara, of the order of warrior priestesses, sitting calmly in a chair beside the window. She rose as the Priestess entered.

"Winter," Tamara greeted her.

"Mother," the Priestess replied.

"It's time to end this," Tamara implored her.

"This needs be done."

"No matter how clearly you believe you see the path, there are always other ways."

"We've been through this, mother."

"Come back to us. It's never too late," Tamara beseeched her daughter and held out her arms.

The Priestess stepped forward slowly into her mother's embrace, allowing her to be wrapped in her arms. She breathed in the scent of her mother's skin and felt her hair against her cheek. She was transported for a moment to a faraway time and place.

Tamara stiffened as the dagger entered her heart. She kissed her daughter's cheek, and her eyes clouded.

The Priestess held her mother a moment longer, then let her body slump to the floor. "You knew how this would end – and still you came. You knew," she accused her bitterly and wiped away the only tear she allowed to escape.

She sat down slowly on her bed and stared at her mother's body. She looked to her bedside bookcase and reached for the history of her mother's people. She sat leafing through the blank pages of the book. *Perhaps it's fitting that their story should vanish with her*, she thought.

"Guards!" she yelled, cradling the counterfeit book in her lap. *This took knowledge, access, materials and talent*, she thought.

Two monks burst through the door, short swords at the ready, and came to an abrupt halt at the sight of Tamara's body on the floor in an ever-widening pool of blood.

"Have this cleaned up," she ordered them, waving vaguely at her feet. "And I want the heads of my consort, my librarian, and my illustrator."

"As you wish, Priestess," the men replied and withdrew.

She sat immobile. *Things are as they must be*, she told herself. *Why else did I leave the book in plain view?* No matter how many times she repeated it, it didn't sting any less.

All the pieces were on the board and in motion.

End of Book 2

Books by Colin Lindsay

Gaia
Gaia Wept

Cassiopeia Rising

B-Rate Gods

Twine
Mya in Pieces

Ella Ethereal

Anna Archivist

The Innocents
Fragile Innocence

Fabricated Innocence

Innocence Reclaimed

The Goddess's Scythe
Raven's Wings

Death's Angel

Queen's Sacrifice

COLIN LINDSAY

is the author of *Death's Angel*, the second book in The *Goddess's Scythe*. He was born in San Francisco and his family now call Ottawa home. He writes for his daughter in the company of an indignant cat.

Made in the USA
Columbia, SC
23 June 2024